Pirate's Redemption

ALSO BY A. T. ROSS

The Word and the Sword series:
The Book of Secrets (Fall 2013)

Short Fiction:
The Lost Mine and Other Tales of Numaloria
The Lost Mine
The Coming of the Fellwraith
The Necromancer

Pirate's Redemption

A. T. ROSS

Brackburn Publishing
www.brackburnpublishing.com

Pirate's Redemption

Published by Brackburn Publishing 2013
www.brackburnpublishing.com
Cover design and layout © 2013 Brackburn Publishing
ISBN-10: 0-615-87901-2
ISBN-13: 978-0-615-87901-7

To Howard Pyle
for all the pirate stories

Chapter One

A Pirate's Request

Massachusetts Bay Colony, 1680 A.D.

John Rackham's heart sank as his mother entered *The Spot*. Behind him the door had been yanked open and he could hear the low moans of the chill ocean breeze before it was pulled shut again. He turned and stared across the tavern's high bar and murky air, stinking with clouds of tobacco smoke, at the thin form of his mother.

Already clutching a bottle of spirits loosely in her left hand, she glanced about the place before spying John. There were about twenty patrons clustered around the tables between them, and she weaved her way between them to the bar, swaying as she came.

"Rum, John," she said, giving him a dull smile, thumping her empty bottle on the counter between them. She was still wearing her housemaid's uniform from work at the Governor's mansion. That meant it had been a hard day. Never a good sign. She looked tired, her eyes haggard, and her hair limp and bedraggled tied up in its bun. "Where's Mr. Burnwake tonight?"

"Upstairs," John replied, glancing at the ceiling as he filled a mug and set it on the bar for her. "Helping a customer."

"Bet he is," she said with a glance upwards, taking a huge swig of rum and grimacing. Hooking her hair bun with a finger, she pulled it loose, her hair cascading to her shoulders in a waterfall of fiery auburn. Shaking her head in relief, she took another large gulp of her drink and glanced around the tavern, her eyes flicking from table to table, sizing up the men who sat there.

"How was work today?" John asked.

"Too long with too little pay, and the governor too handsy," his mother replied without looking at him. She worked as a maid in the Governor's mansion and had done so for as long as John could remember. It was harder work than many supposed, and the Governor's behavior made it all the worse. She had tried keeping that aspect of the job from him for as long as she could, but whether from weariness or inability, eventually she had given up.

She used to speak of her employment as temporary, until John's father would return and free her from the life of household service. Her eyes used to light up whenever she said this with a strength John had not seen in her for many years. Gradually that light had dwindled and gone out with the passage of years, though every once in a while he would catch sight of her gazing out to sea with that same light in her eyes, past the ships docked in the harbor to the open water beyond.

"I'll be over here," she said, gesturing to a nearby table crowded with several rough-looking sailors. *The Spot* was a disreputable dive for sailors that sat on a rise perhaps a half-mile above the wharf, commonly frequented by the disreputable sort of seaman who looked the part of a pirate. Since starting work there the year before, John had witnessed twelve knife fights and on two occasions a man had been shot for cheating at cards. Yet this never

8

discouraged his mother from making an appearance. "Keep the rum coming," she called out to him from over her shoulder, marching over to the table and sitting down in a spare seat. The sailors grunted at her, eying her up and down.

"Deal me in," she told them, throwing a few coins on the table. John knew the rest of the story without having to be told. His mother would play and drink and flirt until closing time, slowing descending into a drunken stupor. He didn't know why she kept returning night after night. It was hardly the sort of place one made a habit of frequenting. John had only taken the job because it was all he could find.

Mr. Burnwake appeared from upstairs, a rotund, squat little man with spectacles and a stained apron tied around his enormous middle. He seemed in good spirits, bobbing his head cheerfully at John instead of slapping at him for being too slow at his work like usual.

"Good even, Mary," he called to John's mother when he saw her. She raised her glass without her eyes leaving the table in front of her.

"How do you be, Mr. Burnwake?" she called out, taking a deep swig of her drink. "How's business this evening?"

"Can't complain," he replied with a guttural chuckle, taking up a greasy rag and wiping down some nearby ale mugs.

Soon enough another patron called Mr. Burnwake upstairs with a problem with their room, and John was left to man the bar alone once again as Burnwake puffed his way upstairs. Being left to tend the bar was not as nerve-wracking as it once had been; most of the sailors kept to themselves and spoke to others as little as possible.

One of the sailors at his mother's table made a joke, and the whole table roared with laughter. His mother, well on her way to drunk, was flirting with him heavily. Feeling slightly ill, John took the opportunity to slip into the cellar to fetch a few casks, wanting to avoid watching her slip away again. He lingered as long as he dared before hauling up another cask of rum. Mr. Burnwake returned not long after and retired to his quarters in the room behind the bar. For the next few hours before midnight, John ran to and from the cellar for casks, scrubbed the floor where one unfortunate sailor had wretched, and swept up the remains of a meal from the floor where a brawl had broken out over a game of cards.

"Let me tell you of my lover!" his mother shouted, her words slurring. She had exchanged her chair for the lap of the sailor with a wide-brimmed hat pulled low over his eyes. John's heart sank again. He'd heard the stories too many times before. As he expected, she told them of her love, a man John had never met, though his presence loomed large by his absence. "Promised me the world, he did," she sneered, "and I gave up everythin' for him in return. But the very night I took him to my bed he vanished, never to be heard from again. Left me all alone."

She never spoke of John's father when she was sober. It was only when rum had loosened her tongue that the stories began to emerge. The attempted mutiny, which his father had put down, cutting the hands off the ringleaders and throwing them to the fins. The treasure hauls where he had executed all the men that had buried it so only he and his captain would know of its location. He had heard them all before, and so he returned to work, trying to tune out his mother's voice.

It was nearly midnight when the door swung open again. John barely glanced at the man who entered. He had seen many just like him before, a bristly shadow of a beard, a tri-cornered hat settled at a jaunty angle over a blue bandana wrapped about his head. The waistcoat was only unusual thing about him, which was a deep brownish-red and glinted with brass buttons. He had never seen anyone wearing that sort of finery intentionally enter *the Spot* before. They didn't usually last an hour. A man had come in once before, wearing a silk shirt. He'd gone flying through the front window twenty minutes later, stripped naked.

The man ignored the sailors around him, drinking, laughing and gambling at cards. John finished tapping the beer cask and straightened, only to find the man standing at the bar, gazing around at the various drinks.

"Rum," he said, his voice gruff. "Are ye serving spirits alone tonight, then?" the man asked, looking at John. "Look a bit young to be runnin' a bar."

"Mr. Burnwake will be back," John said nervously.

"Well, I'm in need of a medicinal remedy to me sobriety," the man said. "Rum."

John filled a tankard and passed it to the man, who took it without comment and flicked a coin at him. John caught it, looking surprised as the man strode through the crowded tables just as the card players burst into loud gaffaws. He ignored them and took a seat against the far wall, where he faced the room and the door with his back to the wall, and drank in silence.

John looked down at the coin. It was a gold doubloon, stamped with the Spanish seal. His mouth fell open and he looked back up at the man in astonishment. It was far too much to pay for a drink. He slipped out from behind the bar and crossed the room to where the man sat, leaning up against the wall on the back legs of the chair. He avoided looking at his mother, who was now drunk and sitting on the lap of the pirate with the biggest hat, her arm around him as he played cards, laughing harshly.

"This is too much," John said.

"What's that, lad?" the man said, looking at him.

"This is too much for a drink," John said, holding up the doubloon.

"Not liable to stop at one," the man said, taking a heft of his drink. "Keep it and we'll settle square when I'm finished. Here."

He tossed another doubloon to John, who caught it, looking dumbfounded.

"What's that for?" he stammered.

"I don't like the look of those lads playin' cards," the man said. "Something about 'em puts me in a right spot of bother. Feel like I might pay their table a visit before night's end and see what's to be seen."

"So what's this for?" John asked, holding up the second coin.

"That," said the man, indicating the second doubloon, "is for the entertainin' part."

"You're going to fight them?" John asked, looking alarmed.

"Only if it comes to it, lad," the man said. He leaned closer and pushed his hat up his forehead with an index finger, fixing John with a stare. "And it'd be a mercy to me if ye could speak of that a bit softer next time."

John flushed red and nodded. "But why would you go and pick a fight for no reason?"

"Old friends," the man said with a sardonic laugh,

leaning back in his seat.

John returned to the bar and put the doubloons on the shelf below the counter, with the cups and tankards. As he straightened, he caught a glimpse of the sailor in the large hat holding his mother on his lap. His eyes were lingering on the place John had just stored the doubloons. Feeling disquieted, John returned to work, but he kept a watch on the bar nonetheless.

The next two hours passed uneventfully. His mother descended further and further into her drunken revelry and the card players grew more rowdy as the night wore on. The man in the corner signaled for a refill every twenty-five minutes or so, and every time John brought him a drink he would hand him another doubloon, and eventually stopped explaining why. John put them all together on the shelf below the bar. The big-hatted ruffian was definitely eying John every time he added one to the growing pile.

One of the card players stood up and stumbled to the bar, laughing. John thought for one wild moment he was going for the stack of doubloons, but he collapsed on the other end of the bar, and began to speak slurringly to Mr. Burnwake. He was inquiring as to the whereabouts of a keepsake he kept around his neck by a leather cord. John could barely understand the man, but apparently it had gone missing. Behind him one of his table-mates was admiring the very trinket, laughing.

As they talked, the fellow in the big hat stood, laughed, and weaved his drunken way between the tables toward the bar. He slumped against it near John.

"Another rum," the man said, drooling on his bristly beard, which fell to mid-chest and had been woven into strands. John filled the tankard and set it on the bar.

13

"Much obliged to ye," the man said, drawing a gleaming knife from his belt and holding it up with a grin. He brandished it, holding it close to his hunched body, allowing him to keep Mr. Burnwake from seeing it. "Now why don't ye pass those doubloons on over te me? Maybe I won't split your gut open that way."

John felt terror spread through his body. Numbly, hands trembling, he reached down and collected the coins, setting them on the bar.

"There's a good lad," the man said, his eyes glinting.

"Hello, Bloody Hands," said the man from the corner of the room, who had just appeared at the villain's elbow by the bar. The man in the big hat turned and looked at the man for a long moment. The vicious smile slipped from his face and an expression of satisfied rage replaced it.

"Billy Jack Thatcher," he growled.

"That's my money you're tryin' to pocket," Billy Jack Thatcher said.

"Only makes things a bit more fair, then" Bloody Hands snarled. "Took all our shares with ye when ye jumped ship, didn't ye?"

"Is that what the captain told you?" Billy Jack laughed. "Well, he always were an opportunist. Knew how to play a tight situation to rob a crew of their shares, the captain."

"Ye low, stinkin' sea carcass!" Bloody Hands said, and his knife lashed out. Before he could get the blade around, Billy Jack had shattered his tankard over the top of Bloody Hands' head, and the pirate dropped to the floor, gurgling unintelligibly.

There was a sudden loud scraping as the rest of the card players stood, bristling, looking at Billy Jack with anger and contempt. As they stood regarding each other,

14

the rest of the clients made a quick, silent exit, slipping through the front door. Mr. Burnwake disappeared into the back room and pulled the door closed, crossing himself.

"Rampart, Gallows, Weaver, Roche," said Billy Jack, nodding to them and tipping his hat. They drew weapons on him, knife, cutlass, and even a pistol emerged from some hidden fold. Billy Jack leaned back toward John, eying the group of four. "Still got those doubloons?"

"Yes," he said.

"Good. You'll need them."

As though everyone knew exactly what was going to happen beforehand, they rushed each other at the same moment with cries of fury. The man with the pistol discharged it at the charging Billy Jack, but he missed and blew a hole in the wall behind the bar, two feet from John's head, who yelled and ducked for cover.

Billy Jack plowed into them, close-lining the first he reached. The man jerked and soared into the air, landing on his head with a crash. The next pirate came at Billy Jack with a knife, cutting and slashing, but Billy caught his wrist and twisted it. The knife clanged to the tavern floor and he headbutted the man, who went down instantly.

A pair of arms grabbed him from behind and he struggled wildly to break the iron grip holding him as the pirate with the cutlass stabbed at him. As the man swung, Billy Jack ducked, then leaped into the air, his foot lashing out. He kicked the cutlass from the man's hand and twisted, throwing his captor off balance. They collided together and toppled with a crash into the card table, sending cards, coins, and cups of drink flying as the legs buckled. Billy Jack landed on top of the man, driving his head into the floor.

He rolled to his feet as the last remaining pirate retrieved his cutlass and rushed forward, shouting curses. Billy Jack stepped at him as he ran and kicked a fallen tankard into the man's face. It shattered and knocked the man backward with a cry. He hit the ground, cutlass clanging from his hands, and was still.

"There, ye see," Billy Jack said, cracking his neck. "That wasn't so bad."

A flying tankard shot over Billy's shoulder and crashed into the table behind him. He spun and saw John's mother, drunken eyes glaring, pointing a rigid finger at him.

"How dare you come back here, Billy Jack Thatcher!" she shrieked and slapped him across the face. This, more than the fight, staggered Billy Jack, and he stepped back, putting up his hands to ward off further attacks.

"Hello, Mary," he said.

"Fourteen years!" she shouted. "Fourteen, and narry a word!"

She took up another cup and hurled it at him. He dodged aside.

"You don't understand, woman!" he bellowed, covering his head.

"I understand just fine, Billy Jack Thather! You run off and left me!"

"I was doing no such thing!" he protested.

She hesitated, squinting at him in suspicion. "What?" she snapped.

"I tell you on me very life, I never ran from you," Billy Jack said, lowering his hands and staring at her.

"Wait," John said, feeling tremors running through his body. "You left her fourteen years ago?"

"I'm sayin' I didn't leave her," Billy Jack said, looking at John.

"John," said Mary, turning to John with a bitter smile, jabbing a finger at Billy Jack, "meet your father."

He goggled at them, stunned. Billy Jack tipped his hat to John.

"The boy did look a mite familiar. Somethin' in the rugged good looks about him," he said, looking at Mary. She shrugged, folding her hands across her chest and glowering at him. "S'pose I've got a tale to tell," he said finally.

"Suppose you do at that," Mary said fiercely.

"Ye mind grabbing me another rum, lad?" John's father asked. He moved to a nearby table and sat down. Mary remained where she was, but John filled a mug with rum, went over and handed to him, and sat, staring at the man that was his father, unsure of what to think. Billy Jack was not a particularly handsome looking man, but John thought he had a strong jaw. There was a scar running from temple to ear he had not noticed before.

"Well," said Billy Jack, taking a swig of rum. "Fourteen years it's been and not one day's gone by that I've not wished to get back to ye."

"Get back to us?" Mary said, trying not to look interested. "What do you mean?"

"Hang it all, woman, I were caught!" Billy Jack cried, slamming his mug down with force. "Somebody tattled as to my whereabouts. After you took to me bed, while you still slept I went ashore to find us a first mate, and hang it all if I weren't caught right then!"

"Why aren't you a dead man swinging from the short rope, then?" Mary demanded. "They hang pirates in Port Royal."

"They were itchin' for it, I don't doubt. But when they learned who I were, they decided to cut a deal. If I showed them where we'd hid all the treasure and helped them catch Bloodbeard, they'd let me go free. Had no choice in the matter, obviously."

He lifted his mug and drained it, though it must have still been half-filled with rum. "Fourteen long years its taken me," Billy Jack said. "Hunting down the crew I used to run with and stealing their treasure right out from under them."

"They made you do that?" Mary said, uncrossing her arms and coming and sitting next to John, looking intently at Billy Jack.

"Aye," he said. "I hated them for it—for a time. 'Bout four years ago I found meself a religious experience." He lifted a small metal cross from within the folds of his shirt and kissed it, before dropping it back out of sight. "After that, I didn't mind so much. The Almighty showed me what manner of man I were."

"So you're free, then?" Mary asked.

"Not entirely," said Billy Jack, and now there was a smile playing around the corners of his mouth. "That actually brings me to me being here. It took me mor'n a year to find out where you'd disappeared to, askin' about you whenever we lay anchor to resupply. I'm not quite free, you see. Took 'em to all *the spots*, save one. Got all the gold we ever left in dirt, except our last take, just before they took me in Royal."

He leaned forward, looking at them with an eager light in his eyes.

"I'm to take 'em to the Isla San Thanatos haul, and then I'm free as a lark."

"You're mad," Mary said, shaking her head. "Can't be

done. Bloodbeard made sure only he could get to that haul again."

"Bloodbeard?" John said, stricken with horror. "Isn't he—?"

"The most feared piratical captain to sail the Spanish Main?" Billy Jack said. "That he be, and more still. But that's not quite the way of things, Mary. I were there with him when he made his boobytraps. I can find the island, and I can get us to the treasure."

"You weren't sailing with him, were you?" John gasped, dreading the answer.

"I were his first mate, lad," Billy Jack said, his eyes hard. "Your mother put in her own time aboard the *Iago*, o' course. That be how we came to make one another's fleshly acquaintance. What were you when we picked ye up in Tortuga, Mary? A serving wench or some whatnot?"

Mary did not answer. John was staring at her in shock, and she was gazing steadfastly at the table, meeting neither of their eyes. It was clear that she had had no intention of telling John about that part of the story, content to let him believe the worst about his father and not a word of her own sins.

"Let me tell ye, lad," Billy Jack said, laughing, "t'weren't a more terrifying sight than old Mary Anne Rackham swinging aboard your ship, cutlass in hand, screamin' like she were a demon straight from the pit!"

Mary was silent. John blinked, trying to process everything that was being said. His entire world was being turned upside down.

"Anyway, I'm here to see if you'll come with me on one last venture," Billy Jack said, sipping from his mug, even though it was empty, trying to collect the last few drops. "One last pirate's journey to plunder the plunderers."

"I'll not be going with you on this or any other mad voyage to hell," Mary said, shaking her head firmly. "I've got a life now, and honest work to be done right here."

"I weren't askin' you," Billy Jack said, waving a hand. "Our ship's sailed, yours and mine, unless I'm rather missin' my guess." Instead, he turned and looking at John. "There comes a time in every lad's life that he's got to learn his father's trade, an' it's high time you learned from mine. I know I weren't there for you afore you grew into a man, but I'd enjoy the chance to make up for that. Got a need fer a cabin boy on board. If ye want it, it be yours. What say ye, me boy? Will ye sail with your old man to witness his last redemption?"

Chapter Two

The Choice

"What do you make of him?" John asked his mother. Billy Jack had remained in the wreckage of the pub with them for a short time, but John had given him no answer then. His mind was struggling to process all that he had learned. John's father had departed about an hour before, and now John and his mother sat across from one another in near silence. John spoke, breaking the silence. "Is he really my father?"

"Of course he is," she said quickly. "Who else would it be? You think I'd know the face of my own lover, even after fourteen years." She drew in a soft breath and looked away, down at the floor of *The Spot* which was still covered in debris from the fight. "And I don't know what to make of him."

"Should I go with him?"

"Do you want to?" she replied.

"I don't know," said John. "I don't really know him, and the stories you've told me . . . ."

"All true," his mother said. "But he says he's changed, and there's some reason to think maybe he has. You didn't know him before, John. A darker, harder man he was. Not like this." She reached over the table and took his hand in her own and held it. "I still don't trust him. Not after what he did, even if it did happen as he says and he were captured. I don't want you going with him, John."

Billy Jack had told them he would be in port for two days, and John did not answer him, nor see him, until the second day. Lost in his thoughts, pulled in two directions at once, he found himself unable to choose. On the one hand, he had no idea who this man was that had emerged out of the night, claiming to be his father. The intimidation of sailing, which John had never liked, was another reason for his hesitation. Let alone to sail along the Spanish Main in search of a lost island and steal the treasure hidden there right from under the most feared pirate sailing the seas, potentially bringing his bloodthirsty wrath down upon them all. John had heard enough of the stories to know that risking the vengeance of a man like Bloodbeard was the last thing he wanted to do. Bloodbeard, it was said, had earned his name from his habit of slitting the throats of his victims and bathing his beard in their blood. Of the many ships he had ravaged over the years, few among the crews had ever survived.

On the other hand was the promise of a new life, a chance to make something for himself. He did not like to admit it, but he resented his mother's determination for him not to go, to remain behind and, potentially, to always remain under her watchful eye. He knew her sudden protectiveness came only from a desperation not to lose her son as she had his father, but John pushed this thought aside.

In the end, he knew there was only one real choice before him, loath as he was to admit it.

The ship lurched beneath John's feet as it rolled with the swells of the sea. The night of his father's unexpected return was three days past, and they had just set out from Massachusetts Bay with light sail near an hour before, tacking south-east.

He had waited to the last minute before sprinting home and telling his mother, in a mad rush, that he was going. She had tried to persuade him not to, but his mind had been made up. She soon realized there was nothing she could do. He found himself angry with her for never telling him she too had been a pirate, let alone sailed with Bloodbeard himself. He felt she had done him an injustice, and was determined to experience what both his father and mother had. The decision had been rash, he knew, but he had had a full day to back out so he supposed some part of him wanted very much to go.

John was on the starboard side of the aft castle, clutching the gunwale and trying not to be sick. Crewmen smirked and laughed as they passed, but John ignored them all, closing his eyes against the world, which was moving too much under his feet. His father, Billy Jack, was at the helm some feet away, gently guiding the sloop as it made its way through the sea.

John leaned over the side and vomited into the brine, then fell back, gasping and wiping his chin.

"Calm seas today," Billy Jack commented, eying John with amusement as he turned the wheel. "Ye'll have yer sea legs soon enough, and no doubt!"

The *Jerusalem* wasn't his father's ship. The Captain was a man named Beneniah Davids, but the crew all called him the Parson, on account of the fact that he was a most religious man, a Puritan by affiliation, who had most of the whole Bible memorized. He it was that had converted Billy Jack, and held prayer meetings belowdecks on Wednesday nights and Sunday worship in the morning for all but the necessary men at the helm and crow's nest.

The Parson and the rest of the crew were British sailors loyal to the Crown, and they had originally served as Billy Jack's guard on the *Jerusalem* when he had first been made to show them the treasure locations. Now, however, the men had developed a camaraderie with one another, as they learned over the years that he wouldn't run off. He wasn't even a prisoner anymore, but one of the crew, first mate to the Parson and the usual helmsman. When they pulled into a port, he was at liberty to go ashore without any questions asked. John later found out that the *Jerusalem* had sailed far out of its way to come to Massachusetts bay colony so Billy Jack could speak to him and his mother. Clearly, it was important to Billy Jack that John come along on this voyage.

"Where are we going again?" John asked, leaning unsteadily against the gunwale and looking at his father.

"Port Royal," Billy Jack said. "One of the few colonies on the Spanish Main controlled by the crown."

"How far?" John croaked. "Another hour or two?" He was being sarcastic, but that didn't stop him hoping it were true.

"Two weeks, more or less," Billy Jack said, scratching his beard thoughtfully.

John felt it would never come soon enough. They sailed for a full week through clear weather, and without incident. John got his sea legs within a few days of their departure from the colony, as promised.

The *Jerusalem* was a sloop, a small ship, perhaps fifty feet, with two decks and a mere eight foot draft in the water. It had ten long guns, a crew of forty and a single mainmast, to which all the sails were attached. "Pirates an' those who hunt 'em prefer the sloop," Billy Jack told him one evening. "They're small and light. With a sloop you can strike a bigger, slower ship faster than lightning, out maneuver them, an' get into coves and the like where a bigger one would run aground on reefs. You can even avoid a full broadside in a sloop; seen it with me own eyes, lad!"

As John soon discovered, the life of a cabin boy was one of many chores and duties. He scrubbed the decks and fetched supper for the Parson and Billy Jack. Helping with the preparation of meals was by far the most unpleasant activity he had to do on the ship; the mess cook was a foul, grunting, sweaty man who delighted in making John slaughter the meat. Because food spoiled so quickly on board a ship such as the *Jerusalem*, as much of the meat as possible was taken aboard while still alive and prepared as need arose. The parts they didn't need were thrown overboard, a chore John detested. The bloody animal parts attracted sharks, and they would form packs and follow the ship for days on end, circling easily, hoping for more morsels—or an unlucky sailor who wasn't minding his footing.

Easily the most terrifying part of the job was being forced to scale the rigging when the sails needed trimmed. The weather had remained steady the first few days, but then the wind changed.

"Wind's shifted! The sails are luffing!" Billy Jack shouted to him, the first time this had happened. "Up and trim 'em, lad!"

John gaped at him. Above him, the sails were fluttering, slack in the wind.

"Into the rigging, lad, an' trim them!"

"I—I don't—"

"Hell's breath!" Billy Jack cried, realizing. "Collins,

take th' helm."

The second mate took the helm and Billy Jack came over to where John was standing. He took John by the shoulder and directed him to the rigging. Snagging the thick, rough ropes in his hand, Billy Jack stepped onto the gunwale and swung himself into the netting and started to climb.

"Come on, lad, up with ye!" he cried. "You're about to learn a thing or two about sailing."

John gazed nervously over the side to the water some ten feet below lapping at their hull. His mind was suddenly filled with visions of himself losing his grip thirty feet in the air and plummeting from the rigging to the dark waters below. But there was nothing to be done, so he cautiously took a hold of the rigging and stood on the gunwale, clutching at the ropes. The glittering sea filled his eyes as far as he could see.

He hesitated, lifting his leg and turning around to face the ship again, inching his foot out into the netting. It held his weight, and so he clambered onto it completely and looked up, clutching the ropes with tight fingers. The rigging stretched away from him and narrowed to a point some thirty feet above. The small platform of the crow's nest was directly above it. Billy Jack had nearly reached the top, so John awkwardly went after him, pausing and clutching the rigging in desperation every time the ship rolled under him. In a minute or two he had reached his father, who was at the peak of the rigging and staring out to sea, enraptured.

"The sea, lad," he said, his eyes lost in the view stretching before them. "Look at her an' behold her might."

John clung to the netting, craning his neck to look out

at the churning ocean beyond them, a bobbing, foaming mass, always flat yet always moving. His stomach lurched unpleasantly at the sight and he turned back, focusing his eyes on Billy Jack and the mast behind him, taking deep breaths.

"What's your trouble, me boy?"

"Don't like heights," John said, forcing himself to breathe regularly. To his annoyance his father threw back his head and laughed, dangling lightly from the rigging by one hand and foot.

"You'll be over that afore we make berth in Port Royal harbor!" Billy Jack cried, grinning. He dragged John a little higher in the rigging so they were more or less side by side. "See how the sails are flutterin' like that? That's called luffing, an' it means the wind's not filling them like it should. Wind's changed, see? It's our job to turn 'em and trim 'em til they're full. Got it?"

Billy Jack showed him how to trim the sails to adjust for the speed and position of the wind, making him crawl out on the sail frame and use the foot ropes for balance. John hated this, inching out away from the ship over the ocean, clutching to the sail, then having to hold himself steady with his legs and back alone as they set about adjusting the sails until they ceased luffing. They pulled on lines and drew up and let down sail for over an hour, clinging precariously over the deep. Finally they finished, and John found that his hands were raw and blistering from the rough ropes. His father slapped him on the back and spoke of it as though they were honorable wounds received in battle. "Soon enough you won't even notice," he cried. "You did well today, me boy! Very well indeed!"

It was with a sore back and arms that John carried the platters of food up to the Parson's cabin for the captain

27

and his father. He was exhausted and it seemed as though every muscle in his body was constantly trembling.

He kicked the door to the aft cabin open and held it with his boot, carefully balancing his burdens in step with the roll and pitch of the ship. He navigated it successfully and glanced about the cabin.

It was spacious by the standards of the ship, about twelve foot square. Most of the men had only hammocks below decks for a living area. An ornate table stood in the middle of the cabin, and a gilded chest of drawers in the corner. There was a mirror propped against a writing desk on the far aft wall, below a set of windows. Candles had been lit and placed on the table, the flames tilting strangely with the movement of the sloop. The places were set, but the Parson and Billy Jack were bent over a map spread over the table, deep in discussion.

Billy Jack shook his head, and said something, indicating a marking on the map. The Parson didn't look pleased, pursing his lips below his great red beard.

"Dinner," John said, joining them at the table and setting the platters down before he lost his balance and dropped them. The two men looked up, and Billy Jack rolled up the map before John could see what was on it.

"Ahh, bless you!" cried the Parson in his booming voice, pulling out a chair and sitting. "A bit of feast restores the soul!"

Billy Jack did not meet John's gaze, but turned and crossed the cabin to the chest of drawers. He slipped the map into one of the drawers, closed it, and pulled a small key from a string around his neck, and locked the drawer. Then he returned to the table and sat, looking at John.

"What was that?" John asked, his eyes lingering on the drawer.

"That's of no nevermind to you," Billy Jack said gruffly.

"Now, now," the Parson said. "Your son's merely curious. He won't be able to alert anyone to our plans, in any case." He turned and looked at John. "We're planning —"

"—our route," Billy Jack finished, looking at the Parson. "We're needing to avoid Bloodbeard or things could get a bid awry."

"And," said the Parson, "we're planning our strategy once we're to the island. There's no guarantee we'll be able to slip through pirate waters without being seen. Always good to be prepared."

John nodded.

"Are we going to eat here tonight?" Billy Jack growled. "Some of us are mighty famished."

John passed out the food and hovered, unsure of what to do. Billy Jack hunched over his food immediately, eating it with his fingers. The Parson bowed his head for a moment, before starting in on his, using his fork and knife to cut his meat.

"Are you going to hover there like a lost parrot?" the Parson asked. "Join us, boy."

John sat, watching the two men eat. His father was definitely not pleased at the interruption in their planning session. He chopped and stabbed at his food, not meeting John's eyes.

The Parson sat lightly in his chair, despite being a heavy-set man with a barrel chest. His skin was leathery from the years in the sun, but his face was friendly. He wore the ordinary clothes of a sailor, not the finery of a merchant captain—the guise they used when sailing in the Main.

"You don't dress like a Captain," John said. "At least, not the sort of captain I expected."

"The only thing finery makes you on the high seas is a target," the Parson said. "I have what I need to keep me warm and nothing more."

"My father dresses well," John said, looking at Billy Jack, who was again sporting the waistcoat he had entered *the Spot* wearing those ten days before.

"You can take the piracy out of a pirate, and he will yet feel need to ploom himself like an overgrown peacock," said the Parson, chuckling.

"Not that it's stopped you from tryin'," Billy Jack grunted.

"I must do my best with the flock I'm given," the Parson said, spreading his hands helplessly. "I fear even my best will not be enough for Billy Jack Thatcher!"

"God's own Spirit had te wrestle with me, Parson," Billy Jack said with a smile. "What more can mere mortals do?"

"Aye, wrestled with you all night, as with Jacob," the Parson agreed.

"Took him all night too," Billy Jack said, grinning. "It were touch and go for a time, before I bested him."

"Don't blaspheme," the Parson said, his voice cold. Billy Jack glanced at him over his food.

"Apologies, Parson," he said, and John was startled to hear the remorse in his voice.

"Besides," the Parson said, "the Lord let you win on purpose." He smiled. "Don't listen to us, John. We're the old dogs of the sea, and we spend our time bickering more and more. Tell me, what of the Colony? Are things well there?"

So John told him about the growth of the

Massachusetts Bay Colony, how the preacher Jonathan Edwards had been the first President of the young Harvard College, how the colony had grown, and about the additional towns popping up. The colonists were advancing west into the wilderness beyond the bay.

"Edwards, eh?" the Parson boomed. "A great man. Puritan himself, you know. I've heard of him. Brings men to tears by his very preaching!"

"The Parson is just envious," Billy Jack said. "The conclusion of his sermons bring people to tears of relief!"

"Bah!" cried the Parson, but he was laughing. "Even better that I'm the captain, then! My crew is captive to my words, or they can leap overboard."

"One of these days one of the men will take it into his head that being a feast for the fins is a sweet relief."

The banter was cheering Billy Jack, who was becoming more of his usual boisterous self by the moment. Soon he was roaring with laughter at the Parson's jokes. The Parson was nothing of the way John had expected him to be. He was jolly, the first to laugh, the first to share a joke. It was a shocking contrast with the Puritans John knew back in Massachusetts; dour, self-righteous and depressing. He found himself liking the Parson very much.

His father, on the other hand, was still something of an enigma. As that meal revealed, his mood could shift at any moment, moving from excited or energetic to the depths of anger or dark scowls. He was a hard man, who demanded perfection from John, but he was also a good man. That much John could tell. He could also sense that his presence on the *Jerusalem* meant much to Billy Jack.

For his part, John could not deny that being with his father meant a lot to him too.

A week and a half out from the Bay Colony, the *Jerusalem* sighted another ship.

"Sail off the starboard!" came the shout from the crow's nest. John's father had been on the aft deck, talking with the Parson over their midday meal. They exchanged looks, dropped their food and rushed to the starboard side, squinting out at the bright water. John followed them and stood next to his father, trying to catch a glimpse of the ship.

The ocean was reflecting the sunlight, blinding him. John's eyes began to water at the sight. He could see nothing at all; the horizon seemed clear.

"Glass!" shouted Billy Jack. "Bring me a glass!"

The helmsman hurried to him and handed him the thin, brass telescope. He pulled it open and raised it to his eye.

"Sail," he said. "Looks like a twin-master."

"Pirate?" asked the Parson.

"They're ten miles out," Billy Jack replied, his eyes still to the glass. "Can't tell yet."

"We're already in Spanish waters," the Parson said. "Let me see that."

He took the glass and lifted it to his eye. John could hear the Parson's steady breathing for a long moment.

"I can't tell if they're even flying colors," he said.

"What's that mean?" John asked his father.

"If they're flying no colors, probably pirate. They'll wait until they're on top of us, then hoist the black flag," Billy Jack said. "If they're Spanish, they'll try to take us."

"Why?"

"We're in their territory," Billy Jack said. "It's called the Spanish Main, after all. If they catch us, they'll slit our throats and leave us for the fins."

He took the eyeglass back from the Parson, snapped it shut and slid it into his belt, then sprinted back to the wheel. He pushed the helmsman aside, and squinted up at the sails.

"Is there anything nearby?" the Parson shouted to Billy Jack, looking worried. "An island, a cove, anything?"

"A few islands," Billy Jack replied. "Nowhere we'd want to go. If they're pirates, they're headed for one of them themselves, most like."

"What are we doing?" John asked.

"Running, lad," Billy Jack said, his voice grim, giving the wheel a terrific spin. The ship surged beneath their feet. He glanced out at the expectant faces of the crew. "Give me a broad reach, lads!"

Sailors sprang into the rigging, scurrying out onto the mast and letting out the sails. Others adjusted the position of the sails to catch the wind, tying the braces fast. John moved to help, but his father took hold of his shirt and held him where he was.

"Stay," his father said. "You're still new to this, an' we've no time for foolin' about today."

"Give me the glass," the Parson said, holding out his hand. Billy Jack handed it to him, shouting at the sailors amid the rigging. The Parson moved to the gunwale and raised the glass to his eye. John looked out across the waves to where the other ship was supposed to have been. Now he could see a gray patch on the horizon, nearly a square.

"They've come about," the Parson said, his eye still to the glass. "Eight miles. Boatswain, give me a reading!"

The boatswain retrieved a rope with thick knots from a wooden locker and crossed the deck. He tossed one end of the rope over the side, and let it run out. The long rope uncoiled like a serpent, rushing and clattering over the side. The boatswain caught the rope and hauled it back in.

"Twenty-five knots!"

"We can do better," the Parson said to Billy Jack.

"No need yet," Billy Jack said, though his eyes were worried. "Shown their colors?"

"Not that I can see," the Parson said. "Pray it's the Spanish."

"I thought you said the Spanish would cut our throats," John said.

"They will, but they're better than the alternative," Billy Jack growled.

"What's the alternative?"

Billy Jack looked at him, his expression grim.

"If those be pirates, then it'll be Bloodbeard."

John felt his blood run cold. "What?" he gasped.

"Those men in the tavern, the ones who tried to steal yer money," Billy Jack was saying, "they're on Bloodbeard's crew. Old Bloody Hands be his new first mate."

"You mean he was that close to us?" John said, beginning to tremble.

"Bloodbeard ranges up and down the coasts – usually to avoid a concentrated hunt by the British or Spanish. He sails up to the Carolinas and waits for the hunt to die away, then creeps back into the Spanish Main. By now, of course, he knows I were in that tavern, an' he'll want to find us."

"You mean he's looking for you," John said.

"Of course he's lookin' for me!" Billy Jack snapped. "I'm his former first mate, who turned on him and has been stealing his treasures out from under his nose for the last twelve years! He'll be wantin' revenge, mark my words, lad."

"Colors ho!" came the call from the crow's nest. "The Spanish crest!"

"Praise God," the Parson said, snapping the glass shut and bowing his head in a silent prayer.

"But they'll still cut our throats, right?" John said.

"Only if they catch us, and that's a might unlikely."

"Why? They've got two masts and twice the sail!"

"Aye, but they're a bigger ship, weighed down with soldiers or treasures and twice the cannon," said Billy Jack. "We're into the wind now. They'd be hard-pressed to catch us. That hull creates too much drag tg catch a sloop like ours. So long as the wind stays in our favor, we've made a clean getaway."

Chapter Three

Trouble in Port Royal

The *Jerusalem* easily outstripped the Spanish ship and left it far behind. Without hours it had vanished behind the horizon, abandoning the chase. They encountered no other ships in the water before reaching Port Royal.

"Land ho!" came the call from the crow's nest early one morning. "Off the port side!"

A quick search of the horizon revealed a dark, uneven smudge clinging to the surface of the waters. John gazed at it, taking in every detail. He had been unsure of coming along with his father, but now that they were this close to an island like Jamaica, he found he was glad he had. The prospect of seeing a land he had never set foot upon sent chills of excitement up and down his back.

It was another two hours of sailing before they reached the bay of Port Royal. They sailed along the coastline close enough for John to see the palm trees and lush, green undergrowth. The island's coast seemed to rise almost straight out of the sea into towering bluffs. The cries of exotic birds could be heard even at that distance and over the sound of the sails and the curses of the sailors.

As they approached the mouth of the bay, John caught sight of a small island, nearly nothing more than a spot of land. Upon this scrap of rock was an iron cage suspended from a gibbet. The corpse of a man had been placed in the cage, and a great crowd of birds were picking over the body, shrieking and feasting.

"What's that?" he asked.

Billy Jack glanced at it and smiled grimly. "Deadman's Cay," he said. "Where they put pirate captains, or especially villainous sea dogs. That's where they were going to put me."

"You?"

"Bloodbeard's first mate, lad," Billy Jack said, with a smile that almost concealed his fear.

The mouth of the bay into Port Royal was wide, and the rocks on either side rose up around it like great solemn sentries over their heads, creating a natural wall between the harsh wind of the open sea, and the bay. At the furthest point the rocks along the port side dwindled to a craggy promontory on a treacherously narrow spit of land. It was windswept and empty beyond the five bodies swinging from a yardarm attached to the rocks. A wooden sign above the bodies proclaimed Pirates Beware.

"Gallows Point," Billy Jack said.

"They really don't like pirates here, do they?" John said, watching the bodies creak back and forth in the breeze as they sailed past.

"That they don't," Bill Jack agreed.

Even in the bay, the water was not free of sharks. John could pick out five or six fins in the water, languidly circling ships or the docks in hopes of discarded meat or the accidental misstep of a dockworker.

"Why are there so many sharks?" he asked his father. Billy Jack glanced at the calm water of the bay.

"With every fisherman guttin' his catch, and the

37

butchers dumping their leftovers in the bay, it tends to draw the fins," he said. "You don't notice 'em after a while. Unless ye fall in!"

The *Jerusalem* weighed anchor near the mouth of the bay and John, Billy Jack, the Parson and four others clambered into a longboat. They rowed through the water to the nearest dock, some two hundred yards away, and tied up at the pier. A few dockhands nearby scurried close and extended their hands, helping to steady the crew in turn as they stepped up onto the wooden wharf.

Billy Jack went before John, then turned and extended a hand for John to grab. After a slight hesitation, John took his hand and Billy Jack hoisted him onto the pier. It felt strange to John to be standing on ground that didn't lurch and roll beneath his feet. The harbormaster approached them, holding a book and quill.

"That's ten shillings to make berth in the bay," the harbormaster said, his voice unpleasantly high-pitched.

"We're not carrying cargo," the Parson said. "We're here to take on supply."

"Ten shillings is for the presence of your vessel in the bay. All other costs are in addition."

"Have you run mad?" the Parson cried. "T'wasn't more than three months since we were here last, and the price wasn't but four!"

The harbormaster spread his hands as though helpless to change the situation, but his eyes gleamed eagerly as the Parson furiously counted out shillings. The harbormaster bit them each in turn, grunted in satisfaction and dropped them in a leather pouch at his side. He sniffed at them aggressively, as though they were hardly worth the trouble, turned and stalked off toward another longboat that had just pulled to shore.

"Let's not stand about lollygaggin'," Billy Jack said.

The pier ended at the shoreline in a muddy path speckled with bootprints, which meandered up a gentle slope into the town of Port Royal proper, and ran even further up to the stone fortress at the crest of the hill overlooking the town.

They set off along the muddy track to the gates of the town. As it was still early morning, few people were about. Kingsmen were everywhere, their typical red coats spattered with mud as they fetched drunks out of the gutters and collected corpses out of the streets from the night's fights.

The town was surrounded by a wooden palisade constructed from logs with pointed tips. They reached the gates, and two surly Kingsmen waved them through without a second glance. The soldiers sat at a small table, playing cards and reeking of gin and horses.

Most of the buildings stretched along the road had two stories; the second stories jutted out over the street, making it appear as though the buildings were tipping inward. Someone was urinating out of a second story window into the street.

As they made their way further up into the town, more people were about. The sun was rising higher into the sky, and several venders wrestled their carts down the road to the wharf to hock their wares. It took nearly a half-hour to hike their way through to the other end of Port Royal and climb the cobbled road to the fortress.

The walls rose high over their heads as they approached, built from mortar and stone. The soldiers about the fort were more alert than those by the docks had been. They paced to and fro, their rifles held in the crook of their arms. The wooden gates were drawn open at their approach and a man was crossing the yard towards them. Four or five redcoats stood on the other side of the gates, fingering their rifles, ready to burst into motion if their company proved a threat.

"Benaniah Davids," the man said when he was within shouting distance, hailing the Parson. "Back at last, are you?"

"Aye," the Parson said, nodding.

The man was dressed in black knickers, a dark waistcoat and a silk, high-collared shirt. He held himself tall, his back stiff. John knew the man was some sort of doorman for the governor—he was dressed the same as the higher servants of the Massachusettes colony's governor.

"I am Isaiah Harolds," the man said, bowing. "Governor Vaughan was informed the moment the *Jerusalem* made port. He's prepared to see you at your earliest convenience."

"That be why we're here," Billy Jack said.

"Ah, yes, the pirate." Harolds glowered at him for a moment, then turned back to the Parson. "This way, please."

He took them through the yard to the steps of the keep. Sentries paced along the walls, and some servants were rolling barrels up a ramp to a storage room. Beyond that, the yard was devoid of life.

They padded their way up the steps to the double doors of the keep. The sentries pushed them open as they approached. The entrance chamber was well lit, fashionable carpet laid on the polished wood floor, silver candelabras resting on mahogany tables to either side. Harolds ignored all this, taking them up a long stairwell that wound its way up to a second floor balcony. This balcony opened out to a hallway that led in both directions, doorways clearly visible on either side. Down the left hall lay another double-door made of dark mahogany. It was towards these doors Howards moved, throwing them open and beckoning the party to enter.

The room within was large and spacious. A large polished desk lay facing the doors, perpendicular to a large bay window that overlooked the fort, the town and harbor beyond. It was at this window a small man stood in the clear finery of a British governor. His long, powdered wig fell below his shoulders beneath a large, festive hat, his waistcoat made of silk and other fineries. He stood facing away from them, gazing out of the window.

"Captain Davids," the man said. He turned and smiled at the Parson, who bowed.

"Your Excellency," he said.

"Clap the pirate in irons," Governor Vaughan said with a flick of his hand towards Billy Jack. The guards at the door stepped up to him and seized him by the elbows before he could move. They fetched a pair of iron cuffs from a nearby table and locked his hands in them.

"What is this?" Billy Jack spat.

"A small reminder, to refresh your memory of exactly who it is that you serve," the Governor said. He turned to the Parson. "Captain Davids, according to what I am told the *Jerusalem* put into port at the Massachusetts bay colony nearly a month ago. This was not part of your instructions, was it?"

"We went under Billy Jack's bequest," the Parson said. "He's been looking for his son for fourteen years, and wanted him to witness his changed heart and mind. He's served the Crown faithfully these years. I thought it would do him good."

"Your son, is it?" Governor Vaughan said, his voice disbelieving. "Where is the young pirate whelp?"

Billy Jack and the Parson turned and looked at John. He opened his mouth to speak, but saw his father give a little shake of the head. He closed his mouth.

"Ah," the Governor said, stepping away from the window and crossing the room for a better look. "So there he is. This man is your father, is he?"

John nodded.

The Governor stared at him for another moment, then shrugged and turned to the Parson. "The problem is this," he said, pacing to his desk. "This man, Billy Jack Thatcher, is a pirate."

"Was a pirate," the Parson corrected. The governor met his gaze calmly.

"Is a pirate, Captain Davids," the Governor said. "I can see you've spent too much time with rogues. You're beginning to speak like them."

"I were a pirate, true enough," Billy Jack growled. "But I've hoisted new colors these last years. If you don't believe my word, I bear letters of marque. Check them yerself."

"I'm very well aware of that, Thatcher, as you were issued those letters of marque by my predecessor," the Governor said. "But the simple fact is, you are a pirate until your purpose to the Crown is completed. One last treasure. One last job. And one begins to wonder what will become of the infamous Billy Jack Thatcher then? If we allow our minds to wander towards the ending of your story with us, we see a great, wide blank spot on the map. Am I wrong? What will you do then, Thatcher? When you have your freedom?"

"Hadn't given it much thought," Billy Jack said. "Spend time with me boy, settle down somewhere. Maybe start a proper family, iff'n his mother can stand to look at me."

"A family!" the Governor barked. "You're too in love with the sea for that, Thatcher."

"What is it you be gettin' at, Governor?" Billy Jack said.

"One cannot help wonder if Billy Jack Thatcher might be succumbing to the temptation of returning to his previous life," the Governor said. "The freedom of the sea after fourteen grueling years in forced service to the Crown. The sight of all that treasure—yours, by rights—must have been a terrible burden to bear, knowing you will never see a shilling of it."

"You've got Billy Jack pegged wrong," said the Parson, shaking his head. "He's been on my crew for all those fourteen years. You learn a thing or two about a man after that long. That's not his life any longer. He's a changed man."

"Changed men don't let others answer questions directed at them," Governor Vaughan snapped. "It appears to me you were all too willing to deviate from your assigned course on the slightest whim of a pirate. Could Captain Davids be in on the plot?"

"What plot?" the Parson snapped. "Have you run mad?"

"Isla San Thanatos is many leagues from here," the Governor said. "Far off our known charts, or so I'm told. It would not be difficult to simply vanish with the treasure, once the island is found, and return to a life of piracy."

"Nonsense!" spluttered the Parson.

The Governor gestured to one of the guards. The man stepped towards Billy Jack, reached into his waistcoat, and withdrew a flap of leather bound with black ribbon. He handed the folded leather to the Governor.

"Aye, those are me letters of marque," Billy Jack said, nodding. "Look them over. Question anyone on the crew of the *Jerusalem*. They'll tell ye straight."

"I'm sure they would," the Governor said, untying the ribbon and unfolding the leather. On the inside were several pieces of parchment. "Yes, this all seems in order."

The Governor moved behind the desk to the fireplace set into the wall. He tossed the letters of marque into the flames and watched as they flared.

"What are you doin'!" cried Billy Jack, struggling against the redcoats restraining him. "Those are my letters of marque!"

"Were your letters of marque, I'm afraid," the Governor said. "It seems clear we cannot trust you. Duplicate letters of marque are being drawn up as we speak. They will be ready by the time you return. Bring the treasure back and your pardon will be restored."

"You mean to set this man to sail without the protection of a written pardon?" the Parson cried. "He's Billy Jack Thatcher! Without that pardon, he'll be the prey of every sailor we meet."

"He is indeed Billy Jack Thatcher, which is why we must take extra precaution. Neither I nor the Crown desire to have him vanish with a ship's hold piled with the King's gold and a full pardon to get him into any port and coast town in the Caribbean." The Governor came around the desk again, staring daggers at Billy Jack. "It is high time you remember what you are," he growled. "Give you a taste of the old life again; hunted down by everyone you meet. Perhaps that will be incentive enough to keep you from falling into temptation."

"Remember who I be," Billy Jack said softly. "What am I, exactly?"

"You're a pirate," Governor Vaughan said. "Once a pirate, always a pirate."

"Is that so, now?" came a voice from behind them. They turned to see a tall man hobbling forward into the room on a crutch. He too was dressed in the fine clothes of high British style, his wig only slightly smaller than the Governor's. He limped with every step, the shadow of a grimace flaring across his face, his crutch clunking on the wood floors with a loud resonance.

"Henry," said Billy Jack, nodding.

The man Henry nodded to Billy Jack as he passed.

"Once a pirate, always a pirate, is it?" Henry said, limping into the room and looking at the Governor with a disgusted glance. "Is this the new policy of Port Royal, or am I to be arrested myself?"

"Lieutenant-Governor," Vaughan said, with a sour look. "I should have thought you would still be crawling out of a gutter somewhere, nursing a hangover."

"There's still time," Henry said. "Now why are you threatening men I have myself already vouched for?"

"You," said Vaughan, "were not a pirate. You were a privateer in the Crown's employ."

"Not a pirate?" said Henry, falling back on his heels with mock surprise. "The Spanish might have a different opinion."

"Who is that?" John asked his father. Billy Jack opened his mouth to answer, but the man Henry seemed to have heard. He turned and pulled his feathered hat from his head and attempted a dramatic bow on his crutches to

45

John, grimacing in pain, though his eyes sparkled.

"I am Admiral Sir Henry Morgan, Lieutenant-Governor of Port Royal and former pirate," Henry said, replacing his hat atop his powdered wig. "I ask you again, Governor, why do you plague these men with threats and unanswerable questions? If Billy Jack Thatcher is a pirate, then I am as well. Clap me in irons."

Morgan held out his hands, bracing his weight on his crutch, and gave Vaughan a significant look.

"Thatcher is under my protection. If you will not arrest me, then unbind his hands."

The Governor smiled, turned without a word and paced to a polished cabinet along the left-hand wall. He opened the top and withdrew a decanter of what looked like brandy and a glass, pulled the crystal stopper from the top, and poured himself a drink. Facing them again, looking thoughtful, he sipped the dark liquid.

"Morgan, your impudence more and more reveals to me you are unfit to have anything whatever to do with the civil governance of our city," he said.

"Civil, is it, burning a man's duly promised letters of marque after fourteen years faithful service to the Crown?" Morgan said. "If that's your definition of civil, then we have finally reached an agreement in our time in office! I shall resign at once."

"Your protests are weak," the Governor said. "We've come so close to undercutting Bloodbeard's supply of coin and I'll not have his first mate escaping to rejoin him. The matter is as simple as that. Release him," he said to the guards.

They stepped forward and twisted a key in the lock. With a metallic rattle, the irons fell away, and Billy Jack massaged his wrists.

"You will be watched carefully in your time here," Vaughan said. "And a guard will be placed on your ship to ensure nothing goes amiss on your voyage." He looked hard at Billy Jack. "It will be as I said, pirate. Return here when your job is completed and you shall be a free man. Flee, or revert to older ways, and know that you will be hunted down like the sea dog you are."

Governor Vaughan nodded to the guards, and the interview was finished. The guards escorted them outside the Governor's office and closed the doors in their faces.

"Well, that went better than last time," the Parson commented wryly.

"Last time he didn't burn me letters of marque," Billy Jack snarled.

"This time you didn't stick your pistol in his face," said the Parson. "Progress."

"It's nearly nine in the morning," said Henry Morgan, looking at them all, his eyes sparkling. "I'd say its time for a drink."

Sir Henry Morgan's plantation was a mile out of Port Royal, set on the top of a bluff overlooking the bay. As the carriage rattled and jostled its way up the wide dirt lane, John gazed out of the window at the rolling sugar cane fields stretching out before them. Black slaves in straw hats were bent over in the fields. He could see the white, pillared mansion in the distance growing gradually closer.

"All of this is yours?" John asked him.

"That it is," Morgan said. "I saw the look on your face in the Governor's office. Did you recognize my name, then?"

"My mother," John said, staring at Morgan. "She told

me of you."

"It's the rare fellow that hasn't heard the name of Henry Morgan," said Billy Jack.

Morgan looked pleased, but said nothing.

"What are you doing in Port Royal?" John asked. "And how do you know my father?"

Henry Morgan laughed, and at that moment the carriage came to a halt in front of Morgan's estate house. The driver clambered down from his perch at the top of the carriage, brushed the dust from himself, and pulled open the door.

Morgan went first, stepping into the sunlight. He was followed by Billy Jack, the Parson and finally John.

"Are you thirsty?" Morgan called back to them, waving at a black woman in a brown dress and tatty apron who had appeared on the porch. She hurried inside, but Morgan did not follow. Instead, he climbed the wooden steps to the wide, white-washed porch, where a rocking chair sat. Morgan winced and grunted with every step, having to brace his crutch on the step higher from his feet and half-haul, half-jump to the next.

He collapsed in the rocking chair and threw his crutch aside as though disgusted by it. He gave a great sigh, closing his eyes in relief.

"What ails ye, Henry?" asked Billy Jack as they joined him on the porch. Morgan opened his eyes and looked at them, hovering in a cluster by the stairs. Realizing there were no more chairs, he grunted and sat up just as the black woman returned, bearing a tray with a bottle of liquor and some glasses. Morgan's drink had already been poured, and he took it eagerly. Sipping, he gasped as his shoulders slumped.

"Monique, fetch some more chairs, if you would,"

Morgan said. The woman curtsied and moments later had returned with some wooden chairs from the kitchen. Billy Jack, the Parson and John sat, and Billy Jack poured drinks out. John did not get one.

"My legs began to swell not two months ago," Morgan said. "The doctor tells me it's the dropsy."

"Surely not," breathed the Parson.

"My health steadily declines," Morgan said. "I am developing a cough, and the doctors fear it may be tuberculosis."

"What can be done?" Billy Jack asked.

"Not much," Morgan said. "But my health is not the only thing that founders. I'm falling out of favor with the King. The royal court is put off by what Governor Vaughan describes as my 'antics.'"

"Are pirates favorably looked upon by the King?" John asked, frowning.

"Yoy don't understand what you're sayin'," Billy Jack said, scowling at him.

"It's all right," Morgan said, smiling at John. "You asked how a man such as myself came to be here. I was a pirate true enough, but I was the right sort of pirate, you see. I plundered the Spanish and gave to the English in the finest tradition of Robin Hood. You can understand my fame, can you not?

"All the same, I was captured, arrested and shipped back to London for trial. Six years ago I was pardoned by King Charles and given to wear the honorable knighthood."

"He's played the politician's game ever since," the Parson finished.

"More or less," Morgan said, "though I find life landward damned tiresome. And now my influence at the court wanes like the vanishing moon."

"Why are you telling us all this concerning yer influence?" Billy Jack said.

"You must take especial care, Billy Jack," Morgan said, leaning forward in his chair with a wince. "I was able to grant your deal with the Crown because of that influence. If my shadow at court fades away entirely, I'm liable to be put from the Port Royal Council, and stripped of my office as Lieutenant-Governor. What Governor Vaughan then decides to do with you, I cannot say. You will be at his mercy and not mine."

"You don't think he plans to betray Billy Jack?" the Parson said, looking aghast.

"Politics is a cutthroat business," Morgan said, taking a long slug of his drink. "A business that exhibits far less mercy than an actual cutthroat. There is no telling what Vaughan will do, but he certainly bears Billy Jack ill will, to say the least."

"Wait," John said, looking startled. "You mean to say —it was you that saved my father's life?"

"Aye, that it were," Billy Jack said, smiling. "Who else do you think could have cut me such a deal? I were picked up, just as I told you, an' it just so happened that Governor Lynch were in charge of Port Royal at the time."

"Lynch always had a soft spot in his heart for Henry Morgan," said the Parson.

"Wrote some lovely letters about me to the King, filled with the very kindest of lies," Morgan said with a smile, taking another swig of his drink and refilling his cup from the bottle. "It was easy enough to persuade him to make the arrangement with Billy Jack."

"But why?" John asked. "Why would you work so hard to spare the life of another man?"

"The same reason Billy Jack made the bargain in the first place," Morgan said. "Self-interest. I was thinking of all that treasure Bloodbeard had hidden away. Billy Jack was looking for a chance to spare himself the rope. That pragmatism forged a strange bond, and it changed us both."

"For the better," the Parson said.

"Speak for Billy Jack on that count," Morgan said. "You've not yet witnessed my habits of 'unseemly fashion' in the taverns of Port Royal, fair Parson."

"The road to redemption is paved with uneven stones, so that even the most stable of sailors will stumble," the Parson said, his eyes laughing.

"I do not know of redemption," Morgan said. "You must speak to Billy Jack on that mark."

"We do, all too often," Billy Jack said with a barking laugh.

"Parson," Morgan said, looking surprised. "I've just noticed you're drinking strong spirits! I had heard you were a Puritan."

"You heard correctly," the Parson said, sipping his rum. "But just because I am a Puritan does not mean I have ceased to be a man. 'Sometimes we must drink more, sport, recreate ourselves, and even sin a little to spite the devil, so that we leave him no place for troubling our consciences with trifles. When the devil says to me: do not drink, I answer him: I will drink, and right freely, just because you tell me not to.' That is my view of things, anyway."

"Not so very much like a Puritan," Morgan laughed.

"Oh, that's not original with me," the Parson said, waving his hand and taking a large gulp of liquor.

"Who said it?" Morgan asked.

"Martin Luther, the first Protestant."

Morgan laughed, a bellow, barking sound of genuine mirth.

"I like the sound of him already," Morgan said. "Keep up your work, Parson. I may be more a Puritan than you think!"

"Are ye going to tell him what else Luther said about alcohol?" Billy Jack said, with a smile. "'Beer is made by men, wine by God'."

"It is true enough," the Parson admitted. "Beer is made by man, wine by God. But rum was brewed by the angels, and of that no man shall dissuade me!"

The men laughed. Even John smiled.

They remained at Morgan's estate until sunset, laughing and talking. Morgan often took his meals at the taverns, and he pressed upon John's father and the Parson to accompany him to his favorite pub. The Parson wasn't much inclined to go, but Morgan insisted they share one last meal together before they set off in the morning. Finally, the Parson relented, on Morgan's word they would be free to get to the *Jerusalem* before it became too late in the night. Morgan agreed, though he did not appear pleased.

His carriage took them back into Port Royal, rattling down the sloppy streets in the cool of the evening. The going was much slower than that morning as the streets were crowded by pirates and filthy sailors, all whooping and shouting and laughing at once, staggering drunkenly into the path of their oncoming horses, and Morgan was forced to lean out of the window and shout at the men to move aside.

Finally, as the sun was dropping behind the rolling hills surrounding Port Royal, they reached their destination. It was a tavern of similar construction to *the Spot*, only this one had a balcony on the second floor. Already several pirates had availed themselves to this balcony, and were dangling their legs through the railing, waving loaded pistols in the air as drunken barmaids slumped on their shoulders. A sign above the door read The Royal Chest.

Morgan limped to the door and lurched inside, the others following. Billy Jack put his arm around John's shoulders and guided him inside, steering him away from the path of a drunk that toppled down the steps and flopped in the mud, much to the laughter of his fellows crowded on the porch.

The interior was crowded by sweaty men, crammed at tables playing card or shoved into corners in knots of twos and threes. The air hung thick about them with smoke and the smell of ale.

"The best tavern in all of Port Royal!" cried Morgan, limping over to a table of card players and sitting. There were friendly cries of recognition around the table, and Morgan nodded to them each in turn as they dealt him into the game.

"Is everyone in town out at the taverns?" John asked his father.

"They say there's a tavern for every ten men in Port Royal," Billy Jack said. "Most of the town's about tonight, I think."

"Why?"

"Sailing be a hard job," Billy Jack said. "Very dangerous, and full of stress. The only way such men can unwind is for their relaxation to be something similarly uproareous."

The sharp retort of a pistol echoed into the tavern from

the street. No one seemed to have heard, or cared. John glanced out of one of the windows and saw a man face down in the mud of the street, his mate standing over him with a smoking pistol.

"That man just killed someone!" John said, looking horrified.

"Welcome to Port Royal," his father said grimly.

The night passed in turns of laughter and shouts of rage in the tavern. Sporadically, men would break out into fights, or a gun would be fired into the ceiling. All the while Morgan sat drinking and playing cards. John watched him lose a thousand pounds on a single game without a blink. He laughed and joked with his other players, and soon was almost entirely drunk.

"He seems to have gone a little far," the Parson said, as Morgan staggered past them to the bar for his fifteenth mug of rum.

"Jus . . . takin' after your Martin," Morgan slurred on his way back to the table.

"He wasn't talking about getting slobbering drunk," the Parson said. "He merely wanted us to enjoy ourselves without the pang of conscience."

"I am . . . joying meself," Morgan said, thumping his chest, which set off his cough. He doubled over for a moment, hacking. Groaning, he straightened and smiled. "See?"

"No, you're miserable," the Parson said. "You're just too drunk to notice."

"Hence my unseemly fashions . . . so objectionable at court," Morgan said. "Perhaps I'm not so much a . . . Puritan as I'd thought, or you'd hoped."

Morgan sat and the table with a thud, then thought better of it and rose again, turning back to the Parson.

"Except," he said, "that you are right and I am miserable." He blinked bleary-eyed at the Parson. "Within sight of the sea and unable to venture on her fair back ever again. How is that for a curse, Parson? I am a dead man, and dry land my murderer. A hopeless, helpless cripple am I. A wastrel of the first order, who drinks himself into a stupor every night because he is trapped in the life meant for a different sort of man. A simpleton forced into the mold of a politician! The sea would kill me in a week if I could go aboard a ship, and so I am left to waste away, left to rot myself into oblivion. If the sea can't kill me, the dropsy will, or the tuberculosis. What say you to that? Enough misery? What does your Bible say about that?"

"It would tell you to stop gambling away money you could use on the treatment of your ailment."

"There is no treatment!" Morgan roared. "The only thing that drives away the pain is the rum."

He turned and sat down at the table and resumed playing cards.

"What's all this yelling about?" came a deep, harsh voice from the doorway behind them. John felt his father stiffen suddenly, his eyes flaring wide.

"God in heaven," Billy Jack Thatcher whispered. The tavern had fallen completely silent, and every head turned to the huge, burly shadow standing in the doorway.

"When I hear shouting, it means somethin' be amiss," the grating voice said again. John turned at the same time as Billy Jack.

A man stood against the night, wearing a dark crimson waistcoat and sported a huge, flaming red beard that fell in tight braids to his belt. His eyes were dark and glinted out at them all, and on his left cheek was a great, deep scar. His belt bulged with pistols, and at his side a wicked cutlass hung.

John knew who it was without anyone having to tell him. He could feel himself beginning to tremble.

Bloodbeard had come.

Chapter Four

Sea Battle

Bloodbeard surveyed the room, taking in the stunned and terrified expressions around him. He took another step into the tavern, and several men John recognized followed him inside, spreading out around him.

"What be the matter with ye all?" he shouted, looking at the solemn gazes around him. "We're not here te loot yer fine port. We're lookin' for a single man and that be all, may the Powers strike me if it isn't true. It be true, be it not, lads?"

"Very true, captain," said Bloody Hands, who John recognized as the man that had tried to rob him in *the Spot*. The others that had brawled with Billy Jack were there too.

"I be lookin' for Billy Jack Thatcher," Bloodbeard said. "His boat makes berth in yer waters, an' I seek 'im. Have ye seen him?"

Bloodbeard clearly hadn't seen them yet, standing in a far corner, obscured by the many packed bodies around them. Billy Jack put a tense hand on John's shoulder and pushed him deeper behind several stricken-looking sailors. John looked at him in fear, but Billy Jack shook his head and gave him a reassuring pat on the shoulder blades.

"Stay here," he said. "When ye get a chance, get back to the *Jerusalem*, understand?"

"What are you going to do?" he mouthed to his father.

"I'll be fine," Billy Jack said, not answering John's question.

John watched his father push his way through the still forms and step out in front of the crowd into the wide open space in the center of the tavern floor.

"Hullo, Captain," Billy Jack said, his voice light and conversational, as if discussing the weather.

"Billy Jack!" cried Bloodbeard, with a huge grin. "Be that truly yerself?"

"It is," Billy Jack said.

"Good," said Bloodbeard, drawing a pistol from his belt as fast as lightning. The discharge from the pistol burst on the confinement of the tavern like a thunderclap and Bloodbeard was obscured by the explosion of powder.

Billy Jack had expected the move, however, and threw himself to the side. Bloodbeard's bullet punched through a sailor standing behind Billy Jack. The man screamed and toppled backward, crimson spreading over his chest.

Instantly there was pandemonium in the tavern. Men were yelling and surging in every direction. Bloodbeard's crew had drawn cutlasses and were trying to make their way through the press towards Billy Jack, but the other pirates had drawn sabers and pistols themselves, and sought to defend themselves. Pistol shots exploded back and forth, and the screams of the dying filled John's ears.

He had been shoved aside in the initial burst of motion, and the pirates around him were bumping and jostling him in their desperation to get clear of the fight. John lurched back and forth as the stinking men knocked him into one another. He lost his balance, toppling to the ground, and a man ran him over, stepping on his hand. John yelled in pain, gritting his teeth until the man's weight had lifted. A knee hit him in the head, and threw him to the floor again. Another pistol discharged somewhere over his head, and he could hear the sound of a hundred feet stomping over the floorboards, and the ring of blade upon blade.

Someone fell over top of him. He could feel the man's sweat and tried to shove him away, but the man took hold of his arm and wrenched him. John surged to his feet, and found that the man was the Parson.

"Go!" the Parson shouted, gripping his sword in a white fist. They pressed into the crowd, shoving and throwing men aside as they made their way along the wall towards the door. John was almost lost in the crowd again, as men were thrown between the Parson and himself. The Parson kicked the man in his way in the shins, and he sank to the ground, howling. The Parson seized John by the collar with his free hand and put his shoulder into the men ahead of them, throwing them aside.

John glanced into the press, but he could not see his father anywhere. His heart leapt into his throat, but he had no choice but to follow the Parson through the press. All he could see were arms and cutlasses waving through the crowd. Another pistol fired somewhere out of sight behind them.

The Parson was clear, rushing out of the door of the tavern and into the street. John plunged after him down the steps, gasping and shuddering.

"Run, boy!" shouted the Parson as confused and terrified onlookers sped past, their heads down.

"What about my father?" John shot back.

"There's no time!"

The front window of the tavern exploded into a thousand shards of twinkling glass as Billy Jack Thatcher plunged through it. He landed hard on the porch, used his momentum to roll off the wooden platform and land on his feet several feet away from where John and the Parson stood. He was singed and bleeding from a wound to his shoulder, but alive. John felt relief flood his chest.

"There might be time to get him now," amended the Parson.

"What are ye waitin' for?" shouted Billy Jack. "Let's be away!"

They broke into a sprint, hurtling down the road in the deepening gloom toward the harbor. John glanced back and saw Bloodbeard fighting his way clear and throwing himself through the window after them.

"Hurry!" he shouted.

There was a loud rumble from the street next to the tavern, and Morgan's coach was reigned in before them.

"Get in!" Morgan shouted, throwing the doors wide and beckoning them inside. Billy Jack adjusted course and the others followed. There was a horrifying, strangled cry of rage from behind them. John turned and looked back, just in time to see Bloodbeard drawing another pistol as he closed the distance. He fired his piece, and the ball blew through the coach driver's head. The body toppled backwards off the top of the carriage and vanished from sight. Bloodbeard dropped his pistol and drew another, brandishing his bloodstained cutlass in his other hand.

Billy Jack threw himself into John and tossed him aside as Bloodbeard fired his second pistol. The ball passed through Billy Jack's long hair and punched into the flank of the horse behind him. The animal screamed and bolted. Morgan was half-extended from the cab when the coach lurched away. The Parson, with one foot on the step, toppled to the ground. Billy Jack hoisted him to his feet, drew a pistol from the Parson's belt in one smooth motion, and fired back at Bloodbeard.

"Run!" he shouted, grabbing John's hand and sprinting down the road after the coach, which weaved drunkenly ahead of them, the horse still wailing in pain. There were the sound of multiple shots from behind them, peppering the silence with ear-rattling thunder. The balls missed, however, spattering harmlessly into the mud around them and splintering into the walls of a building to John's left.

They charged down the slope toward the wharf, which lay a few hundred yards away, below them. John's heart was thundering in his ears, his lungs aching, his breath coming in ragged gasps. The coach ahead of them had disappeared down a different street, but there was no time to worry about Morgan now.

Another spurt of gunfire rang out behind them, but Bloodbeard's crew seemed to be too far behind and running too swiftly to get a clean shot. They reached the docks as the pirates behind them reached the gates of the port. They were maybe seventy yards behind, but their shot seemed to have been used up.

"Get to the longboat!" Billy Jack shouted to the Parson. "Get John aboard!"

"What are you—!" the Parson said, but Billy Jack thrust John across the distance between them into the Parson's arms, hefted his cutlass, turned and rushed the charging pirates with a war cry.

"No!" John shouted, struggling wildly. The Parson's grip was too strong for him to break free, however. Billy Jack threw himself into the line of pirates, sword flashing. The ring of crossed swords reached John, who watched with a horrified fascination as his father parried and thrust at their attackers.

Movement caught John's eye to his left. Morgan was hobbling from another gate towards the dock, nearly flying on his crutch. His face was screwed up into a fierce grimace against the pain, but he made good time. He carried a lantern in his hand and a jar of a thick, syrupy liquid.

"Get to your longboat!" Morgan shouted. "I'll take care of the pursuit!"

The Parson dragged John further down to the end of the dock, where their boat lay moored. He threw John into the boat and followed, fumbling with the oars.

John could focus on nothing but the duel taking place on the shore. Billy Jack was ducking and weaving around his opponents, slapping aside their attacks and following with his own.

Bloodbeard stalked through the gates of the palisade, striding confidently down towards the fight. With a hoarse bellow, Bloodbeard threw one of his own men aside and slashed at Billy Jack, who parried. The other pirates backed away as the two men fought, their blades clanging and ringing out in the moonlight.

Billy Jack dodged away from a thrust intended for his gut, and chopped with both hands for Bloodbeard's shoulder. The strike was deflected, and Bloodbeard grabbed Billy Jack by the throat. Billy Jack kicked him in the shin, forcing Bloodbeard to release him, howling.

Instead of continuing the fight, Billy Jack turned and

sprinted for the docks. The other pirates tried to stop him, to reach him with their blades, but he was through their line in time.

The Parson had the oars and had begun to pull for the *Jerusalem*. The longboat was already ten feet from the docks, bobbing wildly on the swells of the outgoing tide. Billy Jack pelted down the pier and skidded to a halt at the edge, looking at them. It was too far to jump, and he couldn't swim it. There was a shark drifting next to hull of a small British frigate tied at the dock some twenty feet away.

"Come on!" John shouted, reaching out as if to catch his father as he jumped. Billy Jack had other ideas, however. He turned and sprinted back up the causeway into the press of pirates surging up behind him, chopping and hacking. He kicked one into the water as he rushed past. The man toppled, screaming, into the brine only feet away from the shark. The beast pounced, the man shrieked, and the water broiled crimson.

But instead of returning to shore, Billy Jack fled down another line of docks, heading for the frigate, pursued by Bloodbeard's crew. John lost sight of him as he disappeared around the other side of the frigate. The sharks in the bay were making for the helpless victim, having smelled blood in the water, and were gathered in a feeding frenzy near the prow of the frigate. The water foamed and churned red.

Bloodbeard was gesturing wildly from the shore, shouting at his men, but John could still see nothing of what was happening. He kept looking to the docks, waiting for his father to reappear.

There were shouts aboard the frigate, and British solders were stumbling from belowdecks, looking confused. In a moment it became clear what had surprised them. Billy Jack Thatcher had appeared on the deck, deep in combat with Bloody Hands and another pirate, twisting and lashing his sword back and forth, parrying both of their blades. The moonlight caught the swords as they flashed through the night air.

The soldiers had gathered their muskets, and charged the fighters, bayonets leading. As Bloody Hands and the other pirate turned to deal with the newest threat, Billy Jack sprinted up the deck to the aftcastle. Sheathing his sword mid-stride, Billy Jack hurled himself to the furthest gunwale, directly above the rudder, and, with a wild yell, threw himself over the side in a great leap.

He hung in the air for a long moment, a dark silhouette against the night, and then as his body was reclaimed by gravity, he allowed his momentum to tip himself forward into a dive. As he arced towards the water, Bloodbeard's form was visible from shore, drawing a pistol. Bloodbeard screamed in rage, there was the crack of a shot, and Billy Jack splashed into the waters of the bay not three feet from the longboat.

His head broke surface next to them, and an astonished Parson and John helped haul him in, soaked to the bone. John had to laugh at the brilliance of it. The sharks had been nowhere nearby, gathered as they were on the other end of the frigate, the bay clear for him to make it to the longboat.

"After them!" Bloodbeard bellowed, moving towards his longboat moored at the docks.

"Excuse me, gentlemen," came the voice of Henry Morgan from across the water. John, Billy Jack and the Parson all watched in wonder at the sight of the crippled man holding a lantern over Bloodbeard's longboat. "Is this your boat?"

Morgan hurled the lantern into the boat, and it erupted in gigantic flames in an instant. John laughed out loud as he realized what Morgan had done. Kerosene. He'd poured lamp kerosene into the boat. Bloodbeard roared in anger as the flames consumed their means of pursuit. He moved to hack Morgan down, but soldiers were surging down the causeway and pouring out of the gates from the city of Port Royal and Bloodbeard was forced to turn and engage them.

As the longboat made its way to the *Jerusalem*, they could see flashes of musket fire and hear the loud pistol retorts from the pirates as they did battle on the shores of Port Royal. Billy Jack gave a hard cough, and slumped to the side of the boat, his hand pressed to his side. His fingers came away slick with blood. He looked up at them in astonishment.

"Hell's fury if he didn't get me," Billy Jack said, his voice trembling. With horror, John realized that Bloodbeard's final shot had found its mark.

"No," he said, unable to think.

"I'll be all right, John," Billy Jack said, coughing again.

As the Parson pulled them swiftly towards the dark looming shape of the *Jerusalem*, Billy Jack forced himself to sit up straight, growling against the pain.

"All hands!" Billy Jack cried. "To arms!"

Life burst into motion on board as the crewmen came stumbling out of their bunks, armed with pistols and lanterns.

"Hurry there!" called the Parson. "Billy Jack's wounded! Get the surgeon!"

"Never mind me," Billy Jack bellowed. "Prime the long guns! The *Iago*'s at berth! Make ready to sail."

There were cries of terror, and sailors leaped into the rigging. Others began drawing up the anchor, while the cannonade crews primed their guns. The longboat reached the ship, and the crew lowered the ropes to secure and draw it up to the *Jerusalem*.

"Leave it!" the Parson shouted. "Just give us a line!"

"That only leaves one lifeboat," Billy Jack said, coughing.

"We've no time to play about," the Parson said.

Lines coursed through the air and fell over the longboat. The Parson took hold of the line and pressed it into Billy Jack's hands. John watched his father stumble to the gunwale, wrap the thick ropes around his forearms and be hauled the six or so feet to the deck. Hands took hold of him and brought him aboard. He disappeared from John's sight.

"You're next, John," the Parson said, handing him the second rope. He helped John wind the ropes about his arms, looping them around his shoulders and under his arms. Then John was hoisted into the air. He pushed his knees against the hull of the *Jerusalem* to keep himself from being scraped on his way up, and in moments a pair of strong arms had taken him by the arms and hauled him aboard. He collapsed on the deck and worked to disentangle himself from the knotted ropes. He could see his father lying awkwardly on the deck some yards away. Two men were bent over him, and John saw that one of them was the ship's surgeon, his medical bag next to him.

Kicking the rope from his legs, John crawled to his father's side and hesitated as he caught sight of Billy Jack's face. It was ashen in the moonlight, and beads of sweat had welled up on his brow.

"Father!" John shouted, trying to touch him. The

boatswain next to the surgeon grabbed his hands and shook his head. "Is he alive?"

"If he dies, it won't be from the shot," the surgeon said. "The ball passed through, and it only bit his side. A rib might be cracked."

"Will he live?" came the Parson's voice. John glanced at the gunwale, and saw the Parson clambering aboard.

"If we can keep the wound clean, he should recover," the surgeon said. "The sea water didn't help much, though."

"See to him," the Parson said. He turned to the rest of the men. "Give me full sail, lads. I'd like to be gone from here."

The sound of gunfire still echoed across the water from the shoreline.

"Sail off the starboard!" came a call from the crow's nest. "It's the *Iago!*"

"To arms!" the Parson cried. "Make ready the guns!"

John could see a ship, much larger than the *Jerusalem*, surging through the mouth of the bay, the sails on its two masts unfurled. The gun ports were open and the long guns extended. There were two full rows of cannons. The *Jerusalem* burst into motion as the wind caught in her sails. She moved forward, straight for the bay's mouth. The ships would pass alongside each other by perhaps ten feet in a matter of moments.

"Brace for a broadside!" the Parson bellowed, mounting to the aftcastle and taking the wheel from the second mate. He spun the wheel frantically. The ship prows were nearly even with one another. "Ready cannon!"

The gun crews lowered their smoldering wicks, letting them hover inches over the primer. There was deathly silence for a heart-stopping moment as the ships drew even. The *Iago*'s guns went off with the force of an explosion, as the *Jerusalem*'s cannons opened up with a deafening clap of thunder. The deck lurched wildly and John was thrown to the ground. Men were screaming as splintering wood cracked all around him.

Hauling himself to his feet, John took hold of the mast and gazed out at the *Iago*, but the clouds of powder obscured his view of the other ship. The aft castles passed each other as the ships drew clear. The *Jerusalem* was through the mouth of the bay and open sea lay before them.

"Are they coming about?" the Parson called out, spinning the wheel.

"No, Parson," the boatswain said, looking back into the bay. There were the echoing retorts of cannon fire from near the shore, and the last glimpse John had of the *Iago* was of its long guns opening up on the fort. Longboats filled with pirates were being lowered into the water, men from the *Iago*'s deck firing muskets towards the redcoats.

The *Jerusalem* was clear of the fight and safely away.

The Parson gave the *Jerusalem* her run, letting her course through the water the rest of the night with full sail, tacking west. Though the men remained ever watchful, no pursuing sail was sighted. It appeared they had gotten away clean.

The ship's surgeon and the boatswain carried Billy Jack into the Parson's cabin. John sat by his father's side the rest of the night and watched the surgeon stitch up the wound. He asked no questions and sat in silence, his whole body numb. He remained there until his head drooped onto his chest and he passed out in his chair.

When John awoke the next morning, he did not remember where he was. He could hear surf rushing along and the creak of wood. He was sitting on a chair, and his neck hurt. Grimacing, he straightened up and felt his back pop.

The memories were coming back, slowly. Bloodbeard. The escape. His father had been shot! He glanced at the bunk next to him and saw Billy Jack, still asleep. His face was flushed and covered in a film of sweat.

"Father?" John said, his voice soft. Billy Jack did not respond. John's heart surged in his throat. Was he dead? He stood from his chair, grunting at the stiffness in his legs, and crept closer to him. Reaching out a hand, John touched his father's arm. It was hot, but had a pulse. John breathed a sigh of relief. Whatever else, his father was alive.

He pushed open the door to the Parson's cabin and stepped onto the main deck. The sun was already high in the sky, glaring down on them all. The sails were full, and the Parson was still at the helm.

Squinting as his eyes adjusted, John cupped a hand over his brow and climbed to the aft castle. The Parson nodded to him grimly, looking exhausted. Towards the prow of the ship, two sailors scrubbed at a dark, crimson stain on the deck. The gunwale nearby bore a gaping, splintery hole.

"What happened?" John said, before remembering the broadside.

"They fired a mite too late," said the Parson. "Only caught us with about half what they thought. Still about ten guns, though, but sloops are fast in the water. Lost three, and a fourth got his arm blown off."

"Are we taking on water?" John said, looking at the remaining evidence of cannon fire along the deck. There wasn't much, and the ship didn't appear to have taken much substantial damage.

"Another advantage of the sloop," the Parson said with a smile. "If we'd been the same size as the *Iago*, we'd be on our way to the bottom. As it is, the *Iago* is taller, see? They were shooting for our heads, not our water line. Most of the cannons missed the hull. A few holes, but we're patching them up."

"And my father?" asked John. "Is he being patched up well? He wasn't responding when I saw him just now."

"Billy Jack's condition is a bit more complicated," the Parson said. "He fell into a fever during the night. Probably something from the sea water that got in his wound."

"Will he live?" John said, his stomach tightening.

"No one can answer that," the Parson said. "Only time can tell us. Billy Jack's a fighter, John. If there's any way for him to come back, he'll fight his way through it, you mark my words."

As they continued to sail west, John did not stray far from his father's side, and the Parson mercifully did not press the point by insisting he take up his duties as cabin boy. The next few days were the hardest John had yet experienced. He slept little and ate less.

The fever had its crests and valleys, and so John's emotions were thrown wildly from despair to elation as his father improved or declined on a daily basis. By the third day, however, Billy Jack's fever was down and he had regained consciousness.

"Me boy," he said, looking at John through puffed, watery eyes. John leaned closer and put his hand on his father's arm. The skin was still slightly clammy, but the feverish heat in it had all but faded. "What be happening?"

"We got you aboard the *Jerusalem* and you fainted from the loss of blood," John said. "You've been in a fever the last three days."

"Nonsense," Billy Jack said. "Men don't faint. They collapse or pass out in heroic fashion." He gave John a weak smile. "What of Bloodbeard? Were we pursued?"

"We got away clear," John said, "I imagine if he'd caught us you'd hear the sound of cannons."

"Good," Billy Jack said, relaxing in the bed. He nodded to himself.

"You should have seen it," John said excitedly. "The Parson led a full broadside against the *Iago*, and then we swept them by out of the bay, leaving them to engage the soldiers of Port Royal. I've never seen anything like it!"

"That does sound a sight te see," admitted Billy Jack, and John could tell he was actually sorry he'd missed the battle.

"I hope Bloodbeard was killed. Or at least captured," John muttered.

"He'll be aboard the *Iago* alive and well, like as much," Billy Jack said. "Weren't nearly enough men on that beach to keep Bloodbeard from the *Iago*. If that be the case, he'll be comin' after us strong, you mark me words, lad. We're not out of this yet."

He shifted slightly on the bed with a grimace and looked at John thoughtfully.

"I do wonder how he made berth in Port Royal without being arrested," Billy Jack said.

"Isn't it a pirate port, though?" John said.

"Yes, but ostensibly no pirates dwell in Port Royal.

Governor Vaughan likes te walk the fine line between pirate and privateer."

"What's the difference?"

"A privateer has the Crown's sanction te prey on Spanish vessels. Pirates rob any ship they can, entirely for themselves. Vaughan can have it both ways, ye see. He can allow the pirates port and still claim Port Royal free of piratical influence since they be all privateers. Bloodbeard, on the other hand, be a straight pirate, one who leaves a trail of corpses behind him no matter where he makes port."

Billy Jack fell silent, and sighed in exhaustion. Though he had slept for three full days, he seemed very weak still, and John knew he wouldn't be able to walk much for a few more days.

"How are we going to find San Thanatos?" he asked.

Billy Jack chuckled, his eyes closed. He opened his eyes and met John's gaze.

"Ah," he said, looking excited. "Isla San Thanatos. A lost island that no map has charted, known only to a few. Shrouded in mist and home to great dangers."

"You're one of the few?" John asked. "That's what you told mother in *the Spot*."

"Ye can't find a place what been lost. Ye can only stumble across it," Billy Jack said cryptically. He leaned closer to John, a mischievous glint in his eye. "Unless ye have a guide."

John hunkered closer as Billy Jack dropped his voice and spoke quietly. "You have a guide?"

"Aye, that we do!" his father said. "Findin' the treasure's only one part of me orders, John. There's a bigger plan in all this."

"A bigger plan?" John said. "I don't understand . . . ."

72

"I can't be tellin' you the plan, but it's all been arranged. Bloodbeard knows we be making for San Thanatos, and he knows I been there. He knows I can be gettin' us through his traps to the treasure haul! He'll make straight there to ensure the gold's still safe. The whole while we'll be riding his sails behind him."

"You meant to find him in Port Royal," John said, staring at his father in disbelief.

"Actually, that were something of a surprise," Billy Jack said. "Our intention was to find him in waters more friendly to his sort, like Tortuga or Barbados."

"So what was he doing in Port Royal then?" John wondered.

"I'm not for knowin," Billy Jack, "but I'd suspect he were following us the whole way back from *the Spot*. Maybe Bloody Hands or another of them overheard us talking about the treasure."

The door to the cabin opened and sunlight flared in the darkness. The door shut again as the Parson paced into the room. He glanced at the bed and paused, his face breaking into a wide smile.

"Billy Jack!" he exclaimed. "Told you he'd fight his way clear, John."

"Bah, no little sting will hold me back," Billy Jack said, laughing. The laugh triggered his cough, and he spent a moment grimacing in pain, hands pressed against the wound in his side as he hacked. When he had recovered, he slumped back to the bed in relief, beads of sweat appearing on his forehead from the pain.

"Nearly sunset," said the Parson. "The wind may freshen for the night. Ought to put some real distance between ourselves and any pursuit."

"Billy Jack thinks the *Iago* won't pursue. She'll make

for San Thanatos," John said. He paused suddenly, and looked at Billy Jack. "How are we going to follow it if it's not coming after us?"

"Let him in on the plan, have you?" the Parson said, raising an eyebrow.

"Only the first part," Billy Jack said. He looked at John. "I was never for saying Bloodbeard won't hunt us. Once he can't find us, he'll set out for the island to make sure we've not gotten there first and made away with his coin."

"So where are we going then?" John said. "How are we supposed to find him if we don't know where he is?"

"Because," said the Parson. "We know where he'll be going. Tortuga. Before he sets out, Bloodbeard will go to Tortuga."

"Why?"

"To resupply," Billy Jack said, but his eyes were shifty. There was something he wasn't telling John. Before he could ask what it was they weren't saying, there was a shout from on deck. The Parson looked up, a frown shadowing his face. A sudden pounding on the cabin door startled John, and he stood as the door burst open and the helmsman entered.

"Sail sighted on the horizon, Parson!" he said.

The Parson moved quickly to his side and headed for the deck. Billy Jack tried to rise and grunted in pain at the effort.

"Don't," the Parson said, waving a hand at him to lie back down, pausing by the door. "Save your strength."

Billy Jack lay back with a sigh. John rose and followed the Parson out, calling out behind him, "I'll tell you what's going on."

The sun was almost directly ahead of them, partially

blocked by the foresails. It was blood orange and nearing the horizon. Sailors were scrambling over the deck and into the rigging. The Parson turned and sprinted to the top of the aftcastle.

"Glass!" he commanded, and the helmsman handed it to him. He extended it and raised it to his eye, gazing through it behind them. John moved to the gunwale beside him, squinting into the darkening sky. He could see nothing but the movement of the waves.

"I don't see anything," he said. The Parson handed him the glass. John raised it to his eye and peered through it. He could feel the Parson's hand steering it in the right direction, steadying it.

"See it?"

"No," John said, shaking his head. Then his eye caught something that didn't belong in a horizon full of water. It was a small thin stick, appearing and disappearing with the waves. "Wait, I do see it!"

"That's the top of a mast," the Parson said.

"What ship?" John asked. "Is it Bloodbeard?"

"Not necessarily," the Parson said. "Plenty of ships in the sea. Could be that frigate we saw in the harbor at Port Royal. Governor Vaughan wanted a contingent of troops to travel with us, but they hadn't arrived when we set off. He could have sent them after us."

The Parson took the glass back and peered through it.

"They're coming on swiftly, boys!" he called. "We've got foresails now!"

"How do you make it?" said the helmsman. The Parson was still studying the approaching ship through the glass.

"Two-master," said the Parson. "Still can't make out the colors."

"What's the plan? Do we run for it?"

"There's the trouble, isn't it?" said the Parson, biting his lip. "We might as well let them catch us if it's the frigate out of Port Royal. If it's truly Bloodbeard then we must run. If it is the frigate and we run, it will only confirm Vaughan's paranoid suspicions."

"Aye, and if it's the *Iago* and we wait, by the time we can tell it will be too late to run," said the helmsman, nodding.

"What's nearby, in the event we must run?"

"A whole lot of nothin'," said the helmsman. "Any haven's gonna be more'n a seven hour sail from here."

The Parson gritted his teeth. He put the glass to his eye again and paused. "We've got colors," he said. "It's the union jack!"

"Bless the Crown," said the helmsman in relief.

"Haul up sail," said the Parson. "Let her ride the waves for a bit."

Visibly relieved, the crew set about pulling up the sails and letting the momentum of the ship carry it forward. John could feel the hull slowing already, the gurgling rush of water under the deck dwindling away. He glanced back at the approaching vessel and found it already closer by at least a half mile. That put it a few miles out yet. From this distance even John could make out the fluttering blue and red flag of the British navy.

"Won't they just make you prisoners on your own ship?" John asked the Parson. "Governor Vaughan didn't seem to trust you or Billy Jack."

"Being a slave for a day is better than being a hunted man for the rest of my life," the Parson said, "particularly for a crime I did not commit."

There was a grunt of pain from below them. John

turned to see Billy Jack limping gingerly toward the steps to the aft castle.

"Get back to bed, you fool!" cried the Parson as Billy Jack stumbled and caught the gunwale with a trembling hand. Instead of replying, Billy Jack began hunching his way up the steps, a dark grimace of pain on his face with every stair.

John rushed down to his father and threw his weight into supporting his father's other side. Billy Jack sighed and smiled at John.

"Thank ye, son," he said. "Ye do a kindness for an ailing man."

They reached the aftcastle moments later and Billy Jack limped to the gunwale and stared out at the ship approaching them.

"Just the Navy," the Parson said. "Looks like the frigate from Port Royal."

Billy Jack had gone pale, however.

"That's the *Iago*," he said, his voice quivering. "It's Bloodbeard!"

The Parson turned and lifted the glass in alarm. "I can't tell, even from here. How can you possibly know that?"

"I spent a few years aboard her, as you might remember!" cried Billy Jack. "We've got to flee!"

At that moment, the British union jack was hauled from the mainmast, and new colors were raised. The flag unfurled in the wind, and John felt the pit of his stomach jolt in fear. It was the black flag, the skull and crossbones. Dread seemed to slither over the *Jerusalem*, enveloping them all in a shroud of silent terror.

"God Almighty in heaven," whispered the Parson. "I've killed us all."

"Not yet ye haven't," Billy Jack said. "She's still some distance off."

The Parson turned to the crew. "Change course! Ready about! Come off the wind and make speed!"

The helmsman spun the wheel as sailors sprang into the rigging and let the sails down again. The ship surged in the water, picking up speed by the second. Already the *Iago*'s approaching pace had slowed as the *Jerusalem* drew close to pulling an even tack with her.

"We'll never outrun her on this tack," said the helmsman, his voice tight.

"We'll not outrun her on any tack in this damned wind!" said Billy Jack.

"The wind dies at sunset. We can make away then," said the Parson, but his voice wasn't as hopeful as his words.

"It sometimes freshens too!" raged Billy Jack. "We need less wind."

"Less wind?" John asked, looking surprised. "Don't we want more wind?"

"The *Iago*'s heavier in the water," Billy Jack said, "which means when there's less wind, the advantage is ours. We sit lighter and need less wind to push us. With the wind at this strength, they'll be in cannon range in five minutes."

"To arms!" shouted the Parson. "Run out the guns!"

"Get to the munitions locker and give every man a firearm and cutlass," Billy Jack told the boatswain. The man nodded and sprinted from the aftcastle and vanished belowdecks. He returned a moment later with a handful of muskets and pistols. He piled them on the deck and there was a mad scramble by the sailors to get one or two of each. Men were buckling swords to their sides, loading pistols and muskets with trembling fingers. All of them looked pale and jumpy. The cannon crews had run out the guns and loaded them.

The *Iago* was swiftly approaching. Men, tiny spots on the deck scrambling back and forth, were now visible to the naked eye.

"Come about," the Parson told the helmsman. "Let's not give them our ass for a target. We can't run at this point anyway."

The helmsman spun the wheel and the ship rocked beneath John. He gripped the gunwale as the ship turned, spinning to sail directly toward the oncoming *Iago*. Billy Jack hobbled to John's side and pressed two pistols into his hands.

"Ye know how to use these, I suppose?" Billy Jack asked. John nodded, which was technically true, though he couldn't use them well. Billy Jack drew out his cutlass and handed it to John. "This be me best sword. Take it."

John looked at his father, and saw fear and pain behind the easy smile etched on his face.

"You ever used a blade before, John?"

John shook his head, unable to find words, or vocal cords that were working.

"It's easy," said his father. "The pointy end goes in the other man." He patted John on the back and gave a weak laugh.

"What about you?" John said, looking at his father. "Won't you need a sword?"

"You didn't think that were me only sword, did you?" said Billy Jack.

At that moment the *Iago*'s guns went off with a deafening blast, lighting up the darkening seas with fire and smoke. Most of the cannonballs fell short, geysering into the water some yards short of the *Jerusalem* with terrific splashes. One or two found their mark, however, and blasted through the gunwale amidships, showing the deck with slivers of wood.

"Turn her into the wind!" cried the Parson. "Let's draw even before she can reload!"

The *Jerusalem* surged forward, the prow crashing through the wave crests with great sprays of water. They were closing on the *Iago*, and fast.

"Brace for a broadside!" bellowed the Parson, hunkering behind the gunwale, gripping his pistols tightly. Billy Jack tried to bend down, but winced and thought better of it and straightened. The crew of the *Jerusalem* knelt behind the gunwale, clutching their weapons. The gun crews hovered, waiting for the Parson's command.

"Get down!" Billy Jack hissed to John, and he threw himself to the deck next to the Parson. The foremasts reached one another as the ships crossed paths. John could hear the crew of the *Iago* screaming and shouting obscenities at them, and the crew of the *Jerusalem* returned in kind. It was empty bravado in the face of a suicidal broadside, the only bluster that would keep a man sane in the face of certain death.

"Fire!" shouted the Parson. John heard the same command from the *Iago* a second later, and then all sound was lost. The *Jerusalem*'s cannons went off like great claps of thunder and the ship lurched wildly in the water from the force of it. The roar died almost instantly and John blinked, hearing only ringing in his ears. The Parson was shouting something, but John could not hear the words. He felt, more than heard, the *Iago*'s cannons firing, every explosion rumbling and vibrating in his chest.

The cannonballs pounded into the hull of the *Jerusalem* and the ship shuddered in the water again. John nearly toppled from his crouch onto the deck and was forced to clutch the side of the gunwale to steady himself. Men screamed as the wood of the deck and sides exploded, every splinter a lethal projectile, the force of the cannon strikes throwing bodies wildly into the air. One sailor was hurtled into the mainmast, his form crumpling grotesquely in midair as he struck the mast and vanished over the other side of the ship. Through it all, Billy Jack stood tall against the night, waving his pistols in defiance, shouting at the attacking ship at the top of his voice.

"Reload the guns!" he could hear his father bellowing.

"Now!" he heard the Parson screaming, the sound coming from a long ways away. Terror thundered in John's ears as every sailor still able to stand jumped to their feet, leveling their muskets at the *Iago* at the same moment Bloodbeard's crew did the same. The cracking thunder of seventy guns going off at once was met by an answering volley from the *Iago*.

John screamed as he closed his eyes and fired blindly at the other ship. The pistols bucked in his hands as they went off and he nearly lost his grip on them. He staggered at the unexpected kick and opened his eyes. Bullets whistled all around him, biting into wood and flesh. The helmsman took a shot in the face and collapsed. Men all along the *Jerusalem*'s gunwale fell, screaming and jerking, to the deck. Some lay still, others writhed and shrieked.

Then all was silence for a long second. With a shout of triumph, the gun crews ran out the cannons again, ready for a second volley.

"Ready!" shouted the Parson, raising his hand. He

never gave the command to fire. The *Iago's* guns ran out and went off before he could open his mouth. The volley blew into the *Jerusalem* with complete devastation. The cannonballs struck the hull below the waterline, punching through the keel like it were paper. Several cannons from the *Jerusalem* were blown clear off their tracks and flipped into the air, crushing men as they landed with great crashes on the deck. Yardarms toppled from the mast onto the deck, tangling the crew in a morass of rigging and line. Without waiting, the crew of the *Iago* gave them a second volley of musket fire, peppering the line of unprepared defenders. Men screamed and clutched at wounds as they died.

The deck had begun to list to the starboard side and John could feel the hull moving sluggishly in the water.

"We're takin' on water!" Billy Jack shouted, firing his pistols again. Two men on the *Iago's* rigging screamed and tumbled into the water between the ships.

The *Iago's* guns ran out yet again and hammered the *Jerusalem*. The deck jerked under John's feet and he was thrown against the wheel. His father limped to him and steadied him, looking at the Parson. An understanding seemed to be reached between them, because after a moment the Parson nodded.

"Come on!" Billy Jack shouted, turning to John, grabbing his shirt and dragging him to the steps leading down from the aft castle. The *Iago's* second tier of guns ran out and blasted the *Jerusalem* a fourth time, and this time John realized how they were reloading so quickly. They had two rows of guns, and were firing them in alternating patterns, one and then the other, allowing first to be reloaded while the second fired. They could keep up an almost constant barrage that way.

His father tore down the steps to the main deck as the ship rocked around them. Men were thrown into the air and one of the *Iago's* volleys managed to strike the mainmast, splintering the wood with the force of a small explosion. Billy Jack staggered to the side of the ship, clutching his face. John's heart lurched in terror.

With a horrendous cracking, the mast shuddered and broke free, toppling ponderously into the water with a giant splash to the sound of cheers from the *Iago*. Billy Jack had risen to his feet again. He was bleeding, but John couldn't see how badly, because his father kept moving, his face turned away from him.

"Where are we going?" shouted John over the sound of battle.

There was a clattering from the port side of the *Jerusalem*. Billy Jack and John turned at the same moment. Grappling hooks had been thrown from the *Iago*, and Bloodbeard's crew was hauling the *Jerusalem* to their side in preparation to board her.

"Cut the lines!" his father shouted. "Hack 'em with your blade!"

They rushed to the gunwale, and John drew his father's cutlass, chopping at the ropes. It took two hacks, but the line snapped. Men all around John had done the same. They cut and chopped at the lines, which broke with twanging cracks.

Another volley of musket fire from the *Iago's* deck blasted into the sailors at the gunwale. The man to John's left fell screaming to the deck, clutching at a wrist that no longer ended in a hand. Other toppled and writhed on the deck.

The *Jerusalem's* deck was listing violently now, so much so that John had to hold onto the gunwale to keep himself steady on the sinking ship. The *Iago*'s cannons rang out again with thunderclaps and flashes of flame in the night. The battered, doomed *Jerusalem* rocked in the water, forcing John to clutch at a loose piece of rigging to keep himself from falling backwards, rolling down the deck and into the water.

"This way!" his father shouted in his ear. Startled, John turned and realized his father had not been part of the group cutting lines. He took hold of John's shoulder with a strong hand and pulled him from the gunwale as another musket volley rang out from Bloodbeard's ship. Musket fire chopped and splintered into the deck around them, sailors falling to their left and right as they rushed to the other side of the ship. John did not know what his father was doing, but he trusted he had a plan to get them out of this.

Billy Jack was limping badly and blood was staining the bandage on his side. The wound had reopened, and as they reached the far gunwale John discovered why. The single remaining longboat lay bobbing in the water a few feet out from the sinking gunwale. Billy Jack must had hauled it over the side by himself, tearing open his wound in the process.

"What are we doing?" John shouted.

"The ship's going down!" Billy Jack shouted over the sounds of gunfire all around them.

"We're going to abandon ship?" John said, looking startled.

"We can't," Billy Jack said. "This be the only longboat left."

John frowned. "So what're we doing with it, then?"

"I'm sorry, son," Billy Jack said. "For everything."

Billy Jack took hold of John, picked him up and threw

him from the *Jerusalem* into the longboat. The wood of the seats bit into John's side when he landed, and he yelled in pain. The longboat rocked wildly with the impact in the turbulent seas.

"No!" John shouted, moving to the prow of the longboat and stretching out back for the *Jerusalem*. He had to get back. He had to be with his father.

"Don't ye dare!" his father shouted, drawing a pistol and aiming it at John. "You'll not go down with this ship, you hear me? Keep going west! That'll lead ye into commercial waters. Some merchantman or another will find you there!"

Billy Jack reached into his waistcoat and drew out a compass. "Here!" he cried, tossing the compass across the watery distance between them into the longboat next to John.

"Now go!" his father shouted, waving the pistol. "And don't look back, son."

John felt hot tears spring into his eyes, and he shook his head. The currents in the water were taking the longboat further and further away from the *Jerusalem* anyway, and there was nothing John could do about it.

"Curse it, boy!" shouted Billy Jack. "Get yerself gone!"

Another volley of gunfire raked through the foundering *Jerusalem*. Billy Jack shuddered as a bullet struck him in the back. He bellowed in pain and collapsed, lost from John's sight below the gunwale.

"No!" John shouted, scrambling for the oars. He fumbled with them, trying to get them fitted. He had to go back. He would row back and get his father.

Cannon fire erupted from the *Iago*. One of the cannonballs found the powder magazine, because the *Jerusalem* lurched wildly. There was a huge, deafening explosion from belowdecks and the ship seemed lift out of the water for one heart-stopping second, the deck swelling and expanding. Then the deck burst upwards and splintered, tossing men like rag dolls high into the air, kicking and screaming. The night flared like midday for the briefest of moments. Fire ripped through the sides of the ship and engulfed the main deck in a huge fireball.

The force of the explosion threw John backwards and sent the longboat surging away from the *Jerusalem* amid a shower of flying boards and flaming debris. Blown completely in two, the sea claimed the remains of his father's ship quickly. John fell hard in the longboat and struck his head on its side with a sharp crack. The last thing John saw was the mangled wreckage of the *Jerusalem* sinking out of sight beneath the waves as darkness enveloped his sight.

He sank into darkness.

Chapter Five

Sailing the Spanish Main

John awoke to burning pain in his head and a strong pressure around his chest. His head lolled for a moment, his eyes burning from the sea water. He caught sight of his longboat, full of water some feet below him, bobbing sluggishly on the choppy sea. Something was scraping along his back, and he seemed to be floating away from the boat with every passing second.

Blinking, John looked around. He was beneath a great shadow, and realize that the tightness around his chest was a length of rope looped under his arms. He was being hauled aboard a ship. There were shouts and grunts from above him as men heaved him to the gunwale. Rough hands seized him and drew him up and over the railing.

He fell to the deck and vomited, coughing up sea water and gagging. He groaned, his limbs shaking as he lay against the flat deck.

"A live one!" came a surprised shout from somewhere over him, and the sound of movement. John was so exhausted and weak that he could hardly lift his head, his eyes staring lifelessly and unfocused at the planks in front of him.

Hands took hold of him once again and lifted him to his feet. He promptly sank to his knees and nearly slouched back to the deck, but the hands hauled him backward and threw him into the gunwale. John sank into a sitting position and was able to see the ship properly now. His heart sank at the sight of it.

He was aboard the *Iago*. Bloody Hands, the man that had tried to rob him in *the Spot*, stood looming over him, grinning unpleasantly.

"Well, well," Bloody Hands said. He turned to the crew behind him. "It's the cabin boy."

There was a growl of frustration from the *Iago*'s aft castle. Heavy bootsteps vibrated in the rail behind John as Bloodbeard descended the steps to the main deck, his face twisted into an intense scowl.

"I care nothing for whelps," Bloodbeard growled, stepping closer to John and glaring at him.

"Will ye be doing it yerself then, captain?" asked Bloody Hands, indicating Bloodbeard's flaming red beard. John's heart nearly stopped in terror at the thought. They were going to kill him, cut his throat and throw his body overboard for the fins, just like in all the stories. He shuddered.

John looked closer at Bloodbeard's beard. It was wet, the red hair darker than it had been the night in the tavern in Port Royal. Was he still wet from the battle? John didn't know how long he'd been unconscious, but the sun was nearly to its midday height. Rivulets of liquid were gently coursing down the beard and pattering onto the deck at the terrifying pirate's feet. *The spot*s were red.

"He's not barely worth the effort," Bloodbeard spat to Bloody Hands. "It's Thatcher's blood I'm wanting, lads!"

John's blood ran cold. Had there been survivors? Did the Parson's blood now run down the barbaric pirate's beard? Rage and blind terror filled him. Had the crew of the *Jerusalem* been murdered one at a time and then thrown overboard? His father clearly hadn't been found yet, but he had been badly hurt the last time John had seen him, collapsing to the *Jerusalem*'s deck just before the explosion. He could feel the press of his pistols in his belt, and the weight of his father's sword at his side.

Bloodbeard seemed to have noticed John's eyes lingering upon his beard.

"This be from yer boatswain and a few deckhands," Bloodbeard said, gesturing to the blood soaking his beard with a chilling smile. "Barely worth the effort themselves. It seems the four of ye were bein' the only survivors."

John twisted slowly on the deck, leaning on the gunwale and rising to his feet on shaking legs, looking daggers at the hulking form of Bloodbeard. The pirate had all but murdered his father, and such a hate was welling up in John that he could barely contain it.

He drew his pistols and leveled them at Bloodbeard. The deck fell instantly quiet. The crew had clearly not thought him even a remote threat; they hadn't bothered to search him for weapons.

John pulled both triggers at the same moment. There were two wet, sputtering clicks and the hiss of damp powder. John blinked in surprise, his rage replaced with fear and a sinking feeling in his gut. Bloodbeard hadn't even flinched when John pulled the triggers. He was staring at John with something akin to amusement and respect. Then the huge man threw back his head and laughed, a booming, harsh sound that echoed across the deck. Several crew members laughed also, though in relief and not amusement.

"That be a mighty brave thing ye just done, lad," Bloodbeard growled, looking at John thoughtfully.

"Deeply stupid, mind ye, but brave." He turned to the crew and eyed them with a malicious glint in his eyes. "This be no ordinary lad!" Bloodbeard cried. "He'll be gettin' no ordinary death from our hands. Time for a small treat, I'm thinkin'! Something we've not been seein' for many a year!" He threw up his hands. "The boy's te walk the plank!"

There were shouts and cheers at this, though John had never heard of it. He noticed the Bloodbeard had turned his back on him. If he could just get his sword out.... His fingers inched towards his belt.

A loud click echoed in his ear as Bloody Hands pressed a pistol into the side of John's head.

"I'd not be reachin' for that cutlass, young master," Bloody Hands growled. "Ye can rest assured me own powder isn't wet." John froze instantly.

Bloodbeard was continuing to speak. "Now then, who among ye hasn't yet gotten a share of the salvage?"

Several men raised their hands, and Bloodbeard nodded, turned and gestured to John.

"Take what ye can use, lads."

Three of the men moved forward and surrounded John. One of them took his pistols and stuffed them in the red sash he had tied around his waist. Another pushed John to the ground and yanked off his boots, holding them up to his own feet, cursing when they were found to be too small. The third drew out his cutlass and examined it. John struggled desperately, his eyes locked on his father's blade, but Bloody Hands trained his pistol on him. John was forced to subside, seething, his chest heaving. He was made to stand while the men tore off his leather vest and shirt and his stockings, leaving him naked to the waist and barefoot. The only reason they did not take his breeches was because they would be too small for them.

The crew laughed and pointed at John's pale, hairless chest. One of the men that had taken John's things made a great show of trying on his shirt, though it was far too small for him, to the great delight of the crew. He pulled it on and found that it wouldn't even close around his hairy chest. He laughed and began to prance and mince about on the deck, pointing his toes and waving his hands around in a foppish manner.

"Not even enough scraps on him fer a parrot to eat its fill!" the sailor crowed as peels of laughter swept through the watching crew. John felt his face flush red.

"Enough of this," cried Bloodbeard. "The plank for the boy! Where be the boy's plank?"

Bloody Hands and a few other men on the crew moved about the deck until they had secured a long board, about fifteen feet long and a foot wide. This they ran out over the edge of the ship and braced it against the mast. Another plank was set over top the end resting against the mast, and they hammered thick iron nails into the deck, securing it.

Bloodbeard drew his sword and gestured with it for John to walk out onto the plank. Understanding now what they were going to do, John felt tremors of terror flit through him. Gingerly, thinking desperately for a way out of this, John stepped onto the plank and stopped. He looked at Bloodbeard and the pirate captain sighed.

"Further out, ye whelp," he growled, jabbing John in the back with the point of his blade. Gasping at the pain, John inched further out onto the plank. He could see the wreckage of the *Jerusalem* scattered about the deep blue waters, drifting over a wide area now with the currents.

"Further out, boy!" cried Bloodbeard, waving his blade at him. John stepped out further and was nearing the edge of the plank. "Lads, be yerselves ready to send this whelp back to the deep?"

There was an enthusiastic chorus of "Ayes!" from the crew. Satisfied, Bloodbeard turned and made to force John further out onto the plank, so that he would lose his balance and fall into the bright waters below.

"Captain!" said Bloody Hands. "The show's not complete without some fins in the water."

"By the powers, ye be right!" cried Bloodbeard. "We need some blood in the water te draw the fins!"

He glanced around as if looking for something, as if expecting to see some buckets of blood laying about unused on deck.

"You should jump in yourself," John called back to Bloodbeard. "That beard would draw them sure as anything."

Bloodbeard laughed again, the sound grating in John's ears. He found a man nearby, and took hold of him. The man was nursing a shoulder wound, his arm wrapped in a bandage. Blood was seeping through.

"Sailor, do ye know where we could be findin' some blood fer these waters?" Bloodbeard asked, his arm around the man's shoulders.

The man looked around blankly, then hesitated when he saw the look in Bloodbeard's eyes.

"No, please!" the man cried as Bloodbeard casually shoved him over the side. The man fell back over the railing and plunged screaming into the water below with a splash. He foundered for a few moments, then stabilized himself and swam towards the hull of the ship, clawing at the siding; there was nothing to hold onto and no way to climb.

"He's not bleedin' enough," Bloody Hands complained.

Bloodbeard sighed and drew a pistol. The man was crying out for help and splashing around below them. Taking aim, Bloodbeard fired, but the man had moved and the bullet splashed harmlessly into the waters near him. Bloodbeard cursed.

"I think the aim be goin' on this pistol," he said to Bloody Hands, shaking his head.

"Let me see it, captain," said Bloody Hands, taking the pistol and examining it. They bent their heads together and began talking about the alignment, gesturing animatedly and shaking their heads, deaf to the man's yells from the water below. The man in the water screamed as a shark dragged him under the surface. Clouds of crimson swirled in the waves as more fins circled and joined in.

"Ah, there they be!" said Bloodbeard, looking pleased. He tossed the pistol aside and lifted his blade again and leaned out over the gunwale to shove John off into the water with the tip of his sword. A crewman, the one that had taken Billy Jack's sword from John, was waving it about and boasting to the men next to him about it. Bloodbeard glanced at them as he extended his arm, and John saw his eyes widen. He leaned back into the ship and gazed at the sword.

"Give me that sword," he said, stalking over to the man. The sailor looked at him in surprise that turned quickly to suspicion.

"It's mine, Captain," he said, fingering the sword. "Part of me share."

Bloodbeard pulled out a pistol and shot the man in the

head. The body collapsed to the deck, the sword clanging to the planks next to his feet. Bending and retrieving the sword, Bloodbeard hefted it and peered at it closely. He turned to John and stalked back to the plank where he stood.

"Boy!" snapped Bloodbeard, brandishing the blade. "Where did ye get this sword?"

John hesitated. He did not think Bloodbeard knew he was Billy Jack Thatcher's son, but he knew that if the pirate didn't know, then he certainly did not wish for the brutal man to find out.

"I found it," John lied. Bloodbeard fixed him with such a ferocious stare that John nearly blurted out the truth. He fought down the impulse and tried to meet the pirate's glare with a matching one of his own.

"Found it, did ye?"

"Your ship was about to board the *Jerusalem*, so I knew I'd need a sword. The explosion knocked me into the water."

"And ye just happened te find this sword lying around, did ye?" Bloodbeard growled, shaking it at him. "The man who owned this sword, did he live? When ye took it, was the man alive or dead?"

"There were a lot of dead men around," John said. "No one claimed it, if that's what you mean."

Bloodbeard glanced at Bloody Hands.

"Maybe he's truly dead, Captain," said Bloody Hands, shrugging. There was an unpleasant glimmer in Bloodbeard's eyes when he turned back to John.

"Boy," he snarled. "Yer name. What be yer name?"

"John Rackham," John said. Bloodbeard was silent for a long moment.

"Is that so?" he said softly. When he spoke next it was

94

in an entirely different tone. He swept his hat from his head and gave a mocking bow. "Come back aboard the *Iago*, young Master Rackham," Bloodbeard growled.

John didn't like the tone or the sudden shift in Bloodbeard's mood, but what choice did he have? He could walk the plank now and be eaten by sharks, or live another day and be killed in his sleep or get his throat cut open. Or, he thought, he may just get the chance to escape.

He made his way carefully on the plank back to the ship. Bloodbeard took him roughly by the hair and threw him to the deck at his feet.

"Where be the boy's effects?" called out Bloodbeard, looking at the crew. "Let's be havin' it all back."

With much grumbling the crewmen tossed what they had taken from John into a pile on the deck. All except the pistols. Bloodbeard kept the sword, sliding it into his own belt. John picked up the pile of possessions and threw on his shirt.

"Lock him in the great cabin," Bloodbeard said. "We'll worry about him later."

Bloodbeard's great room was spacious, far more so than the *Jerusalem's*, filled with all manner of finery. A writing desk sat off to the side, and John was surprised to see it. Could a barbarian like Bloodbeard even read? John thought, his mind laced with hate. A stateman's table, long and narrow, stretched the length of the room, and the light filtered into the room through a line of delicately designed windows that stretched from starboard to port.

It was to these windows that John moved as soon as the door had closed and he heard the click of the lock. He searched for a latch or hinge, anything that would allow the windows to open, running his hands over the glass panes. After a moment's fruitless examination, John realized the windows did not open, at least not enough for him to go anywhere. Small individual panes of glass could be opened or closed, but John couldn't even get his head through them, let alone escape that way. Without a longboat, it would be pointless to jump from the windows anyway. There were too many sharks cruising through the water.

He sat by the windows, gazing out of them at the waters beyond for the space of nearly an hour. The *Iago* slowly circled *the spot* of the *Jerusalem's* sinking, and John knew they were hunting for his father's body. There were dozens of corpses in the water, floating face down and bobbing in the currents. One by one they were prodded with long, wooden poles. When they did not move, the ship would move on.

John was still in shock, and wasn't processing the events of the night before. He knew his father had almost certainly died, if not from the bullet that struck him in the back, if not from the explosion, then from the sharks. And if he'd managed to avoid those, Bloodbeard would find him and slit his throat, letting the blood of Billy Jack Thatcher spill down his beard.

He knew there would have to be a reckoning with those emotions, but for the moment he was mercifully numb to the pain. There was a dull ache in his stomach, and he was exhausted and bitterly chilled. He drew his knees up to his chest and wrapped his arms around them to keep warm.

The day drew onward, and at last the *Iago* put sail to the *Jerusalem's* watery grave. They must have given up hope on finding any more survivors. About ten minutes after they had set off away from the wreckage, Bloodbeard himself unlocked the door to John's prison and entered. The hulking pirate drew the door closed behind him with a snap, and relocked it. His eyes found John instantly, and Bloodbeard paused, looking at him huddled by the window. The large man made his way to the writing desk and sat in the chair with an aggressive clunk, never removing his eyes from John.

John simply met his stare. He did not know what else to do. He was too tired to do much more than that.

After a pause, Bloodbeard lifted Billy Jack's sword and dropped it to the desk with a clang. He sniffed.

"Your story don't add up, lad," he said, with a growl. "Ye knew Billy Jack Thatcher, an' that be no mistake."

John nodded, not knowing what to say, his chest tight with fear.

"I thought it were as much," Bloodbeard mused. "Ye don't just up an' take the sword of Billy Jack. Nor his compass either." He dropped the compass John's father had tossed into the longboat with him onto the table next to the cutlass. "Found it in yer longboat."

John returned his eyes to the window, and watched *the spot* the *Jerusalem* went down slowly dwindling away to nothing behind them.

"Billy Jack Thatcher is dead," Bloodbeard said. John looked at the brutal pirate in horror and alarm, his stomach clenching. He quickly pressed his face back into a more neutral position, but Bloodbeard hadn't seemed to notice. "Found his floating corpse not half of one hour ago. He looked much the worse for wear since our encounter in Port Royal."

He looked at John and rose from his seat.

"Ye knew the man Billy Jack," Bloodbeard said again.

"I knew the cutthroat. But I'm wantin' te hear of the man, the cowardly, betraying sea filth that's been thieving from me these last fourteen years!"

John told him. He saw no point in not doing so. His heart was numb, but his mind kept him on track in the story, and he even had the presence of mind to exclude all references that would make it appear that Billy Jack was anything more than the first mate aboard the ship. He told Bloodbeard of how his last shot in the harbor of Port Royal had found its mark, and how Billy Jack had collapsed into a fever for the next three days, how he had fallen of a musket ball to the back. Almost laughing with delight, Bloodbeard gripped the pommel of Billy Jack's sword a little tighter, his eyes gleaming with malicious pleasure.

John felt sick at the sight, and fought to keep himself under control. Bloodbeard rose, his hands trembling with delight.

"I'll never be havin' the pleasure of running the man through with me own blade," Bloodbeard said, "But he died an empty, broken man. I can live fair with that."

The door to the cabin eased open and Bloody Hands entered, holding a bucket of what looked like seawater. He dropped it on Bloodbeard's desk.

"Have ye hear'd the news?" Bloodbeard cried, rising to his feet and clapping Bloody Hands on the shoulder. "Billy Jack Thatcher died a broken man!"

Bloody Hands grinned, showing off his rotten teeth.

"This calls for celebration," Bloodbeard said. "We'll feast te that!"

"Aye, Cap'n," Bloody Hands said, nodding. "I'll tell the mess cook."

Bloody Hands departed then. Bloodbeard put his head over the bucket, allowing his beard to hang over the water. He lowered his head and submerged his red beard, rubbing and washing it free of blood. John watched him with morbid fascination.

"Didn't expect meself te keep all that blood on the beard, did ye?" Bloodbeard said, with a wicked smile. "Attracts the flies."

All John could think of was to somehow get to a dagger or his father's sword and cut Bloodbeard's throat. He could feel the tears coming, his head pounding from suppressed agony and rage. He grit his teeth and swore that he would not break down in front of his father's killer.

With a sigh, Bloodbeard straightened, his beard dribbling water back into the bucket and onto the desk. He took a cloth from a drawer in his desk and massaged the bristly red hair until it was dry. He straightened his braids, patting them flat, and looked at John.

"Ye were a friend of Billy Jack's," Bloodbeard said. "Always had a mind te take cabin boys under his wing."

The large, hulking man stepped closer to John, coming out from around the desk and drawing near until he was no more than four paces from where John sat.

"Know this. There ain't ever been a man Billy Jack has cared about. He were a friend te no man! Always manipulating, always interested only in what others could bring him. In the end, he left them all marooned. When they no longer served his purposes."

Bloodbeard was a step closer, and John could see a fury in his eyes.

"Do ye know what happened te our last cabin boy?"

John shook his head.

"He was shot through the neck by Billy Jack Thatcher. Last night, in the battle."

Bloodbeard's eyes searched John's face for another moment, then he turned and strode to the desk. He took up Billy Jack's sword.

"One last thing ye might want te know," Bloodbeard snarled. "This were me own sword before Billy Jack stole it from me. Just like everything else."

With a growl of fury, Bloodbeard drove the sword into the floor of the cabin and left it there, quivering in the deck. Striding to the door and wrenching it open, Bloodbeard turned and looked back at John.

"He never told ye that, did he?" Bloodbeard said. "There's not a single man Billy Jack Thatcher ever spoke truth to. Did ye know him at all, I wonder?"

The door slammed shut, but did not lock, and the last thing John saw of Bloodbeard was a cruel smile. It was then that John knew what he was going to do. He wasn't going to escape the *Iago*. He was going to stay. He was going to kill Bloodbeard, if it cost him his own life.

He sat there trembling, watching the light dwindle to nothing as the sun set through the cabin windows. The sounds of rejoicing pirates on deck made him feel all the worse. Alone, broken, numb, and terrified, the image of his father falling from sight on the deck of the *Jerusalem* rose up in his mind unbidden and unwanted.

The tears came then like a sudden flood, an uncontrollable torrent. He knew his father was really gone, and he wept.

The thunder of boots on deck, harsh laughter and fiddle music woke John. It was late, and the night had settled fully over the seas. The world beyond the cabin windows was dark and empty. He rose, his legs stiff, and made his way to the door of the cabin. He remembered that Bloodbeard had not locked it when he had left.

Of course, there was no reason to lock it. John wasn't going anywhere, even if he had wanted to. Not with sharks in the seas below them and the *Iago* well away from land. Even if he could get a longboat, there was no way he would be able to put to shore in one.

He pulled open the door and stepped back out onto the deck of the *Iago*. Pirates were everywhere, slouched against the gunwales, sitting cross-legged on the deck and howling with laughter, playing cards, drinking from barrels of rum. Two or three had fiddles and pipes, and were playing a lively jig, though drunkenly and slightly out of tune. Most of the crew was drunk, staggering here or there, waving their cups in the air to keep balance on the rolling ship.

The feast Bloodbeard had declared earlier was fully underway. John watched with a sick curiosity as the pirates fought like dogs over every scrap of food. There seemed to be no organization whatever concerning the distribution of food, and men were left to fend entirely for themselves. As one grabbed a slab of meat, another sailor would lean across him and seize it. They would fight, kicking and biting, down the deck until one gave up and the other emerged the victor, scarfing his meal as quickly as possible, lest any other man take it into their head to do to him what he had just done to another.

The only man that seemed to be sober and at work was the lookout, hunched in the crow's nest. The mate of the watch sat next to Bloodbeard on the aft castle, along with the helmsman and the quartermaster, none of whom were paying the slightest attention to their duties.

A crewman on the other end of *Iago* rose, swaying dangerously. He lifted his mug into the air.

"A toast!" he shouted, slurring slightly. "Te the death of Billy Jack Thatcher, may his soul burn in immortal agony in the Pit!"

John felt his anger flare again, but could do nothing as the rest of the crew responded in a deafening cheer, raising their glasses and shouting, "To the Pit!"

"A curse upon the King!" shouted another, and the pirates all drank with bellows of appreciation.

"A curse upon the Higher Powers!" cried another, eliciting another rousing cheer.

"Master Rackham!" came Bloodbeard's voice from the aft deck. John turned and saw the muscular pirate reclining on the deck, an array of foods spread before him. Bloodbeard beckoned him up to the aft castle with the casual wave of a hand.

John slowly made his way up the steps, watching Bloodbeard without ceasing, his heart in his throat, wondering if he would get his chance to murder the foul brute that very night. He paused at the top of the steps, taking in the sight of Bloody Hands, slumped against the gunwale, his hat resting over his eyes. The helmsman, quartermaster and mate of the watch all stared at him as he drew closer.

"I were wonderin' what would draw ye from me cabin, Master Rackham," Bloodbeard said, drinking from a large, bejeweled goblet. "Sit ye down and eat yer fill."

John looked at the food scattered about the deck in front of Bloodbeard, but did not move.

"Were ye interpretin' that as a request?" Bloodbeard growled. Reluctantly, feeling his heart swell with hate, John sat. He could hardly see straight from his rage, his fists clenching involuntarily.

"Ye've got a fierce spirit, boy," Bloodbeard said. "I could see that from the moment ye tried te shoot me dead on me own deck. Ye'll be lookin' te recreate the experience, I wouldn't doubt."

The captain laughed, a harsh, grating thing, his foul belly shaking. Trying to keep himself under control, John pulled a plate of roasted meat toward him and began to eat. It was only then that he realized just how hungry he was, and quickly returned for seconds.

"Know this, Master Rackham," Bloodbeard said, leaning so close to John he could smell the encrusted sweat on him and the stink of his breath. "I sleep with two eyes open, a pistol under me pillow, and a blade between me teeth. Wouldn't have been captain of such a crew for long if it be different. Is it not the truth, Mr. Coll?"

"Very true, captain," said Bloody Hands, whose real name was apparently Coll. "Many a crewmate's lusted after yer job."

"What be happenin' te them when they tried?"

"Ye gutted 'em like mackerel an' bathed yer beard in their blood, were it not so, Captain?"

"That it were," Bloodbeard said, his eyes never leaving John's face. For his part, John met the gaze with as much hate and nerve as he could manage. He knew he was terrified of the huge killer; would his nerve fail him when the moment came?

"Your men drink to the devil," John said, helping himself to a bowl piled with hunks of bread.

"We're thievin' cutthroats, lad," Bloodbeard said. "We're every one of us damned men already. It's our lot in this life. We must be enjoyin' ourselves in the now, afore

103

we're taken by the Angel o' Death to our allotted punishment in the life everlasting. Eat, drink, and be merry, an' all that."

"For tomorrow we die," John recited the rest of the Bible verse automatically.

"Aye," said Bloodbeard, taking another huge swig of rum. "And tomorrow we might just be dyin'."

"Why?" asked John. "Where are we going?"

"I'll not be tellin' ye that, young Master Rackham," Bloodbeard said, with a laugh.

At that very moment, another crewman stood and lifted his glass.

"Te Tortuga!" he bellowed. "Te strumpets an' fornication!"

This elicited the loudest cheer from the crew yet, and the clink of glasses and the hoarse laughter of lusting men filled the night air. John looked back at Bloodbeard and raised an eyebrow. Bloodbeard said nothing, grinding his teeth.

"I'm not fer trusting Billy Jack Thatcher, even in death," he said. "We go te Tortuga te take in supply, and then it's off te check on me treasure. Treacherous man as he were, Billy Jack were not likely te keep the location of Isla San Thanatos a secret. Like or not, the Royal Navy may well be on its way te reclaim me gold. I'll not leave it lie there and allow Billy Jack Thatcher the last laugh."

"Sail ho!" came a call from the crow's nest. "Sail off the port side!"

Bloodbeard glanced at Bloody Hands, then rose and stalked to the port side of the aft deck and peered into the darkness. John stood, staring with them. Sure enough, another ship had come upon them in the night. It was already close enough that they could see its sails reflected from the lights of their own lanterns. Men scurried about on the other ship, having clearly seen the *Iago* at the same moment they had spied the approaching vessel.

"To arms!" bellowed Bloodbeard, his eyes wide with excitement. "We take 'em for our own, lads!"

The men burst into motion at once, lurching and staggering to their stations in drunken stupors, flailing about as the ship rolled on the swells of the seas. One or two vomited as they tried to move across the deck. Another man, pulling himself up into the rigging, took a bad step and plunged shrieking into the dark waters below.

"You're mad!" John gasped. "Everyone's drunk."

"Gives the men a boost of courage," Bloodbeard cried, drawing his blade, an evil glint in his eye as he brandished it across at the far ship. "That be how we took the *Jerusalem*, after all. Run out the guns!"

The other ship had banked hard away from the *Iago*, but the helmsman compensated, and the *Iago*'s prow turned to pursue. The helmsman, for all his precision, clung to the wheel in an attempt to keep himself upright, looking slightly green in the face. The gun crews were staggering back and forth, running the guns out. Peering over the gunwale to the waters below, John saw the *Iago*'s gun ports open and the noses of twenty cannons run out.

"Hoist the colors!" Bloodbeard shouted to Bloody Hands, who nodded and pounded down the steps. He disappeared belowdecks for a moment, then returned with the black flag. He drew it up the mainmast until the skull and crossbones gazed morbidly down on them all, grinning out across the darkened sea at their prey.

The *Iago* had drawn close behind, and John could see the other ship was a small schooner, about eighty feet in length and maybe five guns to a side. Unneeded crew from the *Iago* had gathered on the deck, distributing swords, guns and boarding hooks to one another, waiting in the darkness for Bloodbeard's command.

"Give her a taste of the *Iago's* might!" cried Bloodbeard. The guns went off with deafening thunderclaps. The deck shifted at the concussive impacts, but not nearly as much as the *Jerusalem* had when her own guns went off.

John could see the devastation unleashed upon the other ship. One of the cannon shots blew threw the rudder, shattering the fleeing ship's steering. Other strikes raked across her bow, and the ship shuddered in the water. Block and tackle snapped, lines went limp, and several yardarms toppled from the heights of the mast to the deck below. The agonized screams of the wounded carried across the water, oddly distorted by the distance.

"Hold the guns!" Bloodbeard cried as the *Iago* surged into reach. As they neared, the fleeing ship was desperately running up the white flag of surrender, the crewmen gathering on the deck in clusters, throwing down their arms and raising their hands.

"Fire!" roared Bloodbeard, and the *Iago's* crew raked the deck of the nearing ship with musket fire. Men screamed and dove for cover. "No quarter is to be given!"

John stared in horror at the sheer pointlessness of the slaughter as the crew unloaded another volley into the enemy ship. More screams, desperate and pitying, met John's ears. Bloodbeard was laughing, his head pitched upward, his eyes wide and dark with cold mirth. Terror swept across John's skin as he took in the horrifying visage before him.

Hooks arced out from the *Iago* into the darkness. The

106

men drew on the lines with all their might, grunting at the strain of pulling the ships together. Moments later the gunwales struck one another, the deck shuddering beneath John. With shouts of challenge, the crew of *Iago* leapt over the gunwales and boarded the far ship as terrified men fled in every direction.

"We surrender!" shouted the helmsman, moments before Bloody Hands shot him through the head. The body crumpled lifelessly to the deck, and the loud pops of musket fire rang out from all directions, little flashes of lightning illuminating the deck around them.

Within moments it was over. The wounded were finished off with cutlass and dagger, the bodies dragged to the far gunwale and thrown into the sea. The crew cheered, waving bloodstained blades in the air.

Bloodbeard brushed past John and stepped aboard the captured vessel. Bloody Hands dragged the captain of the captured ship from his cabin where he had hidden himself, and threw him to his knees before Bloodbeard. The huge man drew a long, curved dagger from his belt and bent over the weeping man. John shut his eyes in horror, turning away from the sight. He could not block out the man's gurgling last breaths or the thunk of his boots on the deck as he thrashed.

Feeling his face flushed with rage and terror, John spied an abandoned pistol laying on the deck of the *Iago* as the sounds of the dying man ceased on the ship beyond. Every eye was drawn to the spectacle. Quickly bending and pretending to be sick over the side, he scooped up the pistol and shoved it into his belt and pulled his tunic over it to cover the bulky weapon.

He turned back to the far ship to see Bloodbeard standing over the corpse of the captain. His hands were raised, his head incline to the sky, his eyes closed as if in prayer. Hot blood was steaming from the dark, wet stain on his beard in the night air.

There was a scuffle from belowdecks of the captured ship, and several of Bloodbeard's crew came into sight from the hatch, hauling before them two figures, one a middle-aged man in a powdered wig which lay on his head somewhat askew, and the other a young girl of about John's age, perhaps a year or two younger.

They were thrown at Bloodbeard's feet, and he glowered down at them. The man was trembling, but the girl, who looked like his daughter, put her hand on his arm to steady him. She was glaring boldly up at the terrifying specter of Bloodbeard without a visible trace of fear.

"Ah, the merchantman," Bloodbeard said, laughing softly. "Tell me, merchant. Where be yer treasures?"

"Please, sir," the man said, "I am a man humble in spirit and poor in coin."

"Come, come," Bloodbeard said with a snarl. "Ye wear the finery of the filthy English gentry, and I demand to know where ye've hid yer valuables! I shant be askin' again."

"My only treasure is my daughter," the man said, looking at the girl clinging to his arm.

"Take her," Bloodbeard said. Several men grabbed her by the arms and lifted her away from her protesting father. She shrieked, kicking and struggling, as they dragged her across to the *Iago*. "Strip her naked and see if our good merchant hoped we'd honor the virtue of a woman enough te hide his valuables on her person!"

"No!" cried the man, lifting his hands in supplication. "Please, I beg you, I speak the truth!"

"A thought occurs to me," Bloodbeard said, stepping closer to the man. "If ye hid yer treasures aboard the ship somewhere, she'll know the place too."

He drew out a pistol and shot the man in the head. The body jerked and toppled to the ground. John's blood turned to ice at the sight. The girl behind him screamed again, the first time she seemed to have shown fear in the encounter.

"Your pardon, merchantman," Bloodbeard said to the corpse in sarcastic apology. "Girls are easier to intimidate. Ye understand, I'm sure."

He seized the body, hoisted it over the rail and cast it into the dark sea. He turned and stepped back aboard the *Iago*, looking at the girl, who stood slumped in the arms of her captors, sobs wracking her body.

"Where did yer father hide yer valuables?" he demanded. She looked at him with eyes full of hate, her lips trembling, but did not answer. "Very well, strip her."

With one single motion, the men holding her tore her dress down the middle. She was left shivering on the deck in her corset and frills, weeping softly. Gritting his teeth, John fought the urge to draw his hidden pistol and stop them from humiliating her. But his pistol was meant for Bloodbeard, not to rescue strange girls he didn't even know. Bloodbeard nodded, and with a lewd smile, one of the sailors took hold of her corset, making to tear it away.

"No!" John shouted, drawing his pistol and directing it at Bloodbeard. The pirate captain turned, looking pleasantly surprised.

"Found yerself another pistol, have ye?" he growled.

"I assure you, the powder's not wet this time," John said, his voice shaking. "You'll not shame that girl like this."

"Won't I, now?" said Bloodbeard. "How long ye goin' te keep that pistol trained on me, boy? Can ye not sleep fer a day, a week? Ye can delay me and not a thing more."

"You will swear she will not be shamed or harmed," John said, desperately.

Bloodbeard chuckled softly, his eyes gleaming with delight.

"Is that so, now?" he said. "And why would I be doin' that? Ye've got no claim te her. The only way for me to let her be is for a crewman to come forward and take her as his share in the plunder."

The pirate turned to his men.

"Which of ye would take the girl as yer portion of the haul?"

There was a chorus of bawdy laughter and several hands went into the air.

John kept his pistol trained on Bloodbeard, his mind whirling.

"I will," he said, surprising even himself.

"You?" Bloodbeard said, turning back to John with a strange look on his face. "Yer not a part of this crew, lad."

"I'll join," John said. "I'll join your crew and take her as my share."

"Join, will ye?" growled Bloodbeard, stumping forward a few steps closer to John. "Thought ye were wantin' to kill me. I assure ye, Master Rackham, if ye think to join up with me crew to try and get yerself into position to riddle me with lead, ye do yerself no favors. Lower yer piece and ye can sign our charter and join."

"Let me sign the charter and I'll lower the piece," John countered.

For one wild moment, John thought Bloodbeard would just draw his sword and cut him down where he stood, but then the tall pirate flicked an irritated hand at Bloody Hands, who turned and entered the *Iago*'s great cabin. He emerged once again with a long parchment, a long quill and a bottle of ink. These he set down on a standing barrel and dragged the whole thing over to where John stood. Reaching down with one hand, his eyes never leaving Bloodbeard, his pistol aimed straight into the pirate's eyes, John took up the quill and made his mark on the parchment, next to a host of other scrawls and marks.

Bloodbeard nodded to John.

"Very well," he said. "Welcome to the crew, young Master Rackham."

"I claim the girl for my share," John said.

"Aye, yes, we've all heard about it!" Bloodbeard growled.

Slowly, tentatively, John lowered the pistol. Bloodbeard did not rush him, cutlass drawn. He did not order anyone to grab him. Gradually, John relaxed.

"Give that pistol to me," Bloody Hands said, reaching out to take it. John took a step back and slid the gun into his belt.

"I'm a member of the crew now," he said, "and as such have the right to be armed."

Bloody Hands turned to Bloodbeard in exasperation.

"Captain!" he said.

"The boy's got the right," Bloodbeard said. "But know this, Master Rackham. If ye ever point a weapon in me direction again, I'll cut open yer stomach, nail yer bowels to the mainmast and make ye dance on this deck til yer dead. Do I make meself explicitly, entirely, utterly clear?"

"Aye, Captain," John said, nodding, fighting down his rage. "The dress for the girl, if you please?"

"The dress'll be stayin' with meself," Bloodbeard said. "Ye asked fer the girl, but said nothin' of clothing. She'll keep what she's got, but not a thread more."

"Then you must give her some trousers and a shirt at least," John said.

"Must I?" roared Bloodbeard. He strode to John and took hold of his tunic, hoisting him into the air so their faces were level. Bloodbeard's eyes seemed almost red with rage. "I be the captain of this ship and must therefore do nothing!"

He hurled John to the deck at the feet of the girl.

"Keep yer share under control, Master Rackham," said Bloodbeard, looking at the girl, who was still weeping silently. "I'll not have her underfoot at every inopportune moment. She's to have me great cabin for the night, but she'll be needin' new accommodations after that. Her rations come from yer own."

Bloodbeard strode to the captured vessel and waved at the crew to get back to work. The men, who had been standing and watching the confrontation, scattered in every direction, hunting for treasures.

John looked at the girl, who did not meet his eyes, but stood, arms crossed over her breasts and swept past him with a sniffle, vanishing into the depths of Bloodbeard's great cabin. John made to go after her, but paused by the door, catching the sound of great, wracking sobs from within. With a sigh, he turned and made his way to the captured ship, stepping carefully over the railings, bound together by grappling hooks.

Great stains of blood lay in dark rivulets along the deck. The crew was busy dragging corpses to the side and tossing them into the sea. They laughed and joked as they worked, stringing profanities and curses together as they did so. Others had crawled into the rigging, hoisting up sails. Even more men were hauling barrels and crates to the deck from the lower decks, throwing them through the hatches into great piles. Bloodbeard and Bloody Hands had gathered with the *Iago*'s helmsman at the aft of the schooner, examining the damaged rudder.

"Get te work there!" shouted a crewman as he pushed past John, shoving a boarding ax into his hands. "Break open those crates an' see what we've caught, eh?"

The ax was weighted heavily in his hands. He hefted it for a moment, watching the bustling activity around him. Then he bent down and pulled a small crate toward him, lifted his arm and chopped into the wood. The ax bit into it nicely, and with a few more hacks, he managed to get the planks to shatter. He pried them up and tore open the crate. Inside were thick rolls of woolen cloth, ready to be woven into cloaks and clothing of various sorts.

He tossed the crate aside and drew another one to him. He hacked into it with ferocity, allowing the crate to take his pent anger and bitter sorrow. He broke open crates for the next hour or so, throwing the loot into piles organized by type. There were barrels of tobacco, crates packed with bottles of rum, whiskey, wine and kegs of beer. Bolts of cloth soon followed, along with a set of china dishes, and several chests of valuables and coin.

One of the men soon after found the ship's charter and identified it as the *Philadelphia*, out from Cuba a fortnight before. A commercial merchantman, the *Philadelphia* was carrying a stock of cloth and furs through one Thomas Hackett, the man Bloodbeard had killed, the father of the girl currently in the *Iago*'s great cabin.

The mess cook emerged from belowdecks with an expression of glee on his face, his arms filled with frying pans and pots of various sizes. He hopped the railing back to the *Iago* and vanished below.

Bloodbeard came up the deck from the aft and stopped next to John. "I'll be interrogating your share, Master Rackham," he said. "Have ye a problem with this?"

"You may not touch her or inflict injury on her," John said.

"Boy, ye try my patience," growled Bloodbeard, looking frustrated. "I've half a mind te run ye through afore ye make my life more difficult than it already be."

John followed Bloodbeard back across to the *Iago*. It struck him then how strange the whole situation had become, and how odd it was that Bloodbeard hadn't simply killed him when he'd been first dragged aboard. Certainly the treacherous pirate had no love for those who disregarded his commands—so why was he allowing John to live, to join his crew, and to protect this girl? None of it made any sense.

The only answer was that perhaps Bloodbeard had worked out who John's father had been, though it didn't seem likely John would live any longer were that the case. Wouldn't Bloodbeard simply cut his throat to exact vengeance and be done with it?

Confused, uncertain and worried, John paused as Bloodbeard threw open the door to his great cabin and entered the darkness within. John followed, wondering what it was the huge man had planned for the girl.

And for him.

Chapter Six

Isabella's Locket

They found her crouched on the bench along the aft wall beneath the windows, nearly the same place John himself had been sitting only hours before. Her face was flushed from her tears, and her arms were still crossed over her chest, her legs tucked as far as they could be beneath her petticoats, the only clothing she had.

Her face was round, and would have been pretty if not for the fact that it was twisted up from grief. No, John decided, she was pretty regardless, but the beauty was broken and marred by sorrow. She did not look up as they entered, nor seemed to mark their presence with her at all as they approached.

"Where did yer father store his treasures?" Bloodbeard demanded, without introduction or pleasantry.

She did not answer, but sat, her head slightly turned toward the windows, gazing out into the darkness, her face streaked with tears. She looked numb, as numb as John had felt when he learned his father had died. He remembered suddenly why he was there on the *Iago*, and felt the fires of revenge kindled again in his heart.

"I warn ye," Bloodbeard said, "not to try me patience. I do not tolerate third requests. Where did yer father hide them?"

She turned her eyes to Bloodbeard and stared at him. John was startled to see them lifeless and empty.

"My father hid nothing," she said, her voice clear. "He always said I was his greatest treasure."

"Ye carried no rings, no jewels, golden lockets, no wasteful trifles men spend on undeserving women?" Bloodbeard spat, the ferocity in his voice startling John. "That I cannot believe, Miss Hackett."

"Believe what you will," she said. "I cannot stop you, nor will I endeavor to try. Every penny my father earned went into our well-being and to my education."

"Did he now?" Bloodbeard said. "A greater fool than I thought, perhaps."

"I would gladly have a father who in your eyes stands the fool than hold in esteem such a man that you respect, sir," she said, glaring at him. "Any man must be wise indeed to raise the ire of the likes of yourself."

Bloodbeard drew his blade with a growl and stepped toward her.

"Captain, do you intend to harm my share?" John said, loudly. Bloodbeard paused, then turned on John, his face contorted with rage.

"By the powers, whelp," Bloodbeard snarled. "Ye do not command me, an' if ye know what's good for ye, ye'll try to do so no longer!"

He turned to the girl, thrust his sword back into its sheath and glowered at her.

"Ye will keep a civil tongue in yer mouth next time ye get the urge to share yer razor-wit, lass," he said. "That is, if yer wantin' to keep it whole and attached to yer jaw. We'll be taking the *Philadelphia* apart to find out what's hid aboard her, then we'll be takin' her as our own. We will find it all, ye can be rest assured of that."

Bloodbeard turned and stalked to the door, slamming it behind them. John thought about following him out, but paused, looking at her.

"I'm not your property," she said to him, though her voice wavered slightly, "and if you think your gallantry will allow you to take advantage of my honor, I assure you that you will regret it if you try."

John blinked in surprise at her hostility. She said the words boldly enough, but given the state of her, John wondered if she could even hold a sword, let alone use one with any sort of skill. He shook his head.

"I saved you," he said.

"I didn't need your help!" she cried, looking at him angrily. "I can take care of myself."

"Can you?" John asked. "Getting stripped naked and leered at by a bunch of dirty men was part of taking care of yourself, was it?"

She was silent, glowering out of the window, her face flushed with embarrassment.

"I'm on your side," he said.

"Really?" she said, with a tone of mock surprise. "Did you not only an hour ago join a pirate crew?"

"To protect you," he said, feeling his voice rise in frustration.

"Yes, well done," she snapped. "Only now you've got the girl all for yourself. Very well played, indeed."

"It's not like that," John cried, looking aghast. "So long as you're my share, no one else can touch you."

She raised an eyebrow at him.

"No one can touch you," he corrected. "I won't, and nor will any one else."

"Promises mean nothing from a pirate," she said softly.

"I'm not a bloody pirate," John said, so forcefully that she turned away from the window and looked at him. "I was captured just like you were, not a day ago. I meant to kill Bloodbeard, until you turned up."

"Why would you want to kill him?" she asked, the life starting to come back into her eyes. "Surely you would never survive?"

"No," John agreed. "But he killed my father, just like he killed yours."

He told her of his mother, until Bill Jack Thatcher had burst into his life and of their adventures, and of the sinking of the *Jerusalem*. She looked mortified when he was done, but said nothing. Her face was pale.

"I can certainly see why," she said. John blinked back tears that had risen again in his eyes unbidden. To keep her from seeing them, he turned and walked over to where Billy Jack's sword still stood in the deck. He grabbed the blade, wiggled it back and forth a few times, and pulled it from the floor. He slid it into his belt and turned back to her.

"Yes," he said. "I didn't want to help you, you know. But I couldn't let them, well, you know."

"Thank you," she said. "How will you do it?"

"I don't know," John said. "Joining the crew was perfect, though. I'm armed, and I can walk about the ship like anyone else. Bloodbeard suspects me, so I'll have to lay low for a while. Earn everyone's trust. And then, one day, I can slip into this cabin, walk over to his bed while he sleeps and shoot him through the head. Or bleed him dry."

"And then you die."

"Probably," John said.

"Wouldn't you prefer to live?"

"If I could, sure," John said. "I don't see much hope for that."

"There isn't much hope," she said, standing and looking at him. "At least, if you're doing it by yourself."

John stared at her, surprised.

"No," he said, shaking his head. "No, it's too dangerous."

"Are you possibly the stupidest boy to have ever lived?" she snapped. John felt a flash of anger course through him. "What's supposed to happen to me once you're dead? You said it yourself, the only way I'm safe is with you here."

"But—"

"Besides, you're clearly hopeless at this sort of thing," she said observationally, giving him a pitying look. "You'll botch the job, more like than not. You'll require an educated person to come up with your plan and work out the details."

"What, and that's supposed to be you? You're a girl!"

"Who else is going to help you?" she snapped. "But keep it up and I won't help at all! You'll fail horribly at it, and I could use a laugh."

"Fine!" he hissed. "Very well, fine!"

"Good!" she said, brightly. "First thing's first. I'll need some proper clothes if I'm to be any use to you at all. Some pants and a shirt ought to do it."

"Right," John said, nodding. "That might take some doing."

"Then do it," she said. "I'll catch my death wearing these things. Besides, the less obviously like a girl I look the better for everyone, I should think."

"Where to find trousers for you?" John mused, scratching his chin.

"Our cabin boy had some spare clothes in his trunk," she said. "Also . . . if I tell you where to find some hidden valuables, do you think you could get them to me?"

"You did have treasures!" John said, his eyes going wide.

"Of course I did," she said, and John was not pleased by the derisive tone of her voice. "They won't mean much to anyone but myself, though. Really, all I care about is a little silver locket. It's the only pictures I have of mother and father."

"That'll really take some doing," John said, sounding doubtful.

"Please, I beg you!" she cried. "It's the only keepsake I have."

"Fine, I'll see what I can do," John said, with an exaggerated sigh.

She told him how to find them, hidden away in a false plank in the floor of the *Philadelphia*'s cabin. He slipped out of the great cabin as quickly as he could and over to the *Philadelphia*, which was still crawling with the crew. He reached the pile of loot mounded up over his head in moments. He remembered seeing the chest he now knew to be the cabin boy's; he had hacked it open with the rest of it and tossed the contents onto the pile. That had been early, so they would probably be low in the heap. He glanced around, but no one was paying him the slightest attention.

He bent over the pile, pulling rolled bolts of cloth and barrels of dried tobacco free, his hands searching, groping. At last he found then, wedged under an ebony chest. He rolled the trousers up and threw the shirt over the one he was already wearing. He glanced toward the hatch to the hold, but knew there was no way he could get down there unnoticed, let alone go poking along trying to find concealed keepsakes.

He stood and crossed back to the *Iago*, slipping back into the great cabin easily. The girl looked up, her face fearful. When she saw it was him, she relaxed again and beamed at him when he showed her the clothes.

"Oh, excellent!" she said, taking the trousers and tunic and examining them. She looked at John. "Do you mind?"

"What?" he asked.

"I'm going to change," she said. "Get out."

"Right, sorry," John said, flushing red as he turned and stepped back out onto the deck of the *Iago*. The night air was chilly and damp, and he could smell the burnt gunpowder still on the wind, along with the moldy smell of the wet canvas of the sails. Men grunted and cursed from the far deck of the *Philadelphia*.

A moment later the door opened again, and he came back through. She stood before him, looking sheepish and uncomfortable in the pants, fidgeting and adjusting the shirt self-consciously. She was still definitely recognizable as a girl, with her long, red hair, though with her hair pulled up and concealed under a hat, she ought to blend in fine.

"Well?" she asked. "How do I look?"

She spun in a circle with a grin, her arms above her head.

"Fine, all except the twirling part," John said, fighting down a laugh. "You'll need a hat."

"I'd like that!" she said, pulling at the trousers. "I don't understand why men wear these things. I feel so . . . exposed."

"We're used to it," John said. "Not many men have

fourteen years of dress-wearing to skew their perspective."

"True enough, I suppose," she said. "What about the locket?"

"We'll have to figure out some other way of getting to it," he said, shaking his head. "There's too many people right now to get it."

She nodded, looking worried.

"They won't find it, will they? They're pretty well ransacking the whole ship," he said.

"I wouldn't think so," she said. "It's in a hidden panel in the great cabin."

"I'm John, by the way," he said.

"Isabella," she said. "Isabella Hackett."

He made to leave her then, so she could sleep, but she begged him to stay. He did not have the heart to say no, especially after losing her father. He knew he would have wanted company had there been any the night before when he himself had been going through the same thing. He knew she was numb, and may be for a time, before the full force of reality hit her.

They slept in fits and starts, her on one end of the bench under the aft windows, him on the other, about three feet between them. She would twitch in her sleep and wake with a start and a little shriek that would jerk him out of his sleep. Both would then drift away again.

They were rudely awoken at first light when Bloodbeard burst into the cabin, clearly still drunk from the night before, and slouched to his great bed. He bellowed curses at them and threw them out. They had no choice but to wander onto the deck as the early morning light of the sun gleamed off the water to the east.

Men lay strewn about on deck, passed out leaning against the masts, the rails, slumped on the fore and aft castles, still clutching rum bottles and loot of various sorts in their fists. Isabella turned to John, a wide smile on her face. He wasn't sure he understood why, until he saw what she was looking at. The *Philadelphia* lay bobbing in the water next to the *Iago*.

"Come on," she mouthed to him and took him by the hand, leading him over to the *Philadelphia*. They stepped across the railing between the ships, careful not to make a sound, and reached the door to the great cabin.

She pulled gently on the latch as John glanced around. Not a body was moving. The door was unlocked, because the latch slid open as Isabella eased the door wide. They moved into the semi-darkness within, squinting around. It appeared similar to Bloodbeard's cabin, with a table scattered with charts in the center of the room, a desk and bed in the corner, and windows along the aft wall.

Isabella did not pause, but moved directly for the table, ducked beneath it, and stretched out on her stomach. John squatted, watching her. She was feeling and pressing at the boards that made up the deck, until, after some minutes, she found what she was looking for. With a soft clunk, she pulled up a board and reached down into the gap it left behind, fishing for something, her tongue sticking out of the side of her mouth.

"Got it!" she said, softly, withdrawing her hand with a triumphant flourish. John saw a small leather pouch clutched in her fingers. She returned the board to its former place with another soft clunk, and they were done.

"Let's get out of here," John said.

The pulled open the door to the cabin, stepped into the morning light again, and eased it closed behind them.

"Who goes there?" a voice slurred from behind them. Heart pounding in his ears, John whirled on *the spot.* Bloody Hands stood some steps away from them, blinking in the light. He was slobbering drunk, his eyes having trouble focusing on them. He swayed unsteadily on his feet.

"Nobody," John said.

"Nobody," Bloody Hands repeated. "Tha's a funny name."

He fell over in front of them with a fleshy thud, and began to snore. Breathing hard, John took Isabella's hand and dragged her away from the sight of the unconscious Bloody Hands. She was busy tying the cords of the leather pouch to her belt, and then tucked the whole thing down the front of her pants.

"There," she said, with a sigh of satisfaction. "That should do it."

"What's in that pouch?" he asked. "Aside from the locket, I mean."

"Shh!" she said, frowning at him. "Later."

Not long after, men began to stir, groaning and swearing. They would have dragged themselves about and lay in the sun the whole day if it weren't for the mess cook. He bustled onto deck before the sun was high in the sky, brandishing his newly claimed skillets. The smell of fried meat met John's nose, and a welcome scent it was. It was this more than anything that roused the *Iago*'s crew. Grumbling and muttering imprecations against the light of the sun and its glare off the water, the men lined up as the cook distributed the food. John waited until he was nearly last to go forward, and got his meal on a wooden plate. It was salted pork and beans. He and Isabella moved away from the clamoring crew and split the food between them.

Soon after, the carpenter's mate appeared and pressed them into service breaking up the wooden crates from the *Philadelphia* and evening up the ends of the planks so they could be used to repair the damage to both ships. These were then handed off to the carpenter's mate, who had set about repairing the captured vessel's damaged rudder. This was a long and complicated ordeal that John and Isabella saw little of, busy as they were using hatchets to chop the wood into sizable bits. The carpenter's mate would swear and curse at them, calling down vows from heaven with their every mistake.

Unused to such labor, Isabella tired after a few hours, her brow prickled with sweat. The carpenter's mate laughed at the sight of her exhaustion. John redoubled his pace, hoping that being a member of the crew did not mean others could beat them for sloppy work. This seemed far from the carpenter's mind, however, and it was barely past midday when the task was completed.

The mess cook appeared not long after, and the men gathered around yet again for their rations. John and Isabella huddled towards the prow of the ship, watching the foresails fluttering and enjoying the rocking of the ship and the sound of water rushing beneath the hull. Bloodbeard emerged from his cabin, drawn by the smell of the food. He received a progress report on the rudder from Bloody Hands as he ate, demanding information in his horrible, grating voice.

"It don't look good, captain," Bloody Hands said. "Totally shot te hell and nary a piece of wood what's long enough te serve as a repair spar."

"Can ye get it to a place where it can be fixed?" Bloodbeard said. "We can make fer an island and chop some lumber there."

"Bensen's doin' his very best, captain. Of that ye cannot doubt."

"Bah!" growled Bloodbeard with a dismissive wave of his hand. "We'll need the second ship once we're getting' to San Thanatos."

A makeshift rudder was eventually constructed, though not to anyone's satisfaction. Bloodbeard insisted on dividing the crew at the earliest opportunity and resuming their voyage to Tortuga. He named Bloody Hands commander of the *Philadelphia* and sent another twenty men over to it. This still left the *Iago* far overcrowded and the *Philadelphia* undercrewed for the good of either, but the pirate seemed to think by minimizing Bloody Hands' crew he could minimize the risk of them turning on the *Iago* or striking out alone. By keeping them needy of the protection and resources of the *Iago*, he ensured the second ship would stick close to their wake.

As night fell yet again, the pirates grew rowdy and reveled in their drunken excess for the second time in as many evenings. Uninterested in watching their antics, John and Isabella ate their food as quickly as they could and slipped belowdecks.

The hatch that descended into the darkness of the hold was wide enough for three men side by side. A treacherously narrow ladder fell away from them into the black. They climbed carefully down to the first lower deck. This one held the galley, food and powder stores. Goats and chickens grumbled to one another in the dark. Next to the feet of the ladder they had just left, there was another hatch that led to the second belowdeck. They followed this one down, careful to watch their footing.

126

Here were the crew's sleeping quarters, including John's newly assigned sleeping place. They had not yet been told where Isabella would sleep.

Isabella lit a lantern and brought it to John's bunk, no more than a hammock strung between two support beams. All of the beds were hammocks, and the effect of all of them dangling limply on every side was rather like being surrounded by hundreds of empty socks, or perhaps blankets draped over clothesline.

Isabella thrust her hand down the front of her pants, fished for a moment, then withdrew the small leather pouch. She untangled the cord tied around the neck, pulled it open and gently upturned it on John's cot. A small silver locket tumbled out, along with a few other odds and ends. There were several small rings and another necklace, this one on a delicate chain, and held only a small milky pearl clasped in a band of gold.

"What are those?" John asked, looking at the necklace and the rings.

"The rings were my father's," she said, her voice soft. She picked out a plain gold band and held it up under the lantern light. "This was his wedding ring. He still wore it, even after mother died . . . ."

She hesitated, and John could see the pain in her eyes. The grief was finally starting to hit her, he realized. She set it down quickly and picked up another ring, this one a thin band of gold with a small green jewel mounted to the top.

"This was my mother's," she said. "Father was never very rich, but he scrounged up enough money for the emerald for her."

Her lip trembled, and he saw her force the emotion away, thrust it aside. She took a breath, and picked up the necklace with a single pearl.

"The eye of the sea," she said. "At least, that's what father said it was. He collected it himself, dove into the shallows and dug up the muscles to find one. There were sharks in the water, but he didn't care. He got mother her pearl, and called it the eye of the sea."

John remained silent, because he did not know what to say. She dropped the valuables to the cot again.

"And the locket?" John asked.

"It opens," she said, her voice wavering. She picked it up and opened it. Inside were engravings, but the words were nothing like anything John had ever seen before. He squinted at it in the dim lantern light.

"Unless you know Latin, I wouldn't bother," she said.

"Latin?" John said, looking at them even harder. "What do they say?"

She snapped the locket shut and looked at him, affronted.

"That's private!" she said.

"Sorry!" John said, holding up a hand. "I just wondered, is all."

"It's okay," she said, heaving a sigh. "I just—I don't think I want to share that. No offense or anything."

"No," John said, though he flushed red and kicked himself on the inside for being a horribly insensitive blockhead. "Yeah, I get it."

There was a rush of drunken laughter from above them, and the sound of boots clomping on the deck. Then a shout. More yelling, and this time they could hear Bloodbeard's voice in the mix. There was the sound of boots scuffling on wood and the crack of a pistol shot. Something heavy hit the deck above them, and was dragged to the edge of the ship. Moments later, there was a muted splash from the side of the ship.

"We've washed up in hell, haven't we?" Isabella asked, her face pale.

"Possibly," John admitted.

"It's not safe here," she said. "They're going to kill us. One way or another."

"Not if we get off the ship ourselves," John said fiercely. "Not if we escape."

"Yes," she said, but her voice was uncertain. Her hands were trembling and she looked at John as though stunned by some new thought. "Father's really gone," she said, and dissolved into tears. So utterly unexpected was this that John stared at her for a full fifteen seconds before his mind caught up. He held out an arm awkwardly and patted her on the shoulder. She shrugged it off with a furious jerk and slapped him across the face, a great sob escaping her lips as she did so.

John reeled, staggering backwards away from her, but the life had gone out of her again and she sank to his cot and lay weeping, her shoulders slumped and breathing ragged.

"What was that for?" he shouted, holding his face. This, it turned out, was the wrong thing to say, and she sobbed all the worse. Frustrated at being helpless to fix the situation, John felt like taking her by the shoulders and shaking her until she snapped out of it, or otherwise punching the side of the hull until he felt better.

There was the sound of footsteps on the ladder. The crew was slowly sidling down to sleep off their drink. He looked at Isabella, but she was too lost in her own world of misery to have noticed. John rushed to the cot and snatched up her valuables. The steps were thundering closer, and he could hear the grunts and laughs of the men as they drew nearer. He fumbled with the leather pouch, then shoved the valuables back inside.

"What are you doing?" Isabella shrieked. She slapped at him again, still not having realized the danger.

"Stop it!" he hissed, dodging her clumsy strike and yanking the drawstrings closed. There were shadows from the hatch leading to where they were standing, and a loud belch greeted the first of the sodden-minded crew. They had only seconds. John turned his back on the men and pressed himself against Isabella. He shoved the bag into her hands. "Quick!"

She had seen the shadows and knew the men were halfway down the ladder. She crammed the bag down her pants again, and screwed up her face into something resembling normalcy. Except that her face was flushed and tears streaked her cheeks.

The first man to the sleep deck stumbled to the nearest bunk and threw himself into it without regard for anyone else. There were grunts from the others as they came stumbling down the ladder and to their hammocks. Slowly the hammocks filled up without anyone saying anything or even seeming to notice they were there. John breathed a sigh of relief.

"There's a few hammocks over there," he said, pointing through the maze of now filled beds.

"Sorry I slapped you," she muttered, then turned and made her way to the nearest hammock. She started to crawl into it, when the man next to her grunted and sat up.

"What are ye doin'?" he bellowed.

"I . . . am going to sleep," she said, her voice betraying her nervousness.

"Not there yer not," the man snapped.

"Where do you suggest I sleep then?" she said crossly.

"These are for crew and passengers only," the man said.

"I'm a passenger. Glad we sorted that out," she said and turned away from him. He shouted a curse and grabbed her on the shoulder. She screamed and backed away as he stood before her, reeking of gin and swaying drunkenly.

"Get away from her," John said, rushing to her side, drawing his pistol and cocking it for emphasis.

The man looked between them, his face twisted up into a look of disgust.

"She ain't crew or passenger, so she doesn't get a bed," the man snarled. "She's your property, boy. Only two places for her."

"What are those?" John asked, holding the pistol as steady as he could in his trembling hands.

"Every crewman gets a hook for his personal effects, next te his bed. Anythin' that's his goes on the hook, or in his bed." The man leered unpleasantly.

"I beg your pardon?" Isabella said, looking aghast, struggling to keep herself from dissolving back into tears. "That's completely barbaric."

"T'ain't my fault," the man said, settling down in his own hammock. "Any share not kept on its proper place is up for grabs by any man what takes a fancy to it. That's why we don't take folks fer shares."

"Come on," John said, pulling her away from the man.

"No!" she said, pulling her arm from his. "I'll not be property! Not yours, nor anyone else's on this horrible ship."

"I don't like it any more than you," John said. "That's the way they think."

"Well, it's not how I think!" she said, her nose in the air. She stormed away from him and over to the ladder, her shoulders shaking. She took the ladder two at a time and vanished abovedecks.

John considered going after her, but after how rude she had been, he didn't really feel like it. He climbed gently into his hammock and pulled the blanket up over him to his chin. He closed his eyes, but could not fall asleep.

Ten minutes later, Isabella climbed back down the ladder and prodded him with an elbow as she climbed into the hammock next to him. He felt her weight against his side, felt the increased weight strain the cloth of the hammock, and felt as she turned her back to him, facing the other direction.

"This is the lesser of two evils, that's all," she muttered.

"What happened?"

"The helmsman and mate of the watch took turns telling me things that ought never to be heard in polite society," she said. "Absolutely scandalous."

John suppressed a laugh.

"Don't get any ideas," she said.

They lay in silence for many minutes. He felt her body begin to quiver as they lay back to back, weeping silently for her father into the night.

Chapter Seven

Tortuga

The next month proved to be the longest John had yet encountered in his life. He had twice the work of anyone else, because he had to help out around the ship as well as keep an eye on Isabella, making sure none of the rest of the crew were harassing her. This was rather more of a chore than he had expected, as Isabella was sure to snap back at any lewd comments directed at her, causing no end of rage among the crew.

"You've got to stop letting them get under your skin," he told her one day about a week out from the taking of the *Philadelphia*.

"And let them get away with it?" she cried. "I'd rather die."

"If you keep getting them angry, you might get your wish," he said.

This seemed to sober her. She paused, chewing her lip, and looked at John, lost in thought.

"What am I supposed to do?" she said. "It's the only thing that keeps them away."

"I think it draws more of them to you," he said. "They enjoy horrifying you. If you didn't allow yourself to be so easily scandalized by their words, they might just give up."

"What do you mean, they enjoy it?"

"They like shocking you. The more you react to them, the more they'll try to shock you."

She straightened, looking affronted.

"Are you suggesting that I'm to blame?"

"Only partially."

"That's so much better. Thank you."

But she seemed to respond to their catcalls less that day. To her immense surprise, and John's immense relief, the taunts lessened somewhat. Nevertheless, some of them remained and they irritated her greatly. She was visibly holding back from shouting.

For his part, Bloodbeard ignored the both of them. He stalked to and fro atop the aft castle or was out of sight in his cabin most of the time, taking his meals alone and away from the crew. He suffered from terrible fits of rage that seemed to have no reason behind them. Every one of them left spilled blood in their wake, whether wound or fatality. Bloody Hands would report daily, unable to find any valuables at all aboard the *Philadelphia*, which only served to blacken Bloodbeard's moods all the more. Ordinarily, John believed, the pirate wouldn't care about such a small thing as hidden personal effects, except that he clearly still suspected Isabella of lying to him about it.

John and Isabella would take their food every night and retreat belowdecks, wanting to avoid the often violent crew as much as possible. None of them seemed to be growing more trusting of John, or at least any more trusting than anyone else aboard ship. Not a one of them appeared the slightest bit interested in trusting the others.

Isabella continued to mourn her father in private moments, when she thought John wasn't looking. He would start awake at night, feeling her shaking next to him in their cot, and she snapped at him more frequently. John's grief for his own father had turned foul, and he found himself filled not with sadness, but with anger. Though he would never say so out loud, he blamed his father for his own death, and this feeling had begun to turn ugly in John's heart. Why hadn't he gotten in the boat with him? There had been time, if only seconds of it, before the *Jerusalem*'s powder magazine had been hit, hadn't there? He must have known he would die anyway, being captured by Bloodbeard, his rational mind would answer. This was something John did not wish to hear, and so he forced the thoughts away, focusing instead on his growing bitterness.

There was also the hint that Bloodbeard had given him, that tantalizing thought—that his father had not been truly honest with him. The implications were far reaching. Could Billy Jack Thatcher have been less than honest with everyone? With the Parson? Could he have been planning some elaborate return to his former life of piracy, just as Governor Vaughan had believed? He certainly had been deeply possessive of that map he had locked away on board the *Jerusalem*. Could that parchment have shed light on the enigma that was his father? Of course, it was far too late to find out.

Connected to this growing uncertainty was the man Bloodbeard himself. He would have John believe that he too had been wronged by Billy Jack Thatcher, that he too was a victim of the man's cruel and incessant schemes. Despite his obvious barbaric violence and cruelty, John thought he saw the man beneath the myth. A dark, vile sort of a man, but a man nonetheless. It surprised him to find that he had begun to see Bloodbeard as a hidden ally, another person who understood what betrayal by Billy

Jack truly meant. This disquieted John not a little, and he wondered who had truly wronged who in the emotional and moral morass he had found himself.

John lay awake late into the night in his bunk, listening to the never-ceasing sound of water rushing along the other side of the hull, noting every creak of the wood around him. Isabella had curled against him in her sleep for warmth against the chill of the nights at sea, and he could feel one of her feet on his own.

"Did ye know him at all, I wonder?" Bloodbeard had said. The words haunted John in his every waking hour, and some of his sleeping ones too. The truth was that he hadn't know his father very well, and had agreed to come along on his voyage on a whim of bitterness. He thought suddenly of his mother, and found that he missed her, despite her drunken ways. She was, after all, still his mother.

He gently put his arm around Isabella, who shifted in her sleep. Her head drooped onto John's chest, and he felt a surge of excited terror run through him as she gave a sigh. Don't get any ideas, she had said. And he hadn't, at least not those sorts of ideas.

Soon enough, he too was asleep.

As the week turned into a fortnight, and then to a third week, the crew grew expectant to spy Tortuga any day. They had spotted a few islands off towards the horizon already, but those were simply small, mostly uninhabited jungles and merely meant they were correctly positioned on their route to the infamous pirate capital and approaching from the south, making for the south-western edge of the island.

John had been given a veritable chest-full of stories

about Tortuga by the crew, eager to put ashore. Over 1,600 prostitutes on the island, imported by the French, said one wide-eyed crewman. Its rivers practically flowed with rum, said another. The northern end of the island was uninhabited jungle, a densely packed forest of great trees, harsh rocks and thick undergrowth.

Isabella was enthusiastically certain Tortuga would be the moment to strike Bloodbeard and escape. John himself wasn't so sure he even wanted to kill Bloodbeard any longer, preferring to simply escape and return home. He had tried to subtly discourage her or stall her plans whenever she brought them up, which she did frequently in their evenings eating alone in the crew quarters.

"But it's simple," she whispered to him as they lay curled in his bunk, her mouth close to his ear. He had rolled to put his face away from her, but she had followed him and was now pressed against his back, her head next to his.

"No, it isn't," John said, feeling guilty for both wanting and not wanting to kill the man that had murdered his father. Frozen in indecision, all he could do was to slow her down until an answer to his dilemma presented itself.

"What do you mean? All we need is to get a longboat. We get the longboat over the side, I climb down and row the boat around to the back windows in Bloodbeard's cabin. You slip inside and kill him in his sleep, break the windows, and climb out onto the longboat. Then we row to shore and barter our way back to Port Royal or somewhere!"

"I still think we'd end up dead," John muttered. He felt her move against his back. A hand touched his shoulder and she lifted herself into a half sitting position, looking over his shoulder at him with a curious expression.

"I thought you said you didn't care," she said.

"Well, now it comes to it, I suppose I do."

"Why?" she said, leaning closer to him. "What's come over you? When I first saw you, you weren't going to stop until you had revenge."

"There's something else going on," he said. "Bloodbeard's not just a pirate. He's . . . it's difficult to explain."

"Not hardly," she sniffed. "He killed my father without a reason!"

"You knew your father," John whispered softly, so softly she did not seem to hear. He was grateful, perhaps, that she had not.

Two days later, land was sighted. The lookout was practically cheering as he pointed it out. "Land ho!" he cried, his arms pointing, almost reaching out to embrace the dim, dark splash of crags in the distance. "To the nor-west!"

Men cheered and shouted, rushing to the railing, hanging from the rigging, all work ceasing while they stared. Bloodbeard burst from his cabin and stalked to the railing some yards from where John and Isabella stood.

"Back to work!" Bloodbeard shouted, after he had taken his fill of the sight of Tortuga in the distance. They sailed on for some hours, watching the speck of land grow into a looming island of high mountains, covered in the thick, dark green of jungle undergrowth.

As the sun approached the horizon, blazing the waters fiery red, the *Iago* drew near the southern tip of the island, making for the mouth of a large cove that opened out into a wide harbor tucked snugly away behind sloping walls of land to either side. Strange bird-calls echoed out from amid the darkness within the trees, barely audible over the grunts of the sailors, the bark of commands, and the rush of water around them.

John and Isabella stood at the railing and watched the Tortuga bay drift ever closer, leaning against it almost shoulder to shoulder. He glanced at her and at the sight of the sheer excitement in her eyes, her grief temporarily driven from her mind, and he grinned.

"What?" she asked, meeting his smile with one of her own.

"Nothing," he said, shaking his head, unsure himself why he was unable to control the grin spreading over his face. She turned to face him, grinning, and the light caught at something gleaming on her throat. John's smile faded as he realized what it was. She was wearing the "eye of the sea," the necklace her father had given her. It was long enough to fall below the neck of her shirt, but short enough to emerge if she suddenly shrugged her shoulders or leaned out too far.

She caught the change of mood in his eyes immediately.

"What?" she asked, looking concerned.

He pressed himself closer to her, blocking her view from the rest of the sailors.

"You're wearing the necklace," he hissed.

Her eyes widened in horror and her hands jumped to her throat. She felt it, her breathing starting to increase.

"I put it on this morning," she said, eyes wide, "before anyone was up. I just wanted to wear it, just once. I must have gotten sidetracked. I'd forgotten I was wearing it!"

"Well, nobody's lunged for it," John said, though he did not add, yet. "Just take it off!"

"Now? They'll see it!"

"I'm blocking the view," John said.

"No, they'll see me reach up and take something off."
She did not look pleased by what she was saying, but
John couldn't really argue against the logic of it.

"Looks like you're stuck wearing it until we can find a
private moment," John said.

"What do I do?" she hissed at him.

"Just walk slowly. Don't lean over. That should keep it
out of sight."

She tucked the necklace back into the neck of her shirt
and gave him a quick smile meant to reassure him she
would manage. It just made John more sure she was
panicking.

The *Iago* dropped anchor not two minutes later. The
bay stretched before them, arcing out in a beachline
obscured by shops and tents and the masts of smaller
fishing vessels and a few larger ships. The white sand of
the beach was littered with people, buying, selling,
yelling, drinking, and carousing.

The longboats were lowered several minutes after that,
and the crew clambered aboard them eagerly. John and
Isabella climbed down the ladder into the last longboat
after Bloodbeard himself. As they reached the boat,
steadying themselves in the bobbing water, Bloodbeard
reached out and took hold of John's hair. He gritted his
teeth in pain as the pirate drew him close, so close John
could feel his rancid breath.

"I have tolerated yer presence with me for long
enough," Bloodbeard said, a dangerous look in his eye.
"Ye will be civil and silent when we make shore,
understand? I be takin' a risk in trusting ye two. Try to
run and I will find ye, and gut ye, fer me own
amusement."

The boat set out for the wharf, two crewmen pulling

the oars. They made the ride in silence, watching the wooden docks draw slowly closer. John noticed there were sharks in the water here too, circling lazily in the bay.

Minutes later they were clambering out of the boats and onto the docks. Yet again John felt the strange sensation of a footing that didn't move with the swells of the sea. He helped Isabella out of the boat and followed Bloodbeard up the shore, where he brushed past the harbormaster, who looked absolutely terrified at the sight of him.

They proceeded into Tortuga proper as night was falling. The sun was already out of sight behind the steep mountains that rose up over them on every side, though the sky was still somewhat light.

Port Royal hadn't been the most civilized place John had ever been, but Tortuga was by many times far more rough in appearance. The buildings looked newer and built from less reliable materials. The communities seemed to cling to the shoreline, and almost as a matter of course, the jungle butted right up against the far sides of the small town. The chirp of tropical insects and the cries of wild monkeys seemed to underlay all the sounds of human settlement.

The settlements of Tortuga were crowded with sailors and whores, running and shouting, drinking and laughing. The streets were crowded and reeked of alcohol, vomit, gunpowder and the stink of encrusted sweat.

Bloodbeard strode through the press, and the people in his way parted almost before he touched them, as though he were forcing them aside by the sheer ferocity of his will alone. Eyes wide with terror, they sped out of his way, whispering and subdued.

He made his way through them, followed by John and Isabella, who were only a few paces behind the towering pirate. Behind them came the long string of his crew, all of whom looked about them at the general atmosphere of wine, women and gambling with expressions of longing, though they dared not break rank until given leave to do so. Perhaps they knew better than to try Bloodbeard's patience.

They seemed to have a particular destination in mind, and Bloodbeard did not slow until he stopped abruptly before a large, two-story house that stood near the center of the town. There were a few growls of approval from his crew at the place, though John couldn't divine why.

Directing half the men to remain outside, Bloodbeard marched up the steps of the large house and threw the doors open. John and Isabella followed, the other half of the men coming after them. As they entered, John realized what it was.

There were girls and women in various states of undress walking about the main room or lounging in soft chairs or cushions. The draperies were all of varying shades of red or pink, and in one corner sat a man with dark eyes, surrounded by five or six women, all fawning and caressing him.

At the sight of so many men arriving, several of the women sat up or turned their mouths up into welcoming smiles. It was a brothel. He felt Isabella stiffen next to him. He took her hand in his and gave it a reassuring squeeze.

A woman with long, flowing black hair and an ill-fitting dress approached. She smiled as Bloodbeard stopped.

"Captain Reach," she said, and it was a moment before John realized she had addressed Bloodbeard. But then, Bloodbeard was obviously not his real name. He swept his hat from his head and gave her a bow.

"Lady Jasmine," he growled, "it has been too long."

"Indeed," she said. "Some of your men will have to wait, I think. We've had a busy night."

"All I'm needin' is Carolina. Be she here still?"

"She is," Jasmine said. "But she is with a client at the moment."

"Which room?" Bloodbeard said, peering up at the ceiling to the second floor.

"She's not to be disturbed," Jasmine said evenly. "Even if she is your favorite."

"I be not here for fleshly pleasures this night," Bloodbeard said, stepping closer to her and clasping her thin neck in his rough, tanned hands. The touch was gentle, but there was a force of will behind it that told her very clearly that she was his to deal with as he pleased. Jasmine seemed to quake under his powerful gaze.

"H-her quarters are room twelve," the brothel proprietor said, taking a step back.

"Thank ye kindly," Bloodbeard said. He swept his hat back onto his head, and turned to his men. "Clear the house, gents!"

With roars, the crew drew cutlasses and pistols, bellowing and shouting, scattering in all directions. Several of the girls screamed, some rising to their feet. Impervious to the fear and chaos around him, Bloodbeard advanced on Jasmine, who backed away.

"Get yerself clear," he told her. She nodded and fled past him to the exit into the darkening street. The other women were rounded up and herded to the doors.

"What the hell do ye think ye be doing?" cried the man in the corner as the women around him ran shrieking from the room.

"Who might yerself be?" Bloodbeard said, stepping towards him. The man pulled himself taller and looked the pirate in the eye.

"I am Nicholus Hornbye, duly appointed governor of Tortuga—"

Bloodbeard pulled out a pistol and shot the man in the mouth as he spoke, hardly slowing in his pace to the stairs. The body toppled and Isabella gave a small scream of horror as it fell, splay-legged, a look of surprise still etched on the face, to the floor.

The large pirate ascended the stairs to the second floor, followed by John and Isabella, who were pressed forward by the advance of the other pirates. When they made the top of the stairs, the pirates burst past them with shouts and growls, kicking doors to rooms open, to the screams and shouts of men and women. All were dragged to the landing and thrown down the stairs.

Bloodbeard made his way almost serenely through the running and staggering bodies to room twelve. Cries and grunts were heard from within. He drew his cutlass and kicked the door with tremendous force. The jam cracked with the sound of a sharp snap and the door buckled open, flinging debris from the jam into the room beyond.

The man and woman within leapt to their feet from the bed with cries of alarm. The man fumbled for a moment, almost losing his balance on the pants twisted around his ankles, struggling to draw his blade. Bloodbeard marched to him in three steps and drove his sword through his chest. Eyes wide, the man trembled for a moment, then went limp. Bloodbeard allowed the gravity of the body to draw his sword downward. The man slid off his blade in one smooth motion as the woman on the bed gave a great sigh of frustration, rolling her eyes at him.

"Ye just cost me five guineas," she said.

"Carolina," Bloodbeard said with a smile. "I've missed ye. Tell me, do ye still bear what I asked of ye those long years ago?"

"Oh, that?" she said, pouting. "Yes, I have." She reached up to her neck and held up a bulky necklace.

Nodding his satisfaction, Bloodbeard stepped over to her, took hold of the necklace and tore it from around her neck.

"Ow," she said.

"Let's go," he said, turning and heading for the door he had just come through.

"That's what yer here for?" she cried, rising to her feet and adjusting her dress to cover herself. "Ye've not come for more . . . recreational purposes?"

"In time, perhaps," he said and stalked from the room without a backward glance, returning to the hallway where John and Isabella waited. She followed him, looking affronted but remaining silent.

Bloodbeard marched back down to the main floor. The building had been completely cleared of everyone except his own men.

"Very good," he said, looking around at them. He glanced at Carolina. "Where's the cellar?"

"This way," she said, glowering at him. She brushed past him, intentionally pressing her body against his. John saw Bloodbeard's eyes harden with annoyance. They followed her through a back room into what looked to be a supply room filled with barrels of drink and crates of food.

"Under there," she said, pointing to a corner piled high. Bloodbeard beckoned to several of the men, and they moved forward, bending down and heaving crates aside, tossing them carelessly behind them. After a moment, a space had been cleared. John could see an iron ring on one end of a trapdoor, flush against the wall, and hinges on the other.

One of the men stooped and took hold of the rusted iron ring, giving it a powerful tug. With a creak of protest, the cellar door opened up from the floor, bits of dust and rotted vegetable debris running down the surface and piling at the base.

"Lantern," Bloodbeard commanded, holding out his hand. A crewman pressed a light into his waiting fingers. He moved closer to the trapdoor, and in the bobbing, flickering light of the lantern, John could see a series of dirty wooden steps leading down into darkness.

Bloodbeard did not hesitate, but marched down the steps. John and Isabella nervously followed, Carolina and two others of the crew coming behind them.

It was dank below the floorboards of the brothel. The steps ended in unpacked earth, and John knew they were under the foundation of the building. The uneven, dancing light of the lantern cast strange shadows. The thin, ghostlike wisps of cobweb was spread over everything, drifting about the rafters, stretched across from wooden ceiling to dirt floor. A few abandoned, long-empty chests sat open against the walls, and the odd cutlass or two lay discarded on the earth, half-concealed under the dust.

"Ye told no one of its existence?" Bloodbeard asked Carolina, swinging around to look her in the eye. She jumped slightly under his gaze, but nodded.

146

"Told nary a soul," she said. "Just like ye asked of me."

Gazing around at the cellar, John caught Bloodbeard's eye questioningly.

"Old smuggler's hold," Bloodbeard said, answering John's unasked question.

The hulking pirate strode to the far wall, where the dirt floor met the wooden sides of the building, and kicked about in the dust for a moment. He paced along the wall a few steps, then knelt and brushed at the grime covering the lowest board of the wall.

"There she be, lads," he said, nodding. He stood and beckoned to the two crewmen who had followed them down. They nodded and hefted spades in their hands. They moved past Bloodbeard to the place he had indicated and began to dig. For several minutes there was no sound made by anyone, except the grinding thunks of shovels on earth.

The men worked quickly, and soon enough they had opened a large hole, nearly three feet across and four down, in the ground. The rhythmic sound of driving shovels into the ground, and then the run of gravel off the metal to the ground, was beginning to lull John into a relaxed state when, without warning, the sound changed. The hard clunk of shovel on wood brought the reverie to an abrupt end.

The men dropped their shovels and crouched down in the hole, brushing at the lid of a small wooden chest banded with iron. They cleared away the loose dirt and stones, took hold of the box's handles, and heaved. It came loose from the ground with a loud scraping sound, and with grunts and groans, the men deposited it on the earth before Bloodbeard, who was smiling with a manic glee at the sight.

He lifted the necklace torn from Carolina's neck, and John saw that what he had taken for a gaudy, tiny brick of gold was actually a box itself. Bloodbeard slid the bottom open and tilted it forward onto his palm. Out fell a small iron key, attached to the interior of the necklace by a chain.

"How'd ye do that?" asked Carolina interestedly. "You was never telling that it opened!"

Ignoring her, he moved forward and crouched over the chest. He inserted the key and turned it. The lock grated loudly, but then sprang open. He pulled the latch on the chest and lifted the lid. John inched closer, peering around the bulk of Bloodbeard's shoulders to get a better look.

The deep recesses of the chest weren't fully illuminated, but it appeared as though it were empty. No, John amended silently, there was something small and flat and brown in the bottom. It looked like a folded parchment, sealed with wax and tied with twine. Bloodbeard took the parchment, withdrew it from the chest, and shut the lid again. He relocked it and stood, slipping the parchment into a deep pocket of his waistcoat's interior.

"Be that the map, captain?" asked one of the men that had dug it up.

"That it be!" said Bloodbeard. "Bury the chest again, and make it as though we were never here."

The men nodded and set to work. Carolina scooted past John and Isabella to cling to Bloodbeard with a sultry expression, thrusting her midrif into his chest.

"Now the digging is done," she said, "shall we play?"

"Ye've done well these long years, Carolina," Bloodbeard said.

"Ye knew I would," she said, smiling at him. "Ye can't hardly live without me, so helplessly in love with me ye be."

A flicker of emotion shot across Bloodbeard's face, though John could hardly tell what it was, it passed so quickly. Bloodbeard pushed her away from himself and looked at her.

"Ye have done well," he said again. "And I thank ye for it. Yer job is done."

He grabbed her roughly by the hair and turned her around so her back was to him. He drew her close and produced a dagger from out of an unseen sheath. This he pressed to her exposed neck. Terrified, her eyes wide, she couldn't move against the strength of the huge man.

"But know this," Bloodbeard said, leaning close and speaking into her ear. "Ye be not the woman I love."

He thrust her forward to the ground, her own weight falling against the tightly held knife, slitting her throat neatly. Isabella wrenched her eyes closed and turned away, throwing herself into John's arms. Automatically, he wrapped them around her as she pressed her head into his shoulder.

Carolina fell to her hands and knees, eyes open wide in shock and terror, her every limb shaking. She gurgled unintelligibly for a moment and tried to crawl to the steps, but sank slowly to the ground to lay in her own blood, trembling and jerking, as she breathed her last.

Bloodbeard had paid no attention to her last thrashings, turning back to the men, who were nearly finished reburying the chest. Pulling a handkerchief from his pocket, he wiped his blade clean and slipped it back into his belt.

"Now she knew what be down here, she'd've tattled to

every man what wandered in," Bloodbeard said to John's look of utter horror and disgust. "A necessary sacrifice."

"Necessary sacrifice?" John repeated, his voice weak and shaking.

"Isla San Thanatos be the greatest treasure haul ever taken by our kind, lad," Bloodbeard said. "There be not a pirate in the water what wouldn't give everythin' he owned in this miserable world to get even a small quarter of it in his hands."

He stepped closer to John.

"Three Spanish treasure galleons, taken all at once," he said. "Their holds bursting with the wealth of the Aztecs, mined in South America and shipped back te Spain. We intercepted 'em on their way an' took 'em all. Nearly all of it still be there, piled, heaped in mounds three times the height of a man! I'll not endanger that, not for the life of a whore. Useful while she served her purpose, though. I be grateful to her."

"All done, Captain," said one of the two men.

"Good," Bloodbeard said, turning to them with a broad smile. He drew two of his pistols and shot them both dead where they stood. Isabella jumped against John again, and he tightened his arms around her.

"Are ye wantin' anything they've got on 'em?" Bloodbeard asked.

John shook his head, stunned at the casual nature of the murders and remembered again with renewed resolve why he had sworn to kill Bloodbeard. He looked at the pirate and took a breath.

"Why?" he asked. "Aren't you just going to kill us too?"

Bloodbeard stepped closer to him, and John felt the urge to run fill him. He forced the emotion aside and stood his ground, clutching Isabella in his arms.

"There's only one way I won't kill ye," Bloodbeard said, gazing at John with an odd expression. "Only one thing will save ye."

"What's that?" John said.

"That'd spoil the fun, by the powers!" Bloodbeard growled, slapping John on the shoulder. "If the day comes when I'm to kill ye, it'll be on Isla San Thanatos or after. For now, ye be safe, Master Rackham. Ye and yer property both."

The hulking pirate brushed past them to the steps and climbed them two at a time, vanishing swiftly from sight.

"Close up this door an' put back all them crates," Bloodbeard barked to them as his left the room.

"Come on," John said to Isabella, leading her to the stairs and up into the storage room. He left her shaking by the door and closed the trapdoor, piling the barrels and crates back over top of it. When he was finished, he stepped to her again. "You were right. Tonight is the night. We kill Bloodbeard, get in a longboat, make for shore and barter passage back to Port Royal."

She nodded at him. He took her hand and led her out into the brothel common area. The last of Bloodbeard's men were filtering out into the street and John followed them.

Bloodbeard stood talking to Jasmine, the brothel's proprietor. As they watched, Bloodbeard lifted a finger and stroked her cheek.

"Will ye keep somethin' fer me?" he asked her.

"Of course," she purred.

Bloodbeard lifted the necklace that held the hidden key and draped it gently, almost lovingly, around her neck, fastening it. She looked extremely pleased and

151

Bloodbeard smiled.

"I'll be comin' back fer it," he said. "One day. Be sure ye have it."

She nodded.

"Ah, Jasmine," Bloodbeard said. "Ye ever were me favorite."

John wondered, with a rush of anger, how many he had said that to, how many he had used the same way. Bloodbeard turned to his men and dismissed them for the night. Cheering, the men surged back into the brothel or towards the taverns.

"Not ye two," Bloodbeard said, pointing at John and Isabella. "Yer to come back to the ship with me."

John and Isabella were silent as they followed the shadowed form of Bloodbeard back through Tortuga and to the docks. As they made their way down the street, John could see figures peering out of windows or slipping as casually as possible from the streets, not meeting any of their eyes.

Once returned to the docks, the silver of the moon reflecting off the clear water, Bloodbeard made them climb aboard the longboat and row him back to the *Iago*. With John on one oar and Isabella on the other, it took them some time to get into a matching rhythm that would direct the boat in the direction they wanted. This was a more complicated process than either of them had anticipated, and coordinating their efforts was made all the more difficult with Bloodbeard shouting and cursing at them as the boat pulled first to the left, then to the right, or made no progress at all in the water. What ought to have taken five minutes ended up being twenty-five, and by the time they reached the *Iago*'s side, they were both sweating in the humid night air and panting for breath.

"Curse ye both to the depths," Bloodbeard growled as he climbed up the rope ladder to the deck. Muttering to himself, John followed, after helping Isabella up. As her legs vanished over the railing, John hauled himself up. Before he had reached the deck, he heard her give a shriek of fear. Panic surged into John's throat, and he thrashed his way to the railing and threw himself over the side onto the deck.

Bloodbeard had her by the throat, a wicked gleam in his eye. She was struggling wildly, but the pirate was so much stronger she might as well have been wrestling with stone.

"Hey!" he shouted and reached for his pistol.

"Don't bother, boy!" spat Bloodbeard. He reached to Isabella's neck with his free hand and seized something small and glittering in the moonlight. With a sick jolt, John realized that Isabella's necklace must have swung free as she climbed aboard.

"The two of ye have lied to me," Bloodbeard growled. He tore the necklace from Isabella's throat. She shrieked again and thrashed against his grip. With a snort, he dragged her forward towards his great cabin.

"No!" John yelled, following quickly.

Bloodbeard burst into the room, nearly knocking the door from its frame in his rage. He threw Isabella to the ground and began to grope at her clothes, searching for more hidden valuables as she shrieked and struggled. Within moments he had found the small leather pouch and torn it free of her belt.

Whimpering, her eyes filled with tears, she crawled towards him in desperation, reaching, trying to get at her father's possessions. He kicked her in the stomach and stepped past her as she curled into a ball, gagging and moaning.

"Stop it!" John shouted, drawing his pistol and directing it at Bloodbeard. The pirate turned and glared at him, such fury in his eyes that it cowed John almost immediately. Though he kept the gun pointed at him, John's arm was wavering in fear.

"Or what?" the pirate threw back at him, reaching into his shirt and producing a small silver key that hung about his neck on a small chain. This was the moment, John knew. This was the moment to kill Bloodbeard and escape. He took several deep breaths as Bloodbeard bent over his desk and unlocked the top drawer on the right hand side. Now was his chance, he told himself furiously.

John faltered at the sight. The drawer was filled with parchments, piled and folded and crammed into every available space. Some of them looked like official letters from some head of state, sealed in red wax and signed with a cultured scrawl: *G. M. V.* Before John could see anything more, Bloodbeard had dropped the pouch, the necklace, and the map retrieved from the chest beneath the brothel into the drawer, slid it shut and relocked it. The moment had passed.

Bloodbeard glanced up at the sight of John training him with a pistol, wavering, and growled. He moved suddenly, stepping back across Isabella's prone form and crossing to John in three steps. John flinched, but his nerve failed him at the last moment and he couldn't bring himself to pull the trigger. The towering pirate tore the pistol out of John's fingers with a snort of derision, turned it over in his hand so that he gripped the barrel, and struck him across the face with the iron butt. Stars winked behind John's eyes and he felt himself topple to the cabin floor next to Isabella. The side of his face was numb, it felt cold, and then hot pain blossomed suddenly. He gasped, feeling tears spring into his eyes and bit his tongue to keep from crying out.

"I warned ye about pointin' pistols at me!" Bloodbeard said, his voice still and cold. "I warned ye about lying to me. Ye haven't listened yet."

John forced himself to his hands and knees, pushing himself up until he was standing on his knees, panting and glaring at him. Bloodbeard laughed, softly, and struck John across the jaw with the butt of his pistol again. He fell back to the deck, groaning, and this time he tasted the metallic tang of blood in his mouth.

"So you're going to kill us?" John slurred through his swelling lip. "Leave our bodies for the fins?"

"Don't tempt me, boy," Bloodbeard said, his eyes glinting.

"You would have killed any one of your crew!" John shouted. "Why not us? What makes us so different?"

"Ye understand nothing," Bloodbeard said, shaking his head. He tossed the pistol back to John, who caught it, looking astonished. "Get yerself out of here and leave me in peace!"

The look in Bloodbeard's eyes was so terrible that John helped Isabella stand and limped from the cabin without another word. She winced with every step, clutching her stomach. She sobbed wordlessly as they slowly made their way down to the ladder to John's hammock. As soon as they had found their way to it in the gloom, she pushed him away, not meeting his gaze, and gingerly crawled into the bed. She rolled over and faced away from him on the cot.

He moved automatically to climb in next to her, but

her voice stopped him. It was soft and dull, as though all the life had drained from it.

"He was unarmed and alone," she said, and the quiet disappointment in her tone made him feel much worse. "You didn't even try to shoot him."

"Sorry," he muttered.

"Sorry," she repeated listlessly. "My father is dead, and sorry does no good. Sleep somewhere else."

"Fine," he snapped.

Frustrated, emotionally exhausted and his face throbbing in pain, John slid into the next hammock over, which smelled unpleasantly of sweat. It was a long time before he fell into a fitful sleep.

When he awoke, he awoke with a start. Inhaling sharply at some shadowy nightmare forgotten upon his waking, he yawned and sat up, running a hand through his hair. It was pitch black in the hold, and now deep into the night.

After allowing his eyes to become accustomed to the murky gloom, he realized that Isabella was gone. He sat up straighter, listening for the slightest sound, hardly daring to breathe. What had happened to her? Quiet as death, he slipped out of the spare hammock and found that his belt was lighter. Reaching down, he discovered that his pistol was gone.

"Damn her," he whispered, fear clutching at his chest. She'd gone after Bloodbeard by herself. He knew she had. He ran as silent and swift as he could to the ladder and climbed up the two decks between himself and the main deck.

The soft gleam of silver moonlight trickled in from the open hatch that led to the main deck. Moving cautiously, heart in his throat, John eased his head up through the hatch. The deck was deserted and shrouded in a thick fog that had rolled down from the Tortuga forests and engulfed the bay in white silence. It was so thick about him that the railings to either side were barely visible, fading into nothing, and the main mast, directly in front of him, rose up and dissolved into cloud like a great specter.

He wasn't alone on the deck, he realized. There was a small silhouette standing by the foremast, nearly invisible to him. John clambered out onto the deck and walked slowly over to Isabella's still form. She stood at the railing next to the foremast, one hand lightly resting on it, the other limp at her side, John's pistol clenched in her fist. Her back was to him, and the breeze that swept in off the Caribbean sea tossed her red hair around her with soft caresses.

"Go away," she said, without turning around.

"I'm sorry," he said and he sounded so miserable that she turned and looked at him. This disrupted the flow of her hair in the wind, and she was engulfed in fiery red curls. Spitting and brushing at it, she pushed it out of her eyes and glared at him.

"You don't sound it," she lied, her voice cold with disdain.

"I should have done it when I had the chance," he said. "I'm sorry. I—he messes with my head."

"I know," she said, quietly. "It's not too late, though. I'm about to take care of it. I was only trying to figure out how to get a longboat in the water by myself."

"I'll do it," John said, holding out his hand for the gun and stepping towards her.

"No!" she said, pulling the gun out of his reach and

behind her back. "You had your chance."

"It's mine to do," John said.

"What if you don't do it? Again?"

"Won't happen," John said. "This time for sure. We're the only three on the ship. We don't even have to get the longboat in the water until after he's dead."

"Oh!" she said, brightly, handing over the pistol. "So we'll both go in together."

As she handed him the pistol, their hands brushed together and John felt a jolt of nerves shiver down his spine. He had the sudden, almost overwhelming urge to kiss her. He blinked and shook the heady thoughts away, surprised and taken aback at how suddenly the impulse had come over him.

Confused, he turned away from her and moved softly toward the great cabin. She followed him closely as he inched closer to the door.

He eased his boots to the deck to muffle the sound of their approach, and behind him he could sense that Isabella had held in her breath. They reached the door and paused, gathering around the latch, shoulder to shoulder.

"I've got to get my things," she whispered to him, her mouth close to his ear. "He locked it in that drawer."

John nodded, his gut jangling from nerves. He nearly jumped when he felt her hand slip into his, her fingers sliding between his and giving him an encouraging squeeze. He glanced at her and found she was staring at him. His legs seemed to turn soggy as their eyes met. He smiled weakly, hefted the pistol and drew back the firing hammer with a click.

She reached across him and took hold of his father's sword, drawing it out of its sheath at his side. She hefted

158

it for a moment, getting a feel for it, and nodded to him. He took a deep breath and pulled the latch.

The door opened in almost total silence. They pulled it wide and stood on the threshold for another moment, gazing into the enveloping darkness within. John took another steadying breath and entered the cabin. He heard Isabella follow, the only sound the faint swish of her pants as she swung the door closed again.

In the deep of the night, the shadows clung to the entire room. Faintly, silver moonlight crept in through the windows along the cabin's back wall, but did little to illuminate anything beyond the bench and the few feet in front of it. They could hear the sound of heavy breathing coming from the direction of the great bed along the starboard side, though almost nothing could be seen from that quarter of the room.

Isabella tapped John silently on the shoulder and pointed his father's sword in the direction of the great desk on the other side of the room. The blade flared with reflected moonlight for a heart-stopping moment and Bloodbeard's breathing became a snort.

Breathless, frozen in place five paces into the cabin, they waited, and after a moment there was the sound of a body shifting in sleep. The breathing normalized again. Exhaling in relief, John gave her a look of anger and mouthed, "I'm going to kill you."

"Sorry," she mouthed back, looking pale. She pointed again, this time without the sword, and John saw a crystal decanter resting on the desktop, only the dregs behind.

"He's been drinking," she mouthed.

She padded over to the desk on tiptoes and gave the top, right-hand drawer an experimental tug.

"Locked," she mouthed. John nodded and moved out

of the center of the cabin to the starboard side, slipping towards the great bed on which Bloodbeard lay. The breathing grew louder as John drew closer in the darkness. He clutched at the pistol with a sweaty, trembling palm as he gently eased forward, unable to see, following the sound of the pirate's breathing.

His eyes were beginning to adjust to the darkness, and he could just make out the edge of the bed and the large lump that lay below its sheets. The foot of the bed was no more than two paces from him. He raised his pistol and moved around the foot, padding up the side to where he knew Bloodbeard's head would be. He stepped forward, the pistol aimed at Bloodbeard's head, which was turned slightly towards his side of the bed. The deep breathing continued, and he moved closer until his pistol was two feet from its target.

Something wasn't right, John realized. With a surge of terror, he realized that Bloodbeard's eyes were open and locked on John.

"By the Powers, boy," Bloodbeard growled, "ye just cannot take a hint."

"Get up," John whispered, his hand shaking as he clutched the pistol.

"Fine," Bloodbeard said, throwing off the sheets and standing. He towered over John, who backpedaled, keeping his pistol trained on the huge man.

"Unlock the drawer, the top one," John directed.

Bloodbeard slowly made his way to the desk. Isabella backed away from him, holding the cutlass out toward him. He stopped by the desk and drew a key from the small chain around his neck. He bent over the desk and unlocked the drawer. Straightening, Bloodbeard stepped back and smiled.

"Ye don't want to look in there, lad," he told John, a wicked gleam in his eyes. "Ye never know what ye'll find."

"Shut up," John said.

"Suit yerself then," Bloodbeard said, his eyes glinting with malicious glee.

John pulled the drawer open and peered into it. It was filled with parchments, so many that the drawer was in danger of overflowing. They covered the small leather pouch of Isabella's treasures.

"These are mine!" she snapped, pulling them out of the drawer. A cascade of parchments tumbled to the ground and the desk. John bent and picked up several of them and made to put them back in the drawer. His eye caught sight of something familiar on the top paper and he paused, staring at it. The handwriting . . . he recognized it.

He unfolded the parchment and found that it was a letter. His eyes dropped to the bottom of the letter, and his stomach gave a horrible jolt. The letter was signed,

always your beloved,
Mary Anne Rackham

Stunned, John forced himself to breathe.

"What is it?" Isabella said, moving closer to him. John pulled the letter out of her reach with a snarl and looked at Bloodbeard, who was still smiling, that terrible glee still in his eyes. John looked back at the letter, his heart hammering in his chest.

Dearest Bartholomew,
I am pleased to hear of your successes

against the Spanish. Your last reached Tortuga only days ago, but I could not wait to write back. I am unable to contain myself, and the excitement to hear that you will be returning to port in a few months is only dampened by my excitement to hold you again in my arms. We must again discuss my signing up with the Iago's crew upon your return; I very much wish to join. Yes, I know what you think of it, but I don't think I have much of a mind to let it go.

The letter went on but John could read no more. He was breathless, unable to inhale. There was a strange pressure in his chest, like a great weight were pressing down on him, suffocating him. He gasped and gave a shudder, the letter falling lifelessly from his hands and fluttering to the deck. His eyes misting, he looked upon Bloodbeard, who stood still and silent against the cabin wall behind the desk, looking at John with disdain and delight. He was nothing more than a black silhouette against the moonlight pouring in through the windows behind him, and appeared to John to be as insubstantial as a long-past ghost returning to haunt him.

"You," John said, the word dropping from his lips like an unclean thing.

"Aye," Bloodbeard said. "Yer mother. Me very own lover."

"That's not true," John ground out between clenched teeth. A deep rage was rising in him, and a dull pain was throbbing in his temple.

"Don't be a fool, boy!" Bloodbeard shouted, coming away from behind the desk and glaring at John. "By the depths, I surely am not! Ye call yerself John Rackham, but I'm knowing the truth! Ye think ye're the son of Billy Jack Thatcher, but there's much he never telled ye."

John was shaking his head, terror and anger mixed equally in his mind.

"Billy Jack Thatcher stole her from me!" screamed Bloodbeard. "He be a lyin', thievin' bastard, and Mary Anne Rackham be his filthy, vile whore!"

"Shut up!" John screamed back, lifting his pistol and pointing it at Bloodbeard.

"Or ye'll be doing what, exactly?" Bloodbeard growled. "If ye're wanting to kill me, ye'll need to be plotting it a bit quieter, and not in the crew's quarters where there's dozens of men to overhear ye."

"You knew we meant to kill you?" John spluttered.

"The whole time," Bloodbeard said with an easy smile.

Behind them, the door of the cabin opened and Bloody Hands stepped into the room, cutlass drawn and pistol armed. John cursed their foolishness in forgetting there were two crews of Bloodbeard's in the bay. How could they have been stupid enough to think Bloodbeard would leave the *Iago* totally empty and unguarded?

With a growl of fury and frustration, John pulled the trigger on his pistol. There was a loud click in the dark, but no shot.

"Yer a heavy sleeper, lad," said Bloodbeard. "Weren't hard to swap yer loaded piece with an unloaded one. How many times it be that ye've failed to bring me down?"

"Three," John said, his eyes locked on Bloodbeard. "Fourth time's the charm."

"Damn ye, boy," Bloodbeard said.

Shaking, enraged at his inability to kill Bloodbeard,

John hurled the pistol at him. The pirate knocked it aside with a casual swipe of the hand, and it clattered to the deck in the darkness.

"You're a liar!" John said. "You can't torture my father, so you torture me in his place!"

"I'm not to be denying it," Bloodbeard said. "How do ye suppose they met, lad? She were mine, and he stole her from me, just as he stole everything from me! Me woman, me treasure, me sword. Everything!"

"I'm going to kill you," John said, his entire body shaking with rage, tears now appearing in his eyes. "If I have to do it with my bare hands, I'll do it, I swear."

"Are ye now?" Bloodbeard said, smiling. "Would ye kill yer own father then?"

Chapter Eight

The Storm

John could do nothing but stare at the huge pirate across from him.

"What?" He heard the words enter the room, spill out from his mouth, his tone listless and flat.

"Billy Jack and Mary only had a single night together," Bloodbeard said, a wide smile of delight at John's horror etched upon his face. He moved into the center of the room, where John stood and bent low, gazing with poorly hidden mirth into John's face. Isabella moved slowly after him, hovering behind Bloodbeard's bulk, looking horrified. "She and meself, on the other hand—well, she were aboard the *Iago* for quite a spell before Billy Jack sullied her with his touch."

So this was it, John realized. This was why Bloodbeard had been treating him differently, the reason he'd been allowed to join the crew. It must be the thing Bloodbeard had hinted would spare John from death by his hand. He believed John to be his son.

Shaking, exhausted, broken, John did not know what to believe. He simply stared at the pirate in front of him, trying to hold back gulping sobs. He didn't want to give Bloodbeard the satisfaction of seeing him weep.

With a cry of anger, Isabella lifted John's sword and

stabbed at Bloodbeard's back. There were roars of fury from Bloodbeard and Bloody Hands, who lunged forward, blade drawn, and caught Isabella's strike before it fell. The blades rang out, and the sword in Isabella's hands was torn from her grasp and clanged to the deck.

Bloody Hands backhanded her across the face. She gave a squeal of pain and toppled. He kicked the sword out of reach, and put his own blade to her throat. Whimpering, she lay on her side, her chest rising and falling in the moonlight. John could hardly muster any emotion for her.

"Get her out of here!" bellowed Bloodbeard, waving at Isabella, hardly sparing her a glance.

"What should I be doin' with her, captain?"

"Put her in the brig," Bloodbeard said. "The boy can join her later."

Bloody Hands reached down and with a rough jerk, grabbed her by the hair and hauled her to her feet. She shrieked as she was hoisted bodily into the air and dragged to the cabin door. Weeping and struggling, she fought and struggled, but in the end both of them vanished. John could hear her protesting the entire way belowdecks, but he did not release Bloodbeard from his gaze.

"I'm not your son," John said, eyes still on Bloodbeard. "You're a pirate."

This brought a chuckle to Bloodbeard, and the pirate turned and stepped back to the desk, collected the letters and returned them to the drawer, then locked it with the key around his neck. John's skin crawled at the tenderness with which he had refolded the letters from his mother. Bloodbeard picked up the decanter of dregs and took a swig. He chuckled again, and looked at John.

"Tell me, lad," he said. "Have ye ever heard tell of a man named Robin Hood?"

John shook his head.

"Lived a few hundred years back," Bloodbeard said, leaning against the desk and taking another drink. "In England. A right evil man came to the throne and started taxin' folk too much. So old Robin Hood hides out in the forest and starts robbin' from the King's Men. He steals all the gold they got on 'em, and gives it back to them what had it taken from 'em. Robbed the rich and gave it to the poor. Became quite the folk hero."

"So?"

"So when Robin Hood does it, he's called a hero. When a man such as meself does it, he's called a thief, a vile scoundrel, and a pirate. Be that fair to yer judgment?"

"What, so you're Robin Hood?" John said, raising a skeptical eyebrow.

"Hell's wrath, boy, of course not," Bloodbeard spat. "But we be takin' from the same sort of folk."

"The rich?"

"Aye, the rich, lad. Ye know 'em. They hoard their wealth and leave the rest of us to scrape out a living as best we're able. They live on their plantations and mansions, giving commands and ordering folk about like they were our betters, boy. Ye know it's true; yer mother works for a governor, do she not?"

John was surprised that Bloodbeard knew that, but he nodded. Bloody Hands or one of the others must have heard her talking about it in *The Spot*.

"But do you give to the poor?" John asked, sounding uncertain.

"Curse it, I be the poor, lad!" Bloodbeard roared. "Well, I were once. Pirates pillage 'cause some folk have too much and others too little. We be the poor, and we're takin' back what be ours!"

Bloodbeard summoned Bloody Hands back to the cabin, and ordered John thrown in the brig. Numb and shellshocked, John put up little resistance and allowed himself to be taken below and placed in the brig, a sizable cast iron cage built for holding mutinous crewmen.

Bloody Hands threw John roughly through the brig's door and slammed it shut behind him. With the jangle of a skeleton key in the lock, Bloody Hands departed. John remained on all fours, his face pressed in the deck, listening to the first mate's receding bootfalls.

Isabella sat in the corner where the bars met the wooden hull, her knees pressed into her chest, her arms wrapped around her legs. She wasn't crying, but John could tell she had been; her eyes were swollen and red, and the faint gleam of moisture remained on her cheeks.

His heart heavy and stomach laying sickly in his belly, John felt dead inside. He slowly pushed himself up from the deck and sat up, looking at her listlessly. She met his gaze with one equally lifeless, and they both understood that their position had significantly worsened. It was the third failed attempt to bring Bloodbeard down, and their only shot at escaping the *Iago* was now lost to them.

"Sorry," John whispered, his voice cracking. He fought back the tears, which took so much strength his whole body began to tremble. He gasped for breath and shook his head, grinding his teeth and clenching his fists together until his fingernails bit into his skin.

Isabella's blank gaze broke, and she pushed herself to her knees, crawled to John and threw her arms around him. Immediately, hot tears broke over John, and he let the pain wash over him. He wept like a man, howling and

168

gasping, his hands clenching and releasing, his legs shaking as he clung to her. She was shuddering and he knew she was crying too, but he was utterly unable to speak. His hands were numb and shook as he clung to her. His entire world was visceral, and the mesh of her hair against his face, the texture of her shirt in his hands, was all he could comprehend.

He pulled away slightly, trying to catch his breath, but without warning, without him even really being sure of how it happened, her mouth found his. It took his brain what seemed like an eternity to catch up and realize they were kissing. His stomach somersaulted in surprise. Startled, both of them pulled away and stared at the other. There was silence between them, broken only by the ship's creaking and their own breathing.

The next few days were spent in the brig, having their food brought to them once a day. The portions were meager, and did not fill the stomach. John suspected that the shipboard cook took almost no time at all to prepare it for them. It was not the usual rations, and once John swore they had delivered him a hunk of raw meat. John and Isabella spent most of their time in silence, sitting on opposite sides of the brig or dozing.

Though Isabella was horrified at the revelation that Bloodbeard might well be John's father—and despite their kiss—he could tell she hadn't quite forgiven him for being unable to bring the bloodthirsty pirate down for the third time. He could see it in her eyes when she looked at him, an injured dullness that he yearned to somehow remove.

Gradually, as the fourth day dawned, they could hear the thump of many boots on deck, and knew that their stop at Tortuga had at last come to an end. What this meant for them John did not know, but at least the ship would not simply rest in the Tortuga harbor while they wasted away in squalor. If they set out again, it could mean being eventually let out of the brig once they arrived on the island.

The sound of heavy footfalls continued long into what John supposed to be the night; in the bowels of the ship where there were no portholes and it was perpetually dark there was no real way to tell the hour, nor keep track of the passage of time. Men began to haul crates and barrels down the main hatch and out of sight to the decks below. Some of these crates included live chickens, crammed into as tight a space as possible, squawking shrilly. Cursing and shouting, several men dragged four live goats down the ladder steps, their hooves thunking and clattering on the deck as they went.

A few hours later, John could hear them heaving up the anchors, and the ship rocked easier in the water as the familiar rush of water outside the hull returned and the ship began to move. Hours passed and the ship creaked, pitching and yawing in the water as they sped their way to what John could only assume was Isla San Thanatos. Eventually, he passed into a fitful sleep.

He was startled awake by the sound of their food being tossed into the cage with them. The thin metal plate rang musically as it landed, scattering what looked like a few pieces of rotten fruit in every direction. Lurching to his feet with a groan, trying to rub the sleep from his eyes, John looked up in time to see Bloody Hands departing.

"What day is it?" John blurted, blinking at the first mate.

"Been at sea a day," grunted Bloody Hands. "At least a fortnight 'til we come te the isle." And he left without a backward glance.

They spent at least another two days languishing in the brig before Bloodbeard himself finally descended belowdecks. John could hear his massive footsteps on the deck above as the hulk of a pirate made his way down the steps from the aft castle and crossed to the hatch. The boots, gigantic on the small ladder, appeared first as he stomped his way down, forced to compress his shoulders and duck his head to get through the opening. Finally, the large, grimacing head, topped this time with a great, plumbed hat.

He met John's eyes from the bottom of the ladder and stood silently for a moment, his face unreadable. John felt his heart lurch and he realized he still did not know what to believe, either about Bloodbeard or Billy Jack Thatcher. Was Billy Jack all that Bloodbeard said, or was Bloodbeard after something else? Revenge of some kind, or was he simply toying with John?

The pirate came across the deck to the brig, his gait casual and unconcerned, but John felt trepidation in his chest as the huge man drew closer, and he realized with a shock that part of him really did want to believe that Bloodbeard was truly his father. At least that way he would still have a father who was alive.

"Boy," growled Bloodbeard. "Be ye ready to behave yerself civil-like?"

John, lost for words and with a sickly weight in his chest, merely shrugged. Bloodbeard eyed him for a long moment, and John found that he could barely meet the gaze. Finally, with a derisive snort, Bloodbeard threw open the gate to the cage and beckoned him out.

John glanced at Isabella, who lay slumped in the far corner, her legs stretched out, leaning against the deck of the ship. Her eyes were closed and her head was bowed, but John was quite sure she wasn't asleep; he knew the sound of her breathing when she slept, and though she seemed to be dozing, the more John looked at her the more tense he realized she was, as though she were listening with all her might.

With a sigh, John rose and slowly walked out of the brig, not looking at either Bloodbeard or Isabella. He turned back expectantly, but Bloodbeard shut the gate again and relocked it with a swirl from his key, which he then tucked into his shirt. Seeing the surprised look on John's face, Bloodbeard smiled at him.

"No need for the wench to come along," he said with a wan smile. "Ye may not believe me now, boy, but that girl be a bad influence on ye."

To John's surprise, Bloodbeard threw his arm around his shoulder and turned him toward the hatch, walking towards it in what Bloodbeard apparently thought was a paternal fashion. He was clearly not comfortable doing it, however, because his arm was stiff and barely touched John, as though the arm were almost hovering over him rather than actually touching him.

John went first up the ladder to the main deck, Bloodbeard following. As he reached the hatch and put his head out into the fresh air, John realized it had been nearly a week since he had last seen the sun. As the ocean breeze swept over him, he closed his eyes and took a deep breath, basking in the cool air.

Crewmen were scattered about the deck, some tying down ropes, others in the rigging, while yet others not on duty lounged in groups, slumped or sitting on deck, playing cards or laughing at crude jokes, all of them drinking.

But Bloodbeard did not move in that direction. He turned and made his way to the aft castle, climbing the stairs to the deck. John followed wordlessly, unsure of what to think. The helmsman nodded at Bloodbeard, who ignored him and settled himself at the far railing, directly above the rudder. John stopped in front of him, but did not sit.

In the distance behind them he could see the other ship they had captured, which Bloody Hands was currently captaining. He looked again at Bloodbeard, who was now gazing in John's direction, wearing an irritated expression.

"Sit," Bloodbeard ordered, but John did not move.

"So you're going to treat me like your son now, is that it?" John said. Bloodbeard smirked unpleasantly at him from beneath his great beard.

"Are ye goin' to stand there all the cursed day?" The pirate captain shifted in his sitting position. "Be this some new protest? Standing yerself to death?"

John sighed and sat, reluctantly, leaving a wide distance between himself and Bloodbeard.

"You're not my father." It was a statement, and John tried to muster as much confidence in it as he could.

"Perhaps ye be right," Bloodbeard said, shrugging. "And perhaps ye be not. But ye've got the fire, lad, an' I've got need of men with the fire."

"The fire?" John asked.

"Aye, lad, the fire," said Bloodbeard, sitting up slightly. "The drive, the passion, that great burning feeling of rage in the pit of yer stomach."

"That's because I hate you."

"That be the very truth of the thing," said Bloodbeard unconcernedly. "All we need do is to find somethin' ye may hate even more."

"Are you going to try and turn me into a pirate?" John scoffed.

"Hardly." Bloodbeard shook his head with another of his annoyingly smug smiles. "Ye already be a pirate, lad. Or did ye forget ye signed up on my crew? Yer name be on me roster below, well enough to get any man hanged good an' dead. We're not to turn ye into a pirate; we're to make ye what ye already be."

This disquieting notion bothered John more than he cared to let on. He forced his face to remain impassive, but thought Bloodbeard could tell how much it effected him. Thankfully the large captain said nothing.

"So," said John slowly, "what of your father and mother? Were they pirates too?"

Bloodbeard threw back his head and laughed. "What be this now?" he cried, looking amused. "Ye tryin' to find some source fer my own villany? Be ye thinkin' that me father didn't love me enough or some such high and lofty notion what would explain my bloodlust?"

John paused, realizing that this was indeed what he had been thinking, and was disturbed again at how keenly Bloodbeard understood him.

"Let me tell ye about me father, boy," Bloodbeard said. "He be a good and kind man, always helpin' others and who loved me dearly. I just liked pillagin' more."

John shook his head and looked away, watching the small square of sail on the horizon behind them bob up and down as the other ship followed in their wake.

"Be that too hard to accept?" Bloodbeard said, looking hard at John.

"No," John said softly, turning back to the large pirate across from him. "It just means you're ungrateful."

It was clear that Bloodbeard had not expected this, and his head pulled away from John ever so slightly, the eyes narrowed with surprise. But he covered it well, and the confusion evident there was immediately masked with rage.

"Mind yer tongue, boy!" spat Bloodbeard, ordering him back to the brig. He was escorted there by a crewman and locked back in with Isabella. Over the course of the next few days the weather turned cold, the wind stiffening, the water choppy and hard. The ship rumbled and quaked as it crashed through the wave crests.

Bloodbeard allowed John out of the brig once a day, and John found that he looked forward to that moment, however brief, more than he cared to reveal to Isabella—who wasn't speaking to him anyway. She would shoot him dirty looks every day as Bloodbeard came and released him, but otherwise made no effort to communicate. John felt she was being tremendously unfair, and was in no way taking into account what he was going through.

On the fourth day to sea from Tortuga, the storm came upon the *Iago* and the *Philadelphia*. The helmsman had turned to Bloodbeard and John, who sat at their customary station, leaning their backs against the far aft gunwale. "We're bein' blown off course," he reported to Bloodbeard as the wind picked up around them. Bloodbeard stood and looked out at the sky, then consulted a compass from his pocket.

"It's fine," he said, nodding at some unseen confirmation from the compass.

Within an hour's stretch, the sky had darkened to a nearly nightfall darkness and the wind howled over them, buffeting at the rigging and sails with gale-force gusts. The crew grimaced against the sea spray the wind gathered and tossed over the ship as they staggered from station to station, trying desperately to secure the ship in time. The sails were reduced to half, and anchors lowered into the water on both sides of the hull to create drag and prevent a capsize.

This they had barely managed to do when the first great swell came upon them, crashing with a thunderous retort against the *Iago*'s starboard side. The deck shuddered under the blow as the wave cascaded over them all. John clutched at the gunwale as the wave blasted over top of him and was immediately soaked to the bone. No one was lost to the water as the wave swept over the ship, though there were shouts and cries of terror as it struck.

The rains came so suddenly that it seemed to John as though the heavens had opened once more to swallow them all. It fell almost horizontally as the howling wind tore over them. John was already fighting numbness in his extremities as a cry rose up from the main deck below.

"Brace!" it shouted, the warning almost immediately lost beneath the crash of another titanic wave. The ship lurched sideways wildly in the water, and John again clung to the side as the wave's crest washed over him. This one was more powerful, the water more insistent to drag him over the side and into the depths. He managed to keep his grip, but only just. With a terrified scream, one man was swept away over the side and lost in the darkness.

Lightning rent the air overhead with a great pulse of fire, momentarily illuminating the sea round about. John's heart lurched in his chest as the scene registered around him. The water was a sheer, alien chaos, rumbling and broiling as far as the eye could see, great ocean swells surging in every direction he looked, some of them higher than the *Iago's* mainmast.

At that moment, as the world was plunged back into darkness, the deck beneath his feet seemed to fall away from him. He staggered as, he realized with a horrified gasp, the ship plunged down into a deep trough between two wave crests. Somewhere to his right, Bloodbeard was laughing like a madman, and then the voice was lost in the wind. The prow of the ship, pointed sharply downward, suddenly leveled without warning, momentum carrying them forward. John staggered to the deck again as the freefall ended abruptly and the prow of the ship drove into the wave crest ahead of them. Water burst upon them in thick, white spray, sweeping from the prow toward the aft. The deck tilted precariously upward and John, who was just righting himself, fell backward against the gunwale. The water from the wave struck every part of his body at once and he was slammed against the hard wood of the railing. Stars danced behind his eyes, and he found he was completely submerged under water. For one horrible second John thought he had been swept overboard, but then the wave tore over him and was gone.

Gasping for breath, John spat saltwater from his mouth and staggered to his knees. The deck leveled again as the *Iago* crested the wave's peak, and then began to tilt downward again as they slid uncontrollably into another trough. The crew was hunkered anywhere they could, and many of the men had lashed spare rope around themselves so that, in case they were taken by the sea, they might be recovered. The helmsman was spinning the wheel futility, his eyes wide with terror.

The ship descended and for a brief moment John's stomach tingled and he felt like he were flying. The freefall ended abruptly again as the ship plowed into the next wave. Water crashed over them, throwing several more men free, kicking and bucking to save themselves as they were lost from sight into the sea. The deck creaked and groaned ominously as it tilted upward again, sailing clear to the peak of the next wave.

"We're bein' shaken te pieces!" screamed the helmsman to Bloodbeard, who stood braced against the gunwale, the only one on the ship standing tall in the face of the storm. A wide, gleaming smile was upon his face. At the words of the helmsman, Bloodbeard strode forward and threw him to the side, taking the wheel himself.

"Ye've just got te have the feel for her!" he bellowed, laughing wildly as they ship tilted forward yet again and descended with terrifying rapidity into the next trough. John clung desperately to the aft railings as Bloodbeard gazed out at the seas surrounding them. "What be yer pleasure, good Lady?" he cried to the waves around them, spinning the wheel lubward. "What's yer mood this day?"

They rose out of the trough more gently this time, though they could not avoid being hammered by the wave. As they crested, emerging from the deep watery pit, there was another crack of fiery lightning, flaring off sails not their own. Every eye was drawn as one to the sight that lay perhaps a dozen yards off the port side. It was the *Philadelphia*, angled badly to ride the wave crests and listing to one side. Men scrambled too and fro upon her deck as the ship drifted inexorably closer to the *Iago*, buffeted by the powerful winds. It seemed they had lost maneuverability.

"Their rudder be shot!" cried the helmsman as the lightning flare died around them and the world was plunged back into darkness. "I saw it clear as day! Shattered, it was!"

Bloodbeard nodded grimly, spinning the wheel again. Incredibly, the *Iago* managed to slide to the starboard side as it sank into another wave trough, though the *Philadelphia* seemed to match the move, drawing inexorably closer.

"They're going to ram us!" John shouted, and the helmsman nodded, terror in his eyes.

"They can't help not te!" he said over the wind. "The wind be their governess now!"

Bloodbeard jerked the wheel wildly, and the ship lurched in the water as the *Iago* desperately attempted to get clear of the *Philadelphia*, but John could not take his eyes off the swiftly approaching ship. It was now so close he could almost hear the screams of the men on the other deck. As it was, the *Iago* crested the next wave with the *Philadelphia* now drawn even with them, angled still closer to them.

"Brace!" shouted Bloodbeard as the deck tilted forward and began to sink into the trough. With the *Philadelphia* still oriented towards them, the ships slid into the trough at the same moment as they were drawn together. "Collision!" Bloodbeard bellowed at the top of his lungs as the prow of the other ship rushed down upon them.

The ships collided with an earth-shattering crash. The wail of voices mixed with the screech of buckling wood. Rigging and yardarms collapsed around them as both ships, locked together in a tangle, struck the next wave.

Water blasted over them all, sweeping anything loose on deck together in a great, tangled mass. John was thrown backward, and felt his stomach lurch once more as he was lifted from his feet and hurled backward. Thick, rough ropes tangled about his neck and chest as he was thrown clear of the *Iago*'s aft rail and plummeted toward the dark waters below.

Something jerked, hard, as the ropes snapped taut, and he altered course, thrown bodily into the barred windows of Bloodbeard's cabin. Pain exploded on his face and chest as glass shattered and dug into his flesh, and he felt his limp body tossed away from the windows as darkness embraced him.

Chapter Nine

An Unexpected Challenge

Waves crashed and thundered in the darkness, the sound of running water louder and then softer in his ears. John's entire body was stiff with terror, still feeling the ship rush upward and then plunging down into darkness again, and then water burst over him.

Coughing, John writhed against the cold shock of the water and jerked awake.

The world was suffused with the red-gold light of dawn, and the surface he lay against was softer than the hard planks of the *Iago's* deck. His vision still blurry, he sat up, feeling pain flare to life in his arms and chest. He winced, then winced again as pain also blossomed sharply in his cheek at the motion. Reaching up to his face, he touched the place of pain. The pain flared white-hot and he jerked his fingers away, hissing between his teeth.

Somewhere to his left he heard another wave crash against what he now realized was sand, and cool water rushed over his legs and back. Groaning, he pushed himself to his knees and crawled out of the sea's reach, before slumping back down to the ground in exhaustion. He blinked rapidly, trying to dispel his blurry eyes and accustom them to the morning light.

As the world swam back into focus, he found himself on a beach of white sand that, from his position on the ground, ran for a great distance away from him before disappearing around a bend in the geography of the place. Further up the beachhead at a distance from the ocean was a line of dark green plants. Several palm trees leered over him from the odd angle at which he lay. He remembered suddenly the storm and being thrown overboard, and a fresh feeling of panic washed over him.

Grunting weakly, he sat up again and from there struggled to his feet. Had he been lost at sea, only to wash up on some abandoned island? Would he be stranded forever? He turned to peer out at the ocean, and paused.

Two ships bobbed in the calm waters some distance offshore. He recognized them and frowned at the unexpected appearance of the *Iago* and *Philadelphia*, having believed both ships to have been sunk in the collision. The *Philadelphia* was listing in the water badly, and both ships were damaged where they had collided, but John didn't think it was irreparable. By the looks of things, the *Iago* would escape serious repairs beyond the replacement of some of the upper hull by the prow and a few crossbars, perhaps a bit of rigging. Men were already hard at work, their tiny forms scrabbling about amidst the rigging.

It was only then that John noticed the longboats resting some ways up the beach. There were three of them, and they had been dragged out of the water's reach, laying on their sides. Many pairs of footprints crisscrossed the beach, most of them venturing directly into the jungles, where broken and trampled foliage signaled their passage. Several other footprints moved from the boats toward where John had lain.

Rubbing his eyes against the glare of the sun, John slowly made his way towards the rough path that had been hacked into the underbrush. His legs felt weak and rubbery, and his chest sparked with pain. Grunting, he lifted up his shirt and found a number of gashes across his chest, probably from where he had fallen against the windows of Bloodbeard's cabin. Sighing, he dropped his shirt and stepped from the beach of white sand into the jungle underbrush, overwhelmed by the sudden cool of the deep shade.

The trail led off beneath the trees, straight through bushes and thickets, which had been chopped back to clear room for passage, and wound its way out of sight. He followed this trail for some distance, which crept through a narrow vale that slumped between two rising hills. Exotic birds shrieked and called somewhere out of sight above John's head.

He had only been walking for five minutes or so when the sound of men cursing floated toward him, and he picked up his pace. Clambering over a fallen log, he came around a bend in the path and suddenly found himself confronted by the sight of about two dozen of Bloodbeard's crew. Five or six of these were hacking and chopping at the unyielding underbrush while the others leaned against trees or laughed in small groups.

John's eyes fell on Bloodbeard himself, still wearing his feathered tri-cornered hat over his shaggy hair; Bloody Hands stood next to him, holding out a map and appeared to be in mid-gesture. Bloodbeard shook his head, but Bloody Hands tapped the map insistently.

They were only perhaps twenty yards ahead of him, and John moved quickly to close the gap. As he approached, his boots caught in some vines that lay loose over the path. Several members of the party jumped, and the man nearest to John spun on *the spot* with a scream of terror, drawing a pistol and pointing it at him. John flinched, throwing up his hands. As wide-eyed with fear as the man was, John was afraid he would actually shoot him dead on *the spot*, but at the sight of him the man relaxed.

"John, me boy!' said Bloodbeard with a pleased call. "I see ye survived."

"Barely, the way I feel right now," John said, massaging the injuries across his chest and grimacing. "Why're all of you so nervous?"

"This be a haunted island!" said the man that had nearly shot John, his eyes widening again. "Death lurks in the shadows."

"Or, as an intelligent person would put it," Bloodbeard said, rolling his eyes, "the place be not exactly uninhabited."

"Not—"

"Savages," Bloodbeard said, with a dramatic look. "Bloodthirsty islanders and their dark gods. They make their camps all over these islands."

John looked at him. "There's more than one island?"

"Aye, that there be," Bloodbeard said. "Ten or twelve, scattered all over nearby, all within sailing distance. The furthest isle out be our destination. Isla San Thanatos, lad. These folk be followers of the migration of animals and the schools of fish from island to island. No telling if they be here now, or on one of the other islands."

"They're man-eaters!" blurted the pirate that had nearly shot him. "Sneak up on a man and steal him off, gut him and roast him over an open flame!"

John felt revulsion and horror spread across his body.

"They eat people?"

The man nodded, glancing nervously at the trees around them as he did so, as if expecting a raiding party of warriors to burst out of the treetops at them.

"We be havin' more pressing matters to fret about," Bloodbeard said, turning back to the map.

"How did I survive?" John said, coming to stand next to him. Bloody Hands jerked the map away to prevent him from seeing anything on it.

"Ye got tangled in some rigging that caught on th' aft railing. Threw ye into me cabin windows an' got yerself some nasty wounds, but we soon fetched ye back aboard," Bloodbeard said.

"I thought for sure I was dead—thought for sure we were all dead." John shook his head at the fuzzy memory of the two ships colliding.

"Bah, th' *Philadelphia* gave us naught but a glancing blow, and we'll soon put the *Iago* to rights. The *Philadelphia* herself could be a might more difficult to repair. Her rudder snapped in th' storm and we need new lumber. The rain and waves spoiled the drinkin' water as well, so we're needin' a fresh supply," Bloodbeard explained.

"There's plenty of trees back toward the beach," John said.

"Can't use 'em," Bloodbeard said. "Termites. The wood's useless to us, an if we bring any aboard, they'll eat the decks out from under us. Got to find clean ones."

John nodded, and the company progressed slowly forward at the struggles of the lead team hacking at the jungle growth with machete and cutlass. After several hours had passed and they had made very little progress, John could feel the frustration and growing concern

185

among the men. Every palm tree that seemed to be the size they needed was chopped into and the wood examined.

At long last, as the undergrowth was thinning and they seemed to be approaching the opposite end of the island, a tree was found that would be suitable for their repairs. The men set to work, enthusiastically felling it with their hatchets. Some minutes later it crashed to the ground, causing a storm of insects to take flight from the bushes and shrubs it flattened. Birds squalled in panic out of sight overhead. Bloodbeard directed eight of the men to take the tree back to the beach and set to work. The coconuts from the tree's crown were gathered eagerly by the crew, stuffing them down shirts or into satchels before they hoisted the tree to their shoulders and marched away back the way they had come.

"The rest of ye, come on," Bloodbeard said, motioning the remaining dozen or so men forward. They pressed through the rest of the foliage and emerged a few minutes later on a beach on the island's other side.

The water here, not reflecting the sunlight, shimmered a deep, crystalline blue. Some ways up the beach to their right, the white sand ended as a sheer rock face erupted from the earth and rose away from them. John's eye was drawn up from the cliff face to the slope that began at its top, arching higher and higher, every inch of it covered in trees and brush. It ended in a peak of dark rock high above, leaving the undergrowth behind part way up its face. A rushing stream of water poured out of the rock and flowed out of sight, further inland somewhere.

"There our spring be," Bloodbeard said, indicating the rushing water as it spilled down in white spray down the peak's harsh mountain face.

"How're we supposed te get all th' way up there?" asked the man that had nearly shot John.

Bloodbeard closed his eyes in frustration, and John edged away from the man slightly. "We're not havin' te get up there," he growled. "We jus' need te find th' pool where it collects."

They ventured back into the jungle growth then, heading uphill. They were forced, because the terrain was more rock than sand or dirt, to pick their footing carefully, and the thick undergrowth began to thin as the soil became less rich and able to hold nutrients for the plants. All the same, it took them several more hours to make it to where the incline really began to grow steep and precarious. Instead of leading them straight up the rock's face, Bloodbeard bid them follow him as he made his way across the mountain face, directing them upwards at a slight angle so that they would be heading up and also oriented in the direction the water flowed.

They could hear it rushing and flowing somewhere out of sight ahead of them before they even saw it, and it was the sound they followed for a few hundred more yards, abandoning the attempt to chop their way through the weeds and instead just lunged and threw themselves through the low-hanging branches, vines, and knee-high ground foliage. The sound got louder and louder as they drew near, and finally John burst through the last of the trees and came into a sizable clearing.

Water thundered from above in torrents, tumbling down the rock face from the hidden spring, and fell into the clear pool below. There was a natural stone lip ringing the pool, and rock sloped down into the waters. It appeared that the water level in the pool had once been greater than now, though John could not tell what may be causing the water's retreat.

Men were pulling off their boots and carefully making their way over the lip to fill buckets and canteens, each of them taking small sips to begin—to test the water's freshness—and then great swigs.

"It's sweet, captain," called out Bloody Hands, who was halfway down into the water. Bloodbeard nodded, then held out his hand for a drink. A pirate passed him a bucket of water, and he raised it to his lips and drank deeply, his eyes closed. Water ran in rivulets down his great, dark beard as he gasped in relief. He handed the bucket to John, who also drank. The cool water shocked his mouth, and he eagerly drank his fill.

"Start passin' buckets back to the beach, while we send fer the water barrels," Bloodbeard was saying to Bloody Hands. "Stay yerself and keep watch here."

"What're ye goin' te do?" Bloody Hands asked.

"We're returning to the beach to see how the rudder repairs are coming," Bloodbeard said, turning and striding again into the jungle. "Come along, Master Rackham."

John followed the large hulk of a man back into the undergrowth and back onto the path they had forged. It took much less time to travel the paths than to make them, and within fifteen minutes they had found their route back to the beach, and after another twenty of walking in silence they emerged back out onto the white sand.

Men were busy with knives and hatchets, cutting and trimming the great log into shape. Others lounged while still others were cracking open the coconuts with daggers and drinking the milky liquid within. To John's great surprise, Isabella was pacing along the water's edge, her pant legs rolled up as she strolled in the surf.

"What in the great fiery blaze of Hades is she doing here?" Bloodbeard bellowed, pointing at Isabella. She turned with a jump, fear etched on her face.

"No worries, cap'n," said one of the crewmen holding a coconut. "She 'splained it all te us."

Bloodbeard looked at the man, who quaked under his fierce gaze. "What?" he barked.

"She—she told us all about it," the man said, now less certain. "Said it weren't fair te keep her locked up an' not see th' sun or feel the waves on her feet."

Bloodbeard stared at the man. "So ye just set her free, did ye?"

"She—well, she 'splained it better her own self," the man said. "What with all her pretty words an all. But we ain't settin' her free, cap'n! Iffn she don't stick close, she'll be stranded here on this island."

John thought for one moment that Bloodbeard would simply pull a pistol and shoot the man in the head, as he had so often done before. The man clearly thought the same, because he had gone pale and shook in terror. With a growl, Bloodbeard pulled a pistol from his belt and pressed the barrel against the man's head. The man's trembling intensified, but Isabella's voice rang out from down the beach.

"I'm not running away," she called out, wandering back towards the gathered group of crewmen, splashing in the surf. "There's no place to run."

"I warned ye about keepin' that mouth of yours shut, girl," Bloodbeard growled, the pistol still aimed calmly at the man, who was watching the exchange with beads of sweat running down his forehead.

"Well, what am I supposed to do?" Isabella said,

looking at Bloodbeard coldly. "It was sopping wet in that brig after the storm, and I hadn't been outside in ages. I felt it were rather inhumane of you to keep me there. I merely explained to your men here that I couldn't exactly escape on a deserted island and that it just wasn't fair for them to go and not bring me along."

"It be the brig!" thundered Bloodbeard. "It ain't about fair."

"Still, here I am," Isabella shrugged. "Kill him if you wish, but you'll need every hand you've got, what with your single crew spread between two ships."

Bloodbeard stared at her, as though utterly lost for words. He mouthed for a moment, blinking. Then, with a cry of rage, he struck the man across the face and he toppled to the ground, groaning and clutching his head.

"He weren't worth killin' at any measure," Bloodbeard said. "Death'd only make him smarter, if anythin'." He turned, seized John by the shirt and thrust him forward in Isabella's direction. He nearly stumbled, but caught himself and righted.

"See te your property, Master Rackham," Bloodbeard snapped. "An' keep her quiet."

"Excuse me!" Isabella said, her voice shrill and her eyes blazing. "I think I have had just about enough of this 'property' business! I'm a human being, same as the rest of you!"

"Rackham," Bloodbeard growled in warning. John stepped towards Isabella and took her by the arm, trying to lead her away from the pirates.

"Get off me!" she cried as she shook him off, turning back to Bloodbeard with a glare. "If the only way to get some respect around here is to be a pirate, then I wish to join your crew."

The words flowed past John before he registered their meaning. He gaped at her, as did most of the other pirates gathered on the beach. Isabella stared at them, hands on her hips, glaring at them all.

"Beggin' yer pardon?" Bloodbeard said. "Not quite sure I divined the intent of yer meaning."

"I wish to join up with your crew, if that's what it takes to stop being referred to as 'property'. You obviously don't have a problem with girl pirates, seeing how you had Mary Ann Rackham aboard."

There was a murmur from the crewmen, and Bloodbeard stepped forward, his eyes like chips of stone.

"Don't ye speak to me about Mary Ann Rackham," he said.

"Fine," said Isabella. "She's just an example."

Bloodbeard swept the great feathered hat from his head and mopped his brow, looking thoughtful.

"Very well then," he said. "Ye can join me crew, under one single condition."

"Fine then," Isabella said, impatiently. "What's your condition?"

"A duel," Bloodbeard said, with a wicked smile. "I've got no openings on me crew, so ye must fight one of 'em to the death."

There were growls and nods of approval from the pirates, many of whom laughed or chuckled at the thought of fighting her.

"Gather forward, lads!" Bloodbeard cried, beckoning the men to line up behind him. "Let her take the measure of ye."

Isabella had gone slightly pale in the late afternoon light, but she swallowed and stepped forward to look at them.

"Are you mad?" John cried, trying to stop her.

She looked at him coldly, and he paused, and then fell silent. She paced up and down in front of them once or twice. Bloodbeard laughed.

"The little lady be havin' trouble deciding," he said, to many hoarse laughs from the crew. "Which of ye wishes te cross swords with her?"

"I'll wrestle her," offered one man, with an unpleasant leer.

"Now, now, let us be havin' a bit of propriety and decency while she decided who'll be the man te kill her," laughed Bloodbeard.

"No, I'm not having trouble at all," she said softly, looking at Bloodbeard. "I've already made up my mind." And before any of them could respond to this, she turned and pointed straight at John himself. "I'm going to fight him," she said, her voice soft, but deadly.

A deep, stunned silence fell over the beach as Isabella glared daggers at John. The crewmen stared, dumbfounded, from John to Isabella to Bloodbeard, and then back to John. It was clearly the last thing they had expected her to say.

Their shock was nothing to the sickened jolt that had washed over John. He looked at her across the beach from him and felt anger begin to rise over his fear and surprise. This was a betrayal of all they had been through together, he felt. She never had been very nice to him, looking back.

"Fine," he snarled, drawing his father's cutlass and looking at her with all the defiance he could muster. She glowered at him, then turned to Bloodbeard.

"I'll need a sword," she said, in a matter-of-fact tone.

"Then ye shall use me own," Bloodbeard said, smiling broadly. He drew his blade and presented it to her with a flourish. He glanced in the direction of John's affronted gaze and shrugged. "Me son or no, I do enjoy a good duel," he said, and the men roared with laughter.

Isabella hefted her blade experimentally, testing the weight. John felt a slight sense of relief at her clumsy swings; from what he had seen, her prowess with a blade was not very well honed. Neither was his, but that made them generally even-matched, and John felt he likely had the more skill.

Breathing slightly more easily, John watched as Bloodbeard's men settled themselves on the sand, loudly placing bets. Bloodbeard himself sat on an upright barrel and removed his hat, watching them attentively.

"Ye may commence," he said, waving a hand at Isabella.

She turned and faced John, who felt his entire body tense with fear, his heart thundering in his chest, his palms suddenly trembling and clammy. He saw the way the late afternoon sun gleamed dangerously off of her cutlass, which she was brandishing toward him with an aggressive look.

"Why are you doing this?" he asked, trying to keep the fear from his voice as she stepped closer to him, diminishing the space between them. She answered him, but not in the way John was expecting. She screamed, and lunged at him, swinging her sword wildly. The crowd of pirates crowed and cackled at the move, one which John easily dodged out of the way of.

"You don't even know how to use that thing," he said, shaking his head. She turned with a growl and came at him, and suddenly he found there to be a great change in her, for no longer did she stumble and wave her sword with abandon; she was as a woman transformed, her

193

poise perfect, her sword held in battle stance, her balance no longer off. She closed the gap in two steps and struck for John's side. He flung his sword that direction and deflected the blow, and jarring pain echoed up his elbow and into his shoulder with such intensity he nearly dropped his blade.

With a cry, he stumbled backward as she received his parry, then brought her sword around again, striking for the leg. He whipped his blade down and around from the inside, slapping her move to the side with a hollow clang.

"As you—might—have noticed," she said between ragged, intense gasps, "my father—paid well—for my education!" She initiated a stunning three-part maneuver, which she executed smoothly, striking, then spinning with John's inevitably parry to come around again, her body unfolding out of a spin and driving her blade out in front of her beyond the range John expected. He ducked aside, giving her blade a ringing, glancing blow, before she spun the other direction, returning to John's now vulnerable right side, her sword bearing down toward his shoulder in a great, two-handed chop. John lurched his blade upward and caught the blow, though the strength of it drove him to his knees.

Completing the maneuver, she abruptly reversed course and darted her cutlass back around to John's other side, seeking an advantage. John had not had much formal training in the way of swordplay but he was not completely inexperienced. He slapped her cutlass to the side once more and, tiring of being on the defensive, entered into an offensive move, stabbing forward with his blade. She parried easily enough, but was forced to draw back out of reach as he pursued her, anger flooding like fire through his veins. She slapped his strikes aside as she backpeddled furiously.

She planted her back foot firmly at the surf's edge and, before John could fully stop himself, he had barreled into her. Both of them toppled backward and Isabella managed to punch him in the head as they collapsed into a tangle of arms and legs in the water. With a crash, a wave broke over both of them, catching them off guard and throwing them apart. Cold burst over every inch of John's body and he gasped involuntarily, swallowing a mouthful of the brine in shock. Choking and gagging, he splashed to his feet, his eyes burning from the salt, trying to see where Isabella had gone.

He caught the sound of a yell from behind him and turned, waving his sword blindly out in front of him. He felt it meet steel with a clang, and the strength of the blow tore the slick handle from his grasp. There was another splash and his sword was gone. He spun to retrieve it, but a weight barreled into him and latched onto his back, and a sudden fury of fists began to strike him about the ears. He bellowed in pain as Isabella's weight threw him to his knees.

He thrashed and twisted, trying to throw her off, but her legs were wrapped tight about his waist and her arms like a vice around his chest. Another wave crashed into them and they plunged underwater. John was thrown into the sand face first and only managed to scrunch up his eyes in the split second before he was hammered down by the water's power.

He was buffeted to the side by the water and the two of them rolled several times under the wave, twisting and struggling. The water receded, and John found himself on his back, Isabella straddling him, clutching at him against the water's pull. The moment it had gone, she straightened, drew back her hand and slapped him across the face. Stars blazed behind his eyes.

"Ow!" he said, reaching up and giving her hair a solid pull. She yelped and fell off of him to the wet sand, kicking him in the ribs as she did. He grunted and reached out to hit her, but she rolled away. It was then that he noticed what it was she was doing. The glint of a sword handle lay half submerged in the sand. She scrabbled at it and yanked John's sword from the surf.

He ducked away as she swung at him wildly, her eyes blazing, as he leapt back to avoid the strike. His feet caught in something at his feet and he stumbled. She swung at him again, though more clumsily than before and seemed to lose her own balance. She nearly fell into him, her head pressed against his shoulder.

"Let me win!" she hissed, then righted herself by giving John an almighty shove. He toppled to the ground and saw in a moment what he had tripped over the first time. It was Bloodbeard's own blade, lying in the sand. He snatched it up and rolled to his feet, spraying sand behind him.

Isabella gave him a tiny wink from her left eye, which faced the waters and was masked from Bloodbeard or the rest of the crew, who were alternately cheering and whooping with every blow. He didn't know what she was playing at, but she gave him no quarter to meditate on the question. She rushed him again, her sword flashing out before her. John swatted it aside and they fell into a rhythm of trading blows, Isabella leading John through subtle facial expressions, telling him exactly where she was going to strike next. He shoved aside his doubt, surrendering himself entirely to her lead, and fell into the flow of their duel, now almost becoming a dance. She swept his sword arm to the side and brushed past him as they traded sides. "What are you doing?" he whispered to her as she went by.

She simply smiled defiantly at him as they turned back to face one another and she fell into another combination of moves that brought them near to one another. "Showing you I can take care of myself," she mouthed as she ducked back yet again and feinted to the right with her blade. John followed her feint, but put no power into it and changed the course of his strike at the last moment, whipping his blade toward her exposed side.

She knocked his cutlass away, grabbed him and threw him from her as he whispered, "So it was all a ploy?" She replied to this by charging him before he could catch his balance from her push, and he backtracked quickly as her blade flashed before her, so quickly he could barely follow her.

"It was not just a ploy," she hissed, darting past, John fumbling to keep up. "I'm very angry with you!" She swatted down his cutting slash intended for her stomach and he practically lost the grip on his sword again.

"Why?" he shot back, looking furious, spreading his hands wide as though indicating he were innocent. She crushed her blade into his own, ripping it from his fingers, and sent her free fist into his gut.

The air blasted out of John's lungs as he fell to the ground flat on his back, landing on something hard and sharp in the sand. He moaned in pain as whatever it was jabbed into his back. Isabella knelt over him, pressing her knee into his chest, making John nearly whimper as the thing poked more insistently into him with the added weight. She bent her head close.

"He's our enemy!" she whispered to him, and her eyes

swept across the beach to Bloodbeard, who was standing and applauding as the crewmen shouted with pleasure or groaned as bets were won and lost. "He thinks you're his son, and he still let me fight you to the death. He doesn't even care if you should be killed."

John stared at the hulking pirate standing far off on the beach, laughing, and he shuddered, deflating under Isabella's weight in despair. He did not know what was wrong with him, that he was so drawn to the foul man.

"Ah, but ye disappoint me," Bloodbeard cried, nearing the pair. "I were promised a fight to the death!"

The cold-hearted way in which the words were spoken, almost carelessly, chilled John to the bones and he knew Isabella was right. She straightened up and stood, tossing her sword aside, a look of revulsion on her face as she stared at John. She turned and met Bloodbeard's eyes with the same expression, and shook her head.

"He's not worth it," she said. "Pathetic. It would be a waste of blood."

Bloodbeard and his crew laughed, the sound roaring over the beach like the hot shame that John felt washing over him.

"Welcome to the crew," Bloodbeard said, giving a little bow to Isabella. "Alas that our charter be not here with us, but once we're safely aboard the *Iago*, ye can make yer mark upon it."

She nodded to him, then turned back to John and strode to his discarded sword, which belonged to Bloodbeard. She straightened and dusted it off, giving John a fleeting smile before turning back to the pirate and handing it back.

"Many thanks," he said, his dark eyes glinting as he

gazed at her.

John groaned and rolled off of whatever he had fallen on, rising to his knees and looking down. Something pale was protruding from the sand, though he couldn't tell what it was. Isabella and Bloodbeard turned toward him as they saw him staring down at something in the sand.

"What—" Isabella started to say, but the words died in her throat. John had taken hold of the object and pulled it out of the ground. Half-buried under a fresh deposit of sand delivered by the sea lay buried a great, elongated bone, bleached white, and as they could all see in the light of the setting sun, it had beed gnawed upon. It was a human thigh bone. With a cry of disgust, John dropped it back to the sand and shook his hand in revulsion.

The men behind Bloodbeard had gone deathly silent, and John saw several frantically crossing themselves.

"Islanders," Bloodbeard said softly, stalking forward and bending close to the bone. He kicked around in the sand for a moment, and uncovered what was unmistakably a fire-pit, dark with cinders and charred wood. More bones lay scattered about in the fire's remains. "A few days old."

Straightening up, Bloodbeard sheathed his blade and looked out at the anchored ships in the bay. "Get back to the ships."

He stopped suddenly and looked up at the gathered men, frowning.

"Where are the others with the water?" he growled.

The hidden spring was found an hour later by the light of makeshift torches. The men were nowhere to be found. They did not respond to the shouts of the crew, who tramped through the jungle underbrush in search of them. All that remained were a few of the buckets, and great, dark splashes of blood on the ground.

Not long after, the drums began to sound, echoing over the distant water. To the terrified and jumpy crew it seemed to come from every direction and yet from none all at once. Bloodbeard and several other disappeared into the underbrush and did not return for some time. When finally they did, Bloodbeard looked grim, but they bore the limp form of Bloody Hands. They lay the body down on the beach and Bloodbeard looked at the men, who were anxious for news.

"They took 'em te a nearby island," he said. "We could see the light of their cookin' fires, but it were obvious we be too late."

"What 'appened te him?" one man said, pointing a trembling finger at Bloody Hands. "'E's dead, ain't he?"

"Not dead," Bloodbeard said. "These islanders use poison darts to paralyze their victims. They like ye alive when they start to cook ye. Bloody Hands weren't with the others. Musta been able to run himself an' hide right quick, afore he could be missed. Found him wedged under some boulders a spell from the spring."

He looked around at his crew, all of them trembling and shaking, clutching their weapons and he shook his head, though in disgust or resignation John could not tell.

"Come, let us be away," Bloodbeard said. "Back to the ships. We'll finish on the morrow. I've no interest in being dragged to hell by these islanders and their devil-gods."

Chapter Ten

Isla San Thanatos

Repairs to the ships took the crew the better part of four days. The rudder had to be extensively crafted from scratch by men who were not greatly skilled in such crafting. Those who were especially bad at wood-shaping were set to work running the *Philadelphia*'s bilges, pumping out the water that was slowly seeping in from a hidden hole in the lower hull. Others were set to work re-rigging the *Iago* or repairing its minor damage.

Bloody Hands had revived after a day's worth of paralysis, though John felt this far to lenient of a fate for the bloodthirsty and violent first mate. John seemed to alternate between chores, doing whatever it was no one else felt like doing. So he frequently found himself working the bilges when others refused, scampering up and down the masts to sling rigging and tie them down, or using hammer and nail to repair the damaged port side of the *Iago*.

He found this incredibly frustrating, since he was back to being treated essentially like a cabin boy again. Ever since the duel with Isabella he had found himself, astonishingly, out of favor, as though losing to a girl proved he was unworthy to be treated like the rest of them. There was still some anger and bitterness toward

Isabella for that, who was now a full member of the crew and strutted about the deck like she was important. He tried not to feel shame and anger whenever she strode past, trying to look at things from her perspective, understand that she felt safe aboard the ship at last, that she was protected by the charter from the unwanted advances of the crew.

Looking at things that way did little to help. John felt even less needed now that Isabella had taken to her new-found independence. For the first time since being captured by Bloodbeard's crew, John felt utterly alone. It did nothing to improve his mood that Isabella seemed to go out of her way to teach John pointers about sword-fighting, and would even attack him with a playful look in her eye at moments when things were slow, shouting instructions at him while the rest of the crew laughed. Even worse, it was actually improving his ability with a blade.

These islands were not far separated from one another, and they could spy one in the distance every few hours as they continued. The excitement aboard ship had become palpable as they drew closer and closer to their destination, Isla San Thanatos. The crew seemed hardly able to contain their increased energy, and fights were more common, and more violent.

On the third day the mists fell upon them, rising over the water as far as the eye could see, shrouding the world in ghostly darkness. As the *Iago*'s prow passed into the fog, crewmen lit the lanterns that hung from various places around the deck. From his position on the aft-castle, John could see the small golden lights wink into life across the water, the only sign that the *Philadelphia* was still with them.

202

"Run out a single gun," Bloodbeard ordered, and a gunner crew scrambled below. "Prepare to fire a sounding shot."

Moments later, John could hear the gun being run out, and then the deafening blast of the canon. Half a minute later, another shot boomed out across the water from the place the *Philadelphia* had disappeared, echoing eerily back and forth between them.

Bloodbeard descended to the main deck and leaned down to the hatch that led below. "Ye keep firing every ten minutes!" he shouted. "Got te keep our positions clear."

Damp whiteness had now obscured nearly everything around them, so much so that the rest of the crew on the main deck below him appeared to the John like they were apparitions in the mist, nothing more than dim shadows appearing and disappearing as they passed in and out of visibility range.

"Boatswain, take soundings of our depth," Bloodbeard said as he returned to the aft castle, emerging from the fog like a great, hulking shadow, towering over John. The man nodded, turned, and gathered up a rope knotted at even intervals. This he dropped over the side, allowing the weighted end to fall away out of sight and splash into the water moments later. He fed the line over the side, counting knots as they clattered past him. Nodding, he withdrew the rope and turned to Bloodbeard.

"Depth of over seventy-five."

Bloodbeard nodded, then lifted the compass that had once been Billy Jack Thatcher's, flipped it open, and consulted it. John felt a sudden flash of anger, which surprised him.

"East by south-east," Bloodbeard said to the

helmsman, who spun the wheel in reply. Another canon blast boomed out over the distant water, answered moments later by a retort from the *Philadelphia*, the echoed sound oddly distorted through the mist. John just caught sight of the flare from the canon's muzzle, and saw that the *Philadelphia* had pulled nearly even with the *Iago*.

The boatswain ran out the rope once more, counting the knots. "Forty-two fathoms!" he called out. Bloodbeard, meanwhile, had drawn out his map and had spread it open on the deck, peering at it closely, his fingers trailing over the parchment. John drew closer to Bloodbeard and gazed at the map over his shoulder. The pirate's fingers rested in a dense clump of jagged circles that could only be the islands around them. Many numbers and markings John did not understand were scratched and scribbled in every available space.

"Dead east," Bloodbeard said to the boatswain, who turned the wheel gently to correct their course. As the ship rolled and shifted beneath them, John saw Bloodbeard's finger slide up the map to come to rest against a scribbled line of markings. John saw the unmistakable word scrawled beside the line of scribbles. Reefs. Dpt, 12 fathoms.

"Are we headed for reefs?" John blurted out.

"Not te fret, Master Rackham," Bloodbeard said, without looking up. "Nor-east," he said to the helmsman.

"Twenty-seven fathoms," called out the boatswain, as the *Iago's* canons thundered out once more. The *Philadelphia's* canon reply was somewhere behind them now, and John craned his neck over the far aft gunwale behind them, but saw nothing.

"Better," Bloodbeard murmured.

"What's better?" John said.

"They be followin' us now," the pirate said, his voice soft in the unnatural stillness of the mist. "I can be guidin' them safely through. There be only one safe path through these waters." His finger still rested on the scribbled image of the reefs on the map, and John felt the hairs tingle on the back of his neck, imagining them drawing closer and closer to shipwreck, the *Iago*'s hull sliced to ribbons on the treacherous rocks.

"Quarter-turn to the north," Bloodbeard called out, and the helmsman, listening tensely for instruction, jumped at the booming voice in the oppressive quiet of the fog. As the ship turned, Bloodbeard's finger slid upward, toward what John realized was a small gap in the reef line.

"Fifteen fathoms!" came the boatswain's disembodied voice from the main deck, his figure long since lost in the fog, and Bloodbeard nodded to himself.

The *Iago*'s canon boomed out once more, and the *Philadelphia*'s answer followed not many seconds after, the sound rolling out across the dark water stretched between them. Bloodbeard's finger inched up, closer and closer to the reef line on the map, and John felt nervous pressure gripping his chest like a vice. He realized that he had stopped breathing, and took a gasping breath before his lungs began to burn too badly.

"Twelve fathoms!" called out the boatswain, and there was a definite nervous edge to his voice now. "Captain, we—"

"Steady!" Bloodbeard grunted. "We got room beneath our feet yet."

The *Iago*'s canons boomed out again, answered by the *Philadelphia*, which was still behind them, close enough now for John to be able to see their lanterns through the mist. The sight was strange and haunting, the vision of twelve or fifteen disembodied lights floating above the water as though the ship behind them were nothing more than a phantom ship governed by the damned.

A strangled cry echoed up to them from the boatswain's position, and then a distant splash. Bloodbeard and John looked up at the same moment. The pirate captain stood, slowly, his blood-red waistcoat unfurling around him like a great sail as he moved away from the map to the steps and peered down to the main deck.

"What be the matter?" he cried.

"The measuring line!" called out the boatswain. "Caught on somethin'. Torn from me grasp, it were!"

Even John could see that it was true, for the boatswain was holding his hands up, blood trickling down from where the rope had torn itself from his fingers with great force and speed.

"Caught on the reef, like as not," Bloodbeard called down to him. "Get ye another, and quick like." He turned to the helmsman as the boatswain quickly disappeared belowdecks. "Looks like we be sailing blind for now," he said, his eyes blazing with a terrible excitement.

The helmsman paled in the fog as Bloodbeard returned to his map with a laugh, knelt down again and placed his finger just beyond the reef line. His finger was close to the edge of another small island in the shallows through which they were passing, and he looked up off the starboard side expectantly. There was nothing but fog, drifting lazily past.

The *Iago*'s canon rumbled in the boards of the deck beneath John's feet, and not a moment after, the answering retort from the *Philadelphia* reached them, still from close behind.

"They passed the reef," John said, and Bloodbeard nodded.

"Rocks ho!" came the call from the *Iago*'s crow's nest. "Rocks off the starboard!"

Every head turned to the starboard side as dark, looming shadows materialized from out of the mist. The helmsman made to jerk the wheel away from the rocks, but Bloodbeard shouted, "Steady!" at him, his voice tense. "There be other rocks in these waters. Keep us steady or ye doom us all!"

The rocks off the starboard side drifted closer, nearly as high as the after castle, jagged and sharp, jutting from the sea like the great teeth of some giant sea monster, black against the fog and covered in moss and lichen. The startled cries of nesting birds reached the *Iago* as the creatures took flight from their homes upon the rocks with a loud rush of wings. There must have been many of them, for the cries were numerous, as were the flutter of a myriad of wings, which arced overhead and circled the ship once, before settling back down on the rocks once more as the *Iago* passed.

A rock loomed out suddenly from the mist, appearing very close to the *Iago*'s port side. There were cries of alarm and the helmsman jumped with fear.

"Hard to starboard!" Bloodbeard commanded, and the helmsman spun the wheel frantically, The ship surged beneath John's feet, and he gripped the gunwale in fear, knowing it was too late, that the rocks were too close—

With a loud, rumbling scraping, the ship passed the rock as the unyielding stone raked along the *Iago*'s port side, though the correction had been in time and they managed to avoid a direct collision. The ship lurched wildly and men were shaken to their knees as the deck heaved beneath them, forcing them to clutch at anything bolted down to keep their feet. And then they were past the rocks, the ship angling off of Bloodbeard's carefully mapped path, lurching towards the rocks on the starboard side at the helmsman's overcorrection. There were shouts from the starboard side of the ship as men screamed in alarm as the *Iago*'s prow swung towards a set of particularly jagged rocks.

"Back to port side, and easy does it!" bellowed Bloodbeard in fury at the helmsman, who was now spinning the wheel desperately back the other direction. A canon shot boomed from behind them in warning, but it was too late, and John could see they would strike the rocks to starboard as well.

With a growl of fury, Bloodbeard rose to his feet and sprinted to the wheel, hurling the helmsman aside and sweeping the wheel back and forth, trying to compensate.

"Bring that map to me!" Bloodbeard shouted to John, his eyes wide and smiling in morbid glee. John bent down and picked up the map as the ship rolled beneath him suddenly, responding to Bloodbeard's insistent guidance. John staggered towards Bloodbeard as the rocks to the starboard side loomed at them, drawing inevitably closer.

As he reached Bloodbeard's side, the great pirate gave a deafening laugh and bellowed, "Brace fer impact, lads!" He gave the wheel another futile spin, but they were caught in the current by that time and surged forward and sideways. There was a horrifying moment of silence as everyone aboard the *Iago* realized they could do nothing but watch as they were swept into the rocks.

John's heart seemed to leap into his mouth, and then the world seemed to come undone. The deck pitched wildly, throwing everyone from their feet, and beneath the surf crashing upon the rocks came the much worse sound of buckling wood. Men were tossed into each other or tumbled from their perches. The man in the crow's nest fell screaming and kicking to the deck below and landed with a horrible crunch. The starboard gunwale splintered and shattered like kindling as it met unyielding stone and buckled, throwing great slivers of wood like arrows into the crew. There were screams of pain, and blood blossomed somewhere below on deck, though John couldn't tell who had been injured or where.

The *Iago* lay pinned against the rock for a heart-stopping moment, seemingly stuck, but then it came free and sank back into the water, drifting the other direction, where there were more rocks, appearing out of the water like they were rising from the deep to batter the ship apart. The wheel was spinning freely, Bloodbeard struggling to his feet on the other side of the aft castle. Clutching the map in one hand, John rose to his feet and lunged at the wheel, which was spinning dangerously fast, hardly more than a blur, and grabbed it. Pain erupted in his arm as the wheel jerked his arm straight down. Crying out in pain, John released the wheel before it tore his arm free and fell backward. The weight behind the wheel! He hadn't expected it to be so difficult to turn.

Bloodbeard was to his feet and had seized the wheel, snarling at it as he was bent nearly double in his effort to stop its spin. With a bellow of rage, he regained control, and spun the wheel the other direction, the port side rocks still looming out at them. The *Philadelphia* behind them fired another warning shot as Bloodbeard leaned over the wheel to the men below on the main deck.

"Check for breaches!" he shouted at them. "Get below and work the bilges! I'll not be sinkin' this close to our treasure!" Men disappeared below, practically diving down the hatches that led to the decks below. Struggling in the other direction, buffeted by running bodies, the boatswain reemerged from below, clutching another sounding rope in his hands. There was a great, jagged gash above his eyes, blood pouring out over his left eye, down his cheek and neck into his shirt.

"Found it, captain!" he shouted.

"Don't need it at th' moment!" Bloodbeard roared, fighting the wheel. He looked at John. "The map! Let me see the map!"

John spread the map wide and held it out next to Bloodbeard for him to see. The pirate was gazing at it and nodding. He reached out with one hand, grabbed John's left arm, and pressed his finger to a place on the map. It was a narrow channel within a huge labyrinth of rocks. "We be right here!" Bloodbeard shouted. "Ye keep our location marked with yer finger, understand?" John nodded, terror in his stomach.

The rocks off the port side were close, but Bloodbeard seemed to have regained some measure of control over the ship. They weren't pitching headlong towards the rocks, though they would probably still hit them.

"Brace!" Bloodbeard bellowed as the *Iago* swept closer to the rocks, its prow turning to the side at the last moment. The back half of the ship had not yet turned and continued to slide sideways towards the dark rocks. The prow missed the rocks by several feet, swinging out the other direction, but John clutched the wooden railing overlook the main deck with white knuckles. It would be close, really, really close.

The back end of the *Iago* connected against the rocks right as the aft castle was passing them. The deck shuddered as the hull glanced off the rocks. Shards of stone broke away from the jutting fragment and clunked to the deck around John and Bloodbeard like deadly hail. A fist-sized stone struck Bloodbeard's shoulder, and the hulking pirate roared in pain, barely maintaining a tight grip on the wheel. John ducked and covered his head with his arms, but the worst seemed to be past them, and the *Iago* sailed clear.

"Map!" Bloodbeard shouted, and John held it out for him once again, finding their location with his finger. Bloodbeard seemed to understand all the markings on the map, nodded to himself and spun the wheel to the port side, swinging the ship around between two more rocks, picking his path carefully and from the map. John slid his finger up through the maze of rocks on the map, keeping their place.

The immediate danger, however, seemed to have passed. The *Iago*'s prow was steady in Bloodbeard's hands, and their route clear. John let out a sigh of relief, his legs trembling beneath him. A crewman, sopping wet and panting, emerged from below.

"Damage?" Bloodbeard called.

"Several breaches, captain," the man said, eyes wide. "Three, maybe four. None of 'em big, but we're already takin' on water in the lowest hold. We're workin' te patch the holes and keep the water out."

"Good!" Bloodbeard said, nodding. "Get below and help the crew," he told John.

John's first response was to argue, but Bloodbeard glared at him, and so he set down the map and descended the steps from the aft castle to the main deck and hurried to the hatch. There were shouts from deep below in the hold. He clambered down the ladder as quick as he could, passing the first, then the second hold until he could go no further, blocked by the bodies of several dozen men gathered around the final hatch. There was the sound of spraying water from below, as well as the shout and grunt of panicked and struggling men.

"What are you doing?" John shouted, over the noise of rushing water. They turned toward him, starting in fear and John wondered if they'd thought he were Bloodbeard.

"There's too much water down there," says one man. "Not enough room for all of us."

"Sounds like they need help!" John said. They looked at him. He heaved a sigh and pulled off his shirt. "Get out of my way!"

He brushed past them and hurried down the last ladder into the deep darkness of the final hold. Water was flowing in through several open wounds in the hull, but there were only about ten men down there. It was mass chaos. The water was only about waist-high, but that would soon change. Several of the men were working the bilges frantically, while crates of food floated around them. The four live goats were crying out in fear and paddling in circles while crates of chickens shrieked and bobbed in the rising water.

John looked back up the ladder. "Get down here," he snapped, splashing into the water. "Form a line and start handing some of this stuff up to the next hold!" He snagged hold of a crate of terrified, squalling chickens and heaved it over his head onto the ladder and held it there while someone came halfway down to take it from

212

him. The weight lifted, and John plunged back into the cold water, catching hold of a barrel and pushing it toward the ladder. Holding his arms above his head, he waded further out toward the holes in the hull.

"How is it?" he bellowed to one of the workers, who held planks and a hammer but stood idle.

"Bad!" the man shouted back over the din. "There be not enough room te work down here!"

"Is the pressure too much to repair it?" John shouted back.

"Haven't tried it yet," the man admitted, shaking his head. "The best we can probably do while we're in th' water is a patch. It'll still leak, but might slow th' flow down until we can get te land."

John nodded. "What do you need?"

"We gotta get some of this water out of here!" the man said. "Almost impossible to patch it otherwise. I'd say a foot or two should do it."

John nodded again, looking around. Several of the men from above had ventured down the ladder and were picking up the supplies and passing them up to the men that stood around the hatch watching. John splashed over to them and waved his arms.

"How many bilges do we have?" he shouted. The men looked at each other and shrugged.

"One or two down here," one man said.

"Are there any up on the higher decks?" John yelled.

"A few," the man said.

"Get them." John looked around. "Are there spare bilge pipes down here?"

The man pointed to three others with no bilges. Suddenly someone appeared at John's elbow. He glanced to the side and was startled to see Isabella's figure, sopping wet and nursing a large gash on her forehead, standing at his side.

"What is it?" she shouted, looking at John, and he realized suddenly that they were all staring at him as though he were the captain and they his crew. Shoving the thought aside, he turned back to the men on the ladder.

"Bring me some bilges. We've got to get some of this water out of here so they can patch the holes!" he bellowed. "If we don't, we'll sink!"

Several of the heads at the hatch had already disappeared. Within a few minutes they had returned, and lowered down three bilge pumps, complete with thick round pump and long stem. These the men took and, splashing through the water—which was now at their ribs—began looking for the places to attach them to the pipes.

John splashed over to them, Isabella following him. "Stand aside!" John yelled to the men on his closest side. "I'll guide it down. You lot, keep hold of your end." He didn't stop to think, he simply took hold of the pump, took a deep breath and plunged under the water. Icy brine swallowed him and sent chills down his spine. He forced his eyes open against the sting of the salt water and felt around for the edge of the pipe. His lungs beginning to ache, he felt the place and guided the pump down on top of it. Kicking his legs, he reemerged into the air with a gasp and spat water with a great cough.

"Go!" he shouted to the men, indicating they should start pumping. They lifted the great handle and worked it up and down. It took three men to bring it down once it had been lifted, but John knew they were flushing the water up through the pipes to the ship's deck and sending it back out into the ocean.

They fought the water for hours. John grew steadily more numb in the cold water as he helped, Isabella alongside him, their quarrels seemingly forgotten. They had a noticeable impact on the water level, which began to drop steady against their efforts. The carpenter was able to secure a temporary patch to the holes, and while water still flowed into the ship, it was not nearly as insistent as before. They were able to reduce the pumping crews to the original number after four hours.

Exhausted and expecting to feel waterlogged for the rest of his life, John staggered from the hold back up the ladder to the main deck. His cloths were soaked through, plastered tight against his body. Panting, his every muscle trembling, he practically crawled onto the deck and lay flat against the rough wooden planks, blinking and gasping.

"What news?" he heard Bloodbeard call from the aft castle.

"Breaches mended," John said, his voice rasping, his throat dry. "Got some patches on, but we'll need to get out of the water to repair the damage completely." Bloodbeard nodded.

The mist still hung close about the ship, obscuring the view. The boatswain was at the gunwale once again, measuring fathoms, and the helmsman hovered next to Bloodbeard, his face pale as he helped navigate. The crew that had not been required for the breaches stood at the prow of the ship, occasionally lending their voices to the navigation, calling out when rocks drew near. The lookout's body lay where it had fallen, crumpled under the weight of his own flesh, arms and legs jerked out in unnatural directions, but it was the face that drew John's gaze. It was peaceful, almost serene beneath the layers of grime and stubble, the sightless eyes soft and gentle as John stared into them.

He realized he had never seen a corpse this close before and a shiver went down his spine. Sure, he'd seen people murdered—mostly by Bloodbeard—but he'd never seen a body so obviously untouched by human hands and yet still so very dead.

"It's horrible, isn't it?" came Isabella's voice from behind him. He looked at her as she stood, her head and shoulders out of the hatch, her hands laying across one another on the deck, her head propped on her forearms as she stared at him.

"No," John said, feeling that his head was muddled from exhaustion. He glanced back at the lookout's prone form and tilted his head. "He could be sleeping."

"He's not," she said. He nodded, still staring at the body.

"Yes," he said. "But it's not horrible, not for him. He died at the hands of the sea, not of man. He didn't get his throat cut or shot in the head by the captain, or run through for his gold or his food. Almost like dying in his bed." He looked at her, and she gave him a strange frown. "You know, for a pirate."

"You need to rest," she said.

He shook his head. "They need me."

"No, they don't. You, on the other hand, need to sleep. You'll do nobody any good if you're staggering around like a ghost."

He knew she was right, but he could barely lift a finger. He struggled to get to his feet, but found he could not. She pushed herself out of the hatch and came over to him, and knelt down beside him. He felt her hands on his

216

shoulders as she helped him sit up and come around to a kneeling position. Then she threw his arm over her shoulder and stood. He gave as much as he could, but depended upon her to remain standing. They went down the ladder together, him pressed against the wood, she pressed against his back, her arms around his waist, as they slowly descended.

Reaching the sleeping area, she helped him limp to his hammock and held him steady as he slumped into it and sighed, deeply. Then she was crawling into it with him, her arms sliding around him, her head draping onto his shoulder. His eyes went to hers and she smiled.

"I'm sorry," she told him.

"For what?" he asked, his voice barely a murmur.

"For hating you these last weeks. I know you're conflicted; I can see it in your eyes every time you look at him. But I'm conflicted too, and I've been blaming you for it."

"Why're you conflicted?"

"Because," she said with a sigh, "you're conflicted about him, and that complicates things. I hate him for killing my father, but I don't hate you, and he may well be your father. And I know you want a father, I couldn't bear to kill him if it would cause you pain."

"I don't know what it would cause me," he said, his voice miserable.

"I know," she said. "Like I said. Complicated."

His eyes drifted closed and he could feel the pull of sleep, but he forced them back open again and struggled to look at Isabella. "Why did you fight me? On the beach?"

"I should have thought that were obvious," she said, maddeningly superior, as always. "I wanted to join the

217

crew to get close to Bloodbeard, but I knew he'd want to torture you by making me fight someone else for it. I knew I wouldn't be able to beat anyone else, they're too big for me to take down."

"But you could beat me?" John demanded, anger flaring despite his fatigue. "Thanks, that really boosts my confidence."

"Oh, don't be stupid," she said.

John turned toward her, eyes flashing. "So I'm stupid, am—"

She bent down and kissed him. Again it took him by surprise and by the time it had registered that they were kissing, it was over and she was rising from the hammock. She stood and bent down over him, a smile playing over her face.

"Rest," she said, and kissed him on the forehead.

Over the course of the next three days, the ships struggled their way slowly and cautiously through the mist and rocks, which showed no sign of abating. The canons boomed out at staggered intervals, and as the light faded, Bloodbeard continued to navigate by the golden light of a lantern. He seemed to be singularly unconcerned for sleep, his eyes wide, his mouth twisted upwards in a perpetual grimace as he concentrated upon navigating them safely through the treacherous waters. He was a still form, a silent sentry that loomed over them all as he turned the wheel this way or that.

The makeshift repairs belowdecks held fast, though men were required to be present and work the pumps day and night, which they took in shifts. They were finally able to keep ahead of the water spurting into the hold, though it was exhausting, tedious work. By the time the fourth day dawned in the mist, John and Isabella were in a constant state of weary limbs and blistered hands from the bilges.

At long last, as the eastern sky behind the fog was lightening, the cloud of mist that had been their constant companion began to thin. It happened so slowly that John would not have noticed it for some time had Isabella not taken his hand in excitement and gestured out past the deck to the world beyond the ship.

"Look!" she cried, pointing. It took John a moment to register what she meant, but suddenly the blank whiteness of the fog lifted slightly and the rocks to either side of their path loomed above them. The water lapping at the hull could be seen below them. Their visibility had expanded quickly and John felt a thrill of excitement course through him. It had to mean they were close. He glanced up at Bloodbeard, who was beaming around them in silent satisfaction.

"Not long now, lads!" Bloodbeard cried, and there was a roar of approving cheers from the men, rising up over the ship in tumultuous waves. John felt his face widen in a smile despite himself. Over the course of the morning, the world around them slowly swam back into focus until, as they neared midday, all that was left of the fog were languid tendrils and thin, wispy tufts.

The scene beyond them was a nightmare realm of thick rocks, densely set in a haphazard, chaotic array, stretching out before them as far as they could see, sinking behind thicker mist in the way back, the world clearing ahead of them.

And then it came, the call echoing down from the crow's nest, the voice tight and full of relief as the words formed and sank down to those that stood below. "Land ho!"

There was a clattering from all around the ship as men dropped what they were doing and rushed to the side of the ship, leaping into the rigging, throwing themselves up on the gunwale, hands pressed against their brows against the high sun, eyes straining to catch their first glimpse of Isla San Thanatos.

John and Isabella raced to the railing, jostling for a place next to the crewmen, who stood gaping. John forced himself to the gunwale, dragging Isabella with him, and for a wild moment could see nothing but rocks and golden sunlight reflecting off the sea's crashing back. But then his eyes found the place, *the spot* they all stared at, and it drew him in. The rocks ended a few hundred yards ahead of them, then a stretch of open, pale sea. Beyond all of this it lay before them, waiting for them, spread wide over a great expanse of land, an ominous mountain stretching up, up, beyond the mist, its peak lost in cloud. John could see long stretches of beachhead, but something about it was different, the beaches were dark. He peered closer, and realized the truth. The beaches were all made from black sand, pure black sand running in a dark ring around the entire side of the island visible to them. A chill of dread ran through John at the sight, for it did not look to bode well for any who stepped ashore, but he also felt that land of any kind was as welcome a sight as he had laid eyes on for many weeks.

"Back to work, all of ye!" Bloodbeard bellowed from his station.

It was another two hours before they had successfully navigated through the remaining rocks, often following a zig-zagging pattern to pass safely through them according to Bloodbeard's map. When the *Iago* finally passed the last rocks and burst into open seas once again, another great cheer rose up from the crew. The water here was a light blue and clear for many dozens of feet down. The rocks seemed to ring the island entirely, making the calm, open waters within the ring into a sort of natural bay.

Bloodbeard did not seem interested in circumnavigating the island for the sights. The *Iago* made directly for a specific spot in the water, and the closer the ship drew, the darker and more murky the waters became as the black sand overcame the white below them. They made anchor about eighty yards from shore, where large waves crashed against the black sand.

"Lower the longboats," Bloodbeard called as the anchors splashed into the water. "We're goin' ashore." He handed his map with the instructions through the rocks to the helmsman and said, "Put this in th' cabin desk." Preparations were made. While some men lowered the boats, others distributed weapons to the rest of the crew, swords and pistols and muskets, all of them loading their weapons, checking their powder and shot. A man pressed a pistol into John's hands, and Isabella got both a pistol and a cutlass. She slid them into her belt grimly.

When everything was made ready, rope ladders were flung down to the boats, and the men, nearly bursting with excitement, leaped over the railing and descended. Bloodbeard was the last to leave, pushing John and Isabella before him, his eyes gleaming with a terrible energy. They left a single crew to keep working the bilges. The boats made shore and as they neared the black sand beaches men jumped out into the water and dragged the longboats out of the water, away from the licking of the waves and left them slumped on their sides.

Now that they were closer, John could see that dunes of black sand stretched a great distance to either side, but also further back into the island itself. The dark ground spread out before them for several hundred yards before disappearing into a thick, green jungle, the interior of which was bathed in shadow. The squalling sound of some exotic bird reached them from higher up in the distant trees. Above it, the great mountain loomed over them, its top obscured by clouds that appeared, on closer inspection, to be darker than typical clouds and to be emanating from the stone peak.

"Spread out," Bloodbeard called, "and be lookin' fer our marker. It be here somewhere about."

John watched the crew spread out over the dark sand, searching in clusters of three or four. Some set off toward the trees, while others combed down the length of beaches to either side.

"That's a volcano, isn't it?" John asked, nodding towards the great, shadowed mountain towering over them.

"Aye, lad," said Bloodbeard, and Isabella stiffened next to John. "Long since dormant." he added, at Isabella's look.

A cry echoed up from along the beach to their left. The three of them turned and gazed down at the small figures of about a dozen men, all of them waving and beckoning to Bloodbeard. He turned and strode away down the beach towards them at a quick pace that John and Isabella had difficulty matching. Several minutes later they reached the place, and by the terrified looks on the faces of the crew, it wasn't the marker they found.

"Take a glance, cap'n," muttered one, stepping back to let the looming pirate through, pointing down at the ground. "It's fresh."

Watching Bloodbeard's back, John and Isabella jogged to keep up as the pirate crouched down and peered at something the crewmen had gathered around. Panting, John slowed to a halt and stumbled closer, leaning in and gazing over Bloodbeard's shoulder at what had so captured all of their attention.

It was a bare human footprint.

"We ain't alone on this island," said one man, and the others murmured their agreement.

"It's no civilized man's foot what left that," said another, shaking his head. "T'ain't wearin' no boots."

"Islanders," Bloodbeard growled and stood.

"What—more of those man-eaters?" John asked.

"Like as not," Bloodbeard said, nodding as he gazed out at the jungle in the distance. "Watchin' us right now as we stand, I wouldn't be doubtin'. These tracks be fresh, only a few hours old."

"Why would they come here?" John said, feeling nervous again. He glanced at Isabella, and found that she'd wrapped her arms around herself as though she were cold, her face pale. He looked back at Bloodbeard. "I mean, it's so hard to get to."

"They be here, lad," said Bloodbeard, "because this be where their heathen temple were built." John stared at him in horror. "Aye, lad, this place were once theirs te perform their human sacrifices long before we drove 'em out. When we first came, the place looked te have been abandoned, but upon our return we found 'em all, gathered for some dark ritual or other. They've killed many thousands on this island, and no mistake. But we drove 'em off before."

"And now they're back," John said.

"Welcome to Isla San Thanatos, me boy." Bloodbeard looked around at the men, his eyes wide with malicious glee. "The island of death."

Chapter Eleven

Earth and Air

They found the marker not long after the discovery of the footprint. It turned out to be a long stake driven deeply into the ground at the edge of the jungle. The crew spread out around it as Bloodbeard approached it, drawing out his map from the inner recess of his great, blood-red waistcoat and spreading it before him.

"There it be," he said, nodding at the stake in approval. He turned his attention to the map, but was distracted at that moment by shouts from behind them on the dark beach. He turned to see Bloody Hands and the rest of the original *Iago* crew making their way across the sand towards them. Some distance from the *Iago* lay the *Philadelphia* at anchor in the bay behind them. There were cries of greeting as the two crews reunited. Bloodbeard clapped Bloody Hands on the shoulder and nodded to him, then returned to his map.

"Draw me up a rope the length of ten paces," Bloodbeard said, without looking up. As the men set to work, Bloody Hands leaned closer.

"Where we headed now, cap't?" he asked.

"Due west, to the island's interior," Bloodbeard said. "Twelve thousand paces."

"Ye heard the captain!" Bloody Hands said, turning

back to the men from the *Philadelphia*. "Let's make ready fer a hike! Wood, flint and tinder, an' get us some rations."

"We'll be the night ashore," Bloodbeard said, finally looking up. "I'm not expectin' to get more'n just the first two afore it be too dark to continue."

"An' get some tents!" Bloody Hands shouted after the men, who had headed back to the longboats.

In minutes the supplies had been gathered and the rope prepared. "Make ready yer weapons, lads," Bloodbeard said. "Never know what we're goin' to find in this jungle."

They set off into the underbrush, and as the trees passed over John's head, he had the sudden feeling of being watched. The light of the sun immediately dimmed under the deep shade of the trees, and he glanced around nervously, knowing that it was unlikely he would be able to see anyone watching them from any kind of distance.

The going was slow as they hacked and chopped their way further inland from the beach. Monkeys chattered aggressively overhead, though John never caught sight of anything more than rustling branches and palm fronds as they scurried from tree to tree. Birds called to one another, and the air was alive with the constant hum of insects.

Two men held Bloodbeard's rope and walked ahead of the rest of the party. One would stand still while the other went ahead, stretching out the rope until it was taut, when he would halt. Then the other would walk past him and stretch it taut again. Bloodbeard followed immediately behind, counting softly by tens. John glanced at Isabella, who had already started to sweat, her forehead glistening as Bloodbeard murmured a few paces ahead of them.

Evening had already begun to fall by the time they reached their twelve thousand paces. The men were tired and John's feet hurt by the time the two men with the rope stopped cold. They had emerged into what looked like a small clearing in the midst of the jungle.

"This be *the spot*," Bloodbeard said. "Find the second marker."

Within moments another shaft of wood was located, driven into the ground next to the trunk of a tree. Etched upon it were several numbers and letters which only Bloodbeard seemed able to decipher. He fumbled in his pocket and withdrew Billy Jack's compass. He flipped it open and looked at it.

"Twelve paces north west from the marker," Bloodbeard said, standing in front of the marker, lining his heel up against the wood. He strode forward across the clearing, counting. When he reached twelve, he halted and pointed down at his feet.

"Here," he said. "Dig here."

Several of the men leaped forward with shovels and began to dig up the earth as Bloodbeard and the rest of them waited. They dug for a half an hour, shaping a great hole in the rich, volcanic soil, until finally, with a hollow thud, a spade struck wood. The rest of the crew shuffled forward to the edge of the pit in anticipation. The men in the hole dropped their shovels in excitement and fell to their hands and knees, clawing the earth away from the sides of what looked to be a chest. There were excited murmurs as the men hauled the chest to the top of the pit and Bloodbeard stalked forward. There was no lock on the chest, so Bloodbeard simply lifted the lid and reached inside. The crew pressed forward around him, craning their necks to catch a glimpse of the treasure.

Instead, they found that the chest's interior was bare, save for a single parchment and a small glittering jewel. These Bloodbeard scooped up, then kicked the lid shut.

"That's not the treasure?" John found himself saying in surprise. Bloodbeard gave a barking laugh.

"Our haul be bigger than that, lad. I was makin' sure no one but meself could ever find it again," the huge pirate said with a smile. He held up the parchment. "Second map."

"And that leads to the treasure?"

"No, it leads to the third map," said Bloodbeard simply. "Earth and air, lad, earth and air." He held up the jewel, which John could now plainly see was an emerald, and with a casual flick of his thumb, tossed it into the group of crewmen. After a brief struggle, one man, grinning, emerged the possessor of the emerald and jammed it into his trouser pocket for safekeeping. There were groans of disappointment from the others.

Bloodbeard looked at the men holding the rope. "North east, nine thousand paces."

Even though they were all exhausted and ready to drop at any moment, the finding of the first map and the emerald seemed to have given Bloodbeard's crew a jolt of renewed strength, for no one complained over the next hour as they worked their way to the next location. North east took them directly towards the mountain which John knew rose up over their heads beyond the tree canopies. At seven thousand paces Bloodbeard called a brief rest. The crew sank to the ground, sitting on the leaves or leaning against trees with grateful sighs. John winced as he rubbed the soles of his feet. Isabella came over to join him, sitting next to him on the ground. She slipped her arm through his and leaned close.

"How are you?" John asked.

"Ready to sleep," she said, unsuccessfully repressing a yawn. "And I've been thinking."

"What about?"

She leaned in closer, dropping her voice. "Well, what happens when we find the treasure?"

"I dunno," John admitted, though he hadn't really given it much thought in the last month or so. "What do you mean?"

"He's not exactly the sort of man who leaves people alive who know about his secret treasure spots, is he?" she said, her voice dropping to a whisper now. "I suppose he trusts the crew, but I know he doesn't trust me and, well, I don't really think he trusts you."

"He thinks he's my father," John said. "That comes with trust, wouldn't it?"

"Perhaps," Isabella said. "But no one can really know whether you're his son or Billy Jack Thatcher's."

John sighed. "Your point?"

"John, my point is that Bloodbeard can't be certain. And if he can't be certain you are his son, then you might be the son of Billy Jack Thatcher. Which would, of course, mean that he might be interested in getting one final revenge on his old first mate."

"No, he wouldn't—"

"Think about it, John! He doesn't care about you. You saw that on the beach when he was perfectly willing to risk you actually getting killed for a bit of sport! This treasure was the last thing Billy Jack Thatcher wanted from Bloodbeard. Don't you think it would be a poetic sort of revenge to murder the boy you suspect to be his son right over the treasure he failed to steal back?"

Ice swept over John at those words. He looked at her, his eyes wide. Then he found himself shaking his head. It couldn't be true.

"No man is that heartless," John said, less firmly than he had intended, his eyes flicking to where the large man stood with Bloody Hands, their heads together, their eyes locked on the map. Bloodbeard's voice appeared in his head, words running back to him from beneath the cellar in Tortuga: If the day comes when I'm to kill ye, it'll be on Isla San Thanatos or after. For now, ye be safe, Master Rackham.

He looked at Isabella. "Say you're right. What are we supposed to do about it? We're already here."

"We have to either keep Bloodbeard from getting to the treasure," she said. "Or you need to run away. Hide in the jungle."

"Run away? Are you mad?"

"It's not a good solution, I know," she said, biting her lip. "But if you were out of sight, he can't kill you. At least that way, you would be safe until we could figure out a way to get you back aboard the ship."

John did not like either option, and had just opened his mouth to say so when he heard Bloody Hands calling out. "All right, back on yer feet! Time's up!"

The light was already fading into twilight, the darkness even more acute beneath the thick jungle canopy. Several crewmen were distributing torches, which shone with bright golden light in the dark, casting strange shadows on the ground and trees around them. Grumbling, the men rose and gathered their things. John winced as he put pressure on his sore feet again, and limped off with Isabella toward Bloodbeard.

They pressed further into the jungle for another

twenty minutes until they reached another wide, open place. The dark ground was flat and there was no sign of a marker. Bloodbeard halted at the edge of the clearing and raise his torch, casting the light further up in the air. In the middle of the clearing, well out of reach, hung a small chest by one end. There was a complex series of ropes woven through the trees in a sort of netting that reminded John of a ship's rigging, only it was stretched sideways across the clearing rather than upright, slung between the trees that made up the jungle's edge.

"There it is, cap'n!" cried one man, who rushed forward into the clearing, his head up and arms outstretched towards the chest. Something happened as the man reached the clearing. He seemed to lose his footing in the dark, stumbled forward and pitched headlong into the ground. But instead of the sound of two solid forms colliding, there was a strange sucking sound and the man screamed, kicking and flailing. The torchlight was brought cautiously closer to the edge of the clearing and they saw that the man had actually sunk into the ground up to his chest as he struggled.

"Quicksand!" shouted Bloody Hands, and all the men shuffled backward nervously.

"That's right, me lads," Bloodbeard said, with a wicked smile. "Quicksand. These spots come bearin' traps fer the unwary. We're not to be wantin' some stranger to get ahold of our gold, now would we?"

"Help!" the man was shouting as he struggled, though the more he moved the further he seemed to be drawn down. Bloodbeard drew a pistol and with a single, smooth motion, pointed it at the man and shot him dead. The gun's retort boomed out across the clearing and echoed itself back several times as the man slumped limply in the quicksand.

"Now," Bloodbeard said, the pistol in his fist still smoldering as he turned to regard the crew, "all that netting up there be rigged to collapse unless ye be leanin' on the proper ropes. Only some of 'em be secured to hold the weight of a man. When ye scale the trees, ye must undo the precise knots I tell ye. As the knots be undone, the chest will swing away from the quicksand and be lowered to where we can reach it."

None of the men looked remotely interested in going up the trees, but Bloody Hand quickly ordered seven men to pace around the outside of the clearing and climb the seven trees which Bloodbeard specified. They did this with much reluctance, but in the end they struggled their way up the palm trunks. The netting was wrapped around the trees nearly thirty feet into the air. At last, after about ten minutes of slow climbing, they reached the netting and eased themselves out over the clearing. Bloodbeard was shouting instructions to them, telling them to count knots. The first man picked at a knot for a moment, and then, without warning, the chest and its rope dropped several feet, swinging below the next man, dangling wildly. So it went for the first six men. They undid their ropes, and the chest swung lower and lower with every knot. John realized that the chest had been tied to a rope that had been wound in a spiral pattern around the clearing, so that it began high up and in the center, and with each progressive knot, swung down and further out toward the edge of the clearing.

The seventh man panicked. He was clinging to his netting with trembling arms and legs, clutching himself to the secure rope and refused to move, even when shouted at. He was muttering words no one could hear and shaking his head. Then he slowly began to unfurl himself from his netting, trying to move backward toward the trunk of the palm tree again, shaking wildly.

"Don't ye do it!" bellowed Bloodbeard, rage edging his voice. The man's feet were touching the trunk of the tree, and he began to turn himself. Without warning, he lost his balance, tipping forward. He caught hold of another rope, which snapped away from the tree, and with a piteous scream, pitched head-first into the pit of quicksand, disappearing up to his knees in the sand, only his feet visible. They jerked and kicked for a while, but finally fell still, slowly disappearing into the ground.

"We need another," Bloodbeard growled. The chest was tantalizingly close, just a dozen yards away and just too high to reach, even with a shovel. Looking at the chest, John realized something. He stepped forward and looked at the tall pirate, saw the hatred and rage in his eyes.

"I'll do it," he said.

Bloodbeard and the men nearest him turned as one and looked at John, surprise etched on their faces.

"Well, well," Bloodbeard said, looking at John curiously. "Why be ye so interested in doin' a man's job, lad?"

"I'm lighter than a man. Less of a risk," John said, with a shrug. "Besides, I'd like to see if I can."

Finally Bloodbeard nodded. "Do only as I tell ye," he cautioned John.

"No!" Isabella gripped his arm and looked at him, eyes wide. "You can't do this!"

"Trust me," John said, with an easy smile that he almost believed himself. He turned and picked his way around the edge of the clearing, pointedly avoiding the sight of the unfortunate man's boots in the quicksand, which still jutted unpleasantly from the liquid soil. He found the tree easily enough, which stood directly opposite to the rest of the crew. He took a small length of rope, threw one side of it around the tree and caught it with his other hand. Taking a deep breath, he rolled the ends of the rope around his wrists, then braced his weight against the rope, and began to climb.

It was slow going, and nearly another fifteen minutes passed as he struggled his way to the top of the tree. His hands burned like fire where the ropes wrapped around them, and his knees hurt from bracing against the tree, every muscle in his back taut and cramped. Shouts of encouragement echoed across the wide clearing towards him. Finally, sweat beading on his skin and trickling down his back and stomach uncomfortably, he reached the netting and hauled himself over onto it, breathing a great sigh as he could relax his back slightly.

"That's it, me lad!" Bloodbeard shouted up at him. "Now find the seventh knot and untie the next one."

Nodding more to himself than anyone else, John stretched out onto all fours, gripping the netting with his hands, and began to crawl. It was tricky finding the right balance on the ropes, but after a few moments he felt more confident. He crept outward, trying to ignore the great distance to the quicksand below him through the darkness, counting knots. Three, four . . . five . . . . Finally he reached the seventh knot on the rope. He spotted the eighth knot about two feet out from the seventh, and he noticed that it was tied to the main netting that supported him.

"There ye are!" Bloodbeard shouted to him, reaching up in anticipation of catching the chest. "That's the one.

234

Free it an' it'll be in me hands!"

John paused, and looked again. The rope connected to the chest below him was attached to his main netting. If he undid the rope, it would swing towards Bloodbeard and the rest of them. If his main netting snapped beneath him it would swing in the opposite direction, back underneath John. He fiddled with the eighth knot a bit, but the long years of hanging had bound it together very tightly. His fingers weren't strong enough to undo it. He drew his pistol, and then looked down at the gathered group of pirates on the clearing's far side. His eyes found Isabella's, and he gave her a slight wink. He hoped she would understand.

It seemed Bloodbeard understood too. The hulking pirate surged forward a few steps into the clearing with a roar. "No!" he bellowed, as John lowered the pistol to the netting suspending him in the air, and fired. The gunshot burst over John's ears with a crack of thunder, the muzzle flare blinding him momentarily. With a great lurching snap, the netting gave way beneath him. He clutched at it desperately, catching sight of the chest sailing back underneath him, away from Bloodbeard. With a sickening lurch in his stomach he was falling, plummeting head-first through the air towards the quicksand below.

Just as he was about to plunge to the ground, the netting snapped taut and John changed direction with a jolt that nearly tore him free of the netting. He was thrown bodily heels over head, flipping right side up as his arm tangled in the netting. Pain sparked in his shoulder, and he was sure he had dislocated his arm as he swung away from the astonished pirates across the pit of quicksand, his heels skimming the soft surface.

As the netting slung him back toward solid ground on

his side of the clearing, he forced himself to release the ropes, and felt himself hurtling through the air, twisting and kicking. He crashed into the underbrush and rolled to a stop. Gasping in pain at his nearly useless left arm, which he was certain was dislocated now, he climbed to his feet and staggered to where the chest lay. It had burst open on impact, but the pale section of parchment gleamed almost gray against the dark.

"After him!" Bloodbeard was snarling from the other side of the clearing. John scooped up the parchment, stood, and ran further into the trees. There were thundering cracks from behind him as the pirates opened up their muskets into the woods. He could feel the passing of their shot as it cut through the leaves around him. Terror in his chest, he plunged further on into the darkness, vines and branches slapping and scratching him across the face.

Shouts reached him from the dark jungle behind, and he realized that he hadn't thought anything about where exactly it was he was going to go once he'd betrayed Bloodbeard and run off with the second map. Curses, closer than expected, caught his ears over the sound of his thin form crashing through the underbrush. He tripped and went down on his face, tasting blood from a split lip. He forced himself up and ran on, throwing himself around trees and over fallen logs in desperation.

He didn't stop as another volley of musket fire tore through the jungle, this time not nearly as close as before, the sound of voices more faint. He hoped he was getting ahead of them as his legs began to ache, his breath coming in ragged gasps. He was utterly away from the light of the torches and could see nothing, running steadily for ten minutes, tripping repeatedly on exposed roots, or crashing headlong into the occasional tree he couldn't see in the dark.

Finally, unable to run any longer, he slowed and fell against a tree, his chest heaving, his heart thundering in his ears as he tried to force his breathing to slow so he could listen for sounds of pursuit. Nothing obvious seemed forthcoming, and he took the moment to regroup his thoughts. He had no idea what he was going to do now, or where he was going to go. He supposed he should find a place to hide, perhaps higher on the mountain somewhere. Maybe he could hide the map and exchange it to Bloodbeard for safe passage home.

Something stung him on the back of the shoulder, hard. He yelped in the dark and swatted at his shoulder as pain blossomed through his shoulder and down his arm. Something thin was sticking in his skin, right through his shirt. He pulled the thin stinger from his back and reached down to touch it. It was long, nearly five inches, and narrow. It felt almost like wood, and tipped at the end—his fingers faltered suddenly and dropped the long stinger, terror flooding him. It had feathers on the end. It was a dart. A strange numbness was spreading to John's fingers and feet, and they wouldn't move properly.

Islanders.

For the second time that day, he felt eyes upon him, and nearly gasped in fear. Pushing himself away from the tree, he lurched into the woods, his legs wobbly, his balance unsteady. Gritting his teeth, he forced himself onward in the dark, limping severely as he gradually lost the use of his legs. He stumbled into a tree, but righted himself just at the point of losing his balance and careened recklessly on.

His right leg gave out and he toppled to the ground.

He couldn't even get his arms to brace his fall and simply crashed to the dirt and lay still, gasping. He could hear the sound of soft, padding footsteps from behind him, and started breathing faster as he panicked. He tried to concentrate on his right arm, tried to will it to move, but the message did not seem to reach his arm. Not even a twitch. This couldn't be happening.

A foot set down right in front of his nose and his heart thundered in fear. There was some sort of bracelet wrapped around the ankle. A voice spoke over his head in a strange language John did not understand, and another answered. Then rough hands seized him by the wrists and feet, and he was lifted bodily from the ground. His head lolled back, cricking his neck with pain, but there was nothing he could do. He could see the dark silhouette of a man in front of him, but could make out no more than that as they set out, carrying him between them.

Hours had passed and the men had not stopped to rest. John dozed fitfully, unable to do anything more, hoping that just once he would awaken to find himself back in Massachusetts and the whole adventure a bad nightmare. It never was.

At long last, the men slowed as the trees thinned out around them. There were shouts in the same unfamiliar language and the man holding John's arms called out a reply. They emerged out of the trees onto what John could see was another black-sand beach. The men turned and carried him for some distance towards what John could only guess was an encampment of theirs. There was the reddish-gold glow of a great fire from ahead, just out of sight from the angle at which John's head hung.

Then the drums began, very close by, less than a dozen yards. Ecstatic, undulating cries went up from what sounded to John like a gathered crowd. The firelight was brighter now, and he could feel the heat of it on his back. The men slowed and brought him very close to the fire, and dropped him to the sand.

It took John a moment for his eyes to adjust to the brightness, but he could tell he had been deposited in the center of a ring of people, among them men, women and children. Most of them were dancing or jumping in place. Both the men and the women wore only loincloths, the only difference being that the men had elongated bones shunted through the base of their nose and had painted some sort of pale paste all over their bodies in the outline of their skeletons. The women were bare breasted, their only decoration great necklaces made from shards of bleached bones. Even at this distance from them, John could tell they were human bones.

John's captors, the men who had carried him all this way, lifted their arms and cried out with great bellows of triumph, and the gathered crowd cheered and laughed as they danced. John knew for a certainty then that they were going to cook him alive and devour him.

The mood around the fire shifted suddenly, and a great, slow chant was taken up by the ring of people surrounding him. The faces of all the people had lit up, as if in excitement, and he tried to will his eyes to move, to locate the source of the change. But he need only to have waited a few moments more, for another man, this one very old, had entered the ring. He was covered head to toe in black paint and feathers, bands wrapped around his arms and legs, necklaces of human bones rattling and jangling from his chest, and on his head rested an ornate headdress. He bore a staff, at the top of which also dangled several toe bones that rattled and shook with his every movement. He gazed down at John, then lifted his hands to the dark skies above and screamed something in that strange tongue. The whole circle joined the shout, lifting their arms and waving them overhead.

The man then knelt next to John's prone form and lifted a small wooden bowl into view. The man dipped his fingers into the bowl and, muttering strange things, began to mark John's face and arms with the same black paint. He wanted to scream, to shout for help, to kick the man in the face and flee, but he could not move.

Holding up a stone knife, the man stood again and began to chant and undulate in front of the fire, which brought more excited shouts from the crowd. The men that had captured him grabbed him by his arms and legs once again, hoisting him into the air and shuffling toward the flames. They were so hot they had already begin to burn on John's exposed skin by the time he was still a yard away.

They were going to throw him on the fire. It was really going to happen. John's heart was thundering in his chest again, his breathing increasing in expectation of the pain to come. The drums and the dance seemed to be building, to be climaxing, and he knew, without needing to be told, knew when the drums went silent, when the dance ended, they would hurl him into the flames and he would die.

The chant built and built, the people around him jerking and convulsing wildly, and then the drums fell silent. John screwed his eyes closed and braced himself as he could for his own end. And into that moment of lingering silence, chaos erupted.

Gunfire cracked into the sudden silence all along the beach, and people were screaming. A body toppled forward into one of his captors, and they stumbled away, dropping John's feet. The other man dropped his arms and John's body slumped to the ground. The man that held him jerked wildly as a bullet caught him in the chest. Dark silhouettes were fleeing and scattering in every direction as more gunfire thundered around John. Then there were yells and commands in English and John felt relief spread through him. Even though it was Bloodbeard that had found him, he couldn't imagine a death worse than being burnt alive. He would take what he could get. Perhaps he'd even get a quick death.

The heathen were gone, and suddenly other forms had surrounded him. He could see boots made of dark leather and people standing against the firelight, nothing more than dark shadows. One man knelt down at his side and looked at him.

"Are you all right, lad?" the man asked, and John found himself startled to be staring into the eyes of, not a pirate, but a redcoat, a British soldier. Confusion blossomed in John's mind, and he was sure he was hallucinating. He blinked—or wanted to—but could say nothing. The man looked up to someone else who was approaching. "He's alive!"

"Thank the heavens," said a voice that John immediately recognized. But it couldn't be right. "Wait— John? John! Bring him, sit him up in the name of all that is holy!"

The redcoats took John and lifted him carefully, sitting him up and supporting his head so he could see the one who spoke to him. His head swung up, supported by strong hands, and he could see a man he recognized, though he was much the worse for wear. Bearing a false, wooden leg and many scars along the right side of the face, he stood leaning upon a crutch, and John found himself gazing up into the marred, but unforgettable face of the Parson.

Wordlessly, the Parson beckoned to someone who was outside of John's field of vision. There was the sound of running feet as someone approached, stepping around the great fire, cutlass bared.

"We sent them runnin', by all of heaven's thundering trumpets! Is he alive?"

The voice fell silent as the dark silhouette standing against the flames of the great fire paused, recognizing John. The figure stepped closer, as though out of a dream or out of death itself, and John's eyes would have widened if he could have moved them. His entire world seemed to melt out from under him as the face burned into his dreams emerged from shadow, one eye now covered by a black patch.

It was Billy Jack Thatcher.

Chapter Twelve

Fire and Water

Billy Jack Thatcher was alive. John's brain seemed unable to process what was happening, and he felt strongly that he had passed the boundary between sanity and madness and lay many fathoms beyond both of them. He couldn't move or speak, but if he could he knew he would be yelling, though whether in anger or relief he did not know.

Billy Jack's single remaining eye was wide, an expression of astonishment etched on his scarred face. Then he dropped his sword wordlessly to the black sand and fell upon John in a great hug, a cry of relief ripped from his throat.

"You're alive," he kept repeating over and over, along with "Thank God Almighty" and "My boy!" John felt helpless rage and relief spreading through him and knew that if he'd been able to move he would be weeping. Billy Jack was weeping, tears streaming down his cheek below his good eye as he stroked John's face. He looked up at the Parson. "He's not—I mean, we're not too late to save him?"

"No, no," the Parson shook his head. "Just the paralysis venom. He can hear and see you, but is unable to reply."

Billy Jack looked back down at John and paused. John himself was startled by the sensation of tears welling up in his eyes, of water running gently down his own cheeks. Billy Jack gasped again and smiled.

"You can hear me, son," he murmured, then turned back to the Parson. "Can we not do something about the poison?"

"Possibly," mused the Parson. "Where is the ship's surgeon? Let's see if his apothecary can cook up an antidote."

"Help me move him," Billy Jack said. "Let's get him back to camp."

Several redcoats shuffled forward and hoisted John up between them, as the heathen had done, though they were kinder on John's head and neck. The Parson stood, pulling what looked to be a long, black cloak more tightly around him, and began to limp forward down the beach in the direction from which they had come. Then, grunting and heaving, they set off down the beach, cutting through the jungle some distance on and trekking their way through the deep foliage for close to a half-hour. The terrain began to slope upwards soon after, the soft, dark soil gradually replaced with rock and crumbling shale, the undergrowth becoming thinner and more sparse.

Up a winding path they hiked, John stretched between them, wishing he could move. Another half an hour's steady travel upward, and they seemed to emerge out from the trees and stood in a cold place on a narrow path. The wind gusted powerfully down from what John saw was the mountain. On the other side of the path, the ground dropped away precipitously, sloping down and away toward the island. He knew, suddenly, that they

244

were upon the mountain side.

After a brief rest, they continued on another five minutes or so before reaching the narrow mouth of a cave. The redcoats entered, following Billy Jack and the now one-legged Parson, keeping pace with Billy Jack despite his limp and the crutch.

The cave mouth was actually a large tunnel of sorts, which wound its way, back and forth, deeper into the mountainside. They followed the tunnel for several turns before meeting even more redcoats, who looked to be sentries carrying torches.

"Halt!" they shouted, raising their muskets in the confined space.

"It be us," Billy Jack said, his voice soft. The men relaxed and nodded to him, stepping aside.

"Is the surgeon up?" the Parson asked them.

"I think he may have retired, Captain Davids," said the first sentry.

"Rouse him," the Parson said.

John did not remember falling asleep, but when he awoke he was in an unfamiliar place, a cave flickering with the golden light of many torches. Groaning, he raised an arm and rubbed his face. The sudden movement caused a wave of dangerous nausea to wash over him and he slumped back onto what appeared to be a canvas cot.

Several white tents had been erected inside the cave, and several cooking fires crackled on the ground, heating pots of food tended by redcoats who had pulled off their red uniforms. Gear and weapons lay scattered about the place, and the camp had the air of having been lived in for some time.

Someone sat beside John, slumped over in sleep, his back pressed up against the cave wall, his head resting against the rock, his one good eye closed, his other eye covered with a black patch. It was Billy Jack, out cold. John stared at him for a long while, lost in thought. He was a broiling pit of confusion, once more unsure of what to think. Relief, certainly, for the rescue and that Billy Jack was alive, but suddenly unsure of what he wanted. In the back of his mind, he hoped Isabella was all right.

With a snort, Billy Jack started awake and sat up in alarm, his good eye wide with fear. Then he relaxed as he registered where he was and slumped back against the cave wall. His eye met John's, and he smiled.

"You're awake," Billy Jack muttered.

"Only just," John said.

"Mr. Thomson, our ship's surgeon, brewed ye up an antidote to the venom," Billy Jack said. "It's a tricky little bugger, that poison. Comes from a toad, ye know."

John nodded. "I still feel sick."

"You'll have that fer a spell, I'd wager," Billy Jack said, sitting up slightly and looking at him.

"Where are the others?" John said, glancing around. "Where's the Parson?"

"Out," Billy Jack said. "They let me stay behind today."

John looked at him. "I thought you were dead."

"Aye, well, I thought the same of yourself," Billy Jack said. "We searched the wreckage of the *Jerusalem* fer a day before picking up th' *Iago*'s trail."

"Who is we?" John said, feeling anger rising in him. "I saw the *Jerusalem* explode."

"It did," Billy Jack said. "That much be true. One of the *Iago*'s canons hit the powder magazine. I caught a shot in

me shoulder, went down on deck. Dunno if ye saw it."
John nodded. "Ended up savin' my life. Fell behind one of
th' canons. It shielded me from most of the blast. Me eye
caught the worst of it, but the force of it threw me
overboard. Knocked me out. When I came to, I were a
long ways away, floating on a bit of deck and it were
nearly morning. Way I figure it, I got caught in the
current, but it sent me back the way we came, towards
Port Royal.

"Funny thing, but Governor Vaughn sent that redcoat
frigate after us. They came across me just about sunrise.
We nosed about a bit, and started finding other men lost
in the explosion. Some alive, some dead, but the Parson
was the worst of it. Lost half his face te his own deck, and
bleeding from his missing leg. We patched him up as best
we were being able, tried to catch up te the *Iago*." He
shook his head. "By the time we got back to the
Jerusalem's restin' place, it were gone and you were
nowhere to be found. We thought . . . you know, that
Bloodbeard had. . . ."

He made a motion across his throat. John nodded in
understanding.

"But I hoped, ye know. Hoped you'd made yer way to
the shipping lanes and been picked up by some
merchantman or other, that you lived still." He sat back
and laughed, shaking his head. "Never in all me years
would I have been expectin' you to turn up here, on Isla
San Thanatos. I'm assuming Bloodbeard found ye, then?"

John nodded again, and then recounted the story of his
adventures since their ways had parted, though he left
out everything having to do with Bloodbeard claiming to
be his father. Billy Jack laughed as John told him how his
presence had irked Bloodbeard to no end and how it was

a marvel the large pirate hadn't just slit his throat, of Isabella's arrival. John could also tell that Billy Jack laughed out of relief that John's time aboard the *Iago* was not of a more unpleasant nature.

"So what of you?" John said. "Are you a prisoner to these redcoats?"

"Nah," said Billy Jack with a dismissive wave. "They treat us right enough, even follow the Parson's orders."

"And how long have you been here?" John said, looking around at the tents in the camp. "Seems like you've been here longer than we have."

"Oh, about a week," Billy Jack said.

"How did you pass us? We never saw you. And how could you find this island anyway? Didn't you tell me you needed Bloodbeard to lead you to it?"

"I hold a map to the island," Billy Jack said. "That's what ye saw myself and the Parson gazin' at that one day in the *Jerusalem*. I had a map of the island, but we wanted Bloodbeard here too, if you see that. We must have passed you after the storm."

"The storm!" John said, excitedly. "Our rudder was damaged and we had to deviate from the course to fix it."

"There you have it," said Billy Jack, nodding. "We had hopes of findin' the treasure before ye arrived, but the map led us on a merry chase in the wrong direction, nearly got us all killed."

"Bloodbeard didn't include the locations of the clues to the treasure, did he?"

"No, but he included some dangerously fatal false ones," Billy Jack said with a sigh.

"Well, I know Bloodbeard's found the first two," John said. "I was with him when he did."

"We knew as much," Billy Jack said. "I helped

Bloodbeard hide the clues and set the traps, but he hid the gold himself. Not a one of us knew th' way to where it all be hidden, and each map tells of the location of the next. The last map tells us the way to the end of the journey. X marks th' spot, and all that. He made it so that it'd be suicide to try fer one of the maps without the previous one to guide ye."

John smiled and reached into his pocket. He withdrew the folded parchment and held it up. "I think I can help there," he said.

Billy Jack frowned as he took the map and unfolded it. "The way to the third map!" he breathed. "Son, ye've done well, more than you know. Bloodbeard'll be after us for sure!"

John was still very unsteady on his feet, but he stumbled after Billy Jack and the redcoats as they emerged from the cave into the bright sunlight of the early morning. Fighting away the nausea, he forced one foot after the other, concentrating on the form of the swift moving men before him.

"Come along!" Billy Jack was shouting, gazing out at the imposing specter of the great mountain looming over them, his eyes focused on the dark cloud that encircled its crown in the distance. He unfolded the map and peered at it.

"Where's the third map?" John asked, reaching him, cursing the residual effects of the poison in his blood.

"Up there,' Billy Jack said, pointing to the mountain's crown, obscured by gray cloud.

"That's a volcano," John said.

"Fire and water, me boy," Billy Jack said with a grim laugh.

They set off for the volcano's summit, hiking up a narrow path that led upward. The ground was not severely sloped, but rose at a gentle pace, covered with gray rock and speckled with the occasional forlorn looking shrub or tree. They climbed steadily for several hours as the sun rose higher and higher into the sky, the day quickly heating to near-scorching levels against the bare rock beneath them. It seemed to reflect the sun's heat. Or maybe, John thought nervously to himself, the heat was radiating from below them and mingling with its solar counterpart. Either way, rippling waves of hot rose off the gray and black rock of the mountainside. Sweat beaded easily on John's brow, running down into his eyes, or into the crevice where his nose and cheeks met. It tasted salty as it rolled down past his mouth onto his chin, and seeped through his clothing, plastering his shirt to his back.

Gasping, Billy Jack finally called a break and slumped against the rocks. The redcoats seemed to have the worst of it, covered as they were in several layers of wool. Several of them looked very weak, their eyes dead with exhaustion. John peeled the front of his shirt away from his chest and, gripping it between thumb and forefingers, moved it back and forth to generate some breeze.

"So how come we didn't see you?" John asked, gazing out at the sparkling water beyond the edges of the island, seeing the *Iago* and *Philadelphia* at anchor in the bay below. "When we arrived?"

"I knew which end of the island Bloodbeard would lay anchor," Billy Jack said. "We took the frigate—the *Janus*—around the other side of th' island, and made our camp high enough to see which way he'd head once ye put to shore. The mountain's high enough to block the view of ship from most angles, so we anchored on the other side, in the mountain's shadow, lurkin' out of sight."

It took another hour to near the summit in the heat. Several times John thought he saw water on distant parts of the mountain, but they all ended up as mirages. His eyes were playing tricks on him. It took Billy Jack frequently consulting the map to put them on the right course toward the location of the third map, but the going was still too slow for John, who envisioned Bloodbeard spotting the eight tiny figures dark against the mountainside and was even now coming to get his revenge.

"Close now," Billy Jack said, the dark, gray clouds at the mountain's summit now much closer, and seemed poised to overwhelm them all if John stared at them for too long. He blinked and kept his head down. The very ground was hot now, blistering against their skin. The redcoats had stripped out of their jackets in the deep heat. They had all wrapped handkerchiefs against their mouths and noses; even to breathe the air was painful, like their lungs were being scorched from the inside. Their clothing utterly soaked with sweat, John hoped very much to be done with it, get the map, and return from the mountain top, back out of the heat.

The ground abruptly leveled for some distance, before the slope began again, rising away to the summit, this time much too steep to climb.

"This way," Billy Jack said, leading them to the left, as the flat ground bent and curved around to the other side of the peak. They trekked that direction for some minutes, the mountain now standing between them and the larger portion of the island. This side sloped down into a gentle decline, turned into a small run of jungle, and then a length of black sanded beach. Billy Jack did not stop to admire the view, however, but continued forward. The heat became more intense of a sudden, and then a sharp turn in the rock opened out into a wide flat pocket where the very air was like breathing fire.

John gasped at the sight before them, the redcoats slowing as they came around the curve and also took in the spectacle. The ground within the enclave was broken open in great cracks, giant billows of gray steam issuing forth from deep within the recesses of the volcano's bowels, a deep, blood red sheen on the rocks. A lone, rickety rope bridge spanned the largest crack that spread from the side they stood upon for more than twenty feet to the closet bit of solid rock, a small island against the cracks. Upon this small island, secured with several ropes, was the third chest.

"There it is, sir," one of the redcoats said, nodding at it. The man made to go to the rope bridge, but Billy Jack threw his arm in front of him.

"Wait," he said, pacing away and staring at the map. "There's a trap, more like or not."

John inched closer to the edge of the fissure, forcing away the pain of the heat against his skin, and peered down into the mouth of hell. Fiery lava flowed sluggishly past at the base of the sheer cliff, perhaps fifty feet down. The intensity of the heat made John's eyes water, and he ducked back, blinking, hoping the brief exposure hadn't melted them.

"Perhaps it ain't a trap," Billy Jack said thoughtfully, folding up the map and handing it to John. He stepped toward the rope bridge, only three thick ropes spanning the chasm.

"What are you doing?" John blurted.

Billy Jack stepped to the edge of the cliff and eased himself onto the bridge. He looked back at John, a smile playing on his lips. "I'll be all right," he said. "Be right back."

He took the two higher ropes in his hands, using them to balance himself with his feet on the one remaining rope. He jerked and wavered for a moment before finding his balance. He inched forward slowly, the hot winds gusting through his nice, brown waistcoat. After what seemed like a century to John he reached the other side and clambered up to the rock island, making his way carefully to the chest. It was tied carefully and tightly with the ropes. Billy Jack paced around the box, looking at the way the ropes were wrapped around it, and John knew he was expecting a trap of some kind.

"Do ye see this?" Billy Jack called out, pointing down at the ropes with a wide grin. "They're rigged!"

"What do you mean?" John shouted back.

"There be a price fer takin' the chest!" Billy Jack said. "You've got to sacrifice one of the ropes on the bridge to get it open."

He bent down and untied the box, setting the rope down next to him and moving to open the chest. The moment his hands released the rope, it leaped away from him as though it were alive, slithering over the edge of the rock. One of the hand support ropes dropped away along with it. John and Billy Jack rushed after their respective ropes, and as they reached the edges of the rocks, they saw the rope, weighted in the middle, plunging into the lava in a burst of flames.

Billy Jack looked at John and shrugged, then moved back to the chest and opened it. He jerked his hands away from the metal binding as if burnt, which, John reflected, he probably was. Nursing his right palm, he reached into the chest with his left and withdrew the map. He then kicked the chest over onto its side, mouth pointed toward John, and dropped the map they had used to get there into it. Stuffing the new map into his pocket, Billy Jack eased both feet out onto the one rope, gripping the other in both hands and began to inch his way back out towards them. They going was much more slow this time around, as his balance was off. Halfway across, Billy Jack's foot slipped on the rope and he nearly lost his balance, falling into the other rope with his chest. For one heart-stopping moment, he lay sideways on both ropes. Then his feet slid completely off their rope and he lurched downward. John shouted in terror, but Billy Jack's fall stopped almost immediately, as he was gripping the other rope tightly in both hands, swinging precariously back and forth over the chasm.

Grimacing, he began to inch one fist at a time towards the rest of them. John found himself on his hand and knees at the lip of the crevice, hands extended out towards Billy Jack. At last he was within reach, and John seized hold of his closest wrist, struggling to help him climb out of the chasm, straining with all his might. Then there were other hands on his, and they were pulling too. Billy Jack's hand, then his arm, then his shoulder and head appeared, and then he was rolling out of the chasm to safety, laying on the rock next to John, gasping in pain and relief.

That was where John told Billy Jack Thatcher of all Bloodbeard had told him, of Billy Jack's lying ways and manipulative nature, of Mary Ann Rackham being his lover, and of Bloodbeard's belief that John was his own son. It came tumbling, pouring forth from him in a torrent and he found he could not stop until he reached the end of the tale, couldn't stop until he had told him of his doubts, his conflict. And at the end, when John at last fell silent, he could see in Billy Jack's eyes that some, if not all of it, was true.

"I'll not deny to stealin' from Bloodbeard," Billy Jack said. "I took much from him. But ou must understand, John, that it were wrong fer me to take from others for the benefit of Bloodbeard in the first place. He's got no claim to gold what's been wrongfully stolen."

"And mother?" John asked.

"Aye, her too," Billy Jack said. "You never did see him with her. She may have loved him at the first, but once she were aboard ship she soon found what manner of man he were. A terrible man with a demon's rage. He beat her so many times I lost count by th' end of her first month at sea.

"We began as friends, you know, your mother and me. I were a comfort to her in a stormy time, a strength in her weakness. We needed each other, and when we finally met that need, only once in our brief time, someone saw, tattled on her and me." He stopped and looked up at the dark sky. "We were goin' to run, ye know. The next day. We put in at Port Royal, and we knew we had to jump ship and strike out on our lonesome or he'd have killed the pair of us. So while she still slept, I went ashore to find us a first mate fer our new crew. Bloodbeard knew, though, and alerted the authorities to me. Had me arrested in his thirst for vengeance. I've no idea how Mary Ann escaped that ship, but she did, and she had you, and I couldn't be more proud of you than a father's got the right to be."

"But what if you're not my father?" John said, his voice

pleading.

"Seems to me ye may never know fer sure either way," Billy Jack said. "You're in a more enviable position than many, lad."

John laughed. "How's that, exactly?"

"Ye get to choose yer father. Since ye can never truly know, you've just got to decide which of us ye prefer. And, between yourself and me, have ye seen Bloodbeard? Do you look anything like him at all? Or do you resemble another, rather more handsome, sorta fellow?" Billy Jack winked at him.

"Something in my rugged good looks, perhaps?" John asked with a smile.

"That be it," Billy Jack said. "That be the very thing of it."

Billy Jack smiled at him, clapped him on the shoulder, then pushed himself to his feet with a grunt and stretched.

"That were bracing," he said to the redcoats. "Did me skin melt?"

"Why'd you leave the map there?" John said, looking out at the island on the other side of the fissure.

"Because," Billy Jack said, "I want Bloodbeard to know someone were here. Each map leads to the next, but Bloodbeard'll not have left that as the only way to find the rest of the treasure. He'll find his way here sooner or later, and I'm wantin' him to sweat a bit."

"I thought you just wanted to steal the treasure and slip away," John said.

"There's more to the plan than that," Billy Jack said, with a maddeningly cryptic grin. "Bloodbeard's a part of this too."

John, regardless of his smile, was still not entirely

convinced. That sick, empty, dead feeling was still within him, and he hated it, hated not being sure, hated being so conflicted. He wanted Billy Jack Thatcher to be his father, but was it really that simple? Did it truly come down to a choice without knowledge, or at least a choice without absolute certainty? Could he make that decision? He rolled to his feet and dusted off his hands while Billy Jack carefully unfurled the third map and peered at it.

"Where to, next?" John asked, stepping toward him.

"It's close," Billy Jack said, pointing. "On this side of th' volcano, down, closer to the water."

They set out again, John wishing for not the first time that they could just be done. He was so thirsty it felt like his insides were on fire, scorching him. Instead of turning back and returning the way they had come, Billy Jack said the map led them the other direction, toward the volcano's slope that faced out to sea. Before they had gotten far, Billy Jack sent away two of the remaining six redcoats. "Find th' Parson," he told them. "Have him meet us here as soon as he can."

The men nodded and set off in the other direction. Billy Jack, John and the rest of the company worked their way down the slope for an hour or so, and John's only comfort was that now that it was past midday, their side of the volcano fell into the shadow of the mountain's peak, providing some comfort against the heat.

They reached the tree line after another three-quarters of an hour, but it was only a small patch of jungle and undergrowth. John knew the black sands of the beach lay somewhere beyond, but that did not seem to be the direction Billy Jack was taking them. They did not make directly for the closest bit of shoreline, but veered away to their left in the jungle, pushing and fighting their way through shrubs and thick vegetation for another quarter of an hour or so. Soon after, the ground began rocky once more, and the trees and plants began to thin out, which improved their speed. Some time after that, John began to catch what sounded like a loud, deep sigh in the distance, and then a rumble of what seemed like thunder.

"Storm?" he said, glancing up into the cloudless sky.

"Cliffs," Billy Jack corrected, nodding ahead of them. "Make the sound of thunder when the waves break on the rocks. They be called the Thunder Cliffs on th' map."

They emerged from the foliage onto a high place on the cliff side. The rock swept past them to a jagged edge not thirty feet in front of them and dropped unexpectedly away. They were perhaps sixty or seventy feet above the water by the looks of it. To their left, waves thundered below and the sea spread before them, cold and glittering silver. To the right, the cliffs rose up beyond them before merging with the volcano's rocky side. It was low tide on the cliffs because below, just visible from where they stood, a line of flat rocks stood exposed, speckled with tide pools and forlorn, abandoned strings of seaweed.

A narrow, steep set of stairs had been hewn into the side of the cliff face, leading down to the line of rocks, and it was to this roughly constructed stair that Billy Jack led them. The steps were slippery with sea foam and the brine, and coated with algae. Making their slow, cautious way down, they reached the flat shelf of rock, which turned out to be a rock shelf normally submerged below dozens of feet of water, but which now stood, at low tide, about four feet above the water level. Waves crashed and thundered against the shelf's edge, bursting upwards in towering geysers of white sea spray. A wave collided with the shelf's edge and exploded over them, arching high overhead and descending in speckles of salty rain.

"This way," Billy Jack said, pointing to a small opening where the shelf met the rest of the cliff. They picked their way around the tide pools, teeming with starfish and crabs, towards the base of the cliff. The mountain loomed over them, darkening the world overhead as they pressed closer to its base, where the shadows were thickest.

The cave was only about three feet wide, and five tall. Billy Jack bent over, ducking his head, and entered without slowing down, vanishing into the black. John felt a slight chill of trepidation, and then followed. The walls of the cave were slimy and dripping with water, and what was more, were not smooth, but rough, with dangerous sections jutting out into the tunnelway at random intervals. He banged his knee and shoulder on rock several times before wondering if a torch would have been a good idea.

"What about a light?" he called out to Billy Jack, a black form against black darkness ahead of him.

"Won't need one," Billy Jack said. "Nearly there."

The ground rose up slightly as they pressed further into the cave. John held his arms out before him and slightly to the sides as he went, feeling for bits of jutting rock. So blind was he that he ran right into the back of Billy Jack, who had stopped dead in the tunnel.

"What?" John snapped, rubbing his nose, which stung from driving into Billy Jack's spine.

"We're here," Billy Jack said, taking another step forward. Catching sight of a slight bit of light in the gloom, John peered under his arm and saw water stretching out before them in some form of underground pool. It wasn't terribly large, but it wasn't small either, perhaps the length of the *Iago* to the other side. Light spilled into the cavern from somewhere above. John supposed there must be another crack in the mountain that allowed small bits of sunlight into the chamber. On the far side of the pool was a small lip of rock, almost inlayed into the side of the cavern. Into this tight space a chest had been shoved, bound there with rope to prevent it floating away or getting dislodged.

Without hesitating, Billy Jack stepped out of his thick, brown boots and waded into the water. Several feet out, he was already up to his chest in the water, so he bobbed for a moment, then dove forward and began to stroke for the far shore. Still getting a feeling of foreboding, John watched him swim away.

Billy Jack reached the other side after perhaps a minute of swimming. His torso bobbed upright at the edge of the far lip of water, held in place by his arms. The outcropping wasn't even wide enough for him to get all the way out of the water. He simply braced himself with a knee on the lip, leaned forward, and worked on untying the knots that bound the chest to the rock. After a moment, they slid free and Billy Jack hauled the chest out of the tiny alcove. The rope vanished beneath the water with a metallic growl and a rumble beneath John's feet. Feeling the sense of foreboding increasing, John stood anxiously at the edge of the water, watching.

"Hurry!" he called out, his voice echoing strangely around the chamber and returning to him. With a deep breath and a strong shove, Billy Jack pushed off of the rock and surged back across the silent pool. After a moment or two, John could see Billy Jack's eyes go wide, and he stroked harder for shore. Had he seen something? John was bouncing on his feet as Billy Jack reached the halfway point back across the pool, hampered by the chest.

Something disturbed the water behind him, ripples gliding in broad circles into the pool. Billy Jack was nearly there, only two-dozen feet or so. The ripples changed sharply in the water, bee-lining for him as he splashed his way back. A dozen yards. The ripple picked up speed, and to John's utter horror, a large dorsal fin broke the water only yards behind Billy Jack.

"Shark!" he shouted, pointing and jumping in terror, but if Billy Jack was equally terrified, he did not show it. He stroked closer with the same even arm movements. The ripple was nearly upon Billy Jack as he reached the rocks. John was bending down, his hands outstretched to haul Billy Jack bodily from the water if he had too. Before he could climb out of the water, Billy Jack spun and was jerked in the water, slamming up against the rock with a yell of pain. The water broiled in front of him, and John realized that he had used the chest to deflect the shark's jaws beneath the water.

Billy Jack was pressed against the rock, the pressure of the impact lifting him partially out of the water, a large gray, conical head emerging too, the jaws clamped on the chest still held in Billy Jack's iron grip. Muscles bulging, Billy Jack released the chest, drew back a hand and struck the shark across the nose with as much force as he could muster. The black eyes rolled in their sockets and the shark released the chest and sank back into the water to escape. As soon as it had slid under the dark water, Billy Jack rolled out of it onto the shore, panting and shaking.

"Come on!" John said, helping him to his feet. Billy Jack waved for him to wait a moment, then dropped to his knees, flipped up the chest's latch, threw open the lid, snatched up the map, then rose on shaking legs and followed John back out and down through the dark tunnel, emerging on the shelf where the redcoats waited.

"Did you find it?" cried the Parson's voice.

The soldiers had been joined by the Parson and the other twenty or so redcoats. Billy Jack held up the map, his eyes shining as waves thundered and sprayed behind them.

"Got it right here," he said with an easy smile. "Tell me, Parson, are you ready to unearth some treasure?"

Chapter Thirteen

The Plan of Billy Jack Thatcher

"Where's Bloodbeard?" Billy Jack asked.

"Marching to the top of the mountain peak," the Parson said. "His crew didn't move much at all in the first half of the day, but they began the ascent several hours after you did. I believe they saw you upon the mountainside and went in pursuit, hoping to catch you before you could divine your way here, to the fourth clue."

"Good," Billy Jack said, nodding.

"But they've seen us," John said. "How is that good?"

"It be good because I were countin' on it," Billy Jack said, turning back to the Parson. "We've a window te make our final preparations, then. Have ye arranged everything else?"

"It has been done, just as you asked," the Parson said, nodding.

"Good," Billy Jack said, nodding and clasping the Parson on the shoulder. "We should move quickly then." He turned and looked at John, a grin splitting his face. "Are you ready for a battle, lad? Are ye ready to witness me final redemption?"

"Battle?" John said, gaping, but the Parson was already giving orders to the soldiers, and the entire company had begun to move. Billy Jack followed them as they headed in the direction the Parson and his soldiers had arrived from, to another set of narrow stairs which led up and back into the main part of the island. John realized they had completely circumnavigated the volcano and were headed back to where their base camp was nestled.

"Aye, me boy! Battle!" Billy Jack said. "We're to plunder the plunderers, an' no mistake! Think they'll give in without a fight in 'em?"

"But why a battle?" John asked. "If they're hours behind us, couldn't we clear out before then?"

"We could," Billy Jack said, "if that were part of our plan. I told you before, gettin' a hold of that gold be only the first part of the plan. You're to play a central role in the second part."

"Second part?" John said, looking nervous. "Why me?"

"Because, lad," Billy Jack said, laying a paternal arm on John's shoulder. "Bloodbeard don't know we're alive. He don't know we're here. All he knows is that you've got his map, and his treasure be in more danger now than ever it were before." He paused and looked at John. "You didn't really think he'd let you walk away from this island after you'd seen where his treasure were, did you?"

John was silent for a long moment. "Yeah, Isabella said the same thing."

"She sounds a right smart girl," Billy Jack said. "I'll like to meet her when this be all over with."

"She's great!" John said. "Except when she tries to kill me. I just hope she's still alive."

"What do she mean to ye?"

"I don't really know," John said, feeling suddenly

264

jumpy and nervous. "I suppose I like her."

"Do Bloodbeard know this?" Billy Jack asked, looking at John.

"I think so," John said, nodding.

"Then she's alive, like as not," Billy Jack said. "He'll need leverage if he's to force you to give yourself up."

It took them several hours to return to their encampment, gather their weapons and belongings and break camp. As the men did so, Billy Jack and the Parson were together in deep, quiet discussion, their heads bent over the map. John wondered again about the secrecy which Billy Jack took great pains to keep, some part of him worried that Governor Vaughn would be finally proven right and Billy Jack was planning to return to his old life. Was Bloodbeard right about him? Was there truly no man Billy Jack Thatcher had ever spoken truth to? It was also strange how unconcerned for time the company was, as hours for Bloodbeard to catch up to them slipped past.

Finally, though, all was made ready, the redcoats bristling with weapons, clutching their muskets as the Parson and Billy Jack set out for the last spot, the location of the treasure. It was across the island, on the north side. As they descended into the jungle in the humidity, John wondered what his fate would be if they really did confront Bloodbeard with fire and steel. John himself had been given four pistols, and his still carried Billy Jack's sword from the night it was given to him on the *Philadelphia*.

"How are you doing, young Master Thatcher?" the Parson said, sliding in next to John.

"Very, very nervous," John said, climbing over a fallen palm tree as they pushed deeper in to the underbrush.

"And don't call me Master Thatcher. My mother's not married, so I'm still a Rackham."

"Your pardon," the Parson said, giving a little bow with his head. There was a strange look in his eye, as though he wanted to tell John something, but then glanced at Billy Jack and fell silent. They paced after Billy Jack for some time, picking their way through the foliage in the late afternoon sunlight.

"Do you think he means to stay?" John asked the Parson, nodding his head in Billy Jack's direction. "Will he return the treasure?"

"He will," the Parson said.

"How can you be so sure?" John asked, almost imploringly. "How can you trust him?"

"I've been with him for over fourteen years. You learn a thing or two about a man after that long, and I'm telling you now, Billy Jack Thatcher is no longer a pirate."

"Yes, but how do you know that?" John pressed. The Parson took hold of John's arm and drew him closer, leaning his head down so that his mouth was next to his ear.

"John, listen," the Parson whispered. "Trust Billy Jack. Trust your father. You don't yet know all of our plans. All things have not yet been made clear to you, but they will be."

"Why not now?"

"There is more to our plan," the Parson said, "but these are the soldiers of Governor Vaughn. We do not trust them, not entirely. Given that the Governor is out for Billy Jack, anything could be used as pretense to arrest him when this thing is finally done."

John glanced back at the redcoats, marching in step, behind them, then returned his eyes to the Parson and nodded slightly in understanding.

They pressed on for several hours, heading for a set of rocky hills and ridges that lay on the northern end of the island. As they drew ever closer to the nearest inland hill, they ran across several totem poles, the shapes of animals carved into its surface. "We're drawin' close to the pagan temple," Billy Jack said, glancing around them at the dense jungle. John felt a flair of fear go through him.

Continuing on, they reached the first ridge and glanced about as Billy Jack glanced at the map. They followed him around to the other side of the ridge where the jungle seemed the thickest it had ever been. They pushed and chopped at the dense foliage around them as Billy Jack moved right to where the ridge rose out of the earth and arched over them.

Before them stood the mouth to a huge cavern, like a gaping maw beckoning them into its darkness. The sides and top of the cavern had been carefully smoothed, great rectangular rocks propped up to form a sort of stone frame. The stones had been etched with images, warriors with spears, villages gathered around a fire, men hunting animals, and darker things, strange shapes, grotesque shadows, pictures of people being cooked alive and eaten. The redcoats took flint and tinder and sparked several torches, the damp wood sputtering at the touch of the flames.

"Come along," Billy Jack said, leading them into the cave, under the stones. Shadows danced and flickered on the walls around them in the fiery, golden light of the torches. The tunnel was smoothed all the way back, creating a wide passage that remained level with the ground. It took a sharp turn perhaps a hundred feet on, flowing to the right. This Billy Jack followed, which came

267

to a square chamber that had passageways leading in three different directions. Barely consulting his map, Billy Jack took the left passage, which was smaller and more narrow. This passage sloped down gradually, and they descended for several minutes in the gloom. Finally, the tunnel opened out into a large chamber and John stared around himself in wonder.

The chamber was a huge natural cavern that rose up around them, the vaulted ceiling invisible in the darkness over their heads. The ground sloped down and away from them to a center point in the cavern, then rose in a series of large, carved steppes back upward. At the peak of the steppes was another flat place. Upon the center of this flat place was a great altar of dark stone. Behind it, rising above it and towering over the entire chamber was a huge statue of a three-faced god. The three mouths were stretched wide, large enough to fit a man laying down. Billy Jack worked his way down the slope to the center of the cavern.

"Is this the place?" John asked, looking around.

"That it is," Billy Jack said. He turned to the Parson and nodded.

"Set to work, gentlemen!" the Parson said, directing the soldiers to work. "Charges on the pillars and walls."

The soldiers were pulling off their packs and extracting bunches of dynamite, others unspooling fuses. They set to work quickly, and before an hour had passed, most of the charges had been placed along the pillars and set into the walls.

There were shouts and the sound of heavy boots falling on rock from the tunnel behind them. Everyone turned, and the Parson frowned. "It's Bloodbeard," he said.

"How do you know?" said one of the redcoats.

"Who else be on this island?" Billy Jack said. "Get yourselves hid, and quick! You all know what to do!"

Billy Jack took hold of John's elbow and pulled him towards the steppes, climbing them to the flat space with the altar, which provided them a high place from which to survey the entirety of the chamber. The men were scattering in every direction, disappearing behind pillars or into places John hadn't noticed were there. Billy Jack pulled him up to the top of the final steppe, and the first thing John sensed, that close to the altar, was the stench. It wasn't made from dark stone after all; it was stained black with dried blood. This was a place of human sacrifice, John realized with a flush of revulsion. Then his eyes fell on the great towering statue behind the altar.

It was made from skulls. Human skulls, all stacked and pressed together to create the form of the three faces. Within the three mouths there were grates and cooking stones. It was an oven of some sort; they set a fire in the statue, sacrificed the people on the altar, then roasted them in the mouths of their gods and devoured them. This was the pagan temple that everyone had spoken of. It was, John felt, like descending into hell itself.

Voices, closer now, were coming from the tunnel on the other end of the cavern, and torchlight flickered in the passage, getting closer.

"Get down" Billy Jack said, running and dropping behind the altar, beckoning John to do the same. John hurried to him and ducked behind the altar too, peering around his edge down into the chamber below.

Torches blazed suddenly in the entrance to the chamber and seemed to hesitate. Then the lights moved forward again into the gloom, down the slope to the great holes in the earth. Bloodbeard led the way, immediately recognizable by his hulking figure. His eyes glinted dangerously as he took in the scene before him.

"Where are they?" one crewman's voice echoed out in the darkness.

"That be a very good question," Bloodbeard said loudly, drawing his cutlass and a pistol and gazing around the chamber. "John Rackham, ye've got somethin' to do with this, I'll not doubt. Show yerself, fer I know ye be here!"

John felt a wave of fear wash over him. He glanced at Billy Jack, crouched on the other end of the large altar. "Go," Billy Jack mouthed to John, nodding. "We've got yer back."

Bracing himself, John took a deep breath and stood, expecting to die from Bloodbeard's pistol the moment he showed himself. But nothing happened as he stood, and so he strode around to the front of the altar, fingering his own pistol nervously.

"Ah," came Bloodbeard's rasping sigh of recognition from below. "There ye be, John."

"Here I am," John said, hoping his voice sounded braver than he felt.

"Ye were hurtin' me feelings, runnin' off into the jungle with me own map, lad," Bloodbeard said. "Most insultin', what after all we been through an' the adventure we shared." His tone was cold, mocking, his eyes like chips of stone beneath his wide-brimmed hat.

"I was worried you'd kill me," John said, feeling tense, every second waiting for Bloodbeard to raise the pistol in his hand and fire. But he did not.

"Ye were worried I were goin' te kill ye?" Bloodbeard said, a pained expression crossing his face unexpectedly.

"But John, yer me own son. Why would I be killin' ye fer that?"

John could sense Billy Jack stiffen next to him at the words.

"Because there'd always be uncertainty, wouldn't there?" John said. "You'd never really know, and you'd want to make sure either way that you got your revenge on Billy Jack Thatcher."

"Well," said Bloodbeard said, with a casual shrug and a devilish grin, "in that ye be most certainly right."

The words hung in the air between them. John felt stunned, even though he'd known it, deep down. He was surprised at how much the words stung.

"I were goin' to kill ye," Bloodbeard said, spreading his hands as though he were helpless. "I were goin' to spill every last drop of yer blood onto me treasure in vengeance." He held his hands over the floor where the treasure was buried. "What with you bein' all the way over yonder, I suppose I'll have to settle fer different blood to spill." He beckoned to another crewmate, who came forward, wrestling with Isabella's small form. Her hands were bound, her mouth gagged. She was brought forward to stand next to Bloodbeard.

"So," Bloodbeard said, sliding his blade back into its sheath and drawing a long dagger, "I'll gut her fer vengeance upon yerself fer betraying me, an' then I'll hunt ye down and slit yer throat fer vengeance upon Billy Jack Thatcher. Then I'll sail back to Massachusetts, find yer dear mother and gut her too." He took a deep breath and gave a satisfied sigh. "It's got a powerful sort o' symmetry to it, do it not?"

"Release her, sir!" came the shout of the Parson, who stood out from a pillar some thirty feet from where

271

Bloodbeard stood. The pirates turned with shouts and cries of alarm. "You will not find your treasure with threats and death."

"But they just work so effectively," Bloodbeard sneered. "Who be you, then?"

The Parson stood tall in the dark. "I am Beneniah Davids, captain of the British frigate *Janus*, and you are all under arrest for piracy, murder, and treasonous acts against Charles II, Royal Sovereign of the British Empire. You will drop your weapons and be escorted to our ship. You are to be sent back to Port Royal for trial."

Bloodbeard moved like lightning, raising his pistol toward the Parson's chest. There was a thunderous crack of a gunshot and John yelled in terror. But the shot came not from Bloodbeard. The pistol in Bloodbeard's hand sparked and was torn from his grasp before he could fire. All eyes swung up back toward John. Billy Jack Thatcher stood tall on the altar's other side, a smoking pistol in his hands. He tossed this to the rocks at his feet and drew another, directing it at Bloodbeard, the firing pin clicking into place in the gloom with a thundering echo.

"Do us a kindness and drop your weapons," Billy Jack said.

"Billy Jack Thatcher," breathed Bloodbeard, his eyes wide in genuine shock. "How the hell—there's no way ye could have survived that explosion!"

"Perhaps I'm back from the dead," Billy Jack said, with a smile. "Perhaps I be a specter come to exact vengeance. But these shots seem solid enough."

There was a deep rage in Bloodbeard's eyes that told John he wasn't about to surrender. "Ye've stolen me treasure then," Bloodbeard said. "Ye've stolen everything from me!"

"You know, that routine gets old after a while," Billy Jack growled, still brandishing his weapon. "You need do nothing but delay and you speed us all to our fate. Come on out, lads!"

The redcoats emerged from their hiding places on every side, surrounding the pirates, and blocking the tunnel that led out of the cavern, their muskets bristling. The pirates shouted in alarm, raising their own weapons, but no one fired.

"Our fates?" Bloodbeard asked.

"Aye," Billy Jack said. "You see, we rigged this whole cavern with powder. Me own gunshot was the signal to light the fuses."

Bloodbeard's eyes widened in horror. "Are ye mad? Ye'll kill us all!"

"Thought you had nothing to lose," Billy Jack reminded him. "You've got about a minute, by the way."

With a roar, Bloodbeard drew a pistol and fired wildly in Billy Jack's direction. The shot punched into the altar and shattered stone. Shouting and screaming, the pirates rushed for the tunnel, brandishing their weapons. They were met with a volley of musket fire, peppering their disorganized line with shot. Men fell all around, the pirates returning fire as the cavern disintegrated into chaos.

Bloodbeard raised his dagger and pressed it to Isabella's neck, beginning to draw it across her throat. John yelled as loud as he could, pointing his pistol at Bloodbeard, leaping down the steppes. The large pirate paused, blood trickling down Isabella's neck in the short, inch-long cut he had started.

"Don't touch her!" John bellowed, reaching the center of the chamber, keeping his gun trained on Bloodbeard.

Gunfire echoed all around them as the redcoats met the pirates' charge. They stared at each other, glaring and motionless as they were surrounded by fighting bodies and flashes of light.

"Think that'll be enough to stop me, lad?" Bloodbeard cried, his eyes flaming with rage. "Don't ye even think about threatening—"

John fired. The shot hammered into Bloodbeard's shoulder. He roared in pain, dropping the knife and releasing Isabella. She staggered, teetering on the edge of the hole, and then toppled into it, rolling down to the bottom, lying at the lowest point of the temple. John leaped after her, drawing his sword. He crouched over her, sawing at the ropes binding her hands. He got through them in moments and tore the ropes from her hands, then reached his hands around behind her head and untied the gag.

"Are you all right?" he said. She nodded furiously.

"Get my feet!" she said. He bent over to do it when her eyes went wide, and she screamed. With a bellow of rage, Bloodbeard surged down next to them, his great blade slashing in the gloom. Spinning on *the spot*, John knocked his strike aside but the blow was so powerful that he felt pain jar up his arms. The force of it hurled him to the side, and he nearly lost his grip on his blade. He scrambled to his feet as Bloodbeard stood over Isabella, raised his sword and drove it downward.

There was a blazing flash of gold as a blade, reflecting the torchlight, descended, deflecting the blow that would have impaled Isabella. Bloodbeard staggered to the side, looking up into the face of Billy Jack Thatcher. The huge pirate thrust himself upright, a wicked smile curling at his mouth.

"I'm going to enjoy runnin' ye through!" he snarled, twirling his sword.

"Only if ye can, captain!" Billy Jack cried.

The two men came together with the ring of blades and began to duel, their cutlasses whirling and flashing in the gloom, their strikes and parries so quick John couldn't even follow them. He fell to his knees beside Isabella, cutting at the bonds holding her feet. They broke loose, and she scrambled to her feet.

"Come on!" John shouted at her, taking her hand and practically dragging her out of the pit. Battle raged all around them, the cavern filled with fighting bodies, the ring of blades and the fire of muskets. Men screamed all around them. One of Bloodbeard's crew spotted them and charged with a cry, hefting his cutlass. There was a burst of thunder and lightning from behind him and a shot blew through the back of his head, peppering both John and Isabella with blood. The body collapsed as the Parson appeared at their side, a smoking pistol in his hand. He dropped the gun and drew his sword.

"We must get you clear!" he shouted.

"No!" John yelled, turning back to the pit where Billy Jack and Bloodbeard fought.

"You can't help him, John!" the Parson shouted. "The charges will go off any moment!"

Grabbing John roughly by the collar, the Parson dragged him away from the hole and through the mass of stumbling and struggling bodies. John could barely resist, though he was hardly processing any of the chaos around him. His father was down in that pit.

A dark shape blocked their path to the tunnels above, a wicked cutlass drawn and held before him. Standing casually in their way was Bloody Hand, grinning maliciously. They stopped short, staring at him.

"Now, now," he said, his voice soft in the darkness. "Ye don't want te be missin' the big show, now do ye? I hear there's te be fireworks!"

The Parson released John and moved between them and Bloody Hands, planting himself in the way, raising his blade. With a cry, Bloody Hands surged forward, sword flashing out before him. The Parson moved at the same moment, deftly parrying his every strike, their blades ringing and grating together. The Parson knew more about a blade that John had given him credit for, and he pressed Bloody Hands backward toward the tunnel, taking the wiry pirate by surprise.

The surprise lasted only a moment, and Bloody Hands planted his feet and pressed into the Parson with wild abandon, laughing wildly as the two men were forced away from John and Isabella, leaving the way through the tunnel clear.

"Get out of here!" John shouted to Isabella, raising his sword and turning to help the Parson.

"Are you the stupidist boy ever?" Isabella shouted at him, looking exasperated. "I'm not leaving unless you're with me!"

There was a blinding explosion from one of the pillars and a deafening roar filled the chamber. Rock spewed in every direction, shredding into men on every side as the world lurched wildly beneath their feet. Both John and Isabella sprawled on the ground, clutching at their eyes. Men had been tossed in every direction by the blast, and the battle had temporarily ended as everyone held their breath, waiting for the rest. Several seconds passed, but the charge on that pillar must have gone off earlier than the others.

With one accord, everyone surged to their feet and sprinted for the tunnel, yelling in terror. John grabbed Isabella's hand and they tore forward. Rough arms grabbed at them and hauled them backward, throwing them to the ground. Bloody Hands stood over them, bleeding from the ears.

"Fireworks ain't over yet," he said, staggering at them, fumbling with his blade. He was pale, and John saw blood flowing freely out of his side and down his trousers. He reached them, raising his cutlass with a bellow. Terror filling him, without stopping to think, John drew a pistol with a shaking hand and pulled the trigger.

The shot punched into Bloody Hands' chest and he lurched backward, barely keeping his balance, clutching *the spot* in his right breast. He stared at John as if stunned, then down at the wound flowering with a dark stain, then back up at John.

"What . . . be . . . that?" he asked, sounding dazed.

"Nothing," John whispered.

"Nothin'," murmured Bloody Hands. "That's a funny name."

He slumped backward and lay still, sightless eyes staring up into the vaulted ceiling.

The Parson staggered toward them, limping on his wooden leg, beckoning them to hurry. They scrambled to their feet and headed for the tunnel, which was still emptying of men. Another dark shape appeared behind them and Billy Jack Thatcher overtook them.

"Faster!" he shouted, sprinting with them to the tunnel. There was another deafening explosion from behind them and the ground shook. The sound of cracking and collapsing rock filled the chamber. John dared to risk a glance behind them as they ran. The entire place was collapsing, the walls of the temple cracking and buckling. Another charge went off, disintegrating another pillar and the collapse intensified.

"Is Bloodbeard dead?" he shouted to his father.

As if in answer, a pistol shot cracked out from behind them, the shot shattering the lip of the tunnel just as they reached it. They tore into the tunnel and surged upward back the way they had come. The ground was shaking and bucking beneath them, shards of rock and clouds of dust tumbling down from the tunnel's roof.

Yet another explosion rocked the narrow world around them, and John staggered. Billy Jack's hands were on him then, pulling him upright and shoving him forward.

"Keep going!" he shouted.

Another figure joined them suddenly from behind. John realized with a jolt of horror that it was Bloodbeard. He cried out in alarm, but the huge pirate wasn't interested in them. He ran beside John and Billy Jack, utterly focused on escaping the collapsing tunnel behind them.

They reached the three way split and took the right hand tunnel, finding themselves in the wide, square tunnel that led out of the hill. Sunlight blazed ahead of them as the world trembled. Cracks burst open along the walls, easily outstripping them and arcing for the tunnel's entrance. Rock fell all around them; a fist-sized piece of mountain struck John in the back. Groaning, he forced himself to keep running as pain blossomed along his spine.

With a deafening sound the stone frame holding up the tunnel shattered, shards of rock tumbling to the ground in front of them. They had mere moments before the whole thing fell in on them. Sprinting forward, John, Isabella and the Parson hurled themselves out of the tunnel into blinding sunlight. There was a roar of collapsing rock and a giant plume of dust blew outward into the world after them, obscuring everything.

Coughing, John turned, blinking his eyes from the grit in the air, and searched through the dust for any sign of his father.

"Father!" he shouted.

"Here," came a gasping voice to his left. A dark silhouette against the pale dust, Billy Jack Thatcher stood tall, panting and wiping the grimy sweat from his brow. Without stopping to think, John threw himself into his father's arms, clutching him around the middle and pressing his face into his shirt.

"You're alive," John breathed.

Taken aback at the sudden rush of affection, Billy Jack looked uncomfortable for a moment, but then wrapped his arms around John and smiled.

"We're all alive," he said.

"Not fer long," came Bloodbeard's growl from behind them. He had two pistols in his hands, one trained on John and Billy Jack each. "I'm gonna relish this."

That was when they noticed they were not alone. Not only were the soldiers and pirates all still gathered around the entrance to the temple, but they weren't fighting. They were, instead, staring out at a far larger number of people that surrounded them, gathered in the jungle right at the foot of the ridgeline.

Islanders.

Dozens and hundreds of them, all staring, with surprised and angry eyes at their destroyed and desecrated temple.

Chapter Fourteen

Dead Men Tell No Tales

There was silence in the clearing at the edge of the ridge line as the Englishmen and islanders stared at one another, as if stunned by the sudden appearance of the other. The eyes of the chieftain roamed across them and then past them to the destroyed entrance to their temple through the dust and debris.

He screamed in rage, lifting a long, ornate spear into the air. With echoing shouts, the islanders attacked. Soldiers and pirates in unison raised their weapons and opened fire on them as they were once again engulfed in chaos. Bloodbeard swung his pistols away from John and Billy Jack and out toward the attacking natives and fired. Gunfire peppered the jungle around them as spears hailed to the ground and screams rose up around John from the wounded.

Flinging his empty pistols into the faces of the charging natives, Bloodbeard drew two more and discharged them into the rush, flung them aside in turn, and drew two more. These he fired into the onrushing press, uncaring of who he struck, flipping the pistols in the air as he strode amid the chaos, seizing them both by the barrels, and hacked into the closest natives with them, clubbing at anything he could reach.

Within moments the soldiers and pirates had been overwhelmed and John could barely tell who was who in the dust from the tunnel and the smoke of gunpowder that obscured his vision. Redcoats were using bayonets and musket butts, while the pirates hacked their way through the hordes of shouting natives with their swords.

Billy Jack lurched into the line of battle, swinging his cutlass with abandon before he was lost to sight. A scream pierced the air, and John whirled, seeing Isabella thrown backward by an islander with a hatchet. He gripped his blade and tore across the ground toward her with a shout. The warrior turned and his eyes widened in surprise at the boy charging him. John slashed at the man, who darted back, gazing at John almost curiously. John seized Isabella by the hand and drew her to her feet, forcing himself between her and her attacker.

The tall, thin man glared at John, as though sizing him up. With a roar, the warrior lunged across the gap between them without warning. John raised his sword defensively when a concussive flash went off next to him and he lost sight of his surroundings in the acrid smoke of gunpowder. Blinded, ears ringing, John stumbled away, his eyes screwed shut in pain against the sting of the powder. Someone had shot the islander before he could reach them.

Hands—soft hands—took hold of him and he opened his eyes, tears streaming down his cheeks. Isabella had him by the hand and was pulling him frantically away from the still form of the native warrior. "Come on!" she said, though he could barely hear her. She was pulling him back towards the ridge line, where the battle seemed most intense. The pirates and redcoats seemed to have banded together, using the rock face of the ridge as a defense to prevent themselves from being surrounded. John could see Billy Jack swinging his blade with wild abandon at the very front of the line, taking down two — three — foes in the spare second John was able to see him.

They pressed through the line and rejoined the Parson, who looked exhausted and pale. Panting, he nodded to them as he fired a musket into their attackers, catching a native in the shoulder. John's hearing was gradually returning, and with it came the snarls and bellows around him, the screams of the dying.

"How are you managing?" the Parson shouted, drawing his blade and cutting down a warrior who had leaped over the line of struggling men. The native went down with a wail and lay still; the Parson swiftly closed his eyes and made the sign of the cross over the body, then hacked into the next.

"Where's Bloodbeard?" shouted John, staring around them at the mass of men all around.

"I wouldn't worry about him," Isabella said, pointing. John followed her finger and found himself staring out, past the line of defenders into the swirling mass of natives surrounding them. The great, hulking silhouette of Bloodbeard stood alone in a sea of enemies, his cutlass slashing at anyone who got within reach. His wide, surging cuts caught two or three at a time, throwing the lithe forms into their brothers who stood behind, his face twisted into furious, grotesque delight at the carnage.

"I wasn't worrying," John said coldly.

Bloodbeard strode toward the line of defenders with a casual gait, his long blade lashing out before him, sending enemies sprawling and clearing a path for himself without difficulty.

"We've a pressin' need te be away from here!"

Bloodbeard bellowed, beheading a heathen with a single stroke. Blood geysered into the sky as the body toppled. Bloodbeard turned away without a second glance.

"Getting to the ships is the best chance!" Billy Jack said, dueling with a warrior with two axes.

At the sound of Billy Jack's voice, Bloodbeard whirled on *the spot* and lunged at him with his cutlass. Billy Jack parried it with a shout of alarm, pressed backward by Bloodbeard's blade until he was able to recover from his surprise. Several islanders got passed the wall of defenders and charged at Bloodbeard and Billy Jack. They turned toward the oncoming natives and, moving as one, cut them down before swinging back at each other in a single, smooth motion.

"Have you run mad?" Billy Jack shouted. "Worry about fightin' them lot!"

As if cued by this bellow, a hail of spears fell amidst the defenders. Screams rose up around John and Isabella as they held hands tightly, hunkering down behind the Parson for safety. Following closely on the heels of this barrage came a charge from the islanders that overwhelmed the defenders on their left flank. With shrieks and cries, the natives charged through the ranks of pirates and soldiers, rushing them with spears and hatchets.

Bloodbeard and Billy Jack turned as one once more and fell into their attackers, ducking and spinning around them, blades flying in every direction, carving destruction with their every strike. They weaved in between one another, staying close to one another and dodging between bodies. John suddenly knew what a terrifying sight it would have been to see those two as friends, working together to take a ship. Their moves were almost

283

like a dance as they cleared their path, every slash with their blades and turn of their heels bringing them back into conflict with one another. Their blades rang together for a few strokes before they were forced apart again, only to find themselves facing one another again a few seconds later.

Their efforts had slowed the onslaught of the islanders and it was time no one was wasting. The Parson grabbed John and Isabella by their collars and shoved them away from the duel taking place behind them.

"This way!" he bellowed to the others, raising his sword in the air and pointing along the ridgeline. Pirates and redcoats from all along their defensively line broke ranks and began to surge toward the opening, firing muskets and pistols blindly behind them as they went, too terrified to look back and see if there were natives on their heels.

John was running too fast to look back as they plunged through the jungle undergrowth, but he could hear the sound of many running feet from behind them. He didn't dare turn and see if Billy Jack and Bloodbeard had followed. Instead, they tore along the path they had beaten out earlier as it wound its way along the base of the ridgeline.

His lungs burning, vines trying to snare his feet, branches and leaves reaching out, scratching at his face, John ran without relenting for ten minutes without hearing anything but the pants and gasps of the men around him. He clutched tightly to Isabella's hand and charged after the Parson, who was hurtling himself along the treacherous path and managing to keep a solid pace ahead of them despite his crutch.

The terrain turned upward and they made their way

as fast as they could through the trees to the crest of what ended up being the hill that turned into the ridgeline. The jungle was thinning before them as the ground sloped downward. Great chunks of sunlight were bleeding through the canopy of palm tree crowns above them and beyond that waited the black sand beach with sparkling, blue water.

Almost reading one other's minds, Isabella and John stopped and released hands, staggering to their knees in the soft dirt. The Parson slowed and looked back at them as pirates and redcoats surged past them through the jungle, ignoring everything but the sight of the water ahead through the trees.

"Wait," John gasped, unable to control his heaving chest. Isabella sat slumped against the trunk of a particularly thick palm tree, her face flushed, sweat pouring down her forehead into her eyes. "Can't . . . go on . . . ."

"We must, John," the Parson said. "We don't have a choice."

John was staring the way they had come, searching for any sign of Billy Jack or Bloodbeard. The jungle was silent except for the sound of the pirates and redcoats running down to the beach in the other direction. The Parson had not waited for a reply, but had simply taken Isabella and helped her to her feet. She could barely stand, so he threw her arm over his shoulder and the two of them went limping down the slope toward the beach.

John forced himself to his aching feet and staggered after them. Gunshots from the beach cracked through the thick, humid air and they broke into a limping jog. What had happened? Had the natives found them on the beach?

They broke through the treeline onto the black sand, swords at the ready, searching for attackers. There was no sign of the islanders, but several of the pirates had fired their pistols into the air, waving their arms out over the crystalline sea.

"What are you shooting for?" roared the Parson, limping out into the crowd of pirates and redcoats. They all jumped at the sound of his authoritative voice.

"We was tryin' te signal the ship," one of the pirates said.

"What ship?" the Parson growled. John realized that every one of the gathered men looked at the Parson as their leader for the moment.

"Look, Captain," said one of the redcoats, pointing out into the waters. A dark blotch in the distance bobbed on the surface of the ocean.

"Anyone have a glass?" the Parson asked, looking around. They shook their heads, but one of the redcoats produced a small looking glass and passed it over to the Parson. He lifted it to his eye and squinted out at the ship. "Too far out to tell whose it is."

The pirates and redcoats glowered at each other, though the truce remained for the time being. The Parson was scanning the shoreline of the beach down the island until the rest was lost to sight as the land curved inland. He stopped and smiled, then lowered his glass.

"Longboats!" he cried, pointing along the northern shoreline. "We can get to the boats and away from the island."

"Hang on," one of the pirates growled, holding up a hand and glaring at the Parson. "What if tha' be yer ship there? I've no interest in getting' clear of these heathen only te find meself headed fer the short noose."

The Parson looked at the man hard, then snapped the eyeglass shut. "If that is our ship, I will give you quarter and we will arrange to return you to the *Iago*."

Any further discussion was forestalled when another pirate, gazing up the beach toward the longboats raised an arm and pointed excitedly. "It be the Captain! Look!"

Every head swiveled in one direction to stare up the beach where the pirate was pointing. Sure enough, the tall, hulking form of Bloodbeard had stumbled out of the trees in the distance. Then a second figure plunged out of the trees to the black sand. John felt his stomach clench. It was Billy Jack, and he still clung to his sword. Bloodbeard turned on him and they began to duel along the black sand. The distant ring of blade upon blade reached the gathered company, which instantly broke into a run toward the sight.

John grabbed Isabella's hand and pounded up the beach with the others, racing along the black sand and struggling to keep lifting his legs again and again. As they drew closer to the figures, John could see them spinning and slashing at one another.

"Stop at once!" bellowed the Parson when they had drawn close enough to be heard over the sound of swords. Billy Jack shoved himself away from Bloodbeard and retreated out of reach of the pirate's great blade. Without slowing, Bloodbeard drew a pistol, turned on *the spot* toward the Parson and pulled the trigger. There was a hollow click and the gun did not discharge. Scowling, Bloodbeard threw the pistol to the sand and laughed. The pirates laughed along with him, somewhat more nervously.

"We have to get off this island," the Parson said. "We located some longboats up the beach from here. If we can make it there, we should be able to get to the ship."

"Ye don't say," Bloodbeard said, growling. "Well, I'll not be boarding any British vessel unless it be surrenderin' itself te me own command."

The redcoats bristled. The Parson waved them back and glared at Bloodbeard.

"I've agreed to allow you back to the *Iago* once we're safely away from this island."

"And what then?" Bloodbeard said. "When we're safely te the *Iago* once more?"

"The truce ends."

Bloodbeard stepped closer, glaring into the Parson's eyes, but if he was frightened he gave no sign. He matched Bloodbeard's gaze until the huge pirate gave a grunt, reached out and took the Parson's hand in his.

"It appears we have an accord, Master Parson," Bloodbeard said. "Since ye be a man of God, I'm bankin' on ye bein' trustworthy on this."

"You have my word," the Parson said.

"Good," Bloodbeard said, nodding to himself. "But know this. When our accord runs itself out and we're enemies once more, I'll be lookin' fer yer face amid the battle. Find me an' we'll introduce one another to yer God."

With a foul grin, Bloodbeard dropped the Parson's hand, turned, and began to march along the beach toward the distant longboats. Flicking his hand, he summoned all of his crew to follow him. The redcoats looked at the Parson uncertainly. He sighed and motioned for them to follow.

Billy Jack, sweating and exhausted, moved to the Parson's side. "Are ye mad?" he growled. "Bloodbeard's not te be trusted!"

"Of course not," the Parson said. "But we need to get off this island. Then we can worry about him."

"He'll not keep his word," Billy Jack said.

"Well, he's walking in front of us. If he tries anything, we shall know," the Parson replied, keeping his eyes fixed on the back of Bloodbeard's head. They made their way up the beach for many minutes and all the while John refused to let go of Isabella's hand. It took all his concentration to keep his feet moving, though he was dimly aware that she kept glancing at him as they walked. He looked at her and she smiled.

"What?" he asked.

"Nothing," she said quickly, still smiling. "I'm just glad you're alive."

"We're not safe yet," John replied. The smile faded and she turned her face away from him but he was too tired to wonder about anything but whether he would be able to keep moving forward.

At last, after what seemed like hours to John, they reached the curve in the island where the trees blocked their view. The longboats lay on their sides in the sand, safely out of reach of the waves and perhaps a hundred yards away. The pirates ahead of them stopped abruptly. They could hear Bloodbeard saying something indistinct and then laughter rose up from the pirates.

Billy Jack sprinted forward, John and Isabella following, passing the Parson in their hurry to see. As John reached the place Billy Jack had stopped, a few yards shy of the group of pirates ahead of them, he felt a chill of dread slither up his spine. There wasn't one ship at anchor offshore, but two.

It was the *Iago* and the *Philadelphia*.

They had been heading towards the pirate vessels the

whole time. Unable to stop himself, John slumped to the sand, too tired to feel emotion. A part of John was grateful he couldn't. Roaring with laughter, Bloodbeard turned slowly and grinned at them.

"Well, now," he said. "This turns th' table, now don't it, lads?"

The pirates roared in agreement, fingering their weapons, a foul glint in their eyes.

"These be our ships, be they not, lads?" Bloodbeard growled, sweeping one hand out toward the ships at harbor. The pirate crew snarled in agreement. "These be our longboats, be they not, lads?" The pirates whooped in agreement.

"We had an agreement, Captain," the Parson said slowly, stepping forward.

"Aye, and now it be a mite more than useless, be it not, Captain Davids?" Bloodbeard cried. "Ye might be a man of God, but I be a mere mortal caught in the sins of the flesh."

"Captain—"

"Ye will come aboard with us," Bloodbeard said. "But ye'll be coming as prisoners, not as guests. There's te be no quarter given te ye or yer wretched crew!" The roars of the pirate crew nearly drown out Bloodbeard's words.

"Don't do this!" Billy Jack shouted to Bloodbeard over the thunderous cries of the pirates.

"Ye dare speak te me!" bellowed Bloodbeard, eyes going wide in rage. "Ye'll never see anything but the end of a cutlass as soon as we're aboard the *Iago*!"

The Parson glanced at the redcoats around him. They were clutching their muskets tightly, eying the pirates. John saw him give a slight nod to them. He squeezed Isabella's hand with his and drew her closer to him. Her eyes were questioning, but he dared not speak. The tension running the few yards between them and the pirates was thick and any slight change could set it off.

"Captain Davids, I'm wantin' te see yer weapons on the sand," Bloodbeard warned.

"I'm afraid that's out of the question," the Parson said quietly.

The pirates raised their guns at the same moment the redcoats did. The space between the two groups erupted into chaos as the deafening crack of muskets and pistols shook the air, great clouds of powder filling the air. The scream of men and the eerie whistle of bullets tearing through the air filled all of John's senses. He could hear Isabella screaming as he threw her to the sand and covered her with his own body.

People were running around them as they lay, and then the sound of cutlasses crossing reached them. John rolled off of Isabella and hauled her to her feet. She gasped as he righted her and looked around. Several men lay on the black sand, but none of them appeared to be Billy Jack or the Parson. The rest were in a great broiling morass, swinging and hacking at one another.

"Come on!" John shouted to her, taking her hand and drawing his own sword. Instead of running into the press, he charged to the side, bypassing the battle altogether—catching a glimpse of Billy Jack and Bloodbeard dueling one another again—and headed for the longboats that lay further up the beach.

"Where are we going?" Isabella shouted as she fought to keep up with him.

"We're getting out of here," John told her between ragged gasps. "We can take one of the boats around to the other side of the island. The British have a ship there."

They were about halfway to the longboats when they heard shouts of alarm from behind them. John knew some of them had figured out what he and Isabella were doing.

"Faster!" John yelled, redoubling his efforts to make it to the boats before he collapsed. Then Isabella screamed and stopped short. Nearly tripping, John turned and saw her staring, not at the pirates and redcoats who were now charging in their direction, but towards the treeline of the beach. Hundreds of islanders were pouring out of the trees onto the black sand, hefting spears and longbows, flowing out of jungle all along the shoreline before and behind them. The others weren't charging, they were fleeing.

The longboats wouldn't be able to fit everyone. Some of them would have to be left behind.

"Run!" John screamed, grabbing Isabella's hand and pulling her into a sprint. They pounded across the sand as the rest of the pirates and redcoats shouted at them. They crossed the stretch of sand and reached the longboats only a few moments before the others. Pirates and redcoats alike paid no heed to each other in their desperation to get away from the overwhelming presence of the islanders.

"Get the other end!" John bellowed to Isabella as they reached the first longboat. He pushed it upright and they began to drag it forward to the crashing waves. A solid thunk startled John as an arrow sank into one of the longboat's wooden seats. "Faster!"

When the boat hit the wet sand it rocked to a halt, throwing John to his knees in surprise.

"Get up, get up!" Isabella shrieked, jumping up and down in terror, her eyes locked on the onrushing natives.

"Get out of the way!" Billy Jack shouted, waving them aside with his arms as the rest of the group reached them. John and Isabella backed away from the boat as Billy Jack and Bloodbeard rushed past them and threw themselves against the sides of the longboat, heaving it off the sand with snarls of effort. Other men, pirate and redcoat alike, seized at any available space along the sides and they carried the boats into the water. John splashed after them into the waves.

The other longboat was already in the water and bobbing wildly as men hauled themselves over the sides, hitting and kicking one another to ensure they would make it. Bloodbeard surged across to the far longboat and hauled himself aboard. This left Billy Jack and the other men struggling in chest-deep water as the waves bucked them up and down.

A hail of arrows fell splashing into the water around John as he bobbed in the brine, searching for Isabella. He finally caught sight of her sloshing ashore toward the Parson, who was struggling to stay upright in the pounding waves.

"Come on, son!" Billy Jack shouted, holding onto the side of the longboat and beckoning John to climb in. John shook his head and pointed back to shore. Billy Jack's eyes fell on the scene and went wide. Turning, John kicked frantically for shore, Billy Jack close behind.

Isabella and the Parson were past the surf and kicking toward them as the beach began to swarm with islanders, all shouting and screaming, hurling spears and loosing arrows at them. Billy Jack reached John just as he met Isabella and the Parson. John seized onto Isabella as Billy Jack took hold of the Parson and, splashing into the water, began kicking hard for the remaining longboat.

Gunfire peppered into the oncoming rush of natives as the men in the longboat opened up on the islanders. John did not slow to see whether they found their marks, but concentrated on reaching the boat. Four more good kicks brought him and Isabella to the longboat's side and then rough hands were upon them, hauling them bodily into the bottom of the boat.

A pirate was wrestling with the oars of the longboat, fitting them to the guides. A redcoat threw himself down beside the pirate and took one of the oars. Together they pulled for the ships in the distance.

There were still men in the water, trying to splash their way into the boat, which was too full as it was, and riding dangerously low in the water. The men already in the boats were forced to start punching and kicking the men in the water to prevent them capsizing the boat as they all attempted to climb aboard. As one tried to haul himself aboard the other longboat, Bloodbeard drew a pistol and shot him in the head. After a few minutes the men in the water gave up and began to swim desperately for the ships by themselves.

"The islanders are in the water!" the Parson shouted, pointing back the way they had come. Sure enough, the a number of them had plunged into the sea and were swimming for the longboats at an alarming speed.

"Pull!" bellowed Billy Jack to the oarsmen, who redoubled their efforts.

Their boat had nearly caught up to the other and John could see Bloodbeard standing in the boat, screaming to the men in his own boat to row more quickly. The huge pirate caught sight of Billy Jack and the Parson, drew a pistol and fired at them from across the water. The shot had been poorly aimed and sprayed harmlessly into the water just shy of the boat.

"Are ye mad!" Billy Jack shouted at him as Bloodbeard drew another pistol and fired again. This time the men in the boat all ducked at the crack of Bloodbeard's shot, which splintered the longboat's gunwale.

Bloodbeard was forced to cease firing when another shout went up around them.

"Boats!" several men cried, pointing back at the island. Everyone turned to look backward and John saw everyone in the other boat gaze behind them as well. The islanders had launched their own canoes, which were lighter and more streamlined in the water. They were gaining rapidly, closing the gap. His heart filling with terror, John turned and looked ahead at the ships. They were still easily a hundred yards off. Eyes wide, he grabbed Isabella's hand tightly.

"We're not going to make it, are we?" she said, looking into his eyes. He found he couldn't answer the question because his voice had seized up. He shook his head and drew his sword.

"We're not dead yet," the Parson said. "Can we get some more men rowing?"

The two rowers shifted closer to the gunwale as two others slide in beside them so that there were two men to an oar. John and Isabella watched the islanders' small water crafts draw ever closer, slowing only to hack and chop at the men still swimming in the water. Horrible screams of pain and terror echoed over the water toward the longboat and Isabella closed her eyes against the sight of the crystal-clear water running red. The Parson whispered a prayer for the men in the water and shook his head. John knew the sharks would not be long in gathering.

"It might have bought us some time," Billy Jack muttered, looking pale. He stood and looked at the frightened pirates and redcoats. "If we make it to the ships it'll be by the skin of our noses. If you've got dry powder or shot, pass it forward for those who have muskets an' pistols."

There was a slow scramble as men rummaged through what they had and passed it over to Billy Jack, who handed it out to those with guns. They set to work reloading as the longboat drew closer to the ships, which lay perhaps fifty yards out now. The islanders looked to John to be about the same distance from the longboat.

"Nearly there, gentlemen," the Parson said to the oarsmen.

The islanders were almost twenty yards from the longboats and closing fast. The natives stood and began to loose arrows at the fleeing longboats again. Arrows whistled around them, splashing into the water and falling into the boat like deadly rain. Men screamed as arrows drove into their flesh, in an arm here, in a thigh there.

"Fire!" Billy Jack bellowed and gunfire erupted from every gun they had like deafening thunder. At least most of the volley seemed to reach its target. Islanders screamed and pitched backward out of their canoes or slumped into their boats. The leading edge of canoes slowed but were quickly surpassed by the others. There were dozens, maybe hundreds of canoes filling the water behind the longboats now, too many to fight.

"To arms!" John heard Bloodbeard bellowing at the *Iago*, which was only yards away. It seemed that the crew aboard the ship had already seen the situation. The gunflaps along the side of the great pirate vessel rose and two decks of cannon ran out, bristling like huge mouths of death against the oncoming islander crafts. John barely had time to register the sight before the cannons went off and the world seemed to shatter around him. He could feel the sound of the volley rumbling in the deepest part of his chest and the howl of cannon balls screaming through the air just over their heads. The volley punched and chopped through the islander's pursuit. Flimsy canoes shattered and exploded left and right behind them, hurling natives into the air and sending great geysers of spray into the air as the volley plowed through the boats and into the water.

They had reached the *Iago*'s hull as the longboats bobbed wildly. Rope ladders were thrown down the sides of the ship and men began to climb frantically up to the *Iago*'s deck before the islanders recovered from the first volley. Billy Jack and the Parson remained until nearly the last, letting the others go first. Then the Parson was sent up, using his good leg and his arms to haul himself aboard. Billy Jack made John and Isabella go before he did, so they climbed as quickly as possible, and John refused to leave the *Iago*'s gunwale until Billy Jack had toppled over the side and was safe.

Bloodbeard was already on the aft castle, shouting orders. In the chaos, no one seemed to even notice Billy Jack or any of the redcoats, who stood on the deck watching the pirates get to work, scaling the rigging, securing lines, or disappearing below to man the cannons.

Another volley of cannon fire retorted out from below, the whole deck shaking. John rushed to the gunwale to see the damage. Bits of destroyed canoe and fountains of water were falling back into the sea by the time he arrived at the side of the ship. The volley was devastating, but a number of the canoes had managed to get under the guns and were quickly approaching the side of the ship.

"Islanders!" John shouted, pointing. Billy Jack was at his side in an instant, peering down into the water below.

"They've got under the guns!" Billy Jack shouted. "Prepare to be boarded!"

The redcoats bristled, reloading their muskets as several pirates distributed guns and swords from below. There was a frantic scramble for weapons, but amid the chaos John was able to get some powder and shot for his pistol. He set about loading it as Isabella took up a cutlass of her own, and two pistols, cramming them into her pockets.

She met his eyes and they smiled at each other. As one, they rushed to the railing with the other crewmen. Standing beside Isabella at the gunwale, John could see that six or seven canoes had reached the side of the *Iago* and several dozen islanders were now scaling the side of the ship, using the cannons and gunports to climb. Cutlasses and cannonade ramrods appeared through the gunports as the cannon crews tried to dislodge as many as they could. One or two slipped and plunged, screaming, to the frothing seas below, but most of the others retained their footing.

The defenders from the gunwale opened fire, the sharp crack of gunfire raking across the deck. Taking aim with his pistol, John fired and missed the native he had been aiming for. The volley caught a number of the natives as they climbed and bodies toppled to the seas. But because everyone had fired, now they all had to re-load, John realized, which meant that the rest of the islanders would most certainly reach the deck. The crew tossed their guns aside and drew cutlasses as the first islanders reached the railing. Blades flashed out, biting into skin and bone. The first wave pitched into the seas and a great cheer went up along the line.

"Breach!" Bloodbeard shouted. John turned with the rest of the defenders and realized, with a jolt of terror, that some of the islanders had flanked them and scaled the other side of the *Iago*. They were now throwing themselves over the gunwale with screams and shouts.

With a bellow, Billy Jack raised his cutlass and charged across the deck, meeting the islanders in battle. Blades flashed out against long knives and hatchets. Men were screaming and grunting, blades were ringing back and forth in the midst of the mass of moving bodies. John grabbed Isabella and hauled her away from the railing as more islanders leaped onto the deck.

The *Iago* was swarming with natives and more were pouring over the sides at every moment. Two of them charged John, who drove into them with his blade, knocking aside the one's attack while Isabella hacked at the other. John's blade caught the native's arm and he cried out as crimson blossomed along his forearm. He dropped his hatchet and leaped back over the side of the ship into the water.

Billy Jack appeared at Isabella's side as he ran an islander through. His blade flashed out and with every stroke another enemy fell before him, clearing a path for them.

"Get to the aft castle!" Billy Jack bellowed, slashing a native across the chest and driving the rest backward out of his reach. John and Isabella sprinted through the chaos, ducking around pirates and redcoats grappling with islanders, dodging wild cutlass and hatchet swings.

Isabella's red hair, soaked to the bone from the water, flew around her as she reached the stairs and took them two at a time, throwing herself to the aft castle deck and rolling away from the stairs. John was close behind, reaching the top of the stairs a second later. The Parson staggered to the ground after him; Isabella and John helped him away from the steps as Billy Jack charged up them, followed closely by several islanders.

Bloodbeard charged for the top of the stairs just as Billy Jack cleared them. The hulking pirate slashed out with all the strength he could muster, catching one of the islanders so hard in the chest that the stroke lifted him into the air and hurled him into those following behind.

Billy Jack got to his feet again and joined Bloodbeard at the top of the stairs, hacking and stabbing at any of the islanders that dared try and breach the aft castle.

"You just saved me life!" Billy Jack shouted as they fought the onslaught of natives.

"Don't be making more of it than ye should," Bloodbeard cried, running an islander through. "I were aimin' fer yerself!"

"Behind you!" cried the Parson from his position on the deck to John and Isabella as four or five islanders climbed over the railing from the back of the aft castle. Isabella shouted, her eyes wide as she hefted her blade and charged, her red hair again flying. John lifted his blade as well and surged forward, meeting the islanders with his sword.

He could see Isabella fighting with a giant native that had a knife in one hand and a hatchet in the other. For all of her training with a blade he was easily her better, and had more weight behind his blows. John was nearly struck in the neck by a hatchet head and was forced to throw himself to the side at the very last moment to avoid losing his head. As it was he felt the hatchet graze his head, nearly scalping him. Fiery pain blossomed on the back of John's head and he dodged, staggering away from his attacker as warm blood flowed down the back of his head and neck.

John cursed at getting distracted by Isabella's fight and dropped to his knees, whirling around for a waist-high strike as his attacker pursued him. The native managed to catch his blade with his knife, deflecting the strike, his other arm coming around with the hatchet. Throwing himself forward into a roll, John felt the hatchet miss him. He finished his roll and rose to his feet, throwing his blade forward to parry another knife-hatchet-knife strike by the islander.

As he came out of his defense, John glanced over at Isabella who was deep in battle with the giant islander as more were swarming the Parson, who was feebly deflecting their attacks with his sword while trying to remain balanced on his crutch. John sprinted forward and caught one of the natives in the back with his blade and the man went down with a howl. That provided enough distraction to the other islander that the Parson was able to run him through.

The first islander John had been fighting had followed him, and John spun, flinging his blade out in front of him in desperation, catching the knife intended for his back. He then drove the hatchet arm out wide, spun again and drove his blade into the man's chest.

Isabella was having trouble with her giant islander, who was able to send her staggering with almost every strike. She managed to right herself and use her light-footedness to dance away from his attacks, though it was close. Her flaming hair danced and flew as she sprinted in for a strike and danced away. So caught up in watching her was John that he nearly forgot she was in dire need of help.

"A little help!" she shrieked at him as he stood, jaw hanging slightly agape as he watched her fight. The time it took for her to shout left her open for a half-second. The hatchet arced in toward her side.

With a bellow of rage, John leapt forward and stabbed the giant islander in the side. The man roared in pain and staggered away. This provided enough room that the hatchet strike swept through the air perhaps an inch from Isabella's throat. Yanking his blade from the native's side, John plunged it into his chest again. The huge native gave a gurgling howl, stepped backward, and toppled to the deck, the force of his fall knocking John into Isabella.

"About time!" she cried, glaring at him as she caught him from falling. They both staggered into the gunwale as her arms went around him. He looked into her eyes and realized his heart was pounding in terror. She could have died right there.

"What?" she asked, looking at him.

John straightened, then took her cheeks in his hands and kissed her on the mouth. He could no longer hear the sound of blade on blade, the screams of the dying and howl of those in battle, the continuous thunder of feet shuffling on the deck. All of his senses were consumed with that moment in the midst of pitched battle.

They broke apart and the world of battle and death came searing back.

"Could you do that later?" Billy Jack bellowed angrily from the top of the stairs where he was still in pitched battle, holding the aft castle from the islanders pushing up toward them from the *Iago*'s main deck.

"Wait!" Isabella shouted, looking cross. "Did you just kiss me because you saved my life?"

"Best get back to it," John said, an uncontrollable grin spreading over his face.

"You did!" she shouted as more islanders threw themselves over the railing onto the aft castle. "Well, I don't need your help!"

"No, of course not!" John said happily, turning to meet the new natives.

"Wipe that stupid grin off your face!" Isabella said, following him and hacking at the natives. "Don't you have anything to say to me?"

John knocked a knife aside and drove his blade through the wielder's chest. The man fell sprawling to the deck as John turned to look at Isabella, flashing her his widest smile.

"Don't die!" he shouted, and laughed at the look of utter astonishment on her face.

Suddenly the thunder of cannon fire reached their ears over the din of battle, and it had not come from the *Iago*. John and Isabella stopped in surprise as the natives they had been fighting turned at the sound of the cannons, fled to the gunwales and threw themselves overboard. They looked at each other in confusion.

A great cry of victory and defiance met their ears from the crew of the *Iago*. When their eyes fell on the main deck they found that the natives were fleeing back over the sides of the ship and into the canoes. As they watched, the canoes turned about and were making for shore as fast as they could.

"What are they doing?" the Parson said, watching them go.

More cannon fire echoed across the water from their starboard side. John looked toward the source of the noise and felt his jaw fall open in shock. Coming around the near side of the island, at full sail and with its guns run out, was a third ship, neither the *Iago* or the *Philadelphia*.

Flying the colors of the union jack and on an intercept course was the British warship *Janus*.

Chapter Fifteen

Show No Quarter

Bloodbeard's wild eyes were wide with surprise as the *Janus* swept down on them from the other side of the island, rushing forward at full sail toward the *Iago*. The British warship was easily the match of the *Iago* and John knew that if it came down to a contest between them it was anyone's guess which would emerge the victor.

"What are they about?" Bloodbeard bellowed, turning to Billy Jack. "If they mean te attack, they'll kill yerself, like as not!"

"They don't know we're aboard," the Parson said, going to the gunwale and peering out at the ship as it grew ever larger.

"Probably heard the cannons," Billy Jack said. "They're likely to think we're dead on the island."

Bloodbeard turned to the remnants of the crew. "Battle stations!" he roared. "Prepare for a broadside! Give me a broad reach, lads!" Crewmen sprang into the rigging, climbing frantically to unfurl the sails before the *Janus* reached them. Others scrambled below to join what remained of the cannonade crews.

Bloodbeard strode to the wheel and spun it as the sails began to unfurl and fill with the wind and the ship started to move in the water. Their speed was sluggish

305

and John realized why.

"We haven't fully repaired the damage to the hull," he told Bloodbeard. "We're running waterlogged. We'll never outrun them like this."

Bloodbeard cursed, glancing back at the *Janus*, which was still gaining on them.

"You can't seriously mean to fight them!" Billy Jack said, stepping closer to Bloodbeard. "We've got barely enough men to sail the ship as it is, and they've got a full crew, not to mention their redcoats."

"Ye be right, by the powers," Bloodbeard growled, releasing the wheel. "If I cannot fight, then somethin' else will have te be done."

He turned suddenly on Billy Jack, drawing his pistols. Billy Jack drew his own at the same moment and they stood face to face, pistols pointed at each other, Billy Jack's single barrel against Bloodbeard's two. They glared at one another and no one dared move.

"Well now," Bloodbeard said, with a malicious grin. "Seems we've got ourselves a stand-off."

"Drop your guns," Billy Jack growled.

"Drop 'em yerself," Bloodbeard spat.

John was frozen in place. He could see Isabella also standing still next to him, and on their other side, the Parson was looking from Bloodbeard to Billy Jack and back again, clearly unsure of what to do.

"If that ship reaches us, they'll rake our decks with cannon fire!" Billy Jack shouted. "We'll all perish, you with us!"

"I'd rather go to the depths an' be welcomed te Davy Jones' Locker than let ye go free!" Bloodbeard bellowed, a mad glint in his eyes.

A thunderous boom of cannon fire broke the

conversation and a ball hurtled over their heads, geysering into the water off the *Iago*'s prow.

"That be a warning to surrender," Billy Jack said.

"They're nearly in cannon range!" the Parson said, looking back.

"Lower your guns!" Billy Jack shouted.

"Never!" Bloodbeard screamed, jerking one of his pistols around to point straight at John. Isabella shrieked, but Bloodbeard did not pull the trigger. Instead, his eyes were locked on Billy Jack's. "Ye drop yer piece or I shoot the whelp!"

"If that ship reaches us, we die anyway," Billy Jack said, but there was fear in his eyes for the first time.

"Don't do it," John said to his father, whose arm was shaking, his eyes locked on John.

"I can't," Billy Jack was saying, "I can't lose you again."

With a muttered curse, Billy Jack tossed his pistol to the deck where it clattered to Bloodbeard's feet, and raised his hands. Kicking the pistol away, Bloodbeard directed them to drop their weapons. Reluctantly, they complied as the warship drew ever nearer. Bloodbeard directed them with his guns, and they were forced down onto the *Iago*'s main deck, where the numerous dead had been left. Stepping over bodies, John and Isabella stopped by the main mast with the others. Bloodbeard gave them a malicious smile beneath his great, red beard, and cocked his pistols.

"What are you doing?" the Parson asked sharply as Bloodbeard raised his guns, both barrels aimed straight at Billy Jack.

"We've no way te run," Bloodbeard growled, that mad expression etched on his face once more. He seemed unable to look at anything but Billy Jack. "So I'll not let Billy Jack slip through me fingers any longer. Say goodbye, Billy Jack!"

Billy Jack was standing shoulder-to-shoulder with John. He glanced down and smiled at him, then turned to Bloodbeard, a grin spreading over his face. "Goodbye, Captain."

"What—" Bloodbeard began, but then John laughed and Isabella gasped. The *Janus* had reached the *Iago* and was drawing even with it as they spoke. Bloodbeard turned and gazed up at the British warship for a split second—and in that split second Billy Jack acted.

He charged across the deck to where Bloodbeard stood, scooping up a discarded cutlass as he went. Bloodbeard swung back to face him just as Billy Jack reached him. There were two simultaneous gunshots as Billy Jack threw himself at Bloodbeard with all his weight. Both men were hurtled to the deck at the very moment the *Janus* pulled even with the *Iago* and the warship's cannons went off with such a deafening blast that the world seemed to disintegrate around John completely. The volley of cannon fire ripped into the *Iago* and the deck rocked and splintered as the gunwales exploded into lethal shards of wood, peppering the deck with long, jagged splinters. There were screams all around John, who was momentarily blinded amid the white discharge from the guns. Pain blossomed in his leg as the deck bucked under him, throwing him down between two corpses.

His ears ringing, he staggered to his feet, his eyes burning from the powder in the air. He squinted around him and saw that several huge chunks of the gunwale had been torn away, several cannon balls having ripped though the deck horizontally, creating wide gaps where the deck had been shredded open to reveal glimpses of the deck below.

There was mass confusion on deck. Crewmen lay screaming all around him while others ran to and fro. The only motion was between Billy Jack and Bloodbeard. Somehow, in the midst of the broadside, Bloodbeard had drawn his huge blade and the men fought furiously across the deck, hacking and slashing into one another.

John caught sight of Isabella's limp form laying face down on the deck some feet from him. He sprinted to her side and fell to his knees, panic spreading in his chest. Fearing she was dead, he rolled her over onto her back and saw that she bore a large gash on her forehead that was bleeding freely. She gave a weak cough and he felt sudden relief spreading through him.

"You're alive!" he cried. Upon seeing him, she sat up and threw her arms around him.

"You're bleeding," she whispered hoarsely, looking in horror at his leg. He glanced down and saw that a long sliver of deck had lashed open his trousers at the calf and while the jagged splinter didn't seem to have remained in his leg, blood was staining his trouser leg and boot.

"I'll be all right," John said. "Where's the *Janus*?"

"It sailed past us," came the voice of the Parson as he struggled over to them on his crutch. "She's circling around to give us another broadside. We've perhaps five minutes."

"We'll all be killed unless we surrender," Isabella said, looking around at the devastation.

"We have to take the ship," John replied. "It's the only way to get out of this alive."

"Agreed," the Parson said.

"But that means . . . ." Isabella started to say, looking at John in terror.

"That's right," he said, nodding. "We've got to kill Bloodbeard."

They turned to the furious duel unfolding on the other side of the deck between Billy Jack and Bloodbeard.

"Billy Jack could probably use some help," the Parson added as Billy Jack was driven backward toward the stairs to the aft castle.

John rose, Isabella and the Parson staring at him. "Leave it to me," he said.

Sprinting across the deck over the bodies of the fallen, John didn't dare stop to think about what he was doing. His father needed his help, and so did the others if they were to make it off the *Iago* alive. Bloodbeard's blade was flashing out at Billy Jack, seeking an opening as he backpedaled up the steps to the aft castle.

Diving out of reach when he had cleared the steps, Billy Jack faltered and dropped to his knees—or that was what John thought had happened, at least. He rose again, clutching his own cutlass and caught sight of John racing to join him. With a laugh his blade dipped to the deck and lifted back into the air with John's sword caught by the guard. Billy Jack flipped John's blade into the air over Bloodbeard's head. It arced down over the steps just as John reached them and he caught the sword out of the air, mounting the steps two at a time.

"So yer both te fight me!" Bloodbeard cried, glancing back and forth between Billy Jack, who stood on his right side, and John on his left. He did not seem the least bit concerned by the turn of events; if anything he seemed eager to begin.

"We're taking the *Iago*," John told him, brandishing his

blade. Bloodbeard threw back his head and laughed maniacally, spreading his arms and beckoning them on.

They rushed at him together, Billy Jack's blade arcing high, John's striking low. Bloodbeard whipped his great cutlass around, knocking Billy Jack's strike with such blinding speed that he could half-pivot and parry John's as well. Astonishment etched in his face, John could barely get his blade back into position to deflect Bloodbeard's responding attack as the hulking pirate spun his sword in his hand and flipping it behind his back to catch Billy Jack's slash at his exposed spine before bringing it around again to cut at John.

Knocking Bloodbeard's cutlass aside, John drove into him with all the ferocity he could muster. Despite the threats on two fronts, Bloodbeard was such the swordsman that he kept pace with both of them, falling into a rhythm with his blade so that it flowed in great arcs back and forth, catching their swords and throwing them aside in enough time to defend both his flanks. Howling with laughter, Bloodbeard caught another sword in the toe of his boot and kicked it into the air, catching it with his free hand and beginning a double-bladed assault on them both in a single, fluid motion. So utterly overwhelmed were they that the assault actually succeeded in driving them back down the steps to the main deck.

Crewmen with muskets and cutlasses were sprinting across the deck, reloading their weapons or hunkering down behind the gunwales as the *Janus*, having circled the bay, approached for a second time. Billy Jack shoved John out of the way as Bloodbeard's huge blade screamed over his head right where he had been standing. Leaping backward down the last few steps to the deck, Billy Jack landed, bringing his blade into position as Bloodbeard descended the stairs, holding his blade carelessly in his hand, a wicked smile playing across his face under his long, tangled beard.

"Ye never could best me, Billy Jack Thatcher!" Bloodbeard cried, as John scrambled to his feet and slowly moved around to Bloodbeard's other side. "Not on yer best day!"

"Only because we've never had the privilege of an uninterrupted fight, Captain," Billy Jack said.

Bloodbeard was pacing slowly toward Billy Jack, eyes glinting maliciously. "Ye always were an arrogant man, Billy Jack Thatcher!" snarled Bloodbeard. With a yell he lunged forward the few steps to Billy Jack, whose blade flashed out defensively under the ferocity of Bloodbeard's onslaught. The ring of blade on blade echoed across the deck as the two men fought through the scattered crowd of crewmen, who were desperately trying to get out of the way while keeping their eyes on the duel and the approaching warship at the same time. John sprinted across the deck after them, trying desperately to keep himself in the fast-moving fight.

Raising his blade over his head, Bloodbeard hammered Billy Jack's parry with tremendous force. Billy Jack staggered back and faltered. John charged into the lull in an instant, stabbing for Bloodbeard's back. With a roar of fury, the hulking pirate turned on John, who was forced to dodge a sloppy horizontal slash meant to gut him from side to side. Bloodbeard pursued John as he retreated, slashing and hacking with all his strength, his blade not quick enough for John and biting in anything that came within reach, chopping into the deck, the mast, even catching another crewman on the arm. Not interested in being forced to meet one of those blows with his own sword, John backpedaled, doing his best to stay out of reach.

"Hold still, ye little bastard!" roared Bloodbeard as John danced out of reach yet again and his strike cut through empty air.

"Brace for a broadside!" came the scream of a crewman by the gunwale. John glanced off the starboard side of the ship and was startled to see the *Janus* drawing even with the *Iago* once more. Billy Jack lunged back into the fight at that very moment. Bloodbeard's attention was turned away from John, Billy Jack's blade stabbing forward toward him as the *Iago*'s cannons fired at the same moment the *Janus'* guns went off.

The roar of the cannons were so loud John felt all of the retorts as a wall of deafening sound, objects exploding and splintering all around him, a hail of cannon balls screaming past him. One caught a crewman straight in the chest and he was hurtled backwards in a geyser of red, his lifeless body crumpling against the far gunwale. Other shots tore through the railing, the deck, the steps to the aft castle, throwing men into the air like ragdolls. Through the whole barrage Billy Jack and Bloodbeard fought on, through the fire and the smoke like two specters locked in eternal combat, the sound of their blades lost to the din of cannon fire.

One of the cannon balls found the *Iago*'s mainmast and punched through it without slowing, blasting the far side of the deck with deadly shards of wood. Crewmen were screaming as John threw himself to the deck to avoid getting caught in the explosion. Debris fell to the deck around him as the mast began to tip, cracking and snapping. He threw his hands over his head as something hard landed on his back, blasting the breath out of his lungs and knocking him to the ground. With a deep groan the mast began to tip, cracking and buckling under its own weight, dragging lines, rigging and sail spars with it, rope snapping and buckling as it toppled ominously forward and collapsed with a sound like thunder across the deck of the *Janus*, locking both ships together.

His ears ringing and eyes watering, John gasped and writhed on the deck of the *Iago* for a long moment, struggling to draw breath into his lungs. Finally, inhaling despite the pain, he shook the agony away and tried to lift himself to his feet. He couldn't and he realized that he had been pinned to the deck by something that felt like a long spar from the mainmast, complete with sail. His position on the deck afforded him a view of the *Janus* and of the duel continuing between Billy Jack and Bloodbeard. Boarding hooks arced into the space between the *Iago* and the *Janus*, and were dragged across the deck, catching on the gunwale.

The crew of the *Iago* stood and peppered the *Janus* with musket fire. Screams from the *Janus* met John's ears as he struggled to free himself, but other men from the *Janus* were already charging across the mainmast that spanned both ships toward the *Iago*. Brandishing their cutlasses, the crew of the *Iago* rushed the sides of the mainmast and as the clang of crossed blades rang out, battle was joined on the deck of the *Iago*.

As the deck swarmed again in battle, John caught sight of Bloodbeard driving Billy Jack backwards toward the prow of the *Iago*, his every stroke hammering into Billy Jack's defenses and throwing him even more off-balance. Gritting his teeth, John planted his elbows and knees and shoved upward with all his might, but to no effect. He had to get to Bloodbeard before it was too late.

Isabella appeared at John's side, lifting tangled rigging and debris off of him.

"Hurry!" he shouted, thrashing under the weight of the beam pinning him down. She glared at him but said nothing. The Parson appeared on John's other side, bloodied and bruised but alive. He knelt and together they began to try and pry the beam from John's back as he pushed from below. Finally it budged slightly and they were able to lift it a few inches off of his back. He wormed his way out from under it as they dropped it with a crash.

The shouts and bellows of the wounded and dying filled the air around them as men from both ships fought across the whole deck of the *Iago*. With a shout of thanks, John sprinted through the maze of spinning and whirling swords and daggers toward the prow where Bloodbeard continued to hack into Billy Jack's defenses. Their swords rang and sparked as they fought, their faces wrenched up into grimaces of rage.

Bloodbeard's huge cutlass caught the tip of Billy Jack's sword and threw it out to the side. Overextended and staggering, Billy Jack's eyes went wide as Bloodbeard's blade stabbed out and bit into his side. A scream tore out across the deck, so grating and broken that it took John a half-second to realize it had been ripped from his own throat. Yanking his cutlass from Billy Jack's body, Bloodbeard gave a howling laugh of triumph as John's father fell to the deck, mouth worked fruitlessly.

John was still a long way from them and knew he wouldn't reach them in time to stop Bloodbeard finishing Billy Jack off. Even as John realized this, Bloodbeard was drawing a long, wicked-looking, curved knife from his belt and grinning in malice at Billy Jack's prone form.

Then someone was swinging across the gap between the ships from the *Janus*, a lithe silhouette John couldn't place through the smoke. As it registered that the silhouette was screaming like a banshee from the pit of hell, the rope arced over the *Iago*'s gunwale not five feet from Bloodbeard and a woman dropped to the deck, drawing her blade and facing him. John stopped dead and his jaw fell open. Standing before him, clad in sailors' trousers and a large, billowing shirt, a bandana worn over her long, flowing hair, was Mary Anne Rackham, his mother.

"Get away from my lover," Mary Anne said, her voice deadly.

Looking aghast, as though he had just seen a ghost, Bloodbeard fell back in surprise. Mary Anne paced forward, her blade never lowering, glaring daggers at Bloodbeard.

"Mary Anne," Bloodbeard said, recovering quickly from his shock. "Stand aside now, woman."

"Lay down your arms and surrender the *Iago*," she said, moving between Bloodbeard and the prone Billy Jack. Without taking her eyes from Bloodbeard, she hunkered down and checked Billy Jack's wound.

Bloodbeard laughed. "There be not a chance in hell," he said.

Mary Anne stood and moved toward Bloodbeard, her every move full of a deadly grace.

"I wouldn't have it any other way!" she cried.

With a scream she lashed out with her cutlass, striking again and again, slapping aside Bloodbeard's parries and pursuing him across the prow of the ship. Never in all his years had John seen his mother like this, hair untied and a wild, blazing look in her eyes, a liveliness he had never known she possessed. She was, astonishingly, nearly the match of Bloodbeard, who was struggling to keep up with her onslaught in his surprise.

John sprinted to his father's side as he was struggling to stand, hunkering down and pressing his hands into the wound in his father's side. Clutching at the rail he was leaning against, Billy Jack pushed John away from him with a grimace and hooked his arm over the railing's side, rolling over and trying to gather his knees under himself to stand.

"Don't," John said, trying to push him back to the deck. Billy Jack did not reply, save for a growl as he clung to the railing on his knees, looking rather like how John imagined he himself had looked when they had first set sail, pale and weak, trying not to be sick over the side of the ship.

Billy Jack picked up his sword in a hand that was shaking involuntarily, gritting his teeth as he pushed himself unsteadily to his feet.

"You can't do this!" John cried, terrified at how much Billy Jack's legs were shaking.

"Get out of me way, boy," Billy Jack grunted, one hand clutching the wet crimson stain in his side, the other shaking as it held his sword. He staggered forward toward the duel between Mary Anne and Bloodbeard.

"No," John said, standing in front of Billy Jack, blocking his way. Gunshots and the ring of blades rose in a great cacophony from the deck below as Billy Jack and John eyed each other. "You've given enough," John said firmly. "Don't give your life."

"This is my redemption, boy!" Billy Jack shouted, shaking his blade at Bloodbeard. "One last treasure. One last quest, an' then I can finally be free! Bloodbeard's life, dead or alive, be the last condition of me freedom!"

"We can't run anywhere!" John shouted back. "The *Iago's* foundering in the water! He's got nowhere to escape!"

"He'll slip away," Billy Jack said desperately. "He always does."

"Why are you really doing this?" John demanded, raising his sword between them. "Revenge?"

"How can you ask me that?" Billy Jack said, eyes blazing as he looked at John.

"Because I think it's true," John said.

"I'm doin' this for me freedom, boy!"

"Will you let him live?" John asked, his voice quite.

"What?" Billy Jack breathed. "You cannot still think—"

"—He's my father?" John interrupted. "No. But I don't want your last act of redemption tempered by revenge."

"He turned me in!" Billy Jack screamed, shaking his sword at Bloodbeard again, his eyes wild. "In Port Royal, he be the one who had me arrested those ten years ago! Saw me with your mother and turned to treachery! He's the one that kept me from your mother all these years— from you!"

"I know," John said softly. "Who else could it have been?"

Those words seemed to take the fight out of Billy Jack; that or he simply couldn't stand any longer. He slumped forward with a gasp. John darted forward and caught him before he fell, shifting Billy Jack's arm over his shoulder and helping him limp away from the duel toward the stairs leading down to the main deck. The battle was slowing below, and despite their inferior numbers, the pirates seemed to be taking the upper hand against the beleaguered redcoats and sailors from the *Janus*.

"I can't leave her," Billy Jack mumbled. "I can't leave her again. Can't lose her again!"

"You're not," John said.

"She'll be cut down," Billy Jack said, gritting his teeth against the pain of his wound.

"No, she won't," came the voice of the Parson from ahead of them as he and Isabella mounted the steps to the prow castle. They both clutched cutlasses in their hands, jaws firmly set against the huge pirate dueling John's mother. As they reached the top of the steps, Bloodbeard stripped Mary Ann of her blade, which soared over the side into the water below. A look of panic in her eyes, she ducked backward as Bloodbeard pursued, his cutlass slicing through the air only inches from her body.

The Parson and Isabella were there in a moment, the Parson's blade slipping between Mary Ann and Bloodbeard, blocking his strike. The deck seemed to reverberate with the deep clang of blades as they clashed, and the Parson staggered under the strength of Bloodbeard's arm.

As the Parson struggled to keep his balance, Isabella held her blade out toward Bloodbeard, who paused, taking in his new opponents.

"Well, now," he growled. "If it isn't the third string. I'm tempted te feel a mite insulted." He glanced down at John and Billy Jack with a smirk. "Be this all ye can send against me? The girl and the country preacher?"

"You've seen me fight, I believe," Isabella said with more confidence than John knew she felt. "You know I've some skill with a blade."

"That ye do, lass," agreed Bloodbeard, "and a fine

319

advantage it were te have been had ye only kept it quiet afore now. I'd have had a mind te underestimate ye." He drew closer, that easy smirk on his face, his blade held at the ready. "But alas," he said, his blade darting out, which she parried easily. John knew it was a test of her defenses. "Yer advantage be spent, an' yer strength be not a quarter of me own."

Bloodbeard rushed in even as he finished his sentence, blade flashing out before him. John's stomach knotted suddenly as Isabella blocked the strike but lurched to the side at the power behind the blow. "Ye see fer yourself the problem," Bloodbeard growled, pursuing her across the deck as she staggered, trying to regain her footing. "Ye want vengeance fer yer own father, but ye be powerless and alone against me."

Isabella's face flushed red as she brought her blade back between herself and Bloodbeard. "I cannot imagine what it must be like," Bloodbeard said, moving slowly toward her, his every step menacing. "All alone out on the open sea, no one te protect ye, no one te help ye. Ye have a great, burning desire te be strong, but ye're not. Ye be weak and helpless, vulnerable te the superior advantage."

Shaking almost uncontrollably, whether from rage or sorrow, Isabella's blade began to droop, her eyes fixed on Bloodbeard's lumbering form. "I'm not alone," she said, her voice wavering.

"Oh, yer completely alone," Bloodbeard said, moving closer. "The only thing that'll make ye feel secure is me own death, but ye cannot bring it about, not if ye tried fer a decade an' more. Yer friends? The welp? Not a replacement fer a father, are they? And when they be all dead, their blood runnin' the length of me beard, what then would be yer fate? Ye'll truly be alone!"

Isabella raised her blade without warning and lunged at Bloodbeard. He slapped it away with hardly a second thought, sending her sprawling on the deck, her blade rolling away from her.

John moved to rush up the steps to help her, but Billy Jack grabbed his arm and looking pityingly at him. "If ye don't stay," he whispered, his voice shaking, hatred burning in his eyes as he gazed at Bloodbeard, "I'll take me vengeance." Grinding his teeth, Finian forced himself to stop.

"Now ye face yer death, little one," Bloodbeard said, an evil glint lighting in his eyes, tightening his grip on the pommel of his blade and moving to bridge the gap.

"No, she doesn't," said the Parson, hobbling between them and raising his blade.

"Master Parson," Bloodbeard said with feigned delight. "Be ye recovered from all that wobblin'?"

"Mock if you wish, Captain Reach," said the Parson. "But the girl is not alone in this fight."

"I be not afraid te cut down a man of God, Parson!" bellowed Bloodbeard.

"Of that I have no doubt," the Parson cried. "The real question is whether you'll be able to."

Bloodbeard moved in, swinging his cutlass. The Parson moved forward with his blade, propping himself upon his crutch, which he braced against the deck. He met Bloodbeard's sword each time it lashed out, stopping the pirate's advance on Isabella. "Upon this rock I shall build my church," the Parson muttered between blows, "and the gates of hell shall not prevail against it."

This only seemed to provoke Bloodbeard, who redoubled his efforts, spinning and slashing out with his blade. Then, feigning a strike to the Parson's left,

Bloodbeard turned his blade the other direction before the Parson could compensate and, with a terrible crack, struck his crutch in two. With a gasp of pain, the Parson fell to his knees on the deck. Twisting his body, he planted the tip of his sword in the deck and attempted to regain his feet, but could not. Bloodbeard simply watched him.

"Tell me, Parson," the pirate said, leaning down toward him as he lay propped on his knees and hands. "What be that most famous of psalms? The twenty-third, is it? Remind me, how does it go?"

"No!" John shouted, surging forward toward the steps to the prow castle. He left an astonished Billy Jack behind with a cry, sprinting to the steps. He could not help hear the Parson's reply.

"The Lord is my shepherd, I shall not want," came the Parson's steady voice. "He maketh me to lie down in green pastures. He leadeth me beside still waters."

John took the steps two at a time, rushing past his surprised mother, who lay prone on the deck. He heard her shouting, but could hear nothing but the Parson's words. He drew his blade in desperation, but knew he wouldn't make it in time.

"Yea, though I walk through the valley of the shadow of death, I shall fear no evil," the Parson continued.

"Ah, yes, that be it," said Bloodbeard, his blade lashing out and tearing through the Parson's throat. His helpless, prone form slumped to the deck. "The valley of the shadow of death."

A jolt of horror and rage filled John at the cold-blooded murder as he reached Bloodbeard and Isabella, his blade whistling out at Bloodbeard's midsection. The pirate batted the strike away, took hold of Isabella by the hair and hauled her to her feet, holding her against him, his crimson-stained cutlass pressed into her neck. John skidded to a halt, watching Bloodbeard with eyes that burned with rage.

"Let her go," John said, his voice soft and deadly.

"I think not, whelp," Bloodbeard said. "Her blood be the price of yer own foolishness."

A noise from behind John distracted him, and he turned his head toward the sound. It was the Parson, lying on the deck, his lifesblood flowing out of his neck and pooling around him. His mouth moved slightly, a soft gurgling noise the only result. Eying Bloodbeard carefully, John took a few paces closer to the Parson, who fought to make his mouth work more clearly. He grunted one last time and then went still, one last unspoken word on his lips. John stared, heart racing, knowing exactly what it was the Parson had said with his dying breath. It was a word John did not want to hear.

Forgive.

He wanted to pretend he had not heard it, wanting to feign temporary deafness, wanted to burn it from his mind. Grinding his teeth, John faced Bloodbeard once more, conflict twisting in his gut.

"Some last words of sage wisdom, whelp?" Bloodbeard snorted. "He couldn't help himself, how could he be helpin' yerself or anyone? His God weren't able te save him from me own hand."

"He would have said it didn't matter," John replied, fighting the boiling rage within him. "Let her go."

"I think not," Bloodbeard ground out. "Ye will suffer as I have suffered! I'll slit her throat so ye will know that ye were bested by meself, that ye might feel the hatred and rage as I have!"

"I won't," John said, stepping forward. "I won't hate

you. Not even if you kill her."

"What be this?" growled Bloodbeard, and nothing John could have said would have shocked him more than this. "Do ye not remember what ye swore te do? Te kill me in me sleep for vengeance' sake?"

"I do," John said. "But I won't do it."

Bloodbeard watched his eyes slowly and John steeled himself against the strength of his gaze. Finally a smile spread over the pirate's face. "Yer bluffing."

John stepped closer. "Maybe. But you don't know for sure, do you?"

"I'm yer father, more as like, whelp!" snapped Bloodbeard. "Ye hate me and I may as well be yer sire. Surely that be enough reason te kill me!"

"Not any more. I have no reason to kill you. My father's alive, my mother is alive. You failed to kill them like you swore yourself."

Bloodbeard blinked. "I shot the lass's father in cold blood," he said. "She'll want revenge herself, like as not. Ye would be ever the hero te do it for her, wouldn't ye now? She'd be ever so grateful." He leaned down and ran a calloused finger across her cheek. She squirmed against his touch, but he held her fast and gave John a wide grin. "But what if ye refuse? Would she care te look upon yerself then? Ye would have had the chance te kill me runnin' on five times and yer nerve's failed ye every time. A girl cannot respect that."

"Perhaps," John said, moving steadily closer. Bloodbeard began to back away, toward the starboard gunwale, glaring in confusion at John. "But the true fear isn't hers. It's yours."

This brought a laugh to Bloodbeard. "Afraid, am I?" he bellowed.

"Afraid of what will happen to you once the vengeance is done. You've lived for so long with vengeance as your only purpose that you cannot imagine others who do not place revenge at the center of their lives. If we did not respond to your hatred, where would you be? Your life would be a lie, a sham."

"Would it now?" Bloodbeard growled, as he backed into the gunwale. Glancing over the side, he said, "I think not. I think if I were te slit her throat now, ye'd rush across this deck te fight me. But I'll not give ye the chance!" He threw Isabella forward to the deck and raised his blade to fell her. John had expected the move, however, and his blade lashed out to stop the blow. For the first time that day Bloodbeard mistimed his strike, which had barely had the chance to begin its descent when John's arrived, whistling for Bloodbeard's head. He jerked back and John's cutlass sliced into the pirate's great red beard.

Staggering backward, Bloodbeard gave an enraged roar and caught John across the chest with his free hand, knocking him backward to the deck. His grating voice seemingly beyond human words, Bloodbeard shrieked animalistically and turned toward Isabella, raising his blade. She screamed and scrambled backward, trying to get out of reach. He hunched down to get within reach of her, his hand seizing her ankle and dragging her closer, the blood in his beard running out onto the deck.

Gasping for his breath, John rolled to his feet. Before he could cross the distance between them, Bloodbeard gave a great cough, straightened and turned to face John, a look of astonishment on his face. He gave a strangled noise from deep in his throat, gazing down at his blood-stained beard.

It was then John realized what had happened. He

raised his own cutlass in surprise, to find a streak of crimson blood along its edge. Blood was pouring down Bloodbeard's neck, flowing through his beard and down his front, soaking it in his own blood from where John's strike accidentally caught his throat. It had been neatly cut.

Gaping like a fish for air, Bloodbeard's cutlass clattered to the deck, his hands finding his throat as he staggered backward. His black eyes burned with rage as they fixed on John, Bloodbeard stumbled over Isabella's prone form and lost his balance. He fell over the gunwale, hands involuntarily scrabbling against the railing to stop himself, but they were too slippery from his own blood. With a howl he dropped out of sight and plunged into the waters below.

John sprinted to the side of the *Iago*'s prow but could see only crimson foam where Bloodbeard's form had vanished. The dark shape of several sharks glided to *the spot* he had vanished and the water thrashed wildly. Closing his eyes, John stepped away from the railing. He held out his hand to Isabella. She took it after only a momentary hesitation, and he helped her to her feet. She threw her arms around his neck, and he held her for a long moment.

Finally releasing one another, they saw Billy Jack and Mary Ann crouched over the Parson's still body. He had an expression of peace on his face, the faintest trace of a smile upon his lips, as though just having finished a boisterous laugh. Billy Jack closed his eyes, averting his face so the others would not see his tears. John saw Mary Ann slip her hand into his.

It was then John realized there was no more sound of fighting from the ship. He and Isabella limped to the steps and saw that the remaining pirates had been rounded up by the British soldiers and crewmen from the *Janus*. The *Iago*'s destroyed deck was crawling with redcoats, bodies lying scattered over both ships.

"Thank ye, son," Billy Jack said, appearing at their side, watching the British round up the remaining pirates from Bloodbeard's crew. "Unless me eyes fool me, it looks as the victory were ours."

"The cost was too high," John said, glancing back at the Parson's still form behind them.

"I'm not sayin' you're not right," Billy Jack said, "but what ye told Bloodbeard were true enough. The Parson wouldn't care. He were called home this day." John caught sight of his father's hands gripping the railing of the *Iago* tightly to keep them from trembling all the same.

They limped their way down to the main deck and watched the British crew work on cutting the *Iago*'s mainmast free and start trying to roll it overboard, off of the decks of both ships. John looked at his mother, who seemed more sober and happy than she ever had in his memory, a new light of life in her eyes as she looked at Billy Jack.

"Why didn't you tell me that mother was here?" John asked his father.

"I wanted to surprise ye, truth be told," Billy Jack admitted. "Didn't figure on the course of things takin' the turn they did. Thought we'd get the treasure and be back at the *Janus* without much of a hitch, and you'd see her and have a pleasant reunion."

"There's always hitches," Mary Ann said, cuffing him playfully on the back of the head.

"But what are you doing here anyway?" John asked, turning to his mother. "We left you at the Bay Colony."

"Ah, well," his mother said. "After ye set sail I changed me mind about staying behind and caught the next ship to Port Royal, hoping to catch you before you set sail again. Arrived a few days after you departed, but in time to come along with the *Janus* when it set out after yo. Found Billy Jack floating in the water, half-dead."

"Pity about the treasure, though," John said. "There was nothing but empty holes in the ground in that temple. I suppose we'll never find out what happened to it."

"Buried under the weight of the mountain," Billy Jack said. "I'm not mourning over it much. More trouble than it's worth, all that gold."

"So the gold wasn't the goal at all," Isabella said.

"There were more to this quest than treasure," Billy Jack said, grinning at John. "We wanted Bloodbeard, dead or alive. We followed the maps so Bloodbeard would follow us, see? The plan were to trap him in the temple and kill or capture him, though that didn't quite work out the way we wanted. That were what me and the Parson were workin' on that day you came into the *Jerusalem*'s cabin with our meal."

"It really was never about the treasure," John marveled, looking at his father and realized how much he had doubted him.

"No amount of gold could be a redemption, lad," Billy Jack said. "Only taking down the villain causing the bloodshed and terror would really satisfy. And you saved me the trouble. Kept it a redemption, not a vengeance, and for that I'm grateful."

"I'll be happy to put this island behind us," John said, looking at the dark shape of San Thanatos beyond them. "I could do with less excitement for the next long while."

328

"That'll be a trick," said Isabella. "We barely made it through those rocks with Bloodbeard at the wheel, and he knew what he was doing."

John stiffened as he remembered what Bloodbeard had done with his map. "He left his map behind, though!" he cried. "The map with the instructions through the rocks. He put it in his cabin before we left for shore!"

He led the others across the deck to Bloodbeard's cabin beneath the aft castle, a thrill of excitement coursing through him. The door opened without resistance and they entered the great cabin. The dazzling golden light of day beamed in through the shattered windows along the far wall. Several cannonballs had ripped through the cabin, decimating the huge bed, and at some point during the battle the desk had dislodged and now lay on its back against the back wall. Parchments scattered across the floor, and John saw that the top drawer Bloodbeard always kept locked had been broken open and sat, twisted and broken, jutting out from the desk, jammed in its own runners, its contents spilled over the back of the desk and across the floor.

"It's got to be here somewhere," John said, and they all knelt down and began to look through the papers and parchments that lay everywhere. Just then the captain of the *Janus* entered the cabin.

"We've placed all the prisoners belowdecks in the *Janus'* brig," he told Billy Jack, who nodded as the rest of them continued to search through the papers. "The *Iago* continues to take on water, though not at a brisk pace and the bilges should hold for now."

"Good," Billy Jack said. "She'll need a new mainmast too, though I'd not want to go ashore again with natives lurkin' about. Think she'll survive passage through the rocks without one?"

"I don't see why not," the captain said. "We might be able to rig a makeshift one to get us to the nearest island where a real replacement might be found."

"Try it," Billy Jack said, "if you wouldn't mind. This ship's part of me redemption and I'd hate to see her come all this way only to founder so far from home."

"That's assuming we can get through the rocks again," the captain said.

"Aye, we be workin' on that," Billy Jack said, indicating the mess of parchments. "Well, everything seems to be in order, then."

"There is one last thing," the captain said, drawing a pistol and pointing it at Billy Jack. Everyone froze where they were, hunched on their hands and knees, too far away to be of any help. Billy Jack raised his hands with a heavy sigh before the captain spoke again. "Governor Vaughan ordered your death upon retrieval of the treasure, to ensure you would not return to a life of piracy."

"Did he now?" Billy Jack growled. "Always a kind man, the governor."

"You can understand his predicament, surely," the Captain said. "Just as well as I understand yours." He lowered his weapon and eased the hammer forward with a slight click. Billy Jack straightened to his full height in relief. "The Parson always spoke very highly of you," the Captain continued, looking hard at Billy Jack. "He trusted you with his life. That's good enough for me, good enough for now. But I warn you. Any attempt to escape or take the *Janus* and we will have no hesitation shooting you."

"Fair enough," Billy Jack said.

"If you return to Port Royal you will surely be killed," the Captain went on, returning his pistol to his belt. "We can drop you anywhere you like along the way and report your death to the Governor."

"Always a wanted man," Billy Jack said, looking frustrated.

John sighed in relief and glanced down. At his feet lay a letter half unfolded, with three familiar initials at the bottom which he suddenly recognized. *G. M. V.* He picked up the letter and scanned its contents, a smile forming on his face.

"What is it?" Isabella asked.

John jumped to his feet and handed the letter to Billy Jack. "Maybe not," he said eagerly. "Maybe not always a wanted man!"

Billy Jack's eyes blazed in excitement as he read the letter. He glanced up at the Captain and gave a wide grin. "Ye can take us back to Port Royal," he said. "We've got some unfinished business to attend to there."

Chapter Sixteen

Pirate's Redemption

Night had fallen swiftly over Port Royal and the clouds obscured the sliver of the waning moon. Governor Vaughan was working late, the candles at his desk burning low, molten wax dribbling onto the varnished mahogany. He sat deep in thought, staring at a parchment before him, his shoulders slumped.

The unmistakable sound of a pistol being cocked brought him out his revery. Yet, he did not move. He smiled wanly.

"Ah," he said. "Like father, like pup."

John gripped the pistol tightly in his hand, training it on the governor, forcing his arm to remain steady. He stared at Vaughan, who finally raised his head and gazed into the shadows where John stood in the shadows near the wide window, meeting his glare with one of his own.

"To what do I owe this unorthodox visit?" the Governor said, standing and moving towards the drinks cabinet.

"Don't move," John said. The Governor paused, looking mockingly surprised.

"Why, John," he said. "Threatening a governor of the Crown's territories is a crime punishable by death. Did you know that?"

"I did," John said.

"Yet you still came," Vaughan said.

"Someone had to," John said.

"But my dear boy, if you're here with a pistol in my eye, that can only mean one thing: Billy Jack Thatcher is no more and you're here for vengeance."

The Governor gestured casually to the doors, and they burst open. Five soldiers entered, leveling their muskets at John.

"It was really quite foolish of you to return here," Vaughan said. "The letters of marque are no good to you. You had to know you would almost certainly be killed. I was alerted the moment your ship made berth across the island. You see, nothing happens here that I don't know about it."

"A trap," John said, looking at the soldiers, though he did not lower his pistol.

"Indeed," the Governor said, moving to the cabinet and pouring himself a drink. He turned and regarded John with something bordering on a pitying look. "I am disappointed, if I may be honest. I cannot imagine what possessed you to come here alone."

"What makes you think he came alone?" came the voice of Billy Jack Thatcher from the balcony overlooking the bay, his own pistol directed at Vaughan. Beside him stood Mary Anne Rackham, her eyes blazing in fury, a pistol in each hand.

"Billy Jack!" said the Governor, and John was pleased to see a flicker of astonished fear in his eyes. The soldiers bristled, and pointed their muskets at the newcomers. They realized this left John uncovered. They seemed unable to choose who to keep covered with their muskets.

"Surprised to see me?" said Billy Jack, stepping into

the room. "Your assassins botched the job."

"So it would seem," growled Vaughan. "The boy was a distraction, I take it?"

"We took the *Janus* around to the other side of the island the moment our glass spied Jamaican soil," Billy Jack said.

"Leaving my gaze directed towards the *Iago*," sighed Vaughan. "Very clever. You're here for your letters of marque I take it?"

"That, and a bit more," Billy Jack said. "You see, I was a mite curious as to why a cutthroat such as Bloodbeard would have been allowed to make berth in Port Royal on our last visit. Seemed a strange coincidence to me, given his particularly bloodthirsty disposition." Billy Jack held up a roll of parchment. "Then we found these aboard the *Iago* after we took her. Recognize 'em?"

He tossed the pile of parchments onto the desk, his pistol still trained on Vaughan. The clear initials *G. M. V.* were plainly visible in the flickering light of his candles.

"They're letters of marque, allowin' Bloodbeard free range over any city or town of his good pleasure. They bear yer signature, Governor," Billy Jack said.

"Ahh," Vaughn said, looking resignedly at the parchments before him.

"We always were wondering how Captain Bloodbeard was able to get into so many ports and take so much treasure," Mary Anne said. "Even when we were part of his crew."

"You've been workin' together all these long years," Billy Jack said. "From even before you were governor. You used your influence in the Royal Court to grant Bloodbeard whatever he wanted, and you've been gettin' a cut of the haul all for your lonesome."

"More than a cut, I think you'll find, Thatcher," said Vaughan, recovering from his shock and sipping his sherry. "Bloodbeard was only ever a useful pawn. Why do you think part of the deal was for you to bring Bloodbeard in dead or alive? He was an unpleasant loose end to be tied up. Neither of you were supposed to escape San Thanatos alive. You've not been plundering the pirate treasure for the Crown, Thatcher. You've been delivering the gold to me, and I've whisked it away to my own private hiding spots. Since I've been governor, not a single piece of eight has made the crossing to England."

"Aye, that be what we figured," Billy Jack said, pointing at the pile of parchments atop Vaughan's desk. "Those aren't just letters of marque. They be personal letters from your own hand to Bloodbeard. We could work out the double-cross easily enough."

"Ah," Vaughan said again, looking at the parchments with a scowl. His eyes flicked from Billy Jack and Mary Anne, to John on his other side.

"You used Bloodbeard to collect the treasure, then used my father to steal the treasure out from under him and into your own pocket," John said, his voice shaking with fury.

"I couldn't be certain Bloodbeard would be faithful to our agreement," Vaughan said. "Your father provided a convenient fallback. One, I might add, that has paid off nicely. It's nothing personal, Thatcher, you understand."

"I'd wager there be no letters of marque for myself," Billy Jack said. "Seein' how it were ye planned for me not to return."

"Don't sound so hurt, Thatcher," said Vaughan, smirking. "Alas, no, there are no letters of marque. I'm afraid I may have told the Crown you were responsible for the loss of all the shipments of gold to England, that you betrayed us."

Billy Jack paled at that, his pistol faltering slightly.

"Dear me," Vaughan said. "It appears I was right after all. Once a pirate, always a pirate, Thatcher."

"Just so, Governor Vaughan," came a familiar voice from the doorway behind the five soldiers. Everyone turned as Henry Morgan hobbled into the room on his crutch, followed by ten more soldiers. "Stand down," he ordered the five still brandishing their muskets. They looked at each other and slowly lowered their weapons.

"Clap that pirate in irons," Morgan said, raising his arm in the flickering candlelight and pointing directly at Vaughan.

"What are you doing, Morgan?" Governor Vaughan snarled.

The soldiers that had arrived with Morgan crossed the room and took Vaughan by the arms, binding his wrists together with metal shackles. Morgan hobbled around the desk, gazing at Vaughan in anger. "Governor Vaughan, I hereby place you under arrest, pending your return to England."

"What are you talking about?" Vaughan snarled. "You have no authority here, Morgan!"

"Oh, by the way," Billy Jack said, looking at Vaughan. "The first thing we were doin' when we put ashore was speak to Henry about the situation."

Morgan pulled a parchment from his waistcoat and flourished it under Vaughan's nose.

"You've been summoned to the Court, Governor. The King wishes to see you. The letter arrived today alerting me that I am appointed acting-Governor in your stead, until a more suitable replacement can be found."

336

"The King?" blanched Vaughan.

"You've fallen out of favor, it would seem," Morgan said. He stepped closer and looked Vaughan in the eye. "If we examined the story of Governor Vaughan, we find he may be facing a great blank spot on his map. The King will be very interested to hear of your partnership with Bloodbeard, I should think."

Vaughan blanched at that. "I—I'll show you where the treasure's buried," he said, fighting to keep the panic out of his eyes. "I'll return it all! There's a map in my desk, it shows the locations, all the places I hid it."

"Your fate lies now with the King," Morgan said, opening the drawers of the desk and rummaging for a moment. He withdrew a large folded parchment and unfurled it on the desk. It was a map of what looked like South America. Vaughan lashed out suddenly with a snarl, spilling his sherry over the map and knocking one of his candles over. It toppled onto the map and letters. They burst into flames and crackled with gusto.

With a strangled cry, Billy Jack leaped forward and snatched a handful of parchments from the inferno atop Vaughn's desk. He drew his hand back, clutching the singed parchments, shouting and cursing in pain.

"Just Bloodbeard's letters of marque," Billy Jack grunted. Morgan ground his teeth and turned back to Vaughan, who was smiling triumphantly.

"Dear me," Vaughan said. "Without the letters, I'm afraid you've no case."

"Ye've been summoned either way," Billy Jack said, glaring at the Governor.

"Take him away!" roared Morgan to the soldiers. "I want him on the first ship to London!"

The readcoats moved forward and took Vaughan by

the arms, dragging him from the room. Morgan pulled out the chair and sat at the Governor's desk, brushing the smoldering ruins of Vaughan's letters onto the floor. "Did you see where the treasure were on the map?" Billy Jack asked Morgan.

"Somewhere in Cuba. That was all I saw before they were burned," Morgan replied. Billy Jack cursed and his shoulders slumped.

"All of it, wasted," he said. "I be still a pirate, even after all this. A hunted man I'll be, til the end of me days."

"Not quite," Morgan said, standing and taking Bloodbeard's letters of marque. They were scorched on the edges, but otherwise undamaged. "A few names changed, the odd phrase or two added, and these should work fine."

"What?" Billy Jack said, looking startled. John laughed as he realized what Morgan meant to do.

"We'll just take out the names and put yours in their place. I can sign, as Acting Governor."

Billy Jack stood, his eyes fixed upon the letters of marque.

"These letters give the holder the right to be an independent captain of a vessel in the service of His Majesty, King Charles II. He may possess up to four ships in his fleet, and has the right to make berth anywhere in British territory."

Billy Jack didn't know what to say. He mouthed words for a moment, then simply closed his jaw and shrugged in delight.

"Tell me, Billy Jack Thatcher," said Henry Morgan, his eyes twinkling. "How would you like to be a free man?"

Billy Jack Thatcher stood next to John on the Port

Royal wharf in the gloom of predawn, watching the last of the supplies being loaded aboard the *Iago*. The ship had been patched and repaired, the treasure removed, over the last few weeks, weeks which John had spent in the company with Isabella and acting Governor Henry Morgan. Despite the company, John had been restless and of an ill-temper until the ship had been ready to sail again.

"There you are," came Henry Morgan's familiar voice from behind them. They turned and watched the him limp towards them on his crutches, beaming up at the ship.

"Henry!" Billy Jack cried. "We weren't expecting you to come see us off!"

Morgan paused on his crutches, looking insulted. "You have been guests in my home these last weeks," he said, hobbling up next to them. "The least I could do is come down to say goodbye."

"You can't come with us," Billy Jack said with a smile.

"My dear man," Morgan said, trying and failing to hold back a smile, "I'm quite sure I don't know what you mean." He gazed up at the ship with such a look of wistful longing that John felt half-compelled to beg Billy Jack to let Morgan come with them. "Might be worth it, though," Morgan whispered.

"What be that?"

"To go on one last voyage even if it killed me. To die at sea . . . ."

Billy Jack put his hand on Morgan's shoulder. "Port Royal needs you, Henry."

"I know, I know," Morgan said, shaking his head. "So where are you off to next, Captain Thatcher? Wherever the wind takes you?"

339

"Much as I'd like that," Billy Jack said, "we got a destination in mind." He rummaged in his long waistcoat and finally produced a folded piece of parchment. This he unfolded and handed to Morgan. His eyes scanned the map, widened, and then shone with excitement. John smiled as he too looked down at the map, the best reconstruction they could make of the map of Bloodbeard's that Vaughn had burned. It had pointed the way to Bloodbeard's other treasure-hauls, hidden along the South American coast and on the island of Cuba.

Henry Morgan tipped his tri-fold hat to Billy Jack and John, grinning from ear to ear.

"Good sailing then, gentlemen."

The next day at first light, as the golden rays of the sun bespoke the coming of a new morning, the *Iago* weighed anchor with Billy Jack Thatcher as captain and Mary Anne Rackham as first mate. It was re-christened the *New Jerusalem* as it passed Gallow's Point. John broke the bottle of rum over the prow. When he did, Billy Jack took Mary Anne in his arms and kissed her.

They set for open water with a broad reach amid the sails. John clambered up into the rigging without hesitation or fear and made his way out onto the yardarms, adjusting the sails. He perched in the crow's nest to watch the sunrise when his chores were finished.

"Mind if I join you?" Isabella poked her head through the opening in the nest and clambered up next to him, her legs dangling over the edge of nest, and leaned back into his chest. John kissed her hair and smiled into the advancing day approaching on the horizon.

She looked up at him. "I never told you what my locket said," she whispered, pulling it out of her pocket and opening it so that the Latin was visible. He peered at the words again: niveus rose orbis terrarum.

"What does it mean?" he murmured.

"The white rose of the world," Isabella said. "It's what my father used to call me."

"It fits," John said, wrapping his arms around her as she draped the golden locket around her throat. Then she slipped her fingers through his and leaned back against his chest again.

They tacked due south, heading for South America, following their best reconstruction of Vaughan's map. It pointed their way to lost treasures. They sat back together watching the sun rise from the crow's nest, relishing the sensation of the *New Jerusalem* rolling under them.

Governor Vaughan returned to London in shame. He could not be convicted because of the lack of evidence, but his reputation was ruined thereafter. He never regained his standing in court and died a broken man.

Henry Morgan died in 1688 of a combination of dropsy, tuberculosis and excess drinking. He was buried in Port Royal. After the 1697 earthquake, Morgan's grave sank into the sea and there lies to this day. He rests in peace in his beloved waters at last.

Billy Jack Thatcher searched for the rest of Bloodbeard's treasure for many years, but found little without the aid of the map. With the little he did find, he purchased two more sloops and spent the remainder of his days combating the pirates of the Caribbean as a privateer for the British Crown. He died in 1723 of a fever.

Mary Anne Rackham was married to Billy Jack Thatcher six weeks into the maiden voyage of the New Jerusalem. She bore him six more children. Two died as infants, but the rest lived and flourished in the New World. She died in 1716.

John Thatcher married Isabella and grew up sailing the Caribbean seas. When he was eighteen he entered the Royal Navy and after a distinguished career rose in the ranks to become an admiral of the fleet, took a commission to supervise the British navy's fight against the buccaneers of the Spanish Main and never left his beloved native waters around Port Royal again. He died in 1768, on the eve of the American War for Independence.

The treasure stolen by Governor Vaughan would never be found. Many spent their lives searching for it, but to no avail.

It remains missing to this day.

A. T. Ross holds an A. A. from Washington State Community College and a B.A. in English Literature from Marietta College. He's been writing fiction since the age of ten, when he discovered *Beowulf* at his public library. He lives and writes from the deep humidity of Ohio. *Pirate's Redemption* is his first novel. He can be found online at www.atrossbooks.com.

A Preview of A. T. Ross's forthcoming YA fantasy

The Book of Secrets

Book One
of *The Word and the Sword* series

Coming Fall 2013

CHAPTER ONE
THE SURVIVOR

"RAT!" The unpleasant, grating voice of Mog Borgrumble burst into Finian's sleep. He jumped, lurching from a half-remembered dream into the sudden shock of full waking. "Get up, you useless, filthy, lazy rat!"

Scrambling to reassemble his mind out of the confusion of sleep, and feeling as if he had been thrown somehow off-balance, Finian sat up out of the pile of old straw that made up his bed and forced a yawn away. It would only infuriate his gargantuan step-mother Mog if he indulged in a yawn. He felt the fact that she had resisted using the willow-switch today was an unseen mercy the likes of which he could hardly expect to see again.

As if hearing this line of thought, Mog slapped Finian on the back of the head for good measure, as if to point out how easily he had really gotten off. His stepmother stood over him, her blotchy, red face pressed close to his, her eyes wide and nostrils flared like a winded horse. She struck an intimidating figure to almost everyone in the village, nearly as wide as she was tall, dressed in a roughly woven dress the size and texture of a sail, and an apron designed for someone several sizes too small roped about her enormous middle, stretched to what looked to be the breaking point. Finian thought it a minor miracle it hadn't split apart in several directions the moment she bent over. Her thick, bristly black hair was cropped short and stuck out in every direction in a great, unwashed mass. It was not just limited to the top of her head; it also spanned the gap between her eyebrows and lined her great, bulging cheeks and ran down her thick forearms. Getting a hug from her was like trying to cuddle a porcupine, not that Finian would know anything about that. The day she hugged him would mark the beginning of some sort of apocalypse, he felt reasonably sure. It was due to her general size and irritable demeanor that rumors around the village persisted that she had a bit of Giant blood in her, gained from some long-ago distant relative.

"Breakfast," she snarled at Finian with a casual wave of the hand towards a small plate that sat on the edge of the crude table which stood in the center of their small hut, around which all the other Borgrumbles were already gathered, devouring their meal with a wild, almost feral, abandon. "Yer to eat quick, an' then gather wood for the cooking fire first thing, so we're not late fer the feast," Mog growled at Finian as she stomped back to the distant corner where a pot grumbled on the fire.

Such was life among the Borgrumbles. After twelve years of experience, Finian knew to expect no different. He rose and collected the plate Mog had left for him from the table, ignoring everyone else gathered around it, and returned to his corner. Looking at the contents of his meal, he heaved a quiet sigh and began to eat what he could with his fingers. The plate was sparsely populated with carrot tops, the green stalks still attached, along with potato eyes and peelings only, and an egg that had gotten horribly scorched in the fire. He started eagerly with the egg—such was a rare treat, and once you got past the burn bits, was not a totally awful experience.

The other Borgrumbles were, with two exceptions, just as nasty and greedy as Mog. She had trained them well, the other nine children, all of whom were crowded around the table as close as possible, in a tangle of elbows and hands, all of them bent over their food like animals. The two exceptions to all of this were Gumtuck, Finian's stepfather, and Gluma, the eldest girl of the brood.

Gumtuck was currently at at the table's far end, squashed between his two eldest sons, Brutanon and Firune, both of whom were nearing the size of their mother, with tiny eyes that glinted nastily if they swiveled your direction. They were taking turns elbowing their father in the ribs as they inhaled their food, pretending it was on accident and winking their beady eyes at one another past Gumtuck's silent, beleaguered form when they thought he wasn't looking.

Finian's stepfather was short, hardly taller than Finian himself, even if he stood on the tips of his toes, easily dwarfed by the other men of the village, and therefore considered by all to be the perfect sort of person to be pushed around when they wanted something. As a result, he was always getting taken advantage of, a reality he seemed too kind and timid to combat in any meaningful way. He was balding, with a rounded face and soft eyes that hardly ever lifted from the ground in front of him, stocky around his middle portions, but surprisingly strong.

"And you," snapped Mog, looking at Gumtuck with a nasty look. "Don't forget te pick up what yer owed from Domyn."

"We never agreed on a price—" Gumtuck started to say, but he was cut off by a rumbling growl from Mog.

"Ye spent an entire day last week helpin' that fool of a woodsman chop his own wood, an' yer te be getting what yer owed!" she said, her face going blotchy. Finian braced for the storm to come and wondered if he could slip out undetected before Mog flew into her rage. It didn't usually matter who got her mad, somehow it would always be his fault. "Honestly, where would ye be without me, ye idiot?"

"The Underrealms, most like," muttered Brutanon, and Firune sniggered into his porridge.

"That's right!" Mog bellowed, a plump finger shooting into the air next to her head for emphasis. "Ye'd be with th' dead from yer own stupidity."

"Yes, dear," Gumtuck said, his voice soft. His voice was almost always soft. Finian couldn't recall a single time he'd ever raised his voice in living memory. There was only one time Gumtuck had ever actually stood up to Mog, though Finian had not been around to witness it. In rare, private moments, he would imagine the expression that must have been exhibited on Mog's face and for a brief moment his world would brighten.

But the only person he felt close to in the entirety of his foster family—of the whole village—was Gluma. From his earliest memories, she had always called him a survivor. A bit squat and plump like the other Borgrumbles, Gluma's resemblance to the unpleasant family there ended. The only help he had in his whole life came from his best friend and older sister who, for reasons unknown to everyone, had not ended up mean and vile like the rest of her family, but was instead as kind and thoughtful a girl of sixteen anyone could wish to find. She had become Finian's support, his secret ally in a world that stood continually against him, and she gave him strength to survive the hard days, when Mog's rage would burn particularly hot, of which he usually would bear the brunt. It had been her to find him, twelve years ago, as an infant, and that bond had never been broken in all the years since.

Gluma caught his eye from where she sat at the table. She jerked her head toward the hut's door ever-so-slightly, indicating that she was going out and wanted Finian to come with her. She pushed her plate away from her and rose, moving in one fluid motion to the door and pushed it open. Finian could feel the chilled breeze of early morning. He dropped his plate and followed her, nearly reaching the door before Mog caught sight of him.

"The firewood, rat! Before the feast tonight!" she barked at him as he escaped through the door which Gluma held open for him. Right, Finian thought, remembering. The feast. Their lord, Lord Meeshan, was hosting some great feast at the manor castle up at the top of the high hill that sat to a mile westward of their village, overlooking the small vale in which their houses rested. So many of the other Lords and Ladies of Nulor were expected to the feast that Meeshan had ordered help from the village gathered up to assist his own kitchen staff in preparing for the event. It was not something Finian was looking forward to. "Gluma, don't get too far, I'm wantin' te introduce ye te that trader from the east," Mog told Gluma, who rolled her eyes. Mog's eyes bugged wide at the sight and she inhaled sharply as if to start screaming, but the two of them ducked out of the hut, swinging the door closed as she let loose on them, muffling the sounds of her reply.

They had emerged into the early dawn, the black of night still clinging desperately to the world that surrounded him, the thatch huts on every side nothing more than tall, dark lumps against the reddish glow of the rising sun.

"Come on," Gluma said in her gentle voice. "I want te show ye something."

They set off through the village as the signs of life slowly began to appear, the smoke of a cooking fire drifting into the air here, a small child peering out of a doorway at them there. The Borgrumbles' hut was situated almost directly off the side of the main and only lane that cut through the village, disrupted in the center by the village square.

Four covered wagons were stationed in the square; they belonged to a caravan of merchants which had only just arrived the evening before, from the eastern part of the Kingdom of Nulor of which Finian knew nothing. Their village was the very tail end of a long trade route, and the merchants usually arrived about this time, early fall, with most of their wares hocked, traded and bartered for already. But the village would get their pick of the remains, and then the merchants would turn back for one of the larger trading towns to weather the cold Nulorian winters.

They passed the wagons quickly, and Finian noticed Gluma kept her eyes low to the ground.

"Why does Mog want you to meet the traders?" he asked.

Gluma was silent for a moment. "She thinks that one of them will wish to marry me if she just gets me around them enough."

"Marry?" Finian said, looking amused. "Why would

you marry a trader?"

"I wouldn't."

They passed the square and reached the village gates a few minutes later. Their village was surrounded by a thin palisade wall of sticks, brush and rope, mostly used to keep out the wild dogs and other scavengers. There were so many places where it needed patching that Finian could hardly see the point of it; most nights the dogs got in anyway and carried off a chicken or two. It would never hold off any real attackers. The palisade gates were simply an opening at the end of the lane that they propped a line of brambles against at sundown.

The nightwatchman, old Edwyn McConnell, had already pushed the brambles aside and the way through sat open. Holding a wooden hoe in one hand as a weapon, and keeping himself upright with a cane in the other, old Edwyn did not strike a particularly imposing figure. He was rumpled and unsteady on his feet, bent at the middle with a hunch in his upper back that pressed his head and neck forward a bit. He wasn't even the official watchman, he just liked doing it so much that nobody had the heart to tell him it was pointless. But he took his job very seriously.

"Who goes there?" old Edwyn called out in a croaking sort of voice, brandishing his hoe at them, gripping his cane tightly in the other hand and wobbling slightly. "Halt and declare yer business!"

"Anybody you need to worry about will be coming from the other side of the fence," Gluma told him, smiling. He eyed her dubiously, then glanced at the fence and cleared his throat.

"Righ' enough, I don't doubt it," he said, shuffling closer and peering at them, his eyes narrowed in suspicion. "Iffn it ain't two of the Borgrumble brood?" he said at last, as though it had taken him a long while to determine this. "And where are th' two of ye off te at this hour?"

"Wood," said Gluma. "Got te get some before we're off te the castle."

"Castle, eh? Wood collectors, eh?" Old Edwyn said with a paranoid sniff, as though every word they spoke was an obvious lie, then lowered his hoe and winced, one hand going to his back. "Very well, very well. But use caution, young Borgrumbles!" He inched closer, as if conveying to them an important secret, raising a gnarled finger in warning. "There may be ruffians afoot." His eyes flicked to either side quickly, as though he expected them to come crashing over the fence at any moment.

"Ruffians?" asked Gluma, looking alarmed, but Finian saw Edwyn's eyes lingering on the merchant's wagons.

"You don't like the merchants, do you?" he asked.

Old Edwyn straightened up and glared out at the wagons more openly from beneath his gray eyebrows. "Bah," he said. "Foreigners. Durn foreigners. Ye know I heared a few of 'em are Dunburians, or so it's been said?"

"What—barbarians?" Finian blurted out, suddenly interested.

"No," said Gluma, her voice firm. "I mean, two of 'em are originally from Dunbur, but they moved te Nulor, didn't they? It's not like they're here te pillage."

Old Edwyn sniffed in irritation. This fact seemed to make no difference to his mind. "Don' like foreigners," he muttered.

They extricated themselves from the conversation as quickly as they could and made their way out of the village and down the narrow slope toward the sound of the nearby stream, ignoring Edwyn's dwindling cries of "Caution, young Borgrumbles! Caution!" Once they located it, they followed it upstream to the top of a rise. Just on the other side of the rise was a copse of trees, all growing dense and close together, which the stream flowed through. Gluma made for these trees, and soon enough they had entered the relative darkness beneath their high canopy.

The trees in the copse were old and thick, their trunks reaching high above Finian's head. The stream gurgled nearby as it flowed between the trees and rocky banks past the village and beyond. Gluma was wandering between the trees as if looking for something, a thoughtful expression on her face.

"What are we out here for?" Finian called out to her, unleashing the yawn he had stifled earlier. She just smiled at him and he knew he would have to wait. He watched as she set off, following the bends of the stream, and trailed her deeper into the wood. She strode to a huge oak tree that sat some distance away, curling its roots around an exposed boulder at the edge of the stream bank. She climbed to the top of the boulder and, leaning against the trunk, stretched up to a knot on the tree that was nearly out of her reach. Arching her feet, standing on her toes, she plucked the knot right out of the tree, exposing a small naturally formed cubbyhole, and withdrew something Finian could not see. She replaced the knot and scrambled back down to the ground, brushing off whatever it was she held.

She approached him and gestured behind her to the base of the boulder, where the water of the stream curved abruptly and had hollowed a little calm place free of the current. Cattails bobbed in the soggy mud between the riverbank and water as the water spun in languid circles.

"That," she said, nodding to the place, "is where I found ye, when ye were a baby."

Finian stopped dead in his tracks, his eyes frozen on *the spot* and a strange thrill of excitement went through him.

"Yeh were in a basket of reeds an' mud when I found yeh," Gluma was saying, and Finian forced himself to pay attention to her every word. "The basket had caught in th' cattails and got waterlogged. Sinkin', it were, and yeh would've sunk with it if I'd not pulled yeh out. Never found out who yer parents were, o' course; weren't a note or nothing. They never did turn up looking for yeh or nothing, so papa decided te keep yeh. Stood up te ma an' everythin'."

She stopped abruptly and he looked at her, worried that she would stop telling him the story. She had never spoken of it before, and the most Finian could do was pick up bits and pieces of what had happened from conversation and from the dark innuendo that Mog threw his way whenever something went wrong in the village, as though he was a bad omen or harbinger of some long forgotten doom.

"I thought it were lost, was why I never gave it to yeh before now," Gluma said, her voice quiet, staring at something in her hands. Finian pulled his eyes away from the place he had been found as a child and looked at her. "Forgot I'd hid it up there."

She lifted her hands and opened them, presenting to Finian what looked like a rumpled bit of cloth that could have once been forest green. It lay dark and still against her palms. He stared at it, unsure of what to think.

"It were yer swaddling clothes," Gluma explained.

"What yeh were wrapped in, on yer little raft. And look here."

She drew the patch of cloth taut and indicated a long, frayed line along its lengthiest edge. "It were cut from somebody's cloak, see? Find the cloak what matches, an' I wager ye'd find yer parents."

Stepping towards him, she pressed the cloak corner into his hands.

"Keep it. It be yers anyway. Th' only real thing yeh have left of yer parents, I surpose."

Finian could barely feel the cloth against his fingers, his thoughts a mass of swirling confusion. He had long ago given up on ever knowing anything about his parents, though he had often imagined it in his dreams. They would arrive in the village square one day to carry him off home again, telling him that it had all been a mistake, that he had always been wanted. He had buried all of it as deep as he could inside. It had been easy to ignore, as he had not known them nor the circumstances of his abandonment, and there had not even been a hint of who they were or where they had gone. That hope, long since pushed aside, seemed to flare to life inside him once more, burning white-hot against his ribcage.

He found that he was clutching the cloak corner with whitened knuckles. He forced his hands to open and found that he was shaking.

"Thank you," he mumbled, still staring at the cloth. "Why are you telling me this?"

Gluma grew quiet, but smiled at him when he looked up at her. "Yeh know," she said, giving a nervous shrug, "in case mama really marries me off te one of those traders. I wanted yeh te know."

"That's not going to happen," Finian said, his voice

firm.

"Come on," she said, turning away from him. "Let's get yeh some firewood fer mama."